STEPHANIE FAZIO

THE NAT MAKES 7

Syafant Press

New York, New York

Printed in the United States of America
First Printing: September 2020

Library of Congress Control Number: 2019921024

ISBN 978-1-951572-11-2

To Andrew. Thank you for being you.

CHAPTER 1

It was a typical Boston spring morning, and my breath fogged the air. By this afternoon, the banks of the river would be sun-drenched and filled with students from Harvard and the BSMU.

My oar cut through the smooth water of the Charles River as I set the pace for the rest of the team. I could tell we were ahead even without our coxswain's shouts of encouragement. The fatigue I fought more often than not had been replaced by the zing of adrenaline.

Push, push, push.

Coach's voice rang in my head in time with each stroke.

The race itself was low stakes. It was against a local Boston team to practice before the BSMU's second-ever crew race against Harvard.

The Boston School of Magical Unity, known as the BSMU, hadn't been allowed into the Intercollegiate Rowing Association because of the unique composition of our team. Four of our rowers, including me, were Natural—people without magical abilities. The other four and our coxswain were Magics.

When I joined the team as a first-year, the BSMU was competing in the all-Magic rowing league. The league was good enough, but all the other Ivies were in the Intercollegiate Rowing Association. When I became captain in my second year, I made a point of meeting with Harvard's captain. After a few Sam Adams, he agreed to an exhibition race against us.

That was last year, when we made national headlines after beating Harvard. This year, after about a thousand emails and several in-person meetings, Coach and I managed to secure the BSMU a spot in the

Intercollegiate Rowing Association. We'd gone up against the best teams and were undefeated.

My shoulders, which had been aching before the race began, were throbbing now. I focused on my form, gritting my teeth against the pain that was sending sharp jabs all down my spine. The pain was familiar, but I never quite got used to it. The rheumatologist I saw once a year always frowned and told me I needed to take it easy. Each time, I smiled, refused the offer of steroid injections, and went back to pushing myself to the edge.

My dad had taught me that hard work and determination were the true ingredients of success, rather than innate talent. This mantra had become my obsession, although I never let anyone see how hard I worked. Thus, everyone at the BSMU believed I set the curve on every test without cracking open a textbook, made class president without trying, and became team captain without hitting the gym.

If only.

The truth was that I was average. Average brains, average brawn…better-than-average looks, so I'd been told. It was my intensity, my desperation to be the best, that made me what I was.

We crossed the finish line far ahead of the other team to muted cheers from the small crowd. BSMU students had spirit, but less so when it was an early morning race, and even less so when it was an early morning race during finals week.

I congratulated my teammates even as I tried to ignore the burning in my back and shoulders. When I got out of the boat, I realized the pain was in my knees, too. My body wanted nothing more than to crumple to the ground. I didn't let it.

The other captain was waiting for me. I went over and shook his hand, congratulating him on a good race. He said something, but I was distracted by the rest of his team.

They had lined up along the dock with their arms crossed, and they were refusing to shake hands. One of them spit in the general direction of our boat. Then, they started chanting.

"Dirty Nats, cheating Mags…dirty Nats, cheating Mags!"

I felt my face heat.

The other captain swore. "Look man, I'm sorry—"

The chanting dissolved, but that was only because my friends had charged them.

If I didn't stop this....

I broke into a run.

Unnatural waves began launching up from the otherwise-calm river. Even though both teams were standing on the dock, the water only soaked our opponents. One of them screamed when a long rope of algae slapped across his face. The waves weren't coming fast or hard enough to do any real damage, but the other guys were acting like the water was acid or something.

If I wouldn't have to answer to Coach about all this later, I'd be guffawing along with the rest of my teammates.

"Knock it off," I ordered my coxswain, a Level 4 Water Manipulator.

"If they're going to accuse us of using magic, we may as well use some magic," he retorted. Raising his arms, he brought the waves together until a waterspout began to form. The swirling water grew higher.

My coxswain moved his hands until the waterspout was cutting through river. It was coming straight for the other team's boat.

"Seriously," I warned, trying to look serious.

One of our power house rowers—who was huge and had a temper to match—body-slammed an opponent in the river.

I grabbed him and yanked him back while the other captain hauled his teammate out of the water.

"He started it!" my friend shouted as I wrestled him back.

"Dirty Nats, cheating Mags!" the chant started up again.

It pissed me off, but I pushed down my anger. We were the only mixed Natural and Magic college crew team in the country. We didn't have the luxury of sinking to the level of these idiots.

"Graysen Galder, what the hell is going on down here?" Coach called out to me through his megaphone.

...a little busy at the moment, Coach.

Our team's Level 5 Teleporter winked out of existence and re-appeared right in front of one of the other guys.

"Kleinman, relax."

The two were shouting and about to come to blows by the time I got to them. I grabbed my friend's arm before he punched the other guy.

"Mag lover!" the moron I just saved from getting punched in the face called out to me. Anger licked at the edges of my consciousness, but I tamped it down.

With our luck, some reporter would be here recording all of this, and our would-be rumble would go viral.

Out of the corner of my eye, I saw the other three Naturals on my team facing off against members of the opposing team. This needed to stop before people got hurt.

"Get your goddamn team under control," I yelled at the other captain.

"You in love with all Mags?" a guy with shaggy hair and yellow teeth asked me and the other three Naturals.

"Shut your mouth, Marcus," his captain growled.

Marcus ignored his captain.

"You boys have Mag girlfriends, too? Probably the only action you can get, even if it makes you baby killers."

Baby killers. Breakers of the third high law…Magics and Naturals who had romantic relationships. There was no worse crime a person could commit than being half of a Magic-Natural couple. There was no greater offense than being accused of being a baby killer.

My mind went white. A torrent of rage turned my blood cold, then hot. My whole body shook.

I was the first one to reach the guy.

He was still chuckling when I slammed my fist into his face. His garbled roar was cut off when I hit him again. And again.

"Galder!" someone called behind me.

I ignored the voice. I blocked out all of the shouting and people around us, until they were nothing more than a blur of color and sound.

I absorbed a wild punch without even feeling it as I kept up my barrage. I didn't feel the ache in my shoulders or knees anymore. I didn't feel anything except for the rage that was too old and raw for me to control. I smelled the copper tang of blood in the air, felt my knuckles split. I saw the guy fall to the ground.

I would have followed him if an iron grip wasn't hauling me back.

"Galder, what the hell's gotten into you?"

I recognized Coach's voice through the haze of my fury.

When I didn't answer, he shoved me. Hard. I stumbled back, and Adam, my dorm suitemate, grabbed me before I lost my balance. I was breathing hard, less from the fight than from those two words circling around and around in my head.

Baby killer.

* * *

"Wow, Galder. I've never seen you lose your shit like that before. Well done." Adam clapped me on the back.

"Yeah, I probably shouldn't have done that," I said, giving him what my teammates affectionately referred to as my *golden boy smile.*

Adam punched me in the arm. "Thanks for absorbing Coach's ire for us. We owe you one."

"Any time," I muttered, waving him off as he and the rest of my teammates headed for lunch.

I sat through Coach's lecture and made all the necessary apologies. I really was sorry. I knew we were the ones who were supposed to be setting an example. Getting into a fist fight—even over bigotry as heinous as the words those guys had shouted at us—reflected poorly on the BSMU.

If my dad knew, he would sigh and shake his head, and his shoulders would droop a little more.

Besides, I wasn't the type of person who lost his temper. I certainly didn't need anyone wondering why that particular insult had gotten so deep under my skin.

After Coach was gone and I was alone in the boathouse, I methodically went through each piece of equipment in our private gym. I jogged three more miles on the treadmill and flipped through the handful of index cards I'd been carrying with me all day.

My teammates thought my athletic prowess came easily to me, just like my classmates thought my intelligence was as natural to me as abilities were to the Magics. Nothing could be further from the truth. Most nights, I fell asleep at my desk with my face pillowed on an open textbook. But the side of me everyone saw, the only side I let them see, was the easy-going top athlete and valedictorian-to-be.

So, alone in our small gym, I pushed myself until my limbs were quivering and I saw dark spots.

The joint pain was getting worse. So was the low-grade fever I'd had since this morning. The rheumatologist my dad brought me to about a decade ago diagnosed me with systemic lupus erythematosus, usually just called lupus. It wasn't fatal, at least not the kind I had, but it was the reason why my limbs swelled and I got periodic fevers. I was hospitalized for the worst of the flare-ups a couple of times a year.

Lupus had no cure, and the pain and exhaustion made it harder for me to do normal college things like pull all-nighters and be an athlete.

No one at the BSMU knew about my diagnosis. During the days I was hospitalized, I told my friends I was out of town visiting relatives. My disease wasn't something anyone needed to know about, and like so much else in my life, it was easier to keep the truth to myself.

By the time I left the boathouse, it was late afternoon. I stopped by the dining hall and grabbed a cellophane-wrapped sandwich. I politely declined an invitation to join a few of the girls from my Magical Law class who were hunkered down with bowls of ice cream and stacks of neon-colored sticky notes. I cut across campus and headed back to my dorm.

I downed my sandwich while I flipped through the five-hundred-or-so index cards I'd made in preparation of this exam. Our last final exam, the law final, was tomorrow. My major was Magic Relations and Cooperation with a concentration in Magical Law. If I didn't get a hundred on the exam, it would just be embarrassing.

I fell asleep at my desk several hours later, still fully clothed and with terms like *magical manipulation in cases of perjury* swimming through my head.

CHAPTER 2

I woke the next morning feeling better than I had the day before. My fever was gone, and a scalding hot shower had taken care of the worst of my joint pain. This exam was my last before graduation.

It was going to be a good day.

I walked into the lecture hall and was assaulted by the smell of stale coffee, greasy breakfast sandwiches, and student bodies that had clearly spent the morning studying rather than showering. Most of the students already in the room were staggering around like zombies…clutching their silver BSMU coffee mugs and rolling up the sleeves of too-big sweatshirts I imagined they had slept in. There was even one girl with bunny slippers and flannel pajama bottoms with unicorns all over them. I respected the bold choice.

Most of my teammates were in this class, and I saw them madly flipping through their textbooks as they tried to cram a few last facts into their brains before the final.

"Aren't you looking bright-eyed and bushy-tailed," Adam said, scowling at me.

I winked at him.

I liked that everyone thought I was smart enough to knock the hardest exam in the school out of the park without opening a book. Everyone who got into the BSMU was smart and hard-working. It felt like a vulnerability to be on the lower end of the IQ spectrum, at least as far as this crowd went.

There were students in this class who could do well after only studying for a few days, but I'd been busting my ass all semester for this test. I'd skipped crew parties, mixers with the girls' team, and weekend trips to New York so I could study.

My friends assumed I was bailing to hang out with various mystery girls. I let their imaginations run wild and never bothered to correct them.

"Bet you didn't even study last night, did you, Galder?" another one of my teammates asked before taking a long slurp from his iced coffee.

"It's Magical Law." I shrugged. "No sweat."

Unlike my classes, working a crowd had always been a skill that came easily to me.

"Yeah, maybe if we had a job all lined up in the Alliance's Magical Law branch, we'd be strutting, too."

"I never strut," I said, trying to look offended.

I might have been strutting a little. But who could blame me? It was less than a week until graduation, and this was my last exam. The team had a post-graduation trip to Hilton Head planned, and then I'd be starting my new job as a Magical Law Specialist in the Alliance. It was the best job offer anyone at the BSMU had ever gotten straight out, and it'd been a dream of mine since high school.

"Gonna get a hundred, Graysen?" one of the girls in my dorm asked.

"You bet."

She blushed when I grinned at her.

"He better," a different female voice announced. "If he wants to close that *embarrassing* gap of .01 between our GPAs."

Penelope, a Level 9 Clairvoyant and the highest rated Magic at the school, stood in the doorway. A group of her friends clustered around her as she came into the room.

Penelope's skin was very pale, but not in a sickly kind of way. I could see why many of the school's Magics said she looked like an angel. Her white-blonde hair, round face, and tiny frame gave her an air of innocence, which only served to confirm the kind soul that lay beneath. She had wire-rimmed glasses and a severe pony tail that made her look the part of one of the BSMU's top students.

She tilted her head back to give me a challenging stare. Penelope and I had been competing for the valedictorian spot for the Class of 2070 since I started at the school three years ago. Our rivalry was a fierce but friendly one. We'd traded the Number 1 spot back and forth so many times the Dean officially declared us co-valedictorians.

We'd loudly condemned the decision, but we were both not-so-secretly pleased about it. It was an honor we both deserved.

"How's it feel to be second-best, Graysen?" Penelope asked me.

I shrugged and tried to keep a serious look on my face. "I wouldn't know. I turned in the extra credit for Laney's class yesterday." I raised my eyebrows at Penelope as I tapped my chest. "You're looking at the guy with a solid 4.0 GPA, which if I'm not mistaken, puts us exactly even."

"Nuh-uh!" Penelope stomped her foot on the ground as she tried to keep a straight face.

I gave her a sympathetic look. "Listen, if it took me all five years to graduate, I might be getting a little stale, too."

Our audience oohed.

"Burn," one of Penelope's friends said, but she was giving me a thumb's-up.

Graduating from the BSMU took five years for normal students—and many stayed for six or seven to earn enough credits. It was the most competitive college in the country, even though everyone across the river still liked to pretend Harvard was the best. I was about to be the youngest graduate in the history of the BSMU, and the first to graduate in three years instead of the usual five.

"Maybe if you weren't so lazy and had three majors like me, it would've taken you the usual amount of time, too," Penelope retorted.

Our friends hooted with laughter.

I glared at Penelope. She stuck out her tongue. That was as long as we could keep up our pretense at anger, and we both laughed.

The BSMU was founded thirty years ago when Magics first revealed their existence to the world, but until recently, the BSMU had separate facilities and programs of study for Naturals and Magics. They even had two separate campuses. Five years ago, the BSMU had taken the belated step of combining the two schools into one. This year, the class of 2070, was the first when Magics and Naturals would graduate together in the same ceremony. It was a change that spoke both to how far the city of Boston had come, and how far it had yet to go.

"Hey, Galder, you going to remember any of us once you're a big honcho at the Alliance?" one of the football players in the class asked.

"Maybe." I grinned and gave him a little shrug, enjoying the audience we'd attracted. "Guess it depends on whether you're buying drinks for everyone to celebrate the end of exams."

Appreciative hollers came from our audience.

"Sit down, Mr. Galder," Professor Brodis grumbled as he strode into the exam room and slammed his *I'm a professor, not a magician* coffee mug down on the desk.

He straightened the already-straight stack of test booklets before scowling at me. "Honestly. You aren't the Director yet."

"Sorry, Professor," I said, but I was still grinning as we all dispersed to take our seats.

There were sighs of resignation as everyone put away their textbooks and index cards. Foil crinkled as the last of breakfast sandwiches disappeared. The dregs of coffee were slurped. There was the rhythmic rustle of paper as Professor Brodis handed out the exams.

I turned around in my seat to get one more dig in at Penelope.

4.0, I mouthed.

Don't mess up, she mouthed back.

Still smirking, I opened my test book. I scanned the questions, reassuring myself I had studied the right material. Rolling my shoulders, I clicked my pen, and began to write.

The exam moved chronologically, beginning thirty years ago when Magics first revealed themselves to the world. I wrote about the killings that had broken out world-wide, known generally as the Slaughters, as Naturals and Magics clashed. Many Naturals, non-magical people, were threatened by the revelation that there had been people with magical abilities living among the rest of the population for centuries. Additionally, many Naturals felt cheated because Magics had been able to use their abilities to gain unfair advantages.

What began as isolated pockets of violence soon escalated to what was on its way to becoming an eradication of Magics. Naturals far outnumbered Magics, but the combination of modern weapons and magical abilities had devastated the entirety of the world's population.

The after-effects of the Slaughters were still being felt in many parts of the world. While the United States had mostly recovered, the US Government had lost control of the country's major cities, which were now governed by pockets of powerful Magics or Naturals. As a result, most of our major cities still hovered on the edge of violence. Only Boston was different.

The Alliance started out in Boston as a small group of Naturals and Magics who believed it was possible to live and work together in unity.

Because of the Alliance, Boston quickly became a kind of sanctuary for Naturals and Magics who wished to co-exist rather than fight against each other. The laws passed by the Alliance and implemented city-wide were beginning to spread to the rest of the country. The result was a slow but sure movement toward ending the barbarism of the past decades.

I put down my pen and stretched my wrist as I perused the next section of the exam, which asked specific questions about the Alliance's Report of Laws for Naturals and Magics. This was the section of the test that had kept most of my classmates up the entire night, but I wasn't worried. I'd been studying for it basically since high school, when I first decided I wanted to work in the Magical Law branch of the Alliance. There was a 5,771-page report on all of the laws that were written to protect the harmonious co-existence of Naturals and Magics. I was probably one of the few people who had actually read the report in its entirety. I knew the document's contents well enough that I could even quote particularly relevant sections.

What could I say? Magical law was fascinating. Seriously.

The entirety of the Alliance's Report of Laws only applied to the citizens of Boston; however, there were three essential laws that every American was required to uphold, regardless of which city's jurisdiction they fell under. They were called the high laws, and there was a zero-tolerance policy for breaking any one of them. Being convicted of a high crime carried the sentence of death.

If you got caught.

The first high law forbade magically-motivated murders. It had been the most effective means of bringing the bloody Slaughters to an end. Any murder that was found to be motivated by magical prejudice carried the automatic penalty of death.

The second high law required every Magic to be Marked. The law was written into being for the simple fact that Magics could recognize their own kind on sight, and thus, could identify Naturals. Naturals had no such inherent ability.

There was no visible means of identifying a Magic, which was why Magics had managed to stay hidden for so many centuries. There was a great deal of resentment among the Natural population about how many of history's unsolved crimes were committed by Magics who had used their abilities to subvert the justice system.

This sense of inequality and unfairness had prompted Naturals to begin the Slaughters. The only way to end the violence had been to give people a sense that they were on a level playing field. Thus, every governing body in the US started requiring hospitals to implant trackers into all Magic newborns. The information from the trackers was kept on secure databases and was only accessible to the police and high-level government officials.

At the age of eighteen, all Magics were required to take the Magical Proficiency & Aptitude Test, usually just referred to as *the Test*, to identify the strength of their abilities. Their magical level, which was scored from 1-10, with ten being the most powerful Magic, was recorded and kept in secure files in the Magical Marking Office.

I had written my final thesis about Marking, and how it suppressed Magic freedoms and slowed the progression of peace between Naturals and Magics. I'd even won an award for the paper. Still, I understood the logic behind the policy, which was the only way to ease the fears of Naturals who felt powerless compared to Magics.

Any Magic who tried to duck the Test or removed their tracker was guilty of breaking the second high law. Any Natural who had knowledge of such a Magic and didn't report him or her was in breach of the same law.

The third high law forbade relationships of a romantic or sexual nature between Naturals and Magics. Collaboration and peace between Naturals and Magics was applauded. Friendships were tolerated. Anything more was unthinkable.

The reasoning behind this law was drummed into every child's head as early as kindergarten. All children born to a couple that was made up of a Natural and a Magic had a genetic malfunction—a deadly bacterium that lived in every Magic but was only activated if the genes were combined with a Natural.

After Magics revealed themselves to the world, Natural scientists learned that Magics had 25 pairs of chromosomes, while Natural humans only had 23. The two additional chromosomes, named Chromosome 24 and Chromosome M, resulted in magical abilities. When combined with the genetics of a Natural, the dormant bacterium produced a deadly growth in the child's lungs in one-hundred percent of cases. The bacteria spread through the air and bodily fluids, causing an agonizing death for both the host and any all-Natural or all-Magic infants it encountered.

The genetic mutation was dubbed the Deadly Acriobacterial from Magic and Natural Descendants. Most people just called them DAMND babies. The disease was also referred to as the "Baby Killer Syndrome," because the bacterium was deadly to all normal infants. It also killed the elderly and any member of the population who was immune-deficient.

Magics were aware of the dangers of reproducing with Naturals and had implemented their own version of the third high law centuries ago. Even with as strict as the law was, just about everyone knew someone who had lost a relative at some point in their lineage because of a DAMND baby.

As a kid, my dreams had been haunted by the pictures in my science textbook of the deranged, grotesque-looking DAMND babies that seemed more alien than human. There was a famous case about a Natural and Magic couple in Missouri who had a baby shortly after Magics revealed themselves to the world. There was a graveyard of hundreds of tombstones, all of them babies and elderly. It had become a tourist attraction for some, and a warning to all about the reason for the third high law's inception.

The penalty of execution, which was carried out promptly for any violator of the high laws, was enough of a deterrent for most people. But no one wanted the brand of being a *baby killer*.

A nauseous sensation tugged at my insides that had nothing to do with the body odor of the football player sitting next to me.

I'd broken exactly two laws in my entire life. Both of them were high crimes. It was a part of my life I was desperate to forget.

The testing room was quiet except for the sound of pens scratching on paper. My pen jerked when a scream tore through the room. A chill raced down my spine at the piercing, tormented sound.

I whipped around in my seat and saw that the scream had come from Penelope. She was sitting rigid in her seat, and her blue eyes had rolled back in her head. Her pale skin was white as a ghost.

"Rough time for a vision," body odor football player said to me in a low voice.

As the most powerful Clairvoyant in the school, it wasn't unusual for Penelope to have a vision somewhere public. I'd seen her do it on a number of occasions. But this time was different. Usually, her face remained blank and she spoke the words of her vision in a monotone. This time, her terror filled the room like it was some living thing.

"No, please," she moaned. "Please don't kill me."

I felt the whole room come alert at that.

I exchanged a look with the football player.

"Crazy bunch," he whispered.

I didn't disagree. Clairvoyants were…odd. Penelope was the most normal one I'd ever met, but there must have been something about seeing all those possible futures that messed with their heads.

Penelope screamed again.

"Leave me alone," she cried. "Please, please don't kill me. I'll—"

Her words cut off. She made a gurgling sound, like she was choking. It raised the hairs on my arms.

Normally, it was frowned on to interrupt a Clairvoyant when she was having a vision. But it was clear this was no ordinary vision. Penelope's friends crowded around her, putting hands on her back and trying to offer her silent comfort. She didn't seem to notice any of them as she let out another choked scream.

Even with her eyes glazed-over and unseeing, she looked terrified. Her face was screwed up in horror. I could see the tension in every muscle in her body. She sat ramrod straight, and her hands had gone bloodless from gripping the sides of her desk.

"No." She jerked in her chair like she was ducking a blow. "No, no, no!"

Professor Brodis strode up the aisle and hovered next to Penelope's seat. He gave her arm an awkward pat, even though it was obvious Penelope had no awareness of anything outside of her vision.

"Please!"

She was sobbing even as she continued to make that horrible gagging sound, like she was choking on her own blood.

Someone needs to wake her up, I thought desperately. No one deserved to feel afraid like this, especially not Penelope. I was half out of my seat, ready to do…something…to help her, when Professor Brodis spoke.

"Who's trying to kill you?" he asked in a low voice.

Penelope's eyes swiveled forward at that moment. I'd never seen so much terror on a person's face. It filled me with an icy cold.

"Who's trying to kill you?" the professor asked again.

Penelope's hand trembled as she raised it to point a finger. I froze, still halfway out of my seat, as I stared at her shaking finger. Her voice was hoarse with fear, but there was no mistaking her words when she spoke.

"Graysen Galder."

CHAPTER 3

After she fully came out of her trance, Penelope apologized to me. She told me what I already knew—that divinations were tricky and her visions were often incomplete.

She gave me a shaky laugh, saying she knew I wasn't a murderer and that I should forget it.

I told her not to worry about it and made some joke about her trying to rattle me during the exam. We'd exchanged weak smiles before turning in our finals and parting ways.

As I cut across campus, I couldn't get the sound of her screams out of my head. I saw her terrified expression as she pointed her shaking finger at me and called out my name. The whole thing was just creepy.

By the time I finished a workout that had my joints shrieking in protest, I had mostly forgotten about the vision. I went back to my dorm and put some work into my valedictorian speech.

I'd been using every spare minute I had for the last two weeks to draft my speech. I kept a pen and pad of paper next to my bed for when I woke up in the middle of the night with an idea about something else I wanted to say.

As much as I was agonizing over the writing of the speech, I knew that when it came time to actually give it in front of the BSMU's 4,000 students and their families, I'd be in my element.

Maybe it was the public speaking experience I'd gotten on my middle school's debate team. Maybe it was all the speeches I'd already given as class president. Whatever the reason, I always got the opposite of stage fright. The bigger the crowd the better, as far as I was concerned.

I'm proud to be a Bostonian, I typed. *We've got the best model for peace and unity that's out there. But we still have a long way to go, and the changes we need aren't going to come from the actions of a few....*

I checked the time and closed my laptop. I showered, made a mental reminder about getting a haircut before graduation, and put on my suit. I was knotting my tie when my door opened and Adam strolled in.

"Well, aren't you looking like the BSMU posterchild I know and resent."

I threw him a quick grin.

"What time's the party?"

"Six, but Penelope and I are supposed to be there early. Pictures with Director Remwald and some other Alliance people."

"The Director's gonna be there?!" Adam did a dramatic flop onto my bed.

"Want me to get him to autograph something for you?" I asked. "Pair of your boxers, maybe?"

Adam scowled. "You're a lucky bastard."

I didn't disagree. Edwardian Remwald was the third director of the Alliance, and he'd recently taken over when the previous director retired. Not much was known about his early years, but I had read that Remwald came from a family of modest means and had worked his way up in the Alliance through his bold policies and dedication to the cause. He was outgoing and more politician-like than the previous director. Like all his predecessors, Edwardian Remwald was a Natural. Unlike his predecessors, he was liked by both Naturals and Magics, which in and of itself seemed like its own breed of magic.

I had seen the Director from across the room a few times during my summer internship at the Alliance. Tonight, I'd actually get a chance to talk with him.

The Dean was throwing a private party to celebrate the joining of the Natural and Magic campuses into a single unit for the Class of 2070. Since the BSMU was the most prestigious university in the country, a lot of important people from the Alliance would be in attendance.

"You going stag again?" Adam asked, sprawling out on my bed.

"Yep."

"I honestly don't get it. It must be harder for you to stay single than it would be just to have an orgy with your fan club and get it over with."

I snorted. It was true my looks garnered more than my share of attention from girls. I was tall and built, thanks to soccer in high school and crew in college. I had the same strong features as my dad, same thick, wavy brown hair. I knew the effect my smile and blue-green eyes had on girls.

I had tried going on a few dates at the BSMU. I even kept seeing a pretty girl from my Slaughters Psychology class. Her name was Jamie…something.

"Guess I'm just not the boyfriend kind of guy," I said, trying to sound like the player my friends assumed me to be and hoping it would end the conversation.

"Jamie was gorgeous," Adam persisted. "And nice. And smart. I can't believe you broke up with her."

I shrugged. I wasn't going to tell Adam that the first and only time I'd spent the night with Jamie, I'd woken both of us in the middle of the night because I was calling out for Kaira.

Needless to say, it hadn't been one of my finer moments.

Jamie had cried—something I didn't have much experience with, since Kaira hardly ever cried. In fact, the only time I'd ever seen her shed more than a few tears was when, as a thirteen-year-old, I'd made the mistake of choosing *Old Yeller* as the movie I was hoping would get me my first kiss. It hadn't quite worked out the way I'd planned. Instead of the make-out I'd been envisioning, I had held Kaira while she sobbed over Old Yeller dying.

Seriously, why does the dog always have to die at the end?

Fortunately, I had always been a fast learner when it came to that sort of thing. The next time my dad had a late night at work, I had chosen *Top Gun* for our movie, and the results were much more to my liking.

Way to have a bro's back, Tom Cruise.

I could have lied to Jamie and smoothed things over, but I hadn't seen the point. Even with the girl pressed against me in my single bed that was barely big enough for me, I'd felt a gnawing emptiness I knew would never be filled by anyone except *her*. So, with a gruff apology, I'd helped Jamie gather her clothes and then I walked her home.

After that, I stopped keeping any company of the nocturnal variety.

I had made my peace with all of it. I'd be like my father, dedicated to my job and the Alliance, rather than to a person. My career was more important than any individual bonds I could form. Really, everything had worked out for the best.

At least, that was what I told myself by day when my brain was awake and functioning. At night, when my defenses were down and logic had left the building, I would wake with the feeling that my chest was being ripped open.

Not that I'd ever confess any of that to Adam, or to anyone else for that matter.

"You want to come tonight?" I asked, mostly because I didn't want to spoil the night by thinking about Kaira.

"Really?" Adam sat up, reminding me of a puppy begging for a cookie.

I shrugged. "Why not? I get a plus one."

Adam leaped up from the bed.

"I'm not kissing you goodnight or anything, you know," Adam warned, already halfway to his room to get ready.

"Then you better bring me flowers," I called back.

✳ ✳ ✳

Half an hour later, Adam and I were cutting across the lawn to the Dean's house. It was breezy but warm. The sun was setting, and it made for a pretty picture with the red brick of the BSMU's buildings and the Charles River stretching out in front of us.

As soon as I opened the door, I was swallowed up in a torrent of well-wishes and congratulations. I lost sight of Adam as the Alliance's Minister of Defense shook my hand and offered me his business card, telling me "whatever you need in your new role, don't hesitate to reach out."

I felt a hand on my shoulder and turned.

My dad was smiling at me.

"I thought you had to work tonight!" I hugged my dad, while a camera flashed somewhere behind me.

"I wouldn't miss a celebration of the Alliance and its future." He squeezed my shoulder and then stepped back.

My dad had never exactly been the warm fatherly figure type. He was serious and dedicated to his work in a way I had always admired. We were close but in an aloof kind of way. I had always gotten the sense that, in his natural habitat, my dad wouldn't have chosen to be a father. At the very least, he wouldn't have chosen to be the primary caregiver. But he'd had no choice when my mom left us shortly after I was born.

I met my mother once, when a middle school family tree project had led me to track her down. The meeting had been awkward, and I hadn't attempted to contact her again. She was a photo journalist who traveled the world documenting the after-effects of the Slaughters. She had been living in Moscow the last time I checked, but that was years ago, and she had probably moved half a dozen times since then. A dedication to the job was something my parents had in common, and which they'd passed down to me.

In spite of my dad's lack of experience with fatherhood, he'd risen to the occasion. I had never wanted for anything. And if my dad had been at work more often than he'd been home, it was an inspiration rather than a source of resentment.

When I looked at my dad, I saw that he was even more haggard than he'd been when I saw him over spring break. He had always been lean, but ever since the night I referred to in my head as *the incident*, he'd become gaunt. Maybe it was something about the candlelight that made him look even more hollowed out, more skeleton than human. My stomach clenched.

"I'm proud of you, son." Lowering his voice, my dad continued, "Now, you'll be able to accomplish what I never could. I know you'll make a difference in the Alliance for both our sakes, since I no longer can."

The familiar guilt that never completely went away held my lungs in a vise, making it difficult to breathe. It was partly my fault that my dad lost his senior-level job in the Magic Marking Office, and with it, his dream of building peace between Magics and Naturals. And everything that came after was my fault, too.

I could have taken away my dad's misery at any time. I could do it right now. All I had to do was tell the truth.

I gave my dad a smile and nodded at him. "I'll do my best," I promised.

"Atta boy." My dad patted me on the back.

"Graysen Galder."

I turned to see Director Edwardian Remwald making his way through the small crowd toward me. I resisted the urge to pinch myself.

Director Remwald looked the part of the most powerful figure in the Alliance. He was even taller than me, and his jet-black hair and beard were neatly trimmed. He wore a pinstriped suit that shouted authority. He carried himself like a man who was well-aware that he was the most important individual in the country.

The Director's security detail stayed back a respectful distance, but I could feel their eyes scanning the crowd behind their dark glasses.

"Congratulations, young man," the Director said. "Tonight is the start of a very exciting time." He turned to my dad, gave him a bright smile, and shook his hand like they were old friends.

"Thank you, Sir," I replied, a little overwhelmed and a lot starstruck.

Director Remwald turned his attention to the small group that had just entered the room.

Penelope, flanked by two people I assumed were her parents, were heading toward us. She wore a white dress and was blushing from all the attention. I thought again about how she was known around campus as an angel. All that was missing were the wings.

Penelope and her family were absorbed into the group along with my dad, the Director, and me. Director Remwald congratulated Penelope before turning to her parents.

"I'm sorry again about earlier," Penelope whispered to me.

"Don't mention it," I said. "You sure you're okay?"

Now that I was looking at her, I saw there were dark shadows under her eyes, and her hands were trembling.

"Oh, yeah." She laughed a little. "I'm just sorry I shouted your name like that."

"Ah! Our posterchildren." Dean Miller slung an arm around each of our shoulders.

A photographer materialized, and we all smiled as the flash threw blinding spots across my vision.

Once I extricated myself from the photographer, I returned to find my dad putting on his jacket.

"Leaving already?"

My dad nodded. "Big day at the office tomorrow." He gave me a broad smile that didn't fool either of us.

My dad still kept long hours, even though his paper pushing job didn't generate enough work to fill even a normal 9-5 shift. He missed his old job the way someone might miss a lost limb.

It was an unspoken rule between the two of us that we never discussed the incident that, even years later, had him mumbling in his sleep about misplaced files.

Apparently, talking in one's sleep ran in the family.

"You want any help?" I asked, wishing one time my dad's answer would be yes. It might lighten the load of guilt I carried.

My dad shook his head and gave me a pat on the shoulder. "I'll see you at graduation this weekend."

Before the incident, my father would have been in his element in this crowd. He would have been surrounded by important people who were eager for his perspective on new legislation related to Marking. Now, he apologized and slunk through the crowd of Alliance members like he had no right to so much as brush up against them.

I swallowed the painful lump in my throat.

Having lost interest in celebrating, I wandered over to the side of the room where most of the students at the party had gathered. The BSMU's best Magics had been invited, and they were showing off their abilities for their Natural audience. I stood off to the side as the school's most powerful Animate Illusionist transformed his nose into a shark's snout. The crowd oohed and clapped.

I pasted an admiring look on my face. There was no doubt the feat was impressive. Most Illusionists could only manipulate a single aspect at a time.

But I knew the most powerful Illusionist ever recorded. She didn't need to use cheap party tricks to impress people with her abilities.

An Earth Magic was juggling seven dirty rocks without laying a finger on any of them. The students were amused. The waitstaff scowled and hurried to shift the plates so dirt didn't dribble down onto the cheese platters.

There was snickering coming from the refreshments table, where an Alchemist had dipped his finger into one of the water pitchers. I suspected the water was now pure vodka, or maybe absinth. Alchemists had a weird sense of humor.

"Dude. Best party ever." Adam slung an arm over my shoulders.

"Let me guess, you've been sampling the water."

A sloppy grin widened Adam's face. "Chyeah."

I extricated myself from my friend's grasp. "Meet the Director yet?"

Adam sulked. "Nah. I saw him leaving a little while ago, and security wouldn't let me near him." Then, he brightened. "But I did meet a couple of senators and the Vice President."

The United States government no longer controlled any of the major US cities, but it still had lawmaking power and controlled the country's military. Its biggest role was to ensure that the whole country kept the three high laws, even if they didn't follow most of the Alliance's other rules.

The US government was old-school and made up entirely of Naturals. Magics weren't allowed to run for office or serve in the military. It operated under the same misguided assumption that had caused the Slaughters in the first place: that Magics weren't human.

It was a stupid argument grounded in fear and prejudice. Alina Freeman, the most widely-respected judge on the US Supreme Court, had made a historic ruling that decided Magics deserved equal rights. Alina Freeman was a Natural who tirelessly championed Magic rights, and she'd been the inspiration behind my early interest in Magical Law.

"Dude." Adam grabbed my arm and gave me a shake. "*Dude.*"

"What?"

"Hot blonde, nine o'clock. Eating you up with her baby blues."

I turned. Even though the room was crowded, I didn't need to ask Adam who he meant. I noticed her dress first, which brought back memories better left in the past. The dress was a color I didn't have a name for, somewhere between blue and green. Righteous indignation filled me at the sight of another girl wearing that dress. It was *her* dress, and the sight of it on someone else was like an insult. But then my gaze moved to her face, and my heart forgot how to beat.

Everything about her was wrong, from the light skin, to the blonde hair, to the blue eyes. Her body was the wrong shape, and she was about five inches too short. Her lips were too thin and her eyes too round. Still, I knew it was her…the one I'd been in love with ever since my pre-adolescent brain understood the word. The one who'd ruined my dad's life.

Kaira Hansley.

CHAPTER 4

Kaira's own Ma and grandma sometimes couldn't recognize her when she was fully illusioned, but I had always known her, no matter what face she wore.

Even though it had been three years since I'd seen her in any form, I knew the expression on her face. I recognized that half-smile and the graceful way she moved even when she wasn't on stage for one of her ballet performances.

Our eyes met while my lungs tried to remember how to draw in air. An entire, silent conversation passed between us before I managed a breath. She tilted her head just a fraction, and then she slipped through the crowd and out of sight.

"Too bad," Adam commiserated, slinging an arm around my shoulder as I tried not to give the impression I'd just seen a ghost. "Guess that means you're coming home with me after all."

I said something back, but I wasn't aware of what. I forced myself to pretend to watch the Magics show off as my heart tried to claw its way out of my chest. I counted the seconds in my head. I waited five minutes.

"Bathroom," I told Adam as I made my way to the edge of the crowd.

I had to shake several more hands on my way to the door. Finally, I made it outside. I looked around. She was sitting on one of the benches in the courtyard. I crossed over the grass toward her.

The sound of my racing heart filled my ears. If the world started falling apart around me at that moment, I doubt I would've noticed.

Tell her to leave, my brain ordered.

I didn't want to see her. I shouldn't want to see her.

"Hi, Gray." Kaira's sultry voice, the one I thought I'd never hear again outside of my dreams, spoke from the blonde's body.

"Hey, Kai." I could barely hear myself over my thundering heart.

For a moment, neither of us spoke. I looked around, but we were alone.

"Why are you here?" I asked. The last time I'd seen her was the night I told her I never wanted to see her again.

The pain of what she had done was still raw, even now.

"I saw the article in the Globe and wanted to say congrats on graduating. I figured this would be my last chance before you became an official member of the Alliance."

Did she think I would arrest her once I started in my new role?

I should. Of course, I should have turned her in years ago. But I knew now, just as I had even when I was shouting at her to get the hell out of my life, that I'd never do anything to hurt her. Even if it meant breaking the second high law.

"Thanks," I managed, when I realized I'd just been standing there.

I stayed a few feet back as I tried to think of what else to say. Being tongue-tied wasn't usually a problem for me.

"Take a walk?"

I should say no. Even here, where it was unlikely anyone would see us together, and even less likely anyone would recognize her, there was a risk. A combination of intense paranoia and pure dumb luck were the reasons why we'd never been caught in all the years we'd been together…loved each other.

I wanted to tell her no. I had never been able to convince myself that I had stopped loving her, but I couldn't forgive her, either. I wasn't *that* pathetic.

I felt my head nod.

We were silent as we crossed the lawn and headed toward the Charles River. It was dark, and as soon as we had gone far enough that no one from the BSMU buildings would be able to see us, I turned to Kaira.

"I can't talk to you like this," I said.

"I wasn't sure you'd want to see me." Her voice was uncharacteristically soft.

"I don't," I said, even though I didn't think either of us was convinced by the lie. "But I can't have a conversation with this." I waved my hand, motioning to the blonde who was and wasn't Kaira.

I was staring out at the Charles, but as soon as I felt her start to shift, I couldn't stop my gaze from being drawn to her.

Her smooth, blonde hair turned into long, coarse black strands styled in a way she had once told me were called *thick twists*. Her light skin darkened.

Kaira's Ma was black and her dad Hispanic, although her dad had died before I met him. The combination gave her almond-shaped eyes and caramel-colored skin that many of my classmates paid a fortune to Magic aestheticians in hopes of achieving.

The last of the illusion melted away, and Kaira…the real Kaira…was left in her place.

Kaira was an Animate Illusionist. For most Animate Illusionists, that meant the ability to change aspects of their own person, and if they were higher than a Level 6, aspects of any other person close enough to touch. Kaira was a Level 10, the rarest and highest score on the Magical Proficiency & Aptitude Test. It meant she could transform her entire appearance, as well as the appearance of any living being within a certain range.

I saw the way the dress showed off her ballerina's legs, something I hadn't noticed on the blonde. She had always been slender from dancing, but she was even thinner now. There was a hardness to her body and expression that hadn't been there before. One thing hadn't changed. She was still the most gorgeous woman I'd ever seen.

I looked away from her before I lost my mind completely and did something I'd later regret. Like reach for her hand. Or kiss her.

"You still have the dress," I managed, because my brain had gone fuzzy around the edges. As soon as the words left my mouth, I realized I was an idiot for reminding us both of that night when we meant nothing to each other anymore.

"I wasn't sure you'd remember, but then I saw your tie," she said.

I looked down. I hadn't even noticed which tie I'd put on. It was the one Kaira had bought for me because it was the same color as her dress.

Another onslaught of emotions washed over me—emotions I had spent years trying to convince myself had cooled.

It was around the time of my high school prom. I obviously couldn't bring my secret Magic girlfriend as my date. Prom coincided with re-elections in the Alliance, and my dad was staying in the office day and night. He was even showering at work. So, I had made the necessary excuses to my friends, and as soon as it got dark, Kaira and I had drawn the blinds in my house and decorated it for our own private prom.

She'd worn the dress she had on now, and we'd had a candlelit dinner in the dining room my dad and I never used. We'd eaten Ma Hansley's leftover lasagna and then had raw cookie dough right out of the package for dessert. After, we'd danced for hours in my bedroom. I remembered the satiny feel of her dress as I held her and the even more satiny feel of her skin when I'd taken the dress off. We'd spent the rest of the night wrapped in each other's arms.

I didn't want to think about any of that.

"How's Ma and Grandma Tashi?" I asked.

"Same as ever," Kaira replied. "You know them."

And I did. I had first met the Hansleys when they moved in across the street. I was ten and Kaira was eleven, and we had immediately become friends. We had both been old enough to understand the ins and outs of the high laws, and we knew enough to keep quiet about our friendship. With the hours my dad kept at work, it wasn't hard to hide how much time we spent together from him. Even though we were neighbors, I don't think my dad would have recognized any one of the Hansleys on sight. But the Hansleys accepted me without question, and I became a fixture in their house.

Even the very real threat of getting caught hadn't stopped our friendship from quickly morphing into something more. We had known on a theoretical level how wrong it was to do what we were doing, but it had felt too right to stop. I had never, not for even a single second, been ashamed of loving her. I had only ever felt a mild frustration that I couldn't brag to the world that the most amazing girl in existence had picked me.

A fortunate turn of events had left Kaira with a house in Back Bay that her paternal grandparents had gifted her when they died. Kaira had convinced Ma that she needed the house to practice her magic where no one else could see her, and it had become our personal sanctuary.

Even with the fact that we never met up in public, we always knew there was a chance we might be discovered. It was a risk we had both understood and accepted. It was the only choice we could make, because not being together was unacceptable.

I never would have guessed the reason everything fell apart would be because Kaira betrayed me.

"You taking any online classes?" I asked.

Kaira was as smart as anyone at the BSMU and a thousand times more talented, but she had given up her chance at a normal future the day she decided to remove the tracking chip in her arm.

"No," she replied. "I've been too busy with work to even think about it."

I felt an old anger flare to life. I knew what work she was referring to…her illegal work…the work that was a direct violation of the second high law. I was also guilty of breaking the same law, since I knew about Kaira and what she did, and yet I'd never turned her in. It was my choice, but I resented the impossible position she'd put me in.

"I don't understand why you'd give up your future for Magics who are breaking the law," I said before my anger overcame me.

"I *am* one of those Mags," Kaira pointed out.

I winced at her use of the slang. It wasn't a slur, exactly, but one didn't refer to Magics and Naturals as Mags and Nats in good company. After three years at the BSMU, hearing the slang sounded wrong.

Kaira brushed a finger along the dark scar that ran down the inside of her forearm from where she'd cut out her tracker.

"And I do what I do because I'm not the only Mag out there who doesn't want to be Marked. Except the others don't have the ability to hide themselves the way I do. They're scared and trying to avoid execution, and I have the ability to help them."

"Naturals have to have passports," I pointed out.

It was a feeble argument, and Kaira jumped all over it.

"It's not the same thing, and you know it." Her eyes were bright with anger.

"Then petition for a change, but do it on the right side of the law. Get your degree and work for the Alliance."

"The Alliance is all politics and mission statements that don't count for jack in the real world. Besides, any organization that thinks it's acceptable to implant a tracker inside me isn't one that will ever see me as an equal."

I started to argue, but then I chuckled. I couldn't help it. It was an argument we'd had a hundred times before. We both believed in the same principles…the same rights for Naturals and Magics…but we disagreed about how to achieve them. Neither of us had ever been able to sway the other.

God, I missed arguing with her.

"Guess it's a good thing we parted ways, huh?" I asked, still smiling a little.

"Yeah, I forgot how I sometimes wanted to kill you," she replied, but the anger in her eyes had been replaced by something softer.

We just looked at each other for a few seconds. The need to touch her was a physical ache in my chest. I curled my hands into fists in my pockets.

"Well, I better get back," she said.

"Yeah, me too."

Kaira stopped walking and looked at me. "Even though I don't respect the Alliance, I respect what you're doing. I just wanted you to know…I'm proud of you. I know you're going to do amazing things." She reached up and kissed me on the cheek. "The Alliance is lucky to have you."

I was frozen in place. A whisper of her familiar jasmine scent had me wrestling for control of my arms that wanted to grab hold of her and never let go.

Kaira shifted back into the blonde she'd been earlier. We walked back in the same direction, maintaining a little distance and not speaking.

My thoughts were pulled back to the last months of high school. While I was submitting college applications, Kaira had started to help unMarked Magics who were trying to stay one step ahead of the police.

We had fought constantly during those months. I had hated that she was breaking the second high law, but I'd hated it even more that she was putting her own life in danger for the sake of strangers who had chosen to remove their trackers. It didn't matter what I said. She had only become more invested in her work. I had my suspicions that she was planning to remove her own tracker, but I'd had no idea *how* she intended to go about destroying her records.

One day, when my dad was home with the flu, Kaira had walked right into the Magical Marking Office illusioned to look like him. She'd sat down at my dad's desk, hacked into his computer, and destroyed every record of herself. Then, she'd walked into the room where all the hard copies of the Testing files were kept. She took hers and slipped out of the office—still illusioned as my dad.

When my dad's boss realized a file was missing, the police had come to our house. My father, who had never committed any crime, let alone a high crime, was taken down to the station in handcuffs.

I still remembered my father, shivering from the fever that had kept him in bed for nearly a week, being shoved into the back of a cop car.

He was accused of aiding an unMarked Magic, which was a violation of the second high law.

The lawyer my dad hired made the argument that there was no evidence of my dad being involved with deleting any files or tracking information. And since there was no way to tell whose file had been deleted—Kaira had been that thorough—the police couldn't mount an effective prosecution.

The eventual determination was that my dad had misplaced the file, and some glitch in the system must have been responsible for erasing the tracking data. It happened from time to time…with so many Magics in the system, there were always files that went missing and turned up some time later. Except those kinds of errors never happened on Joseph Galder's watch. And this particular missing file never re-surfaced.

The case was thrown out before it reached court, both sides having decided carelessness was to blame.

Most people would have been relieved to be exonerated from a high crime offense, but for my dad, the decision had been devastating. My dad loved his work as much as he loved me—more, maybe. He'd been one of the most dedicated members of the organization, and he was demoted to scanning in copies of restaurant receipts from Alliance officials for reimbursements.

As soon as my dad was arrested, I knew whose file had gone missing. I'd begged Kaira to tell me that it hadn't been her.

I could still see her standing in the kitchen of her Back Bay house, a determined and unapologetic look on her face, as she told me what she'd done. Our fight had been brief. At the end, I'd told her I never wanted to see her again and walked out the door.

I could have forgiven her for breaking the second high law. I could never forgive the permanent damage she'd done to my father.

She had the ability to illusion herself to look like anyone. But she'd chosen my father…whether it was out of convenience or something more vindictive because of his high-powered role in the Magical Marking Office, I didn't know.

Even now, I didn't let myself think about the state I'd found my dad in after I'd gotten back from breaking up with Kaira.

The bandage on my aching wounds had been torn off at the sight of her, and I felt raw and exposed all over again.

"Kai."

She turned to me.

"Yes?"

Why'd you do it? The question that had plagued me for the last three years was on the tip of my tongue.

I shook my head. It didn't matter now. She had destroyed my dad's career and almost destroyed his life. She had done it, and that was all that mattered. Besides, there had never been a future for us, only a beautiful illusion.

"Take care of yourself," I said finally.

She gave me a bright smile that didn't reach her now-blue eyes.

"You too, Gray."

She headed toward the road, and I turned to cut back through campus.

It was still early enough that I could go back to the party, but I didn't feel like trying to put on a good face right now. I decided to head back to the dorm and read those policy updates the Alliance just put out.

I was crossing the quad when I saw the flashing blue and red lights of at least a dozen cop cars. As I got closer, I saw ambulances and two fire trucks. Police were everywhere. They wore bullet-proof vests and held guns in their hands.

And they were all standing right outside my dorm.

CHAPTER 5

I had never seen so many police in my life. They were milling around the lawn outside my dorm, surrounded by a gaggle of onlookers. I wondered what the emergency was, since the police just seemed to be waiting for something.

"There he is!" someone called.

I startled as several people began to point at me. Then, the police were swarming me.

My hands were yanked behind my back and my face shoved against the dorm's brick wall. Lights from a dozen flashlights blinded me, and the harsh voices of as many policemen was deafening.

"What—" I turned, but my head was slammed back against the wall with so much force I saw stars.

"Graysen Galder," one of the cops said in a voice that was so loud and full of menace I was sure it carried across the whole quad. "You are under arrest for breaking the first high law."

I was still a little stunned from being thrown against the wall, so it took me a moment to process the cop's words.

"Magically-motivated murder?" I managed. "I don't understand."

Something hard and unyielding hit my lower back. More hands came to restrain me, even though I wasn't struggling. I was too shocked to do anything.

My hands, now weighed down by handcuffs, were given a vicious yank. I stumbled across the lawn with four cops holding onto me. They steered me toward one of the police cars.

"There's been some mistake," I said, squinting against the blinding flashlight beams and headlights. "I didn't kill anyone."

"So that's how you're going to play it, huh?" One of the cops gave me a shake.

"Heard he was a smart shit," another cop said. "Better read him his rights. Kid's a law genius or something." He hauled me close enough that I could smell the stale cigarettes on his breath. "Not that it'll help you a lick once you get in that courtroom."

I was aware that more students had joined the crowd of onlookers, and they were staring at me with expressions ranging from horror, to disgust, to hatred. No one had ever looked at me like that before.

My logical brain told me that I just needed to understand what had happened, and then I could begin to untangle this disastrous mistake.

"Who was killed?" I asked, gritting my teeth as I was shoved against the side of the squad car. Rough hands patted me down.

This was insane. I had never carried a weapon in my life.

"You have the wrong guy," I tried again.

"You Graysen Galder?"

"Yes, but I—"

"Then we've got the right guy. Scumbag."

One of the cops opened the passenger door.

"Graysen Galder," he said in a voice loud enough for all the onlookers to hear, "you are under arrest for the magically-motivated murder of Penelope Heppurn."

Penelope?

"No." I shook my head. "I saw Penelope a little while ago. We were just at a party—"

"Yeah, we know," the cop replied. "Don't worry. We know everything. All you have to worry about it is how that orange jumpsuit will look on you when they fry your ass."

My blood went cold.

Before I could begin to process the implications of what the cop was saying, the crowd parted for a group of EMTs who were wheeling a stretcher down the cobbled path from my dorm. There was a body-sized lump on the stretcher zipped up into a black bag.

One of the cops motioned for the EMTs to stop right next to us. A different cop zipped open the bag enough to display the victim's face.

I sucked in a breath. Penelope's pale face was spattered with blood, her white-blonde hair clumped and crusted with it. Her blue eyes, open and vacant, still held the terror of the last seconds of her life. I stared at the slash mark across her throat.

A horrible, keening cry came from nearby. Penelope's mother was standing on the lawn, surrounded by police. She was screaming and reaching toward her daughter's body as her husband and the police tried to calm her.

A few girls I recognized as Penelope's friends hovered just past them. They were holding each other and sobbing.

This couldn't be. It hadn't even been an hour since I'd last spoken with her. I had to be hallucinating. Penelope couldn't be dead….

The cop zipped up the bag and nodded for the EMTs to take the body away while I tried not to throw up. I couldn't speak. I could barely breathe. Someone had murdered Penelope, and everyone thought I had done it.

"It wasn't me," I managed when I found my voice. "We were friends. I would never—"

"You were seen walking back to your dorm with her by no fewer than ten witnesses," a cop said, sounding a little bored now.

"You mean to tell me that isn't your artwork up there?" another asked.

I looked in the direction the cop was pointing. That was when I saw the window of my own dorm room: second floor, two from the left. Across the glass window panes were the words "MAGS GET OUT." The words had been written in blood.

A voice in the back of my head was screaming, *This isn't happening. You're dreaming. Penelope isn't dead….*

Adam, my closest friend at the BSMU, stalked up to the cop car. He got as close as the police would let him. I thought he was going to start throwing punches or yelling at the cops that they had the wrong guy. Instead, he glared at me.

"You had us all fooled, didn't you, Galder?"

"What?"

This had to be some kind of nightmare. If I could just wake up….

"You had us all thinking you were this perfect specimen of humankind, and here you were planning *murder*. You sick fuck."

Then, he spit at me. He was too far away for the slimy glob to reach me. It splatted onto the pavement a few feet away.

"Adam, wait—"

I shoved against the cops holding me before remembering my wrists were shackled and I was surrounded. Something hard and metal collided with the side of my head, and for a few seconds, I blacked out.

I was still struggling to get the words out to explain that they were all making a terrible mistake…that I'd been set up…when I was shoved into the cop car.

It wasn't me! I wanted to scream as I stared out the tinted window at my fellow students' hate-filled looks. *I would never do something like this.*

Sirens blared. The retinue of cop cars bumped over the lawn and screeched out onto Storrow Drive. My handcuffs clanked together as we hit a pothole.

The cop sitting in the passenger seat turned to stare at me through the grating. "Hotshot valedictorian falls just like the rest of us." He smirked. "Think you're better than everyone else, don't you?"

"What? No."

The cop just huffed out a laugh and turned back around.

I sat in numb silence as the car and our escort blew through Boston traffic, sirens blaring. My mind was filled with the image of Penelope's bloody face and those awful words written across my window.

The car didn't stop until it reached a metal gate. The driver rolled down his window to talk to the men in the security booth. One of them laughed, and they waved at each other like this was just another day at the office.

The barbed wire-wrapped gate rolled back. Three cameras turned to follow the squad car's progress as it rolled forward. I caught sight of the sign posted above the fence.

Federal Correctional Institute of Boston, the sign read.

I had read about this place. It was a maximum-security prison, and the only prisoners kept here were ones who had been accused of breaking a high law. It was a small building, which made sense because none of the prisoners stayed long. High crimes were tried within a few days, and those who were convicted were immediately sentenced to death.

I felt like I was going to be sick again.

I forced myself to breathe. Panicking wouldn't help anything, and if I was going to get myself out of this mess, I'd need my wits about me.

I was yanked out of the cop car and escorted inside the building. Buzzers sounded as different metal gates opened and closed, bringing me deeper and deeper into the prison.

I was shoved into a tiny room with nothing but a table and two chairs on either side. The floor was concrete. Three of the walls were cinder blocks. The fourth was a one-way mirror. I was pushed into one of the hard metal chairs, and my handcuffs were attached to a short chain that locked me to the table.

"Start thinking about what you want for your last meal," the prison guard said as he gave my shackles a tug to make sure I was firmly attached to the table.

"Nah," his partner said. "High crime violators don't get a last meal request."

"Oh, right." The first one grinned down at me. "Hope you like soggy green beans, then."

Still chuckling, they slammed the door, leaving me alone in the interrogation room.

CHAPTER 6

It was impossible to tell how long the interrogation had been going on, but I guessed it had been hours. My voice was hoarse from answering all the questions, and my head pounded from the horror of it all.

Pictures were strewn across the table before me, making it impossible for me to think about anything else. There were pictures of my dorm room with Penelope's bloody body crumpled on the ground. There were pictures of my bed, which was covered in blood. There was a pile of my own clothes on the floor, covered in blood. There was the bloody message on the window.

Everywhere, blood. So much blood.

"Your fingerprints are all over the room," the detective said again.

It was the third or fourth time the detective had said this. I knew the repetition was meant to trip me up and expose inconsistencies in my story.

"Of course my fingerprints were in my bedroom," I ground out. "I'm not disputing that it's my room. I'm disputing that I'm the one who killed Penelope."

The detective opened a folder, pulled out a few sheets of paper, and slid them across the table to me.

"Is this your valedictorian speech?"

I stared at the papers. The words were typed on regular printer paper.

Welcome, Class of 2070, and congratulations to all of us!

That was, in fact, the opening of the speech I had been working on before the party. That was where the similarities ended, though. The speech in front of me was full of hate and slurs against Magics that I couldn't even think, let alone write. It wasn't a valedictorian speech; it was a rant against Magics and the Alliance.

"This isn't mine," I said. The chain rattled against the table as I slid the papers back to the detective.

"It was on your computer," the detective countered in the demeaning way he'd been speaking to me all night.

"Then whoever murdered Penelope must have put it on there." I lifted my chin at the papers on the table. "I didn't write this speech, and I didn't kill Penelope."

"Well, that's strange, isn't it?" The detective gave me a mock-puzzled expression.

"Why would I go to the BSMU and take a job in the Alliance if I hated Magics?"

"A good question, and one I would like the answer to before your execution." The detective studied me for several seconds. "I'm told you're the most well-liked student at the BSMU. My people couldn't find a single person who had a bad word to say about you." He rearranged the pictures on the table between us until one of Penelope, smiling and alive, was on top.

My chest squeezed. I still couldn't wrap my head around the fact that she was gone.

Not gone, I reminded myself. *Murdered. And everyone thinks I'm the one who did it.* I refused let myself panic, though, as much as every part of me strained in that direction. I just needed to explain myself. I needed to understand what had really happened.

"Maybe," the detective said, "you're not used to sharing the spotlight, and you decided to take matters into your own hands. Maybe, in a jealous rage, you decided to kill that *Mag* so you wouldn't have to share the stage with her."

"That's insane," I said, unable to keep silent any longer. "And I don't use that word."

"Even amid all of this," the detective gestured at the crime scene photos spread out between us, "you're cool as a cucumber. You haven't broken down or shed a tear like anyone else in your position would have. Are you a sociopath, Graysen?"

"I'm not a sociopath," I replied through gritted teeth.

Some of my numbness had worn off enough for anger to poke through.

"Every bit of evidence you've shown me is circumstantial," I said. "Did you find my DNA on Penelope's body?"

"Alright, Mr. Fancy-Ass Lawyer." The detective leaned back in his chair and crossed one leg over the other, like he was playing along. "You didn't need to touch her. All you had to do was slash a knife across her throat."

"And where's the murder weapon?" I demanded. "I haven't seen any pictures of it. Were my fingerprints on that, at least?"

"You disposed of the murder weapon," the detective replied. "My guess is you threw it in the river." He leaned forward. "Am I right?"

"So, no murder weapon," I continued, ignoring the detective's question. "And no DNA evidence. Penelope could have been killed by anyone. Like I've already said, I wasn't in my room at the time of the murder. Anyone could have gotten the building code, and my door was unlocked."

"That's right, you did mention you hadn't been in your room since before the party." The detective smiled as he flipped back through his note pad. "Where did you say you were again?"

It was the fourth time the detective had asked some version of this question, and it was the part of my story that got complicated. I focused, making sure to repeat the same version I had given the last three times.

When I finished, the man consulted his note pad. "Ten students and one faculty member saw you walking to your dorm with Penelope."

"Maybe it was someone who looked like me," I said. "It was dark. They might have gotten confused."

"That's an awful lotta confusion at a school full of smart people." The detective scratched his stubbled jaw. "Do you have a doppelganger someone forgot to tell me about?"

"No, but—"

"And of course, let's not forget the room of fifty-three students, including yourself, who heard Penelope's premonition. Or has your memory failed you on this point, too?"

"I remember," I grated out. "I also remember her telling me that her visions are often inaccurate and show only partial truths."

The detective looked down at the transcript of Penelope's vision. "I'd call this particular premonition pretty damn accurate."

"It *wasn't* me."

"Your alibi is leaving the party alone and wandering around alone on a night when you should have been celebrating with your nearest and dearest," the detective said. "Does that sound weak to you?" He directed his gaze at the one-way mirror separating the interrogation room from whoever was watching on the other side. "That sounds weak to me."

I knew how it sounded. If I was on the other side of the table, I'd be saying exactly what this detective was saying now.

If I told the detective about who I'd been with, I would prove my innocence in Penelope's murder. And I'd also be admitting my guilt in breaking the other two high crimes. And I'd get Kaira arrested along with me. As much as I'd rather be executed for the crimes I'd actually committed—not something as heinous as murder—I wasn't about to drag Kaira down with me.

"I'm telling you the truth. Penelope was still at the party when I left. She was with her parents."

I held the detective's stare as we faced off. Finally, the man sitting across the table sighed.

"I guess we're done here for now."

As soon as he'd finished speaking, the door opened and two prison guards came into the room. They unhooked my handcuffs from the chain on the table. They locked shackles onto my ankles, too, and I was clumsy as I got up from the table and followed the guards out of the room. The only sound was the rhythmic clank-shuffle-clank noise I made with each step.

We stopped outside one of a dozen identical cells. One of the guards scanned his badge and then tapped a long series of letters and numbers into the keypad. A loud buzzer sounded and a red overhead light flashed as the metal door slid back.

It was all so surreal I couldn't bring myself to feel the fear and grief I knew was buried somewhere inside me. Part of me was still convinced this was just some nightmare that I'd wake up from and laugh about with my teammates. The other part was sure there was some logical explanation for what had happened, and the detective would come chasing us down at any minute to tell my guards they had the wrong man.

These were the thoughts that filled my mind as I was shoved into the tiny cell. The buzzer sounded again, and the door slammed shut.

CHAPTER 7

I was brought out of my cell some time later and taken to a different room that looked much like the one in which I'd been interrogated. I sat handcuffed to the table for what could have been minutes or hours before two guards returned, escorting a man in an expensive suit.

I recognized Emmanuel Blytheman, the lawyer my father had hired after the whole scandal with Kaira's missing file. The lawyer took his seat across from me, put his briefcase on the floor beside him, and stared politely at the guards until they left the room and shut the door behind them.

"Graysen," Emmanuel said. He hesitated only briefly before reaching across the table to pat my shackled hand.

"I didn't do it," I said, my voice as fierce as I could manage after so many hours of interrogation.

Emmanuel reached down and opened his briefcase. He pulled out a stack of papers and put them on the table. Then, he took a pair of glasses out of his breast pocket, carefully polished the lenses with a microfiber cloth, and put them on.

I could tell from his deliberate movements that the man was staving off the inevitable bad news.

"It doesn't look good, Graysen," he said, frowning at the papers. "The prophecy and the witnesses are pretty irrefutable, and your alibi isn't going to hold up in the trial."

"It's the only one I have because it's the truth," I said.

I had never felt more helpless and out of control in my life. It made me want to scream.

Emmanuel Blytheman sighed. "Your trial is tomorrow."

My stomach turned over.

"Tomorrow?"

I knew that high crimes were tried and convicted quickly, but…tomorrow? I needed more time to figure this out. There had to be some explanation for what had happened, I just needed more time.

"Can we delay at all?" I asked the lawyer.

"My team's working on it, but there doesn't seem to be much room on this one. The Magic community is…quite angry."

"I understand. Penelope was my friend, and I want justice for her, too. But they've got the wrong person."

"I'm trying to arrange for your father to visit you before tomorrow," Emmanuel said as though I hadn't spoken. "There are strict rules about visitors, but I might be able to arrange something so you can…."

Say goodbye.

He might as well have spoken the words, because they were written all over the lawyer's apologetic face.

"Is there anything that can be done?" I asked, feeling a wave of hopelessness crash over me.

Emmanuel gave me a small shake of his head and grimaced. "I'll do what I can to convince the jury there's enough reasonable doubt, but—"

But don't get your hopes up.

The lawyer cleared his throat. His eyes shifted around the small room as his hands fumbled for another stack of papers in his briefcase. I looked at the header on the top sheet, and my breath caught.

It was a will.

I was good at keeping my pain to myself. I'd done it for years—both with my disease and Kaira breaking my heart. It was the only reason why I wasn't weeping and sniveling right now. That, and the knowledge that my self-control was all I had left. If I let go of it, then I'd have nothing at all.

Besides, it wasn't like crying or begging would make me look less guilty. I had read the certainty on the detective's face, and I could see the apology on my lawyer's. It didn't matter what happened at the trial tomorrow. As far as everyone who mattered was concerned, I was guilty. End of story.

"Do you have any assets you'd like me to allocate?" the lawyer asked, still not looking at me.

I felt myself shaking my head. I had a few thousand dollars in the bank from last summer's internship, but nothing else of value.

"I understand." The lawyer softened his voice. "Are there any messages you'd like me to deliver, or anything of that nature, just in case?"

My thoughts immediately went to Kaira. But it wasn't like I could ask my lawyer to go seek out an unMarked Magic to say…what?

And after what I'd been accused of, none of my friends or teammates would want anything to do with me. My reputation was destroyed. A sick, twisted feeling grabbed hold of my insides and squeezed. I tried to rub my eyes before remembering my wrists were shackled to the table.

"Just my dad," I said, my voice not much louder than the lawyer's. "I'd like to see him, if I could."

The lawyer nodded in understanding. "I'll see what I can do."

He stood, looking relieved to be done with this hopeless and pointless meeting. "Keep your chin up, Graysen. Blytheman and Associates are on your side. We'll raise hell at the trial tomorrow."

I watched the lawyer knock on the door, and then he was escorted away. My two guards took me back to my cell.

I sat on the square frame of my bed, which was without a pillow or mattress, and tried to think. Someone—not me—had murdered Penelope. If I could figure out who it was, I could get out of this mess.

If ten witnesses had seen Penelope and I together, could it have been an Illusionist? I discarded the idea as quickly as it came to me. First, the detective had said that there were no Marked Magics placed anywhere near the scene of the crime at the time of the murder. Second, it was unlikely there were any other unMarked Animate Illusionists besides Kaira who were that powerful. And Kaira had been with me while the murder was taking place. Third, a Magic would never have killed one of their own and written an anti-Magic slur on my window. The perpetrator had to be a Natural.

The motive was clear enough. The murderer hated Magics. The fact that it was the first year when Magics and Naturals were graduating from a combined campus, and the fact that Penelope was the Magic valedictorian, was motive enough for anyone who didn't like the even footing that Naturals and Magics were now on.

People who didn't believe in equality between Naturals and Magics didn't go to the BSMU, which meant the murderer wasn't a student at the school.

But even with that knowledge of who the killer *wasn't*, I was no closer to having a suspect.

CHAPTER 8

There was no clock or window, but I thought it must be nearing early morning. My cell had a sink, a toilet, and the square platform that I thought was supposed to be my bed. Aside from the bright white light that shined mercilessly on me from the ceiling, and the cameras spaced in each corner of the cell, there was nothing else to look at. It was obvious this place hadn't been designed for a long-term stay.

I tried pacing, but there wasn't enough room in the cramped space to do it effectively, and it grated on my nerves the way the cameras angled to follow my every step. With little other choice, I sat on the square platform and buried my face in my hands to block out some of the blinding light.

I kept hoping to hear the buzzer sound and my door open, and for a guard to tell me that my father was here. It hadn't happened yet, and the minutes until my trial continued to tick by.

I didn't think my father would believe any of what the police were saying. Still, I needed to explain things to him. I needed him to hear the truth from my own lips. Mostly, though, I just wanted to see a face that wasn't filled with hate and accusation before my trial.

Since my mom left, my dad and I had been each other's only family. Now, I would be leaving my dad, too.

I felt exhausted and sick to my stomach. All my joints were aching in reaction to the stress and anxiety of the last several hours. But the physical discomfort wasn't enough to distract my mind from the horror of what had happened, and the position I was now in as a result.

I didn't want to die. All of the *what if's* and *if only's* hovering on the edge of my consciousness were enough to drive me insane.

Too bad insanity pleas didn't work for the high crimes.

If only I had stayed at that damn party instead of leaving with Kaira, I'd have an ironclad alibi. And Penelope might still be alive.

In spite of everything, I still felt too many emotions where Kaira was concerned. Would she believe I had done this? Would the rest of the Hansley clan?

Take care of yourself. Those were my last words to the person who, in spite of everything that had happened, I loved with every fiber of my being.

I let my head fall back against the cinder blocks. All the pictures the detective had shown me swam through my mind. I had been so consumed by my own impending execution that I hadn't given much thought to Penelope and what her family was now facing. Now, I couldn't get the image of her bloody face out of my mind. I couldn't stop hearing her mother's screams.

There hadn't been a magically-motivated murder in Boston in years, and now, everyone believed the top Natural student at the BSMU, a school that boasted about its mission to promote understanding and equality between the two groups, had committed the most heinous of anti-Magic crimes. I couldn't even begin to contemplate the ramifications of this murder.

Who would do something like this?

My academic brain couldn't let go of the question, even though it would very soon be irrelevant…to me, at least. I would go to my grave, and the killer would walk free.

Would the person murder again? The thought of someone like that out and about in the world without anyone the wiser made me feel sick.

I wrapped my arms around my bent knees and huddled in on myself, trying to ignore my too-quick pulse and the coldness that had stolen over me.

I tried not to think about being led into the sterile room where some prison doctor would administer my lethal injection. The process was supposed to be fast and painless, but I'd heard of at least a few botched executions that had caused the inmate a long, agonizing death.

I knew enough about pain not to be anxious for more.

Regret washed over me as I thought about the future I would never have.

I'd had so many plans. I'd had aspirations. None of them were worth a damn anymore.

Maybe this was all some kind of twisted cosmic justice for breaking the other two high laws without being caught. The difference with those crimes, though, was that no one had been hurt when I broke those laws. Still, some part of me appreciated the irony that I was about to die for the only high law I hadn't broken.

I had never thought loving Kaira or lying to protect her had been worthy of the high crime designation, but some part of me couldn't deny the circuitous justice of where I now found myself. My one comfort was that Kaira wasn't in the cell next to mine.

Without warning, the cell's harsh white light winked out. Everything was thrown into darkness. I couldn't see anything except the red blinking lights in each of the four cameras. There was a mechanical whine. Then, the cameras went dark, too.

My first thought was that they were going to execute me without a trial. My second thought was that whoever had murdered Penelope was here for me. The buzzer sounded at my door.

I jumped to my feet. I searched the darkness for something I could use as a weapon, but of course, there was nothing.

My pulse raced as the cell door slid back with maddening precision. There were multiple voices and flashlight beams on the other side.

"Are you sure this is the right one?" an unfamiliar female voice asked.

"Smith said—" a rumbling male reply began, before it was cut off by someone else's "Shhh!"

Three flashlight beams swept the inside of my cell.

"Gray?"

After a stunned silence, I found my voice.

"Kaira?"

CHAPTER 9

Three people crammed into the cell with me, their flashlight beams bouncing wildly and filling my vision with starbursts.

"What are you doing here?" I asked, bewildered and still trying to figure out if I was hallucinating.

"What's it look like?" the other girl—not Kaira—asked. "We're prison breaking your ass."

"I don't—"

"Gray, come on."

Kaira grabbed my hand and tugged, but I didn't move. I hadn't gotten a good look at her face. It was possible this was all some kind of a trick. And who were those other two people?

Given my impending execution, I shouldn't have been worried about getting murdered. But too many strange and terrible things had happened tonight. I couldn't even be entirely sure that my brain, in some kind of self-preservation mode, hadn't fabricated all of this in my desperation to live. Distrust and wariness prevailed, and I hung back.

"A little short on time here, Gray," would-be Kaira said, tapping an impatient foot on the ground.

"How do I know it's you?" I asked.

She huffed before flashing her beam of light on herself, which made her features warped and shadowed. It made me even more distrustful of what I was seeing.

There was another male voice that sounded like it was coming through a cell phone, but none of the people in here seemed to be holding anything except their flashlights.

"Smith, shut up for a second," Kaira said. It certainly sounded like her voice, but again, I couldn't be sure it wasn't my own brain playing tricks on me.

The cell phone babble went quiet, and Kaira turned back to me. "When we were twelve, you dared me to illusion both my cousins into warthogs. I did, but I didn't have enough of a handle on my magic to know how to turn them back. They had snouts for two days, and I was grounded for a month."

"Ohmygod Kaira, you didn't!" the other girl in my cell exclaimed.

"We need to get moving," the guy standing beside her said.

That had all happened just like she'd said, but....

"Someone else might have known that story," I said. "Or everything you're saying could be a figment of my imagination," I muttered.

The woman who gave every indication of being Kaira sighed. "Go sweep the hall," she told the other two. "We'll be right out."

That other, faraway male voice had started to yell again. Kaira reached up and clicked something near her ear. I realized she had on a headset, and the voice had been coming through the earpiece. The other guy's voice abruptly cut off.

Kaira waited until the other two had left the cell before coming toward me. I wondered if the killer had been an Illusionist after all, and now that person was here for me, too. Or maybe it wasn't Penelope's killer, but an Illusionist who wanted to kill me for what had been done to Penelope....

My racing thoughts turned to a quiet hum in the back of my mind when Kaira reached up and slid her hands around my neck.

"It's me, babe," she whispered.

My breath caught. Before I could recover, she kissed me.

There was nothing illusory about our kiss or the way she felt when my arms came around her. There was no one else on Earth who could make me feel like this.

I would have stayed just like that, holding and kissing her, until they came to drag me off for my trial. But she pulled away.

"Convinced now?" She was breathless, too.

"Um...."

"Good. Let's go."

I let her pull me out into the hallway, which was still lit, although I had just enough brain space left to notice all the cameras were turned off. Kaira flipped the switch at her ear. She winced as a torrent of shouting came from the other end.

The huge guy who looked like some kind of bodyguard scanned the hall, his eyes squinting against the harsh light. A tiny blonde who looked younger than the rest of us…maybe eighteen or nineteen, was bouncing on the balls of her feet.

"Can we go yet?" she asked, her voice breathless with barely-contained excitement.

"Hall's clear," the guy said.

"Come on!"

I followed the three of them to the end of the hall where another door blocked our path.

"9174AXJ," the voice yelled over Kaira's headset. She punched the code into the keypad, the buzzer sounded, and the door opened.

"Go left!" the voice shouted.

We obeyed, our shoes slapping the cement as we sprinted toward what I hoped was the prison's exit.

"Guards on your six," the voice announced over Kaira's headset.

I slowed, expecting the big guy and I would do what we could so at least the girls could escape.

"No, keep going," the tiny blonde called to me.

She stopped running and blew on her fists. All of her skin that wasn't covered by clothes, from her face to her ankles, turned a metallic silver.

"Stop!" a voice shouted. The air filled with a popping sound, and something pinged off the wall next to me.

"Rubber bullets," the big guy said, holding up one of them like it was supposed to make all of us feel better.

"Bri, take care of them," Kaira yelled.

Out of the corner of my eye, I saw the blonde girl race down the hall. She thrust out one silver, metallic fist. The nearest guard was flung against the wall and slumped to the ground. His gun went skittering across the cement floor. Bri didn't glance back at him as she lunged for the others.

The next one went down after one sharp jab of Bri's metal leg. He didn't get back up.

It was her against six armed guards. She barely made it up to most of their shoulders, but within a few seconds, she had turned the guards to moaning, barely-conscious bodies on the ground. She was so fast, not one of them managed to get a shot off before they went down.

"Damn," I muttered.

I was the only one who seemed surprised.

"More ahead," the voice on Kaira's headset announced.

Bri was vaulting back across the hall. She did a crazy front flip over a guard who was rolling on the ground and clutching his stomach. She looked like a tiny ninja, except she was dressed more like a southern belle. And her skin was silver.

She put down all three of the guards racing toward us before I finished taking a breath.

"You've got about thirty seconds before the next batch," the voice on Kaira's headset warned.

"Michael, do your thing," Kaira told the big guy.

Nodding, he crouched down next to one of the guards lying on the ground.

"You didn't see anything," he said in a low, soothing voice. "Everything is normal. No one and nothing is out of place." He put a hand on each of the guards and repeated his words.

He was obviously a Whisper, and a powerful one. Most Whispers could only make suggestions to people, but it seemed like Michael could convince anyone of anything.

Who the hell were these people?

Michael was scowling when he stood back up.

"You'd make my job easier if you didn't knock them around so hard," he told Bri.

"Got a little excited, I guess," Bri replied with a shrug.

"Get moving, you idiots!" the voice shouted from Kaira's headset.

Kaira punched in the code he read her for the next door. This time, I counted ten guards, all of whom had machine guns. I didn't think these ones were filled with rubber bullets.

Bri raced down the hall. I flinched at the sound of gunfire. I think I shouted something, but I couldn't hear anything over the roar of the guns. Bri stood there, tiny and silver, and utterly unconcerned. The bullets struck her and pinged off her metal skin. Shouts filled the hallway as the bullets ricocheted off her and went flying back at the guards.

I was rooted to the spot, barely able to comprehend what I was seeing. Bri didn't share my paralysis. She sprinted after the guards, who had flattened themselves on the ground to avoid their own bullets. She kicked their weapons out of their hands and had them writhing in pain in ten seconds flat.

Michael Whispered to each of the guards. They seemed to go into a trance afterward and just lay on the ground, blinking at the ceiling and looking mildly puzzled.

"Hurry up!" the voice yelled over Kaira's headset.

We continued our mad dash.

Incessant chatter continued to come through Kaira's earpiece, and she was talking back.

"I don't care about how you do it," she was saying. "Just make sure those outside cameras are down and fry whatever recording they've already got."

"Too many guards coming to fight," the voice called.

"Damnit, Smith!" Kaira winced and rubbed at her ear.

"You've got approximately eighty seconds before they're on you," the voice said in somewhat less of a shout.

"Change of plans," Kaira said to Bri. "Knock them out."

I winced in sympathy as Bri went from guard to guard and clocked them on the head with her metallic fist. The guards were still placid from Michael's Whispering, and they didn't so much as make a peep as Bri stalked up to each one of them and rendered them unconscious with a single blow.

When Bri stood back up from the final guard, she no longer looked like the silver-skinned southern belle. In her place was a fearsome-looking male guard, complete with the full guard's uniform. If I didn't know Kaira's illusion work when I saw it, I would have thought I was losing my mind.

When I looked at Kaira, she was gone. In her place was a large woman with light skin, brown hair, and a scar down her left cheek. It was an exact match for the guard lying on the ground in front of her.

Michael had become another one of the guards, and when I looked down at myself, I saw I was a black man with a beard, just like the guard who was slumped against the wall beside me.

"Gray, get his gun," Kaira commanded me.

I did, the weapon feeling heavy and unnatural in my hands. I caught sight of my reflection in the glass above the door. I looked terrifying.

"Alright," Guard Kaira said. "Act natural."

We walked out of the last set of barred doors and found ourselves in the prison entrance, which was swarming with guards and police.

"What's happening?"

"Where's the prisoner?"

"That way!" the guard I thought was Bri yelled, pointing down a different hallway.

It was chaos as the guards and police pushed their way through the narrow corridor.

"We'll check the front," Kaira announced, walking purposefully toward the doors that led out of the prison. She waved to Michael, Bri, and me. "You all, with me," she commanded.

The sky overhead was still dark, but floodlights bathed the entire front of the prison in harsh, white light.

I followed Kaira and the others. They were striding toward a white, unmarked van idling right outside.

"Hey, what are you doing?" a voice called from behind us.

"Keep walking," Kaira commanded.

"Hey! *Hey!*"

Kaira broke into a run. The rest of us followed. Bullets pinged off the outside of the van. The door opened, and we threw ourselves inside. The last one—Michael, I thought—slammed the door. There was a tinny rattle as bullets struck the outside of the van.

"Go, go, go!" someone shouted.

The woman in the driver's seat slammed on the gas. Tires screeched, and then we were peeling away from the curb.

CHAPTER 10

The van streaked down the access road between the prison building and the exit, but two cop cars were quickly gaining on us.

The interior of the van was open, with long, cushioned seats on either side. Kaira sat between Bri and Michael across from me. I was sitting next to a guy who was dressed in a pinstriped suit with a hot pink shirt and purple tie. He started to wave his hands like he was dancing.

"Oopsie, that wind can be so pesky," he said.

I looked out the window and saw a dumpster fly through the air and land on the road behind us. It blocked off the road and forced the cop cars to come to a screeching stop.

Holy shit. The guy just lifted a dumpster…with his mind.

"That's enough, A.J.," Kaira warned. "I don't want them to have any guesses about who we are."

"But what about my party tricks?" the guy, A.J., whined. He swept his long bangs out of his eyes by flipping his head in slow motion, like he was on *Baywatch* or something.

"You can show us and we'll ooh and ahh when we get home," the Indian woman in the driver's seat said.

I lurched forward as the van came to a halt at the guard booth at the end of the access road.

"Open your window," Michael ordered the driver.

The big guy leaned around the front seat and stuck his head out the window. He spoke to the guards in that same low, calming voice he'd used before.

"Open the gate," he told the guard. "Don't let anyone else get through after us. You don't remember what any of us looked like, or even how many of us there were. You don't remember anything about us at all."

Nodding, the guard ducked into the booth, and then the prison gate was sliding back.

The two cop cars, which must have detoured onto the grass to get around the dumpster, were speeding toward us.

A.J. flicked his hand, and the first cop car fishtailed. The one behind it slammed into the first.

"Silly Nats don't know how to drive a car," A.J. cackled.

"Motorcycle police coming up on the right!" the Indian woman yelled.

Bri blew on her fists, and her whole body turned metallic again. She opened the van's rear door.

I cringed out of instinct at the sound of bullets pinging off Bri's impenetrable skin.

I watched in muted horror as she catapulted herself out of the van. She held onto ropes attached to the van's ceiling, and her feet glided atop the asphalt like she was some kind of extreme water skier…minus the water and the skis. Fiery sparks flew behind her as she skidded along behind the van.

If we weren't fleeing for our lives, it would be one of the coolest things I'd ever seen.

When one of the motorcycles got close, Bri balanced on one titanium leg and kicked out with the other. The motorcycle and its rider crashed to the ground behind us.

I looked away before I could see what kind of shape the motorcycle's rider was in.

Bri swung herself back into the van, closed the door, and blew on her fist until her skin turned normal again.

My hands were clammy, and I let out a shuddering breath. No one else in the car reacted. It was like this was something she did all the time.

"You should have let me have that one," A.J. complained. "I wanted to see if I could make him go like E.T."

"You know, the part with the bike," he continued, when no one replied.

"I can't concentrate with A.J. babbling," complained a guy, whose voice I recognized as the one that had been yelling through Kaira's headset.

I hadn't noticed him at first because he was sitting behind a work station that had been built into the back of the van's interior. There were three laptops balanced on the desktop and a tangle of wires at his feet. I couldn't really make out the guy's face because he had the hood of his sweatshirt pulled up, and his long, greasy hair hung on either side of him like a curtain. He was still wearing his headset, even though Kaira had pulled hers off.

"Boyfriend, until you can lift a car in the air, talk to the hand." A.J. made a *talk to the hand* gesture I hadn't seen anyone use since middle school.

"I'm over here making us disappear," Computer Guy shot back. "You know how many cameras are in that prison?"

Kaira held up her hand to stop A.J. from retorting. "Smith, can you get us green lights all the way?"

"Well, yeah, and—"

"And scramble the Nat police's communication. I don't want them following us."

Smith's fingers didn't touch any of the keyboards, but I could see the screens flickering and changing as he manipulated them with his mind.

Techies were rare, especially powerful ones. And Smith was clearly powerful—at least a Level 8—if he could turn off all the prison's cameras and affect the police's communication.

The van screeched down the road. When I looked back, I realized no one was chasing us anymore.

A.J. sat back and fanned himself. "Whew, that one got the ticker pounding." He elbowed me in the ribs and winked at me. "You were really locked up in there."

I was still trying to process what exactly had just happened and couldn't think of a single word to say.

"What's the matter?" A.J. asked. "Kitty cat got your tongue?"

I just shook my head, still trying to wrap my brain around the fact that I was no longer in prison.

"We did all this rescuing for a mute?" A.J. complained. "Kaira, you promised me a new friend."

"Ignore Whiny Pants," the woman driving the van said, glancing at me in the rearview mirror.

"Keep your eyes on the road," Michael told her, as we all grabbed for something to hold onto when the van lurched around another corner.

"That's *Sir* Whiny Pants to you," A.J. retorted, seemingly unperturbed by the hazardous driving.

My heartbeat started to slow, and as it did, I was hit by the revelation that Kaira and five other high-level Magics had just broken me out the highest security prison in all of Boston—possibly in the country. The sky outside was lightening, and in a few short hours, I would have been sitting in a courtroom full of jurors who undoubtedly would have convicted me. I would have been executed by day's end.

"Who the hell are you people?" I asked.

"The Nat speaketh!" A.J. applauded.

I looked at Kaira. "Why?" I managed.

Her fierce gaze softened, but her tone was flippant when she said, "Because I didn't see anyone else rushing to save you."

"I—" I began. "I mean, thank you. All of you." There were six people in the van besides me, and of them, Kaira was the only one who wasn't a complete stranger.

Why would these Magics risk their lives for someone they'd never met?

"How did you even know?" I asked.

There was a chorus of snorts and guffaws from the five strangers, but Kaira's eyes were full of sympathy.

"You're all over the news, Gray."

Right. Of course I was. Twenty cop cars parked on the quad, and ten-thousand students with cell phones. It was all just too much. My brain was rapid-firing, but everything ground to a halt when my thoughts snagged on one person.

"My dad," I choked.

"Joseph Galder is under surveillance," Smith said from behind his laptop screens. "Three detectives in the house, and four more in two separate patrol cars outside 136 Bolter Street, Beacon Hill."

"What Smith is trying to say," Kaira said, "is that your dad is fine, but we can't get near him."

"I need to talk to him. To tell him—"

"Phone and Internet lines tapped," Smith said, like he was some kind of Techie robot.

"He's being investigated as an accomplice," Kaira explained. "You can't try to contact him until the cops and surveillance are gone."

"Especially now that you're a fugitive," A.J. added helpfully.

A fugitive.

I tried to swallow the lump in my throat, but my mouth had gone too dry for me to manage it.

Ten seconds. That's how long it took for the police to slam me up against the side of the dorm and lock the handcuffs on me. That's how long it took for the life I'd been working toward every day for the last three years—hell, every day since the start of high school—to come crashing down around me.

"I'm so sorry, Gray," Kaira said in a quiet voice.

"Why did you all risk…everything for me? Now they'll be searching of all of you, too."

My words were met with more laughter.

"Sweetie, the authorities were looking for us long before your pretty face came along," A.J. said.

"They're all unMarked like me," Kaira explained.

"We're colleagues," Bri said, her voice full of pride.

The van turned onto the Mass Turnpike. It was the beginning of rush hour, but somehow, Smith managed to keep us moving through traffic. The van swerved and darted around cars in its path, much to the irritation of Michael, who kept telling the driver—whose name I learned was Yutika— that she wasn't allowed behind the wheel anymore. Yutika had shot back that she was from New York City and hadn't even driven a car until she was nineteen, a fact which didn't make me feel any more comfortable about having my life in her hands.

The others in the car bickered good-naturedly, like breaking a death-row inmate out of a maximum-security prison was just another day at the office.

My mind had gone a little numb, like it had been stretched to the breaking point and needed to go into sleep mode before it overheated. I stared out the window without really seeing anything as we got off the Pike and drove through the quieter streets in Beacon Hill.

"We can't go to the house," I said as soon as I realized where the van was heading. "If the cops find it, you'll never be able to go back there."

"He knows about the house?" Yutika asked.

"You certainly were neighborly, weren't you?" A.J. raised an eyebrow. "The closest I ever got to my neighbor growing up was when Mrs. Troll sprayed me with a hose for getting too close to her side of the fence."

"Was her name really Mrs. Troll?" Bri asked.

"No, but it suited her," A.J. replied.

"Don't worry," Kaira told me, speaking over the others. "Ma illusioned the house, so no one'll be able to find us."

Ma Hansley, Kaira's mom, was a Level 8 Inanimate Illusionist. I had always thought that together, Ma and Kaira could rule the world.

"Did she know you were going to do this for me?" I asked, my voice coming out rough.

"I didn't discuss it with her," Kaira replied.

A flood of guilt hit me.

Ma Hansley had lost most of her family, including her father, brothers, and husband—Kaira's dad—in the Atlanta Slaughters when Kaira was just a baby. She was a fierce mamma bear to anyone she considered family, which for Ma included half the neighborhood. Still, I didn't think Ma would be okay with Kaira taking such a risk. *I* wasn't okay with her taking such a risk.

The van slowed as we entered a narrow alley behind the houses. The van took a right, and I winced as it headed straight for a brick wall. Instead of either turning or hitting the wall, which was what I was honestly expecting with the way Yutika was driving, the van slid right through the illusion. We lurched to a stop inside a narrow garage.

"We're ho-ome," A.J. announced.

CHAPTER 11

ood job, team," Kaira said as we piled out of the van.

Smith grunted and handed me one of his laptops, which I took to mean that I should carry it inside.

The moment I stepped into the house, I was assaulted by memories. This was the house Kaira's paternal grandpa had left her in high school. It was where Kaira and I had spent all of our free time. It was the only place we had ever really felt safe.

Back then, though, the inside of the house had looked very different from the way it did now. The house had been empty of furniture when Kaira first inherited it. We had scraped together our savings from various summer jobs and bought a couch, a table, and a bed off eBay. They had been the most adult purchases of our lives, and when the furniture was successfully delivered, we had just sat on the couch and giggled like two evil maniacs for about a week straight.

We had hauled up the heavy pieces of the bed set—which had arrived deconstructed—to the master bedroom. I had brought my old stereo over, and we blasted music while we built the bed. For some reason we couldn't work out, the bed had ended up being slightly tilted and smaller than advertised. Still, neither of us had complained.

The house looked nothing like the way I remembered it. The small living area was bursting with two couches, two coffee tables strewn with Smith's electronics, and three oversized bean bags. Colored lights were strung all along the top of the wall, and there were books, bags of potato chips, empty soda cans, and other odds and ends scattered over every surface that wasn't taken up by electronics. The place wasn't a complete mess, but it had a thoroughly lived-in kind of feel.

From the way the others sprawled out on the furniture, it was obvious they lived here with Kaira. I didn't quite know how to feel about the fact that these people had made their home in a place that had once belonged to Kaira and me. At the same time, it made it easier for me to keep my memories of this place in the past where they belonged.

I was startled out of my reverie as banging erupted in the kitchen. A.J. sat on top of the island with his legs crossed like he was some kind of a flamboyant Buddha. He was waving his hands as pots and pans flew through the air around him. He swayed his arms and hips, and the kitchenware responded with a synchronized dance of their own. Even A.J.'s tie started to levitate when a particularly excited pot almost collided with a casserole dish. It looked like a scene straight out of *Beauty and the Beast*.

"A.J. stress-cooks," Bri told me. "He's pretty good, too."

"He'd be even better if he didn't insist on making everything vegan." Yutika made a face.

"Do you have any idea how many cows are slaughtered each year?" A.J. called back from the kitchen. "This house will not be complicit. Do you hear me? Not complicit!"

Yutika opened her mouth to retort, but whatever she said was drowned out by the opera music now blaring from the kitchen.

Yutika raised her voice to say, "We all know you don't need those hand motions to levitate anything. You just think they make you look cool."

"Can't hear you!" A.J. shouted over the opera music.

"I'm Yutika," she said, holding out her hand and giving me a friendly smile.

Yutika was short and a little chubby. Her thick black hair was wild, and she kept blowing at her bangs to get them out of her eyes, which made her look continually windswept. She also had a gap between her front teeth that was on prominent display whenever she smiled, which seemed to be often.

"So, you're the resident getaway driver around here?" I asked.

Her smile broadened. "Not usually. This was kind of a one-time special occasion since I was the only one with free hands. Usually I'm just in the back with my sketchbook."

When she saw my puzzled look, she clarified, "I'm a Creator."

I had never met a Creator before, but I knew from my ABCs of Magical Abilities class that Creators could bring objects to life by drawing them on paper.

It was considered impolite to ask a Magic directly about her ability and level, but I figured we were past that given what we'd all just been through together. Besides, I was curious.

"Could you bring a cow to life just by drawing it, then?"

A.J.'s wail came from the kitchen, although I wasn't sure if it was from the suggestion of creating a cow or whatever was now making smoke waft over the stovetop.

Yutika rolled her eyes in A.J.'s direction, but she was smiling. "My magic goes a little funky with anything alive, but hypothetically—"

"No, no, no! No cows!" A.J. shrieked.

Yutika laughed as she swatted at the fork that had zoomed from the kitchen to buzz around her. "My job around here is more functional. I make all the money and any documentation our refugees need—plane tickets, passports, getaway vehicles…. You may have noticed the van we picked you up in was built to our specific needs—that's 'cause I drew it that way."

"You mean this isn't the first time you've broken someone like me out of prison?"

"Prison is actually a first for us," she said.

"We've also never saved a Nat before," Smith, the Techie, said from behind his laptop screen.

I wasn't sure how much to read into his gruff tone, so I didn't say anything.

"I was the first initiate into the Six," Yutika continued. "Well, after Kaira, anyway."

"The Six?"

"Six Magics," Yutika said, pointing at each of them.

"I see," I said.

Kaira came over to sit on the couch's armrest. She draped a casual arm over Yutika's shoulder.

I gave up on trying to think of a delicate way to ask the question and just blurted out, "Are you all unMarked?"

"All unMarked, all Level 10s," Bri replied.

"I told you," Kaira said to me. "There are lots of Mags who don't want to be monitored. Since we had the magic and resources to save ourselves, we're paying it forward by helping other Mags in a bad situation."

"Not just a lone criminal anymore, then?" I asked Kaira. I hadn't meant the question to sound confrontational, but I heard the emotion in my own voice.

"These criminals just saved you from execution," Michael, the big guy, spoke for the first time.

"Be nice," Yutika told Michael, swatting the back of his head. "The Nat's been through a lot. He's probably in shock."

I didn't try to argue with that.

Bri smiled at me. "Nice to meet you, by the way. I'm the Six's Steel, in case you hadn't already figured that out."

"Steel, as in—"

"Well, it's a bit of a misnomer, actually. My body turns into titanium, not steel, but there isn't a designation for that on the Test. So, I just call myself a Steel to make things easier."

"Bri is our newest recruit," Kaira said.

"Newest and coolest," Bri said. "I'll fight anyone who disagrees."

The others put up their hands in surrender.

"I'm the coolest!" A.J. argued from the table, where he was overseeing the silverware and dishes that were setting themselves.

I was having trouble processing all of this. These people were all acting like they were just a group of friends living and working together. None of them seemed to notice, or care, that they were breaking more laws between them than I could count.

Of course, it wasn't like I was one to talk. Especially not now that I had escaped from prison.

Part of me still expected to wake up only to realize someone had slipped some hallucinogen into my drink during the party….

"You're getting that slack-jawed look again," A.J. said, coming over to peer at my face. "Are you going to faint? Tell me if you're going to faint. I hate being surprised by that sort of thing."

"A.J., let the man breathe," Kaira ordered.

"Don't you want to go to college?" I asked them when I'd regained my personal space. The BSMU valedictorian side of me was trying to process all the lost talent of six Level 10s living outside of the law.

"The Alliance puts Level 10s in boxes and studies them like animals," Smith said without looking up from his screen. "There was a blog post just yesterday about—"

I lost whatever else he was saying as the room erupted in groans, *give it a rest's,* and *not again's.*

"If you ask Smith, there's a conspiracy for everything," Yutika explained, rolling her eyes. "The government is planning to poison our water, the Alliance is trying to take us apart with tweezers and study us in petri dishes, and Russia is spying on us through our cell phone cameras."

"Yeah, we'll see who's laughing when you all get carted off for some science experiment, and I'm safe and hunkered down in some basement somewhere."

"Probably your mom's," A.J. said. "We all know you're grungy enough to pull it off."

A comb zoomed in from another room and started carefully brushing through A.J.'s already tangle-free black hair, as if to emphasize his own non-grunginess.

"Not all Techies live in their parents' basement," Smith replied with a scowl. "That's just an over-used trope people who don't know their ass from their hard drive use to make themselves feel better."

"I *was* hiding out in my parents' basement after I ducked my Test," Bri told me. "I would have been stuck down there forever if my parents hadn't found out about Kaira and asked her to help me. Now, I get to help other people. Pretty awesome, if you ask me."

"So, you help suspected criminals like me disappear?" I asked, still trying to get a handle on exactly what Kaira was involved with.

"You're the first criminal we've ever helped," Yutika said.

"Wrongly-convicted criminal," Kaira corrected. "And no." She turned her attention on me. "Most of the Mags we help are living in other countries where the Slaughters are still bad. They find out about us, and we help get them to Boston."

"It's not as simple as she's making it sound," A.J. said. "We have to create new files for them, fake a tracking history, and then there's the business of living arrangements and employment—"

"We get them a house, money, help them with a job, and get their kids into school," Bri added. "Sometimes, we need to go to wherever they're from and help get them out of the country. Gangs who are using them for their magic and threatening their kids…that kind of stuff."

It sounded like a good deed, but—

"What makes you any different from Valencia Stark and the UnAllied?" I asked.

My answer came in a chorus of scowls.

Valencia Stark, a Level 5 Rain Bringer, was universally disliked by Naturals and most Magics. She had founded a group called the UnAllied, which advocated for Magics to separate from Natural society and enslave any who were less powerful.

In addition to being completely bigoted and the exact opposite of everything the people of Boston championed, the concept was also ludicrous. Naturals far outnumbered Magics. Not to mention, the US military was composed solely of Naturals. Unless Magics liked the idea of being outnumbered a hundred-to-one and taking on the country's war arsenal, it was safe to say Valencia's plan wouldn't end well for anyone who attempted to see it through.

The woman was as nuts as the Naturals who still tried to argue that Magics weren't human.

The handful of Magics who listened to Valencia were equally crazy. She was arrested just about every other day for making it rain on everyone who came and went from the Alliance building. She liked to stand on the building's steps and spout nonsense, most of which was inaudible due to her insanely thick Boston accent.

Her biggest function in Boston society was to be the punchline for late-night comedy.

"We're not extremists," Michael said. "We're not trying to start any more Slaughters." His frown deepened.

"And we don't want war between Mags and Nats," added Yutika.

"What do you want?" I looked right at Kaira.

"Privacy," she answered, her eyes ablaze. "The right for Mags to go about their lives without their heart rate and every magical flare showing up on some computer somewhere."

"Where that data is just one good hack away from being shipped off to Russia or anyone else who's willing to pay for it," added Smith.

"What if Penelope's murderer is an unMarked Magic?" I asked quietly. "And the reason he or she got away with the murder is because there's no way to find them?"

"I guess it's possible the murderer was another unMarked Illusionist like me," Kaira said, sounding doubtful.

"What reason would a Magic have for killing another Magic and writing those slurs…about Magics?" Bri asked.

The others shrugged.

"Penelope Heppurn was murdered by a Nat," Michael said. "No Mag would have ever done that to her."

Before I could reply, A.J.'s sing-song voice called, "Breakfast is served, my lords and ladies and everything in between!"

A seventh chair flew in from some other part of the house, and we all crowded around the table that was now laden with steaming dishes. In spite of the earlier grumblings about vegan food, no one hesitated to dig in…with the exception of Smith.

The greasy-haired, hoodie-wearing caricature of a computer geek sat pushed back from the table with a laptop balanced on his knees. He took a case out from under his chair, pulled out an instrument that looked like some kind of sensor, and carefully hovered it over a single-serve vanilla pudding cup.

I watched in fascination as Smith moved the sensor all around the pudding cup, inspected the seal, and then took a spoon out from his hoodie pocket, which he also scanned. Only after the whole laborious process had been completed did he peel back the lid and take a bite.

"Seems like a lot of effort to go through for pudding," I commented to Yutika, who was sitting next to me.

"Smith thinks the government is poisoning our food," she said with a shake of her head. "He reads these conspiracy theory blogs and is practically peeing his bed on a nightly basis over everything he thinks the government is planning to do to us."

"All he eats is ramen and pudding," Bri added, scrunching up her face in disgust. "And he only drinks grape soda because he says the Alliance is poisoning our water."

"I didn't say they're poisoning our water. I said they *could* poison our water. All they'd need to do would be to—"

He stopped talking as he hovered his sensor over the can of grape soda, bending his ear to it in deep concentration. Once he was satisfied, he inspected the tab, opened the can, and took a long drink.

"So gross," Bri said as Smith took another slurp. "You could at least have enough dignity to go for orange soda rather than grape."

"Meanwhile, when the rest of you are lying on the floor and foaming at the mouth, don't come looking to me for help." Smith raised his soda to the rest of us in either a salute or a farewell—I wasn't sure which.

"If I'm foaming at the mouth, how am I going to ask you for help?" Yutika retorted.

Smith scowled and hunched down behind his computer, clearly done with socializing.

A.J. sniffed. "Snubbing my food is just *ruuude*. And do you have any idea how many artificial ingredients are in one of your precious pudding cups?"

Smith just grunted and slurped his grape soda.

"Do you have a first name?" I asked Smith. I was trying to get a handle on all of these people and their role in this new life of Kaira's.

Smith looked up from his screen and glared at me. "Why you asking? You a Russian spy?"

"Um…could I do that without speaking Russian?"

Bri and Yutika giggled.

"None of us know Smith's real name," Kaira said. "He's very private."

"Or where he comes from, or who his family is, or if he owns anything besides solid-colored hoodies," A.J. said, doling out slices of a vegetable casserole that actually smelled pretty good.

Smith just squinted at his screen, ignoring us.

"Our history is our own business," Michael said from the other end of the table. "It's the whole point behind what we do for other Mags."

"Doesn't stop the rest of us from being curious about the people we're living and working with," Yutika shot back.

I noticed the confrontational look Yutika gave Michael before they both looked away.

"My grandparents immigrated from Indian and settled in NYC," Yutika told me. "I'm the first Level 10 in my family, and when my parents found out my level, all twenty-five Sharmas—I'm talking aunts, uncles, cousins, second-cousins, second-cousins-twice-removed—decided to move to Boston so I'd have access to the best schools." She smirked. "Grammie and Gramps weren't exactly pleased when I put my fancy college degree toward illegal work with the Six. Luckily, my Hindi sucks, so I just pretend like I don't know what they're saying when they start lecturing me."

Yutika craned her head toward the front door and widened her eyes in fake-surprise. "And look at that. No government people breaking down our door now that I've spoken my family history out loud."

She looked at Michael again. He just shrugged and glared down at the vegetables on his plate. I wasn't sure if anyone else noticed how the big guy's cheeks had turned red.

Conversation flowed easily, and I felt like I was at a friend's house whose whole family was at home. The Six teased and grumbled at each other, but there was obvious history and trust between them—Smith's paranoia aside.

After the last vegan waffle was gone and there were only crumbs left from A.J.'s "veggie surprise extraordinaire," Kaira cleared her throat.

"There's something I need to say."

Everyone went quiet as she pushed away her plate and rested her elbows on the table.

"I appreciate everything you all did tonight. I couldn't have done it without you, and I'll never forget it." She didn't look at me as her eyes moved around the table to the others. "I was clear about the expectations when you joined the team, but what you did tonight wasn't in your job description." Kaira looked at me then, and I saw my own anger and feelings of injustice reflected in her eyes. "Gray was set up for this murder, and things are going to get ugly before all this gets resolved."

I felt overwhelmed as I watched Kaira captivate the room. She had always been a force to be reckoned with, but I had never seen her command a group the way she was now. She was all confidence and business. It was incredibly sexy.

"This is what we do," Bri said into the silence that followed. "It doesn't matter that he's a Nat. He's being unfairly persecuted by the system, and he needs help. This is exactly our job description."

I felt a sudden rush of warmth toward this small, ass-kicking titanium girl who I'd met only a few hours ago. At the same time, I was being buried beneath a crushing sense of helplessness. I never leaned on other people for help. I was the one who solved problems and got things done. Now, though, I didn't have a choice.

"This time is different," Kaira said. "And not just because he's a Nat." She looked at each of the Magics sitting around the table. "I'm not gonna lie. Graysen's important to me, and this is personal. It's not like our other jobs, and you'll be more at risk if you help us. If any of you want to sit this one out, I'll understand."

No one moved or spoke. For a group of people who seemed to have no trouble finding their voices, the silence was weighted with meaning.

"Did you kill Penelope Heppurn?" Michael asked me.

"No," Kaira and I replied at the same time.

There was a fiercely protective look in Kaira's eyes that warmed me to my core. There wasn't a hint of uncertainty in her rigid posture, like she was ready to do battle with anyone who suggested I was anything but innocent. I appreciated it more than I could have ever put into words.

"I was set up," I said in the next pause that followed. "There was evidence…a lot of it. Whoever killed Penelope had the whole thing planned to a T."

Fury welled inside me at the memory of the detective's note pad, filled with damning evidence against me.

"Did you get a copy of the report?" Smith asked.

I gave him an incredulous look, but the other guy was serious. "There wasn't a photocopier in my jail cell," I replied dryly.

"Too bad," Smith said, clearly missing the sarcasm.

"The only way to clear Gray's name is to figure out who set him up," Kaira said. "I'm going to put all of my time into finding the answers he needs. The rest of you can either help us, or you can go somewhere out of the line of fire until this is done."

"We're the Six," Bri said. "And I don't scare easily. Count me in."

"I, for one, will be glad to expand my resume with saving a Nat," A.J. announced. "Plus, he's hot. You know, for a Nat."

"Really, A.J.?" Yutika said with a roll of her eyes.

"Not to mention he's a *Nat*," Bri pointed out. "Just because we regularly break the second high law, it doesn't make us complete barbarians."

"Besides, Gray doesn't swing that way," Kaira told A.J.

"How do you know?" A.J. shot back.

I had a strangely disembodied sense as I sat and listened to the others argue about my sexuality and the barbarism of people who broke the third high law.

"Are you gay?" Kaira asked, her voice calm and her expression revealing nothing.

"No," I replied, trying my best to keep a straight face.

"There you have it," Kaira said.

A.J. gave me a pitying look.

"*Anyway*," Kaira continued. "What about the rest of you? Are you up for this job?"

"Yeses" chorused from around the table.

My throat felt scratchy. "I'm not sure how to thank all of you," I began, but the others waved away my words.

"We don't stand on ceremony around here," Michael said. "We help people who need it."

"And you definitely need it," Bri added.

"The manhunt is on the way," Smith announced.

Instead of turning his laptop around so we could see what he was seeing, he flicked his hand at the blank wall next to the table. A dozen different images appeared on the wall. They were as clear as if they were coming from a TV screen. Smith waved his hand, and one of the images expanded and moved to the center of the wall.

It was my dad's house, surrounded by police. There were two of them standing right outside my front door, and I could see cop cars lining my street.

Smith flicked the image away with a wave of his hand, and one of the others zoomed to the center. It was a live feed of the hallway of my dorm. There was police tape over my doorway, and cops ducking under the tape as they came and went.

"Is there audio?" Kaira asked.

Smith closed his eyes, and then the cops' voices filled the kitchen.

"There's more blood in this room than was left in that poor Mag's body," one cop said, kneeling to snap a photo of my bloody clothes.

"Sick son-of-a-bitch," another replied, studying the tape outline of Penelope's body on the floor.

I clenched my jaw until it ached.

The next screen Smith enlarged was Memorial Drive, where police cars were flying through traffic, their emergency lights flashing.

And the last image was a live NBC news feed. I flinched when my picture flashed across the screen. It was the picture that had been taken at the party—*had that really been just last night?*—except Penelope and Director Remwald were cropped out. The news anchor was telling viewers to call 911 if they caught sight of this "armed and extremely dangerous criminal."

"That's enough, Smith," Kaira said, her tone sharp.

I blinked, and then the wall was blank again.

"Keep track of what's happening and let me know if they figure out we're involved," Kaira said to Smith.

He nodded and then ducked his head behind his screen again.

"Alright, everyone," Kaira said. "Let's all get a few hours of sleep. We'll meet back up in the afternoon and start working through the evidence we have. I want Graysen exonerated as soon as possible, so it's going to be a hard push until this mess is cleaned up."

"Where are we putting the Nat?" A.J. asked.

"There's the office off my bedroom, and I have an air mattress he can use," Kaira said.

For the second time today, I had the sense that I was listening to a conversation about some stranger. Who was this person who was causing so much trouble?

For as long as I could remember, I had been in control of my life. If I wasn't happy about something, I made a change. If something wasn't going right, I fixed it. It was such a foreign experience to be dependent on other people. I hated it.

"It might be better for him to stay down here," Michael said. "Bri and I can take turns keeping an eye on him."

"We didn't break Graysen out of one prison to turn him into a prisoner in our own house," Kaira said, her voice low and dangerous. "I thought I was clear on that point."

"I'm just saying—"

"No, you aren't." Kaira glared at him until the big guy visibly shrunk down in his seat. She turned her scalding gaze on the rest of the Six. "Graysen is innocent. We're going to figure out who killed Penelope so Gray can go back to his life and the real killer can get what he deserves."

The Six clearly knew better than to try to argue with her.

"Now, we're going to get some rest," Kaira said, inclining her head at me. "I suggest the rest of you do the same."

Kaira headed for the stairs, motioning for me to follow. A.J. muttered something about how messy it would be to have to clean up all of her blood, which she ignored.

"My room's at the end of the hall," Kaira told me in a voice loud enough for the others to hear.

I knew which room was hers. It was the same one that used to be ours.

CHAPTER 12

When I stepped inside the room, the first thing I noticed was that my old stereo was still there. The bed, however, had been replaced by a larger, non-tilted one. The rest of the room was decorated with ballet posters and family photos. Kaira's clothes were everywhere. They were draped over the desk and chair and piled on the window seat.

Kaira had always been messy and had more clothes than she could wear in a lifetime, a fact I had never hesitated to tease her about. I almost smiled, remembering how I was always tripping over her shoes and finding parts of her outfit strewn around the house. I'd once found one of her belts in the refrigerator.

"Make yourself at home," Kaira said, shutting the door and locking it.

I turned to face her. I felt…odd. I had never expected to be back here, with her.

Kaira put the back of her hand to my forehead. Her touch was cool and comforting, and I had to stop myself from leaning into it.

"You have a fever," she said, going over to the bathroom and rifling through the medicine cabinet.

She came back with two ibuprofen and a glass of water. She handed them to me without a word.

"Thanks," I muttered, taking the pills.

Kaira was the only person from whom I'd never tried to hide the effects of my disease. Even my dad didn't know about how frequent my joint pain and fevers were. But even though Kaira knew how bad the pain sometimes got, she'd never fussed over or pitied me. She'd just given me ibuprofen or drawn me a scalding hot bath and let me get on with it. It was one of the things I had always loved about her.

I looked at Kaira, who was watching me.

"What the hell am I doing here?" I asked. "I'm a fugitive. My dad's being investigated. I need to turn myself in. Once I explain everything—"

"Sit," Kaira commanded, putting her hands on my chest and pushing me over to the bed. "Take a breath."

I sat on the edge of her bed. My mind was racing.

"I'm guessing you tried explaining things. They locked you up for it."

"But my dad," I began.

"I'm not going to read about your execution in the papers," Kaira said, her voice cracking from emotion. "Do you hear me? I need—" she cut herself off, turning away while she collected herself. When she turned back to face me, she was calm again.

"We're going to figure out who's behind this. Once we have the evidence to prove your innocence, you can go back to the police."

I knew she was right. I had tried to explain myself, but no one had listened. I knew no one on the jury would have listened, either. My conviction had been written in stone from the moment this nightmare began.

"This whole thing has been one big slap of irony," I said, letting out a humorless laugh.

"How do you mean?" She sat on the bed next to me and kicked off her shoes.

I looked at her. "I get arrested for the only high crime I haven't committed…. I've always been against Magics being unMarked, and now, a bunch of unMarked Magics are the only reason I'm still breathing." I shook my head, still chuckling.

I had always believed the Alliance's justice system would serve and protect as it was meant to.

"Guess I'm going to need to start thinking of career alternatives," I said, feeling more than a little unhinged.

"You're going to get your life back," Kaira said, her voice all ferocious determination. "We're not going to rest until you do."

I was quickly remembering why I had fallen for Kaira. If I wasn't careful, I was going to slip right back to where I'd been before everything happened.

Focus, I ordered myself.

I raked a hand through my hair. "Whoever did this isn't just going to leave a trail of breadcrumbs for us to follow."

Kaira clenched her fists and pressed them into her eyes. "If I hadn't taken you away from that party, you would have had an alibi." She swore.

In that moment, it all made sense to me. Why Kaira would risk her own life to help me after we'd been less than nothing to each other for years.

"You're doing all of this because you feel like you owe me."

The second I saw the hurt fill her dark eyes, I wanted to cut out my own tongue.

"I'm sorry," I began, but she interrupted me.

"I feel horrible that I'm the reason you don't have an alibi, but that isn't why I came to the prison."

"Then why did you come?" I asked, my voice coming out harsher than I meant it to.

"Because," she paused, searching for the words. "Because it's you, Gray. And because, no matter what's happened between us, I know you would have done the same for me."

Would I?

It wasn't really a question. I had lied for her when telling the truth—or at least part of the truth—might have saved me. I would have gone to my death without ever regretting what I had done to protect her. I knew without a shadow of a doubt that if our positions were reversed, I would do whatever I could to help her. Just like she'd done for me.

"I'm sorry," I said again. "This is just—"

"I know." She put a hand on mine, but then pulled it away before her familiar warmth had time to settle into my bones.

I got up and started to pace. I wanted to fix this…needed to. I just didn't know how. It was like I was trapped inside my own mind. All burners were firing, but I didn't have the information I needed to get myself out of this situation. I was a helpless victim, and it was driving me crazy.

I stopped pacing as another thought occurred to me.

"What did you tell the others about us?" I asked Kaira.

She shrugged. "I said we were neighbors growing up, and that I knew you well enough to know you'd never do something like this."

I just nodded because I didn't know what else to say.

"Let's get some rest," Kaira suggested. "You're no good to anyone if you're too exhausted to think."

I nodded again. The ache in my joints was getting worse, and I knew if I didn't get at least some sleep, I'd have trouble walking tomorrow.

Kaira went over to the dresser where the drawers were belching clothes. She opened the bottom drawer and took out a pair of athletic shorts and soccer T-shirt I recognized. As she handed me the clothes—my clothes—I saw her cheeks darken in embarrassment. It was a rare emotion for her.

"I'm surprised you didn't throw these out," I said, my voice coming out rough as I took them from her.

"Guess I forgot I had them," she said without meeting my gaze.

I knew her well enough to know she was lying.

I took the clothes to the bathroom and closed the door. Kaira had seen me naked plenty, but it didn't feel right to change in front of her anymore.

As soon as I put on the T-shirt, I understood why Kaira had been embarrassed. The lettering and image of the soccer ball were unrecognizable from so many washings. The green athletic shorts were faded, too. The clothes smelled like her, and not in a they've-been-in-her-room kind of way. The jasmine-scented lotion she always used to put on before bed—and clearly still did—was all over the clothes.

When we'd been together, Kaira had slept in my T-shirts. I had laughed about how she stole my clothes when she had so many of her own, but I had not-so-secretly loved seeing her in my too-big shirts. I was surprised she'd still done that after we broke up.

I had tried to lock away my memories of her in a place where they wouldn't touch me. I didn't understand why she wouldn't have done the same.

Before today, I had known where we stood. I didn't know why she had to confuse the issue by acting like I mattered to her.

I turned on the sink and splashed cold water on my face.

There were too many more important things going on than Kaira and me. Being back in this room, with her, was strange enough. I didn't want to dredge up memories that were better left in the past.

When I came back out into the bedroom, she had changed, too. She was wearing a pink tank top and tiny flannel shorts that made it impossible not to notice her miles-long legs. Even though I didn't want her anymore, I couldn't ignore the simple fact that she was the hottest woman on the planet.

"Where's the air mattress?" I asked, going into the tiny office connected to the bedroom.

"There isn't one." Kaira climbed into bed and raised her eyebrows at me. A challenge. "But I didn't think you'd appreciate sleeping on the couch downstairs. Yutika got drunk and puked all over it last weekend, and I'm pretty sure it still smells."

"Got it," I muttered.

"I'll let us sleep until this afternoon," Kaira decided as she set an alarm on her cell phone. "That way we'll get some solid rest without losing the entire day."

"Sounds reasonable," I agreed, still hovering by the foot of the bed.

Kaira turned off the lamp on her nightstand and snuggled down into the blankets. It was like so many nights we'd spent in high school…back when convincing our parents we were sleeping over at a friend's was our biggest challenge…back before Kaira ruined everything. We had lived for those nights.

All it took was a quick recollection of the past twelve hours to remind myself that everything was different now.

I got into bed, staying on the far edge and facing away from Kaira.

I didn't think I'd ever be able to sleep…not with my arrest, the detective's photos still swimming through my mind, and Kaira lying in the same bed as me. But the sound of her even breathing calmed me. Being this close to her, wearing my clothes that smelled like her, felt right in a way I knew it shouldn't. It was comforting, and I found myself drifting off in spite of everything.

* * *

The next time I opened my eyes, it was to the piercing sound of Kaira's alarm. I was disoriented, and I tried to sit up to take in my surroundings. Something was keeping me in place, though.

Not something, I realized. *Someone.*

Kaira and I were tangled in each other. For several moments, I thought I was still dreaming. It wouldn't be the first time I felt the phantom of her in my arms, only to wake and remember I was alone in my dorm.

But this time was different. She was warm and real. Her chest rose and fell against mine. My arms were wound all the way around her, holding her to me, and our legs were all twisted together.

It was early afternoon, and light filtered in through the skylight above the bed. I looked down at the woman in my arms and fought back the urge to kiss the top of her head.

"Kai."

"A few more minutes," she mumbled, snuggling into me.

This time, I couldn't stop myself from pressing my lips to her hair. The easy intimacy we'd always had was as natural to me as breathing. I wanted nothing more than to stay like this forever.

But then I remembered why I was here.

"Kaira." I started to move, trying to un-pretzel our limbs.

I felt her wake up. She lifted her head, realized how we'd been sleeping, and gave a little "Oh," of surprise.

I didn't look at her as we got out of bed. I pulled my suit pants from the night before over my shorts. I didn't want to wear the same clothes I'd been arrested in, but it was better than trying to explain to Kaira's housemates why she happened to have clothes that fit me lying around.

A knock came at the door. Kaira shut the door to the office so no one would be able to see the lack of air mattress inside.

A few seconds later, A.J. pranced in carrying a stack of clothes.

"I come bearing presents!" he announced, handing me the clothes. He peered around me into the bedroom and seemed to relax when he caught sight of Kaira. I had the distinct impression A.J.'s real reason for coming by was to make sure Kaira hadn't been murdered.

After everything the police and news reporters were saying about me, I couldn't exactly blame Kaira's friends for worrying about her.

"They're Michael's, so they'll be a little big, but we—I mean *I*—figured you might want some variety," A.J. chattered. "Once we have some time, I'll go shopping and get you stuff in your own size. Your body's too pretty to hide behind baggy clothes."

"Thanks," I said, when A.J. paused to take a breath. "I appreciate it."

"Don't mention it." A.J. gave me a bright smile and skipped out of the room.

The rest of the Six were already downstairs. They had congregated around Smith, who was sitting on one of the couches. He had a computer on his lap, two others on the cushion next to him, and about twelve empty grape soda cans littered around.

"Where we at?" Kaira asked Smith.

"Same place we were five hours ago," the Techie replied. "Nat and Mag cops are equally clueless. They're searching for Graysen and aren't even considering other suspects. The Dean of the BSMU put out a statement that the school in no way condones his actions and is urging the public to come forward if they see him."

"Blah blobbidy blah," A.J. said with a roll of his eyes.

"Any luck with tracking down the camera footage from outside the dorms that night?" Kaira asked.

Smith frowned. "That's another thing. I hacked into security at the BSMU. Their firewalls are pathetic, by the way. Like, embarrassing. A four-year-old must have set up their systems, because a six-year-old Nat could hack them—"

"Smith," at least four voices said at once.

"Wha'?" he stopped with a can of soda raised to his lips.

"Focus," Kaira told him. "What's the problem with the camera footage?"

"That's what I was just saying. It's gone."

"What do you mean, it's gone?" I asked.

"I mean, it's gone. Someone wiped all the cameras between the Dean's house and your dorm."

Kaira and I exchanged a look.

"Do you think another Techie wiped them?" I asked.

Smith shrugged. "Could have been anyone. Like I said—"

"Yeah, the six-year-old," Bri cut in. "We heard you."

I slumped onto the couch. "So, all we know is that someone—likely whoever killed Penelope—deleted the camera footage and then disappeared?"

"I did come across one interesting tidbit," Smith said.

We all leaned forward.

Smith looked around at the rest of the Six. "Remember that Level 8 Alchemist who got in touch with us a while back about a new identity?"

"Yeah," Kaira said slowly. "Bobby something. He said he needed to disappear, and then at the last minute, he changed his mind."

"Waste of a week of my life," Yutika grumbled. "Those were the best fake files I've ever made."

"Bobby Axelrod," Smith said. "He put in a call to Mag authorities about an hour before Graysen's arrest, saying he wanted to report a murder that was about to happen at the BSMU."

The room went quiet.

"And?" Kaira prompted.

"The line went dead before he could say anything else. This morning, his wife issued a missing person's report."

No one spoke while we digested that information.

"We need to talk to his wife," I said. "Maybe she knows something."

"Or she can at least point us to someone who does," Kaira agreed.

Smith's eyes roved over the screen. "She works at a Mag club downtown, and she's listed on the schedule for tonight."

I peered over his shoulder, and saw that Smith was shifting windows and opening new tabs without touching the computer. It was amazing.

"Alright, then we'll go there tonight," Kaira said.

Smith nodded. "She's a Level 2 Alchemist, so I'm guessing she's a bartender. He turned his screen around so everyone could see the woman's image.

Nancy Axelrod was a plain-looking woman, with light skin, brown eyes, and sandy-blonde hair. She wasn't thin or fat. I guessed from the picture that she was in her forties.

"Well, it's a place to start," Kaira said.

"What do we do in the meantime?" A.J. asked.

Kai pointed to Yutika. "Get the Axelrods' files out of storage. We might have use for them yet." To Smith, she said, "See if you can find out where Bobby is now.

"The rest of you, let's finish up with the family in the safe house. After them, we're not taking on anyone else until Gray's case is solved."

"Where are you going?" A.J. asked as Kaira slipped into a pair of heeled ankle boots she'd discarded next to the couch.

"Gray and I are going to Ma's," she replied as she pulled a sweater over her tank top. "She texted me and said Grandma Tashi heard from Penelope."

I stood up. Kaira's grandmother was a Medium. She was a Level 5, which meant that she could only talk to the dead when they sought her out. If Penelope had visited Grandma Tashi, then maybe Kaira's grandmother knew who the real killer was. The testimony of a Medium was good enough to hold up in court. My heart began to race as my mind swam with possibilities.

"Are you sure you want me to come?" I asked.

I had practically grown up in the Hansley house, but after everything the media had been saying about me over the past day, I wasn't sure I'd be welcome there. Besides, I was a fugitive. Anyone who so much as glimpsed me without calling the police was putting themselves at risk. I couldn't stand the thought of any of the Hansleys being in danger, especially on my account.

"I think I'd better stay here," I decided.

As much as I wanted to hear what Grandma Tashi had to say, I knew Kaira would pass on the information as soon as she got back.

"Ma wants to see you," Kaira said. "Come on."

CHAPTER 13

We walked the three blocks to the Hansley house in silence. Kaira had illusioned me before we stepped outside, and I caught sight of my reflection in a passing window. I was shorter and thinner, and all of my features were unrecognizable. It was more than a little unsettling whenever Kaira did this. Unlike with her, who I could recognize no matter what illusion she was wearing, I didn't recognize a single aspect of my own reflection. It was enough to mess with a person's head.

Even though it had been years since I'd been to this house or seen any member of the family that affectionately referred to themselves as the Hansley clan, I felt that familiar sense of at-homeness as soon as I stepped inside. Voices were coming from the kitchen, which was where the Hansleys usually congregated.

I followed as Kaira walked through the narrow hallway between the foyer and the kitchen. As we passed the mirror on the wall, I saw that my illusion was gone, and I looked like myself again.

I grabbed Kaira's arm and pulled her back before she reached the kitchen.

"Are you sure it's a good idea for me to be here?" I whispered, feeling anxious in a way I never had in her house.

"G-Baby, you will always be welcome in my house." Ma Hansley, wiping her hands on a flower-print apron, came out of the kitchen.

Ma's real name was Marcy, but she'd always treated me like one of the family, and I'd been calling her Ma since I was a kid.

Ma squeezed past Kaira and folded me into her plump embrace, surrounding me with a familiar warmth and smell of fresh cooking that made my heart expand.

Ma stepped back and took my face in both her hands. She was shorter than I remembered—or maybe I was taller. Otherwise, she looked exactly the same. Her chin-length black hair was straightened and flared out at the ends. Where Kaira was tall and thin, and almost too beautiful to be real, Ma looked like someone you could go to when life sucked and you needed comfort. When Ma hugged me, it was like being engulfed by a marshmallow with attitude. Her face was round and didn't have the sharp definition of Kaira's, but they had the same eyes. Ma had the *I love you, but don't think I'll take any of your crap* look down pat.

Since I was a kid, whenever I was sick or had something to celebrate, Ma had been there with delicious homemade food, advice whether I wanted it or not, and hugs. I hadn't realized until this moment just how much I'd missed her.

She didn't say anything about how long it had been or ask me why I'd stopped coming over, and I wondered what excuse Kaira had given her family for why I was constantly around one day and then gone the next.

"Good lord, look how handsome you've gotten." Ma smiled up at me. But as she searched my face, her smile turned to a frown. "Too skinny, though. Come."

I managed to exchange a quick grin with Kaira before Ma took my hand and dragged me toward the kitchen. Kaira's two cousins, Cora and Desiree, were sitting at the table.

The Hansleys were originally from Atlanta, where the Slaughters had been fierce and terrible. Ma's brother and his wife—Cora and Desiree's parents—had been killed in the Slaughters when their kids were babies, along with Kaira's dad and grandpa. Ma and Grandma Tashi had managed to get what was left of the family out of Atlanta and, eventually, to Boston where her in-laws lived.

"What's *he* doing here?" Desiree, the older of Kaira's two cousins, demanded. She even sniffed and turned her head, like I smelled.

"Hello to you too, Desiree," I said, giving her a pleasant smile.

Desiree rolled her eyes at me.

Kaira lightly smacked the back of her cousin's head. "Don't be a such a—"

"Maaaa!" Desiree whined. "Kaira punched me!"

Kaira gave me an exasperated look.

Desiree was now fifteen, but she'd been a bratty teenager since she was about six. She was a Rain Maker like Valencia, and they were known to be a moody bunch. Desiree was certainly no exception. Her long, black braids had been dyed so that they went from different shades of purple at the bottom to blue at the top. She clicked inches-long purple nails against the top of the table. Even that small motion conveyed her irritation. Kaira and I had always joked that Desiree's real magic was being constantly pissed off.

The light over the table buzzed and flickered as moisture started to condense around the bulb.

"Desiree Hansley, if you make it rain in here and get my lasagna soggy, I swear it'll be the last thing you do," Ma called from the stove, where I caught the smell of tomato sauce simmering.

I couldn't help but smile at the familiar routine. I remembered Ma and Desiree's epic fights, which began with a downpour and ended with Ma feeding Desiree homemade donuts or something else sugary and delicious.

"Hey Graysen." Cora, Kaira's youngest cousin, gave me a shy smile.

"Hey Cora, whatcha working on?" I asked, coming over to look at the book she had open in front of her.

"Studying for my Test." She turned the book so I could see the magical transfiguration diagrams on the open pages.

"Isn't it a little early to be studying for that?" I asked.

Cora was thirteen, which meant her Test wasn't for another five years. Besides, it wasn't exactly an exam one could study for.

"I'm not very powerful," she said, looking ashamed, "so I need to work harder. And I want to go to a good college."

"You're plenty powerful, and you'll get into whatever school you want," Kaira told her.

Cora was an Inanimate Illusionist like Ma. Unlike Ma, though, she had to be looking at the object and concentrating on it to keep the illusion.

Ma's ability to create an illusion and maintain it when she was somewhere else—like the garage door at Kaira's house that appeared to be a brick wall—was much more difficult. Ma had once told me that only a professional multitasker, *aka a mother*, could keep up illusions indefinitely from afar.

It was even more complicated for Animate Illusionists, since their magic had to account for changes and movements in the subject they were manipulating. Kaira and I had tested her range once. It was over a mile.

"Where do you want to go to college?" I asked Cora.

"If I could go anywhere, I'd want to go to the BSMU like you." Cora gave me another shy smile.

"He doesn't go there anymore," Desiree said before I could reply. "They kicked him out for being a *murderer*."

"Shut your mouth, Desiree," Kaira warned.

"Make me," her cousin muttered under her breath.

Kaira lifted a shoulder. "Challenge accepted, Cuz."

A fat, hairy baboon was now sitting at the kitchen table.

Cora pointed and started to laugh until tears poured down her face. I tried to hide my own grin and failed.

"What?" the baboon demanded in Desiree's voice. "What the hell did she do to me?"

Kaira smirked.

Cora slid a makeup mirror that was on the table to her older sister. The baboon picked up the mirror and looked at herself. She screeched, which was oddly just the sort of noise I would have expected from a real baboon.

"Bitch, make it go away!" Desiree screamed, lunging at Kaira, who hid behind me and used my body as a shield between her and her cousin-turned-baboon.

A freezing rain started to fall right above my head.

"Your butt is blue," Cora gasped, holding her side.

"That's enough, girls."

Grandma Tashi stepped into the kitchen. At one look from her, Kaira's illusion fell away and I stopped getting rained on.

"Hi, Grandma." Kaira, dripping wet and shivering, stepped out from behind me to give her grandma a kiss.

I gave Grandma Tashi a little wave. Unlike Ma, Kaira's grandmother had always slightly terrified me. She was tiny and birdlike, with sharp bones jutting everywhere. She had the look of someone who had seen the worst that humankind had to offer and had come out the other end. Grandma Tashi had lost her husband and son in the Atlanta Slaughters. Still, she had communicated with her newly-deceased family and used the information they gave her to get what was left of their family to Boston. She was as much a parent figure in Kaira's life as Ma.

"So," Grandma Tashi said, giving me a hard stare, "we're letting murderers into the house now, are we?"

"Don't I always tell you not to believe everything you see on the news?" Kaira asked her grandmother.

"Don't you talk about my G-Baby like that," Ma called from the kitchen. She pointed a wooden spoon at Grandma Tashi, ignoring the tomato sauce that dripped onto the floor. "This boy doesn't have a murderous bone in his body."

"That's not what Penelope says." Grandma Tashi raised her pointed chin and glared at me.

"With all due respect," I began, but Tashi interrupted me.

"Boy, don't you be playing at respect when Penelope done told me herself that you're her killer!"

"You're gonna throw your blood pressure all outta whack again if you keep hollerin' like that," Ma said, coming over to the table with two plates balanced on each arm. "And if you keep throwing around accusations, I'll leave you lying on the floor after you give yourself a heart attack. See if I don't."

The two older women glared at each other.

"Penelope said—"

"How many times have I said no talking about dead people while we're trying to eat?" Ma shot back. "Put the poor boy off his appetite, and he's skinny enough as it is."

I was desperate to know what Penelope had told Tashi. Maybe she knew something that would offer me a clue about who the real killer had been. But one look at Ma told me I wasn't learning anything until after we'd eaten.

Ma slammed the plates down on the table. She stood with her hands on her wide hips, glaring until we all sat down.

I looked down at my plate and saw a huge slice of Ma's homemade lasagna with two pieces of buttery garlic bread.

"You didn't have to do this," I said, touched that she had remembered my favorite meal and feeling bad that she had put herself out for my sake.

"After everything you've been through, the least you deserve is a home-cooked meal. Now, dig in. That's Ma's soul food right there, and you'll feel better once you eat."

I had no appetite, but I forced myself to eat enough that I wouldn't offend Ma. A heavy silence gathered around a table that was usually full of chatter and good-natured arguing. I glanced at Kaira, who just shrugged and rolled her eyes.

Desiree got up and switched on the tiny TV on the counter.

NBC was showing a live feed of the front of the Alliance building, where a single dark rain cloud hung over the building. It was raining fiercely, even though the screen showed it was sunny everywhere else except for the Alliance building.

Valencia Stark, self-proclaimed leader of the UnAllied, was standing on the Alliance steps. She was a sight to behold, with her wild, cherry-red hair and zebra-striped dress plastered to her skin from the downpour. The rain streamed down the thick, round lenses of her glasses, which made Valencia look perpetually bug-eyed. She clutched the over-sized leopard-print purse she was never seen without as she shouted to the small group of angry-looking people surrounding her.

"My follow-ahs and I will nev-ah stop fighting for Mag rights," she shouted at the camera. She had the thickest Boston accent I had ever heard, which somehow made her seem even crazier with all the dropped R's. "We've let Nats think they can control us. We need to take back this country and our lives. We will not live in fear!"

The small group surrounding her shouted and raised their fists in solidarity.

"Penelope Heppurn was a dah-ling. 'Mags get out' he says? I say *Nats* get out!"

The spectators roared in agreement. I felt sick.

"That's enough," Ma said, switching to a different channel. "We don't need any of that nonsense in this house."

"She's kind of got a point," Desiree said, moving noodles around on her plate.

"You bite your tongue," Ma told her. "Valencia wants a war. How many times do I got to tell you that any time there's a war, both sides lose?"

"I just don't get why the rest of you pretend like Nats are our equals," Desiree persisted.

"They are," four female voices replied at once.

This argument was a familiar one, but I sensed there was more anger behind Desiree's words than just her usual teenage, Rain Maker angst. She wasn't just trying to get under my and her family's skin anymore. She looked like she really believed what she was saying.

"Valencia's crazy," Kaira told her younger cousin. "And the only ones who follow her are criminals and outcasts."

"Nuh-uh," Desiree argued. "Ever since Penelope," she gave me a look that could kill, "kids at school are saying—"

"That's ignorant folk talk," Ma said. "And I didn't bring you up to be ignorant."

Dark clouds appeared in the kitchen. "I think Valencia's got a point," Desiree said again. Her eyes turned gray with the impending storm.

"That is not how this family does," Grandma Tashi told Desiree. "And put that rain away, you hear? You'll give your old grandma pneumonia."

Desiree wasn't dumb enough to cross Grandma Tashi, but I could still feel the anger radiating off her as we all turned our attention back to the TV.

Ma had switched to CBS, which was covering one of Director Remwald's press conferences. He was standing at a podium, flanked by the BSMU's dean and other important Alliance members I recognized.

"…make it clear the hateful, despicable acts of one individual will not tarnish the progress that has been made in this administration…."

I watched numbly as my hero looked into the camera and condemned me.

I felt a strange mix of emotions. I was angry at the real killer for what he'd done to Penelope and the position I was now in as a result. And underneath that anger was guilt. I knew it was irrational, since I hadn't done any of what they were accusing me of, but I still felt badly for putting the BSMU and the Alliance in a position where they needed to defend themselves.

I had always wanted to enhance the peace and goodwill between Naturals and Magics. Now, I had somehow been dragged into an unspeakable crime that was causing irreparable damage between the two. I hated that the institutions I believed in were threatened because of a crime tied to my name.

There was clapping and the flash of cameras as reporters in the audience shouted questions. One of the reporters stood up.

"Director Remwald, have the authorities identified whether Graysen Galder is working alone or with accomplices?"

Remwald leaned into the microphone. "The murders seem to be connected, but we don't yet know if Galder is acting alone or if—"

Ma switched off the TV with a huff.

"Murders? As in plural?" Kaira asked.

"Haven't you heard?" Desiree gave Kaira and me a smug smile, pleased to know something we didn't. "Jonas Meddlesworth was found dead in his house. The murderer wrote 'Die, Mags' in his blood."

I stared dumbfounded at Kaira.

Desiree continued, "Everyone assumes Graysen did it, since the crime scene looks like what happened to Penelope."

"Two murders in two days," Ma said, shaking her head. "What is this city coming to?"

I was stunned. There hadn't been a single magically-motivated murder in Boston in years. Now, there had been two murders in two days. And not just any murders. First Penelope, and now—

"Jonas Meddlesworth," Kaira said. "Why do I know that name?"

"My dad's old boss," I managed, my mind still racing.

"That prick Level 3 Alchemist at the holiday party?" she asked me.

"Don't speak ill of the dead," Grandma Tashi snapped.

I nodded at Kaira. It was the last winter Kaira and I were together, and my dad had thrown a party at our home for his bosses, since he was up for a promotion. I had convinced my dad to invite the neighbors, which conveniently included the Hansleys.

Everyone had pretended to be impressed while Meddlesworth spent the first half of the night breathing into open wine bottles and claiming he had transformed them into the most expensive wine in the word. He'd spent the other half of the night hitting on Kaira, even though the man was in his fifties. It was the closest I had ever come to actually committing murder.

Kaira pulled her phone out of her pocket and started scrolling through what looked like a hundred texts.

"We've gotta go," she said, her eyes still scanning the texts.

"Could you tell us what Penelope said to you?" I asked Grandma Tashi.

Kaira looked up from her phone at that.

Grandma Tashi sat back and folded her bony hands on the table. "Penelope came to me last night. That poor angel had her throat cut. She said she left the party early because she had a headache. She said Graysen caught up with her as she was crossing the quad, and that he said he needed her help with something.

"She went back to his dorm room, and when he closed the door, he turned to her and said, 'This isn't personal.' And then he killed her."

I couldn't speak. This murderer, whoever he was, had used Penelope's trust in me to lure her to my dorm. *My* room. The thought of her, locked inside my room with her killer, was too much for me to bear. I stood up, not seeing anything except for that frozen expression of horror on Penelope's bloody face as the EMTs wheeled her away.

I was dimly aware of Ma shooing Grandma Tashi and Kaira's cousins out of the kitchen. When it was only Ma, Kaira, and me still there, Ma took my shoulders and forced me to look at her.

"This is not on you, G-Baby. You hear?"

I just shook my head.

I felt Kaira's hand on my back, a silent show of support.

"I was there when she had her premonition," I said, my voice scratchy. "She sounded so scared. I should have—"

"What?" Kaira asked, fury and challenge radiating from her voice. "Turned into a Clairvoyant yourself and figured out that some psychopath was going to murder her? Sat around your room and twiddled your thumbs just in case someone stopped by needing you to rescue them?"

I didn't know. All I knew was that Penelope, one of the kindest people I'd ever met, had died a horrible, brutal death at the hands of someone who had convinced her it was me. I should have done something…even if I had no idea what that something might have been.

Ma tucked me more firmly into her embrace, forcing me to divert at least some of my attention to getting enough air.

"You can't go back in time and change something you never couldda seen coming," Ma said. "I'm grateful Kaira got you out of that hellhole prison, and I know that the two of you have the brains and determination to find the real killer." She tapped my nose. "No one messes with my brilliant boy and gets away with it."

"Thanks, Ma," I managed.

"If you need any help, you just say the word," she said. "Lord knows I don't usually get involved in Kaira's work, but this is different. You're family."

She kissed my cheek before releasing me. "Now, before you go…."

Ma went over to the counter and handed Kaira three huge, covered trays. I took two out of her hands before she collapsed under their weight.

"Top one's A.J.'s. I used tofu crumbles to get a little extra protein into him," Ma said.

"Thank you for everything," I told Ma as she followed us to the door.

She gave me another hug, which was awkward with the giant dishes in my hands. "Keep your chin up G-Baby," she told me. "The truth has a way of coming out, eventually."

Grandma Tashi, who was coming down the stairs, frowned at Kaira and me.

"If Penelope visits you again, could you please ask her if she remembers anything else about that night?" I asked Kaira's grandmother.

"Boy, I don't get to ask the dead nothing. They come when they wanna come, and they say what they wanna say."

✳ ✳ ✳

As we walked back to Kaira's house, we both tried to make sense of what we'd learned.

"What I don't get is why someone would go to all the trouble of making himself look like you," Kaira said. "I mean, why not just wear a ski mask?"

"Unless the killer really was an Illusionist," I pointed out.

Kaira shook her head. "First off, I can't imagine there's another unMarked Animate Illusionist who is powerful enough to pull off that complete of a transformation. Second off, like Michael said, there's no reason a Mag would do something like this. It just doesn't make sense."

None of it made sense. I had been over and over every piece of the puzzle, and nothing was lining up. My analytical brain was screaming in protest.

Kaira chewed on her lip. "And what about that thing Grandma Tashi said about it not being personal? It certainly looked personal."

"Maybe Penelope was drugged," I suggested. "A hallucinogen maybe, or something to make her think the guy was me?"

The more I thought about it, the more it made sense. The murderer could have fooled the witnesses from afar with some makeup, a wig, and the right clothes. But maybe there had been a different kind of magic at work to make Penelope believe the man who approached her really was me.

The detective who interrogated me hadn't said anything about drugs, but he hadn't exactly been forthcoming with information.

"Any mid-level Alchemist could make something like that," Kaira said, nodding. "And the Alchemist who made the potion might not have been the one to give it to Penelope. Maybe a Nat bought the stuff and then—"

"Hey," I said, stopping on the sidewalk as a thought occurred to me. "That guy who called in the murder before it happened—"

"Bobby Axelrod," Kaira supplied.

"Didn't you say he was an Alchemist?"

Kaira's mouth formed an O of surprise. And then, a slow smile spread across her face. "You think he made the potion that killed Penelope?"

"Or maybe it was Jonas Meddlesworth, and this Axelrod guy somehow found out about it. Either way, it seems like a pretty big coincidence that two Alchemists are now involved in all of this."

"It's certainly more than we had a little while ago," Kaira agreed, her eyes bright with excitement.

"Can Smith get access to Penelope's toxicology report?"

Kaira pulled her phone out and texted with one hand while she used the other to balance the tray of food.

I felt the first spark of hope since my arrest. An Alchemist's drug would explain at least why Penelope thought I was her killer, even if it didn't explain who had administered the drug or why he would have wanted to frame me. Still, it was a start.

CHAPTER 14

When we got back, everyone was in the living room. Smith had a live feed projected on the blank wall. It showed the interior of what I assumed was Jonas Meddlesworth's bedroom. I had never seen the inside of Jonas' house, but I recognized his wife. She was sitting with two detectives, shivering under a blanket wrapped over her shoulders. The white carpet next to the bed was covered in blood.

Those horrible words, "Die, Mags," were written in blood on the wall.

"Hey, congrats on getting framed for another murder," Yutika said without looking up from the sketch pad she was drawing on.

"You've been a busy little bee," A.J. confirmed. "Buzzing here, killing Mags there—"

Kaira shut him up by dropped the pan of lasagna into his hands. A.J. oofed, exclaimed something about Ma's cooking, and skipped off to the kitchen.

"Well, at least we know for sure Graysen isn't the killer, since he was definitely at Ma's when this one happened," Bri said.

"There was never any question about that," Kaira replied, a warning in her voice.

Bri's grin faltered. "I was just saying—"

Her words trailed off and were replaced by Smith's muttering. He was sitting on the couch with his eyes closed.

"Who's he talking to?" I asked, sitting down next to Yutika and glancing at her drawing. It was of a hundred-dollar bill.

"Video camera drone," she said without looking up from her sketch pad.

Smith continued his quiet mumbling. "A little to the left. Back an inch. No, get back behind that tree! You want to give yourself away?"

"That camera's got great resolution," I said, impressed. There wasn't even a hint of graininess.

"Yeah, Smith and I make a pretty good team."

At the puzzled look I gave her, Yutika glanced up from her drawing. "He tells me exactly what he wants, and then I draw it. I keep trying to convince him to sell some of the cool stuff we've come up with, but then he gets going about the Alliance using it to spy on citizens…so I'm stuck doing this."

I looked down at her sketch pad, where the drawing of the hundred-dollar bill was no longer a drawing, but an actual one hundred-dollar bill.

"That's incredible," I said, admiring the crisp bill.

"I know." Yutika grinned as she started on another one.

I watched as a few strokes of her pen produced Benjamin Franklin's likeness. A few more, and the *United States Federal Reserve System* seal appeared.

I turned my attention to Smith. "Any chance that video has audio capabilities?"

Smith scoffed, and without opening his eyes, said, "The Nat wants to hear what's going on."

A few seconds later, a set of speakers in the corner of the living room crackled to life. Cops' voices and movements came through the speakers and coincided with the images projected on the wall. The audio narrowed, and the conversation between Mrs. Meddlesworth and the detectives came into focus.

"Ma'am, did your husband have any enemies who might have wanted to harm him?" one of the detectives asked.

"No," she sniffled. "My husband was a model citizen. Everyone adored him!"

I exchanged a look with Kaira. I hadn't been a fan of my dad's boss before the scumbag hit on my girlfriend. The man might not deserve to be murdered, but that didn't mean I could bring myself to mourn the guy.

"Was it that Graysen Galder?"

I jerked my attention at the wall, where Mrs. Meddlesworth was staring at the detective. "Did that Magic-hater murder my husband, too?"

"We believe so, Ma'am," one of the detectives replied.

"I just don't understand why he hasn't already been executed. How do you people just let someone as dangerous as him escape?" She sniffed and wiped the tears from her eyes. "If you people were more competent, my husband might still be alive."

Kaira came and stood beside me, her shoulder just touching my arm. It wasn't something any of the others would notice, and it said everything I needed to hear. I was grateful.

"Smith, what do we know?" Kaira asked.

The Techie opened his eyes, and the feed immediately cut off.

"No DNA evidence at the scene. Mag cops believe it was a single intruder. No one seen coming or going from the residence. Graysen's their only suspect, but only because they don't have any other ideas." He rattled off the facts of the case, all of which were infuriatingly useless.

"Oh, and Meddlesworth quit his job at the Alliance six months ago, but he was still getting an income of fifty-thousand a month from an untraceable offshore account."

Everyone stared at Smith.

"Fifty-thousand a month?" I repeated.

"You could have led with that little tidbit," A.J. muttered.

"Do you think he was involved with drugs?" Bri asked.

"It would make sense why he was making so much money without any record of a job," Michael said.

"And don't forget about Bobby Axelrod," Kaira said. "What are the odds that one Alchemist calls in about Penelope's murder and goes missing, and then another Alchemist shows up dead with the same calling card as Penelope's murderer?"

It was obvious there was some kind of a connection, I just couldn't figure out what it might be. What did two Alchemists most likely involved in some kind of illegal drug work have to do with Penelope? And why did they choose me to frame for the murder?

"Were you able to get Penelope's toxicology report?" Kaira asked Smith.

Smith waved his hand, and images of enlarged documents filled the blank wall. My heart raced as I stepped forward to study them.

It took about five seconds for all of my hopes to fall. My only theory about how the killer might have tricked Penelope crumbled into dust.

There was no trace of drugs or anything unusual. She didn't even have any alcohol in her system.

I sunk down on the couch.

"It was a good theory," Smith said with a shrug.

"Maybe Axelrod's wife will tell us something useful tonight," Bri said, giving my arm a sympathetic pat.

Over a quick meal of Ma's lasagna, Kaira and I told the others what Grandma Tashi had said. No one else had any ideas about what might have led Penelope to believe I was her killer. We all agreed that we'd know more after tonight. I hoped our optimism wasn't all for nothing. I didn't think I could handle any more dead ends.

"Okay, cats and kittens." A.J. clapped his hands, and the lasagna trays re-wrapped themselves and put themselves in the fridge. "Time to get club ready." He rubbed his hands together in anticipation.

"Here we go," Michael muttered.

"I'm gonna need some eyeliner from you." A.J. pointed at Bri, who grinned and nodded at him. "And you." He pointed an accusatory finger at Michael. "I want you in those fancy pants I gave you for Christmas. Don't think I've forgotten about them."

Michael scowled. "I don't wear fancy pants."

"No, that's right, I forgot. Because you're *boring*." A.J. rolled his eyes up at the ceiling and heaved a dramatic sigh. "Well, lucky for you, I have someone new to play dress-up with."

"He's talking about you," Yutika told me.

Two shopping bags zoomed across the room. One of them would have hit Michael in the head if he hadn't ducked. They came to rest on the floor next to my chair.

"I picked up some clothes for you," A.J. told me. "Suits, casuals, jammies…I wasn't sure if you were a boxers or briefs kind of guy, so I got some of each…."

"Thank you," I said. "But I don't have any money. When I was arrested—"

A.J. waved a hand, and the hundred-dollar bills Yutika had stacked on the coffee table rose into the air and did a little dance.

"Oh, right." I grinned. "Thanks."

"Don't mention it." A.J. glared at Michael and Smith. "*Some* people don't appreciate men's fashion." He straightened his turquoise bowtie. "I have higher expectations for you, Nat."

I was suddenly concerned about A.J.'s idea of fashion, but I decided not to say anything. I'd wear a paper bag to this night club if it would help get me answers.

The Six scattered to their own rooms to get changed. I stayed downstairs, the mammoth toxicology report blown up on the wall like it was mocking me, while I unwrapped the first set of clothes I found in the bag.

They weren't as bad as I was expecting. The pants and shirt were more fitted than the clothes I usually wore, and the colors were brighter, but at least there were no bow ties or polka dots. It was certainly better than wearing the suit I'd been arrested in.

Michael and Smith were the first ones back downstairs. As far as I could tell, neither of them looked any different from when they'd gone up.

"A.J.'s going to be pissed," I commented, coaxing a smile out of the big guy.

Yutika came down next, and I noticed the way her glance went right to Michael. I wondered if the feeling was mutual. My answer came when Yutika bent down to pick up a few of the bills from the coffee table, and I saw Michael check her out.

My stomach did its own little flip when Kaira came down the stairs. She wore skin-tight black pants, black heels that got her almost to my height, and an orange top that bared her stomach. I turned away, even though all I wanted to do was devour her with my eyes.

"Looking good, Girlfriend!" A.J. told her.

Understatement of the century, I thought.

Bri and A.J. were the most dressed up of the bunch. A.J. was in a pastel-purple suit with a yellow shirt and black bow tie. His shoes were purple; too. I didn't even know they made purple dress shoes.

Bri was wearing a white dress and had curled her blonde hair. With her red lipstick and pearls, she looked like she belonged on one of those rounded bridges under a tree covered with Spanish moss. All that was missing from her southern belle routine was the accent.

I didn't notice much else after that. I was too busy sneaking glances at Kaira out of the corner of my eye as she moved around the room.

"I'm a genius," A.J. said as he scrutinized my outfit. "That shirt totally brings out the Turks and Caicos of your eyes that I bet all the Nats go loco over."

I couldn't help myself. My gaze flicked to Kaira. She was studiously examining one of Yutika's hundred-dollar bills on the coffee table and didn't look up.

Smith handed all of us tiny Bluetooth earpieces that were almost impossible to see unless someone was right on top of us. Apparently, Smith always stayed in the van when the Six were on a job so he could do his Techie thing. The others did the more hands-on work of ferrying their client out from wherever they were trying to escape. The Six seemed to take all of our preparations in stride, but I had the surreal feeling I was playing James Bond or something. I had to stop myself from requesting that my martini come shaken, not stirred.

When we filed out of the house and into the garage, the white van the Six had used to break me out of jail was gone. It had been replaced with a blue one of a different make and model. I didn't remember the license plate on the other van, but I guessed this one was different.

I turned to Yutika. "Your work?"

"You know it."

I shook my head in amazement. "I'm glad you guys are on my side."

I was rewarded with a smile from Kaira.

Michael drove, which made for a decidedly smoother ride than when Yutika had been behind the wheel. He parked in a handicapped spot right on Commonwealth Ave. Yutika did a quick sketch on her note pad. I watched as the drawing became a real handicapped tag, which Yutika passed up to Michael to hang from the rearview mirror.

"We're all going to hell," I muttered.

The others grinned and shrugged, looking less than apologetic as everyone except Smith piled out of the van.

When I caught sight of my reflection in a dark window, I startled before remembering I was now a Hispanic man with tattoos and a shaved head. It wasn't a bad look on me, all things considered. At least Kaira hadn't turned me into a girl, which she'd done on a few occasions. That had really been trippy.

I followed the others down a side-street and tried to be cool as I stepped into my first Magic club. It wasn't exactly against the rules for Naturals to go into Magic clubs or vice versa, but there was a tacit understanding that bars and clubs weren't usually places for mixed company. There was so much justifiable unease when it came to the third law, that places involving alcohol and scantily-dressed patrons catered to Naturals *or* Magics…not both.

My illusion wouldn't keep Magics from recognizing I wasn't one of them if they bothered to look, but the Six had assured me no one would pay enough attention to me to realize I was a Nat.

As soon as I stepped inside, it was immediately obvious that this was like no club I'd ever been to.

The dancers on top of the bar were Contortionists, literally becoming boneless as they twisted into positions that would be impossible for anyone with a skeleton. Drinks zoomed across the room and delivered themselves.

There was a band, but no musicians. The electric guitar, cello, and keyboard were playing themselves. I knew there must be a group of Magics somewhere who were controlling the instruments, but I couldn't see them through the crowd.

The club was packed. If Bri hadn't gone first, using her titanium body to cut a path for the rest of us, we never would have made it to the bar.

Smith's voice crackled across my earpiece. I tried to be subtle as I pressed the earpiece farther into my ear. It was so loud in here, I barely heard when Smith asked, "Any sight of her? Nancy Axelrod, age forty-four. Alchemist, Level 2. Height: five feet six inches—"

"I see her," Kaira said through my earpiece. "Far left of the bar."

"She won't hear me over all this noise," Michael's deep voice replied.

"She doesn't look like she's in the mood to chat without Michael's persuasion," Yutika observed.

As I looked at the bartender, I realized Yutika was right. Nancy Axelrod was nervous. Her eyes kept shifting around as she worked. She spilled a drink she was handing over the bar because her hands were shaking.

"Everyone spread out and keep an eye on her," Kaira's voice said into my earpiece. "We'll get her on her way out of the club."

I knew it was the right play, but it didn't make the situation any less infuriating. I needed answers.

"What do we do in the meantime?" I asked, trying not to let my frustration come across in my voice.

"This is a party, Boyfriend. Enjoy yourself," A.J. told me.

Right.

"Michael and I will stay close in case she decides to leave early," Kaira said. "The rest of you, hang out near the exits in case she tries to bolt. And turn off your mic when you don't need it so we don't get so much backfeed."

I turned off my microphone and let the crowd push me away from the center of the dance floor. I found myself near the back entrance of the club with Yutika. It was quieter and less crowded back here, and it gave us a view of the bar, as well as the club's front door.

"I forgot it was you for a second," Yutika giggled, giving my arm a friendly punch. "You look super bad-ass with that illusion."

"Oh, right." I glanced at my unfamiliar reflection in the mirror on the back wall. "I don't think Kaira's ever given me the same face twice. It's going to give me an identity crisis one of these days."

"You two have known each other for a long time, haven't you?" Yutika asked.

"Since we were kids," I replied, keeping my gaze focused on Nancy Axelrod.

"Kaira's my hero," Yutika said, fanning her face. "I want to be just like her someday."

I laughed. I didn't say anything else for fear of saying too much.

"Seriously, though," Yutika said. "You must know her better than any of us." A thoughtful expression came over her face. "I've been living and working with her for years now, and I feel like I don't really know much about her. It's weird. I mean, I've met Ma and her grandma and cousins, but I don't *know her*, know her."

"I guess being unMarked has made her a little less willing to share things about her past," I said, giving Yutika a non-committal shrug.

I couldn't be sure, but I guessed Kaira kept her distance from her friends for the same reason I did. At the BSMU, I was friendly with everyone, but I never got too close with anyone. It was difficult to get close to people when I couldn't tell them why I didn't date or why I made periodic trips to my dad's house to make sure no new pill bottles had appeared in his medicine cabinet.

The day I'd walked out of Kaira's life, I hadn't just lost the woman I loved more than life itself. I'd lost my best friend.

I cleared my throat. Nodding at the packed dance floor, I said, "This place is nuts."

"If you think this is crowded, you should see the holidays at my house. Five-hundred Indian relatives crammed into a kitchen this big." She held her thumb and forefinger together until they were almost touching. "Honestly, it's a max capacity issue. If my house was an elevator, we'd get shut down."

I laughed again.

"So, how long have you been…um…working with Kaira?" I asked.

"Two-and-a-half years." She looked at me. "You don't approve of what we do, do you?"

I shrugged, but when Yutika raised her eyebrows, I said, "What you guys are doing weakens the Alliance and makes the whole system worse off."

"I think you're walking proof that the system is already broken," Yutika replied.

I wanted to argue with her, but a part of me wondered if she was right.

As quickly as the thought came to me, I rejected it. The Alliance was the reason Boston hadn't succumbed to the Slaughters like every other major city. It was the reason why we weren't being governed by some tyrant. It was the only way to bring true unity between Naturals and Magics.

A.J.'s voice in my earpiece said, "If Michael doesn't stop staring at our mark like he's an assassin or something, she's going to know we're here for her."

"Come on, Michael. Dance with me."

I jerked my attention to where Kaira was leading Michael away from the bar and into the crowd of people dancing in front of the musician-less band.

A surge of emotions I didn't want to feel took hold of me.

It wasn't that I was jealous. Even from here, I could tell from Kaira's body language that she had no interest in him like that, and Michael was keeping his hands firmly in friend territory. It was just that I wanted it to be my hands on her waist.

We were done, I reminded myself. We'd been done for three years, and I'd been doing fine. I still missed her…still loved her, but I could get through the day without constantly thinking about her. It was just now, being within sight of her…. That, along with everything else that was going on, was making me a little crazy.

I forced my attention back to Yutika, but her narrowed gaze was on Michael.

I checked to make sure my microphone was turned off before saying to her, "You could go cut in, you know."

"I didn't. I wasn't—" Yutika turned to me, and then she laughed. "Okay, I might have been."

I grinned at her. "I'm sure Kaira wouldn't mind."

Yutika glanced back at the dance floor.

"We work together. And Michael is…hard to get to know. All any of us know about him is that he came from Detroit."

I winced. Detroit was infamous for having the worst Slaughters in the country. It had been even more violent than Atlanta.

"You don't need to know his life story for a dance," I pointed out, wondering what the hell I was doing.

"I guess you're right." Yutika blew out a breath and threw a few fake punches, like she was a boxer going into the ring. "Wish me luck," she told me.

"Good luck."

I kept one eye on the bartender as I watched Yutika weave through the crowd toward Michael and Kaira. She tapped Michael on the shoulder. Kaira smiled and stepped back.

I assumed Yutika and Michael were dancing, but I wasn't looking at them anymore. Everything in the club had faded. All of my attention was drawn to Kaira like a magnet.

She moved to the side of the dance floor where she was partly hidden behind a column. Some guy immediately went over to her and spoke into her ear. It was so close to her mic that his words almost blew out my eardrum.

"Dance with me, Gorgeous," he said.

She shook her head and turned away from him, toward me. Our gazes locked.

I should stay put. I knew that. I had never been the self-destructive type.

Then again, I reflected, *maybe I had*. I'd fallen in love with a Magic and broken two out of three high laws for her sake. I had convinced myself we'd find a way to be together and have the life we both wanted. At the very least, I was delusional.

These thoughts were just background as I was drawn through the crowd to her by an invisible tether.

It's just a dance, I told myself as I held Kaira's gaze, asking her without needing to say a word.

I tried not to think about how we were in a crowded club, where anyone who bothered to look would know I was a Natural.

We positioned ourselves behind the column so she could watch the front door and I could keep an eye on the back exit. Kaira slid her arms over my shoulders. Mine came to rest on her waist, and I pulled her closer before I could stop myself. This undeniable connection between us had always been here, and even after what had happened, it hadn't gone away. If anything, it was stronger than ever.

I drew her deeper into the column's shadow, where we'd be hidden from view of most of the dance floor. I was distantly aware of the other Six's chatter over my earpiece. I looked around once, just to make sure none of the others were watching us. I didn't think they were. Besides, we were surrounded by people on every side. No one would see the way we were holding each other.

It must have been the desperation of my current situation that emboldened me. I would never before have risked touching her in public in case any Magics noticed I wasn't one of them. But the couples surrounding us now were too busy grinding and making out to pay attention to anyone else besides their partners.

Kaira rested her head on my shoulder and moved her hands up my neck until she was playing with my hair. I felt her heartbeat quicken in time with my own.

I slid my hands up to the bare skin at her waist and then back down to her hips, wanting to feel her every curve as I drew her all the way against me.

She made a soft sound that raised my temperature several degrees. When she lifted her head from my shoulder and I caught sight of the expression in her dark eyes, I lost the battle I'd been waging with myself. I leaned in.

An earsplitting scream made me jerk back.

CHAPTER 15

It's the Nat!"

"Penelope Heppurn's murderer! He's here!"

"Graysen Galder!"

People were pointing at me. There were more screams. I barely avoided a glass bottle that was aimed at my head.

Kaira swore. "I'm sorry!"

I looked down at myself. My illusion was gone.

"Kill the bastard!"

Another projectile came through the air. This time, it was a knife. I caught it in the air, miraculously getting the handle rather than the blade.

"Get out of here," I yelled to Kaira, but when I turned back to her, she was gone. In her place was…me. And then the other people around us turned into me, too. There were at least ten identical versions of me.

"What the—"

"An Animate Illusionist!"

"Kai!" I shouted, searching the sea of carbon copies of myself for the one person I was desperate to protect.

A version of myself went hurtling through the air, attacked by some invisible force. Another had red sparks erupting from his head.

Kai. Where was Kai?

"Six, get to the door," Kaira's voice called into my earpiece.

"Kaira Hansley, get this illusion off me," A.J.'s voice shouted over my earpiece. "Frat boy is not a good look on me."

One of the illusions of me erupted in flames. It was horrible, even more so to see it happening to an identical version of myself.

There was the sound of glass shattering and more screams. A fire extinguisher flew through the air, bashing two Graysens in the head.

By now, half the bar was filled with identical copies of me. If I wasn't so worried about where the Six were in this madness, I'd be more disturbed about all the ways I was seeing my body punished.

"Kaira!" I yelled. Where the hell was she? Which one was she?

Half the people in the bar looked like me, and the place had turned into complete pandemonium.

I caught sight of Bri, her skin glittering titanium, as she blasted through a crowd of Magics who were punching one of the Graysen's senseless.

I had to stop this before someone got killed. I looked around, searching for some way to end this insanity, when I caught sight of the bar. The bartender…our bartender…was gone.

My heart leapt into my throat. I scanned the crowd, frantic. She was our only lead on the murders. If she disappeared, we had nothing. Somehow, my attention snagged on her white bartender shirt, which glowed under the fluorescent lights. I shoved my way through the crowd toward her.

"Stop!" I called.

The bartender glanced back at me. I saw her eyes register fear. And then she ran for the back exit. I went after her.

I realized I still had the knife in my hand, and I waved it around to part the people punching, hurling magic, and screaming at each other. The bartender went through the fire exit, setting off the fire alarm. In addition to the screeching of the alarm, the sprinklers turned on. I barely felt the spray as I forced my way to the back door.

I crashed through it. I glanced both ways, saw the bartender sprinting down the sidewalk, and raced after her.

Fear made her fast, but I was faster. Nancy started to cross the street. Cars honked. With an extra burst of speed, I caught up to her. I tackled her, yanking her back onto the sidewalk before she got hit by a car.

She kicked and clawed at me.

"Stop," I gasped, using my weight to pin her to the sidewalk.

She screamed. Porch lights came on.

"I'm not going to hurt you. Just calm down."

I felt her teeth sink into my forearm.

I wrestled her back down and then raised the knife to her throat. "Stop," I commanded.

She went still.

Some part of my brain registered that I was holding a knife to a person's throat, but in that moment, all that mattered was making sure this woman didn't get away. I hated that look of terror in her eyes, but if it was the only way to get what I needed....

I got off her, keeping the knife pointed at her throat.

"Get up," I said, using the gruffness in my voice to let her think I might actually use the weapon.

I used one hand to wrap an arm around her shoulders, keeping the knife lightly touching her neck. I used my other hand to turn my microphone back on.

"I've got the bartender," I said, wondering if anyone could even hear me over the screams and bedlam coming from inside the bar. "If you can hear me, get to the van and pick us up at the corner of Warrenton and Charles."

"Bobby was wrong about you," Nancy sniffed.

I didn't have a chance to ask her what she meant.

"Gray?" Kaira's worried voice cut through the sound of sirens in the background.

My knees went weak with relief.

"Kai, are you okay?"

Whatever she said in reply was lost in the squeal of tires. The blue van stopped in front of the curb. The door opened.

"Get in," I told the woman.

She was crying. I felt like a complete asshole, but I didn't feel bad enough to let my only chance at answers get away.

I wiped down the knife's handle with my sleeve, feeling more criminal by the second, and tossed it into some bushes before climbing into the van.

The woman whimpered as I squeezed in beside her, but Michael was sitting on her other side and was already speaking softly to her. Within seconds, her tense posture relaxed and a tentative smile replaced her look of terror.

"Yes, yes of course I will," she said to whatever Michael had Whispered to her.

It was a relief to see the Six back to looking like themselves. My gaze cut straight to Kaira. She was sitting next to A.J., and a quick scan reassured me she wasn't hurt.

My relief at seeing her unharmed turned to anger when I realized the danger she'd been in. Every Magic and probably most Naturals wanted me dead. And she had illusioned herself, and the rest of the Six, to look just like me.

"Don't ever do that again," I told her.

Kaira let out a shaky breath, but she didn't say anything.

"I mean it," I growled. Staying angry was the easiest way to avoid thinking about how something could have happened to her.

Kaira replied with a silent look of challenge that made me want to yell at her until I turned blue in the face. Or haul her into my arms and kiss her senseless.

"I'm not gonna lie," Bri said, blowing on her fists until they turned back to human skin instead of titanium, "that was the most fun I've had in…well, forever."

"It was like eating shrooms and then going into one of those houses of mirrors," A.J. said. "Equal parts interesting and terrifying."

"You all had one simple mission. Get the bartender and get out," Smith grumbled from behind his screens. "Destroying a club and drawing the attention of every Mag and Nat cop in the city isn't exactly going to help our cause."

"It's my fault," Kaira said. "I let Gray's illusion slip. I'm sorry."

"It's not like you to get distracted enough to lose one of your illusions," Yutika said. "What happened?"

"I—I lost focus. I'm sorry."

I felt my face heat with shame and self-loathing. Kaira and I had destroyed a bar because of an almost-kiss. People got hurt. Some might even be—

What on Earth had I been thinking?

The simple answer was that I hadn't been thinking…at least, not about anything other than Kaira.

"Well, the police just arrested all twenty-two Graysens still inside," Smith said.

"They'll be back to themselves in a few minutes," Kaira said. "We're reaching the edge of my range."

"That is super impressive," Yutika said from the driver's seat as the van screeched to a halt at a traffic light.

"Meanwhile, have any of you said boo about how I levitated the whole goddamn bar to block the door behind us?" A.J. huffed.

"That was pretty sweet," Bri said.

A.J. winked at her.

I turned my attention to the bartender, who was speaking quietly to Michael. His eyes widened, and then he asked her, "Can you tell my friends what you told me?"

Nancy hesitated. Michael said something in her ear again.

In a hurried voice, Nancy began to speak.

"It all started about six months ago, when Bobby said he'd gotten a big promotion at the Alliance. He started acting weird after that. He worked all the time, and when he was home, he was always taking strange calls when he thought I was asleep. He was getting nervous, too. He installed a security system in our house and insisted we keep our blinds drawn day and night."

Nancy looked at Michael, who gave her an encouraging nod.

"Then, a few months ago, I got a notice in the mail that we were overdue on our cable bill. Usually Bobby pays the bills, but he'd been so busy with work I assumed he just forgot. When I went to transfer the money, I noticed there was almost a million dollars in our account." She laughed nervously. "Bobby and I could barely pay our bills. School loans, car payments, and alimony payments from Bobby's first marriage. You know how it goes."

"Of course," Michael told her.

"Well, anyway, I was so flustered, I called Bobby's cell. When he didn't answer, I called his office." She took a gulp of air. "He'd been real insistent that I only call him on his cell, but it was a million fucking dollars. Can you blame me for wanting to talk to my husband?"

"Not at all," Michael said.

"That was when his secretary told me that Bobby had left the Alliance six months ago. She didn't know where he'd gone to work, only that he wasn't at the Alliance anymore."

The van was silent as she took a nervous little breath.

"When Bobby came home that night, I confronted him. He yelled at me for calling the office, and then he told me he was working in some secret department that no one knew about. He said it was so secret he couldn't even tell me about it."

"I knew it!" Smith exclaimed, victory lighting his eyes. "I knew the Alliance—"

Kaira put up a hand and gave him a warning look.

"Go on," Michael told Nancy.

"That night, he was on the phone again, so I listened. I couldn't hear much, but he kept mentioning *the Lab*."

"Do you think your husband was involved in a drug lab?" Michael asked.

"Yes." She whispered the word, but we all heard it.

It was what I assumed, too. It would explain Bobby Axelrod's sudden increase in wealth, paranoia, and unwillingness to tell his wife what he was mixed up in. Except, something felt like it was missing with that theory.

"Don't drug dealers usually pay in cash?" I asked no one in particular. Not that I had any related experience myself, but I'd seen enough crime shows to know that drug dealers didn't wire money into bank accounts.

"Smith—" I began.

"Yeah, yeah," the Techie said from behind his screens. "I'm working on it." He was muttering and swearing as his computer screens blinked and flashed.

"Interesting," Smith said a few moments later.

"What?" Six voices asked at once.

"I can't see where the money came from, but I can see that an additional $250,000 was wired into the account yesterday morning at 8:00am."

"So?" Yutika prompted.

"So, the other Alchemist, Jonas Meddlesworth, was found dead at 8:02am. Don't tell me you think this is just some kind of coincidence."

I turned to Nancy. "Did your husband know a man by the name of Jonas Meddlesworth?" I asked.

Nancy's lower lip trembled. "He's the one who's been on the news because he got murdered."

We all nodded.

"Did your husband know him?" Michael asked.

Nancy shook her head. "I'd never heard that name or seen his face before the news started covering his murder."

"That doesn't mean our two Alchemists weren't acquainted," A.J. pointed out.

"Bobby and Jonas had to have been part of the same organization," Kaira said. "There's no other explanation."

But there was still the matter of Penelope. What could she possibly have to do with two Alchemists involved in drug production?

"Nancy, what do you know about your husband calling in to report a murder at the BSMU?" I asked.

Nancy's eyes widened with terror as she glanced from my face to my right hand, where I'd held the knife before tossing it into the bushes. She gave a little yelp of fear and scooted away from me and closer to Michael.

I shoved my guilt to a dark corner of my mind where I'd come back for it later, once I had the information I needed.

"No one's going to hurt you, Nancy," Michael said in a soothing voice. "Can you please answer his question?"

Refusing to look at me, Nancy said in a tremulous voice, "I didn't know Bobby did that."

My heart sank a little.

"One more question," I said. "What did you mean when you said Bobby was wrong about me?"

She looked at Michael, who nodded at her.

Nancy swallowed. "Well, we were watching the news a few nights ago, and they were doing that story on you and Penelope graduating at the top of your class at the BSMU. Bobby turned off the TV, and I swear, his face had turned green. He said something like, 'Poor things, they both seem like such nice kids.'"

She glared at me. "But *nice* boys don't threaten people with knives."

I wanted to apologize and ask for her forgiveness. Instead, I asked, "Did Bobby say anything else? Did he mention any names of anyone who might have been involved with Penelope's murder?"

Nancy looked at Michael. "I'm sorry, but that's all I know."

"You did great," he told her.

"Stop the van," Kaira told Yutika.

I crashed against my seatbelt as the van came to a stop.

Kaira leaned forward in her seat. "I want Nancy in her right mind for this conversation. No manipulation."

Michael Whispered in her ear. Immediately, her tension returned and she scooted as far away from me as she could, giving me a death stare.

"Nancy," Kaira said in a commanding voice. "We believe you're in danger. My friends and I can keep you safe. We can help you find a new place to live where you'll be able to start over. You'll have money, a new file, somewhere to live, and anything else you need. Will you let us help you?"

"You kidnapped me." She pointed an accusing finger at me. "He—he threatened me."

"I'm sorry," I said, feeling awful.

"You'll have to forgive the Nat," A.J. said. "He's having a tough week."

"We can protect you from whoever your husband's mixed up with," Kaira told Nancy. "Six of us are unMarked, so we have a lot of experience at this."

"I just want to go home," Nancy said, her chin trembling.

"Your home might not be safe," Kaira said.

"Honey, let us help you," A.J. chimed in.

A tear slid down Nancy's face. "Please, just let me go."

"Can we at least drive you home?" Kaira asked.

Nancy shook her head and motioned for Michael to open the door. He did, and she jumped out.

We all watched as Nancy stumbled down the street, turning back to give us a frightened stare, before turning a corner.

"Want me to keep an eye on her tonight?" Bri asked.

Kaira nodded. "Someone might come after her."

"I'll go with Bri in case anyone shows up who's worth talking to," Michael said.

"My fists can be pretty persuasive, you know," Bri told him as they got out of the van.

"Call me if you need anything," Kaira told them.

Once they were gone and we were on our way back to Kaira's, A.J. said, "Okay, so what do we know?"

"Bobby Axelrod and Jonas Meddlesworth were definitely working for the same people," Kaira said.

"And now Jonas is dead and Bobby is missing," A.J. said.

"And Bobby knew about Penelope's murder before it happened," I added.

Everyone was silent for a moment as we tried to find the missing connections.

"My vote is that they're working for a secret Alliance department that doesn't officially exist," Smith said, his voice rising in excitement. "I read a blog post the other day by a lady who swears the Alliance is nabbing Mags off the street, preserving their bodies, and shipping them off to China for Mengele-like experiments."

"You need therapy, Smith," A.J. said, scowling at the Techie. "You know that, right?"

"Even if any of what you just said was possible, the Alliance is a government organization," I said. "It has a budget just like any other government, and it certainly doesn't have spare millions sitting around to fund these supposed secret departments."

Smith huffed.

"Bobby Axelrod, Jonas Meddlesworth, and Penelope are all somehow connected," I said. "We just have to figure out how."

"Gotcha."

We turned to look at Smith, who brushed back the greasy strands of his hair to reveal a victorious expression.

"What've you got?" Kaira asked.

"Bobby Axelrod used his credit card an hour ago at the Watertown Motel."

"That's not far from here," I said, looking at Kaira. "If Bobby is still there—"

"Directions," Yutika demanded.

"Turn around," Smith said.

I clung to the edge of the seat as the van U-turned and barreled back in the other direction.

"Oh Lordy," A.J. complained.

"If you don't like my driving, then one of you can be the getaway driver," Yutika grumbled. "NYC girl here, remember? What am I supposed to know about driving, anyway?"

"Well then, get around to making driver's licenses for the rest of us," A.J. retorted.

Yutika's comeback was drowned out by the simultaneous chime of several cell phones. A.J. and Kaira pulled their phones out of their pockets, while Yutika took both hands off the wheel to look at hers. Kaira snatched Yutika's phone away before we all died.

There was a chorus of curses from everyone except me.

"What?" I asked, craning to see the bedazzled screen of A.J.'s phone. "What happened?"

A.J.'s phone floated in the air and hovered in front of my face.

The bolded headline read, *Chief Justice Alina Freeman found murdered in Boston hotel room.*

CHAPTER 16

My whole body went numb.

Alina Freeman was the first Natural judge to rule that Magics were officially humans, and thus, deserving of all the rights and protections as Naturals. The effects of her death would be…incalculable.

I snatched the phone out of the air and scrolled through the news article.

…stabbed brutally seven times. A Magic whose identity has not yet been released has been arrested for the murder. He is being held at the Federal Correction Institute of Boston while he awaits trial. If convicted, his execution will be held early Monday morning.

Valencia Stark, head of the UnAllied, will be holding a rally this Saturday to protest the execution. Magics nation-wide are outraged that Graysen Galder, the chief suspect in two Magic murders earlier this week, has yet to be apprehended.

It would seem Galder started a trend of prejudice and violence, which other disturbed people—both Naturals and Magics—are eager to perpetuate….

My stomach turned over.

Before I could even begin to process what Chief Justice Freeman's murder would mean for the Alliance and the ever-more fragile bonds of peace between Naturals and Magics, everyone's phones started dinging and buzzing at once.

"How many times do I need to tell you to get rid of those things?" Smith grumbled. "Do you know how easy cell phones are to track? Bloggers are saying—"

"Someone tell me what the hell is going on," Yutika demanded.

"Mags," Kaira and A.J. said at the same time.

"People are panicking," Kaira clarified. "We're getting inundated with Mags who want to disappear."

"At least trade out your SIM cards once in a while," Smith persisted.

"If it were up to you, there'd be no way to get in touch with any of us," A.J. said.

"Um, yeah," Smith replied.

"Right. Because that'd be great for business," A.J. retorted. "We'll help you, but only if you can crack through ten firewalls to get our phone number."

"That's not how firewalls work," Smith said.

"What do we do now?" Yutika asked before A.J. could continue the argument.

Kaira rubbed her neck. "Okay. Smith, I need you to find out everything you can about the Mag they've convicted. Find out if he's actually the guy, or if he's another scapegoat. Text me if we need to do anything about him."

Kaira turned in her seat.

"A.J. and Yutika, you both go back to the house and start sorting through all these Mags. Figure out which ones we can help and get the process rolling. And Gray and I will need a car."

Yutika was drawing before we had come to a full stop, and she didn't seem to notice when the van lurched over the curb. She flicked her pen across the sheet of paper.

"Done," she announced a minute later. She rolled down her window and tossed the paper out.

I followed Kaira out of the van and stepped closer to get a better look at the drawing. Yutika was the first Creator I'd ever met, and I was fascinated.

The drawing lay on the pavement for several seconds. Then, the image of the car lifted itself right up. It left behind a hole in the sheet of paper as the 2D drawing of the car stood on its flimsy wheels.

As I watched, the flat image began to expand. I heard the sound of crinkling paper, and it was as though the sketch's fibers were somehow multiplying. The flat paper car became a 3D paper car. It looked like something out of a pop-up book for kids.

The soft, papery exterior hardened into a metal shell. It reminded me of a toy car. At least, it did, until it started to get bigger.

There was the groan and creak of metal shifting into alignment. Small rubber tires and plastic hubcaps sprung from the remaining paper.

"You better back up," Kaira said, observing my fascination with an amused look on her face.

I did, going to stand on the curb next to her without taking my eyes off the tiny car. It was wobbling back and forth on its new wheels. It started to grow. Fast.

One second, it was the size of a toy. The next, a real-life black sedan was parked next to us. If I was still standing where I'd been a few seconds ago, I would have been crushed underneath the car.

The windows rolled down all by themselves, and I caught the hint of new car smell. *Eye of the Tiger* was playing on the radio.

"That is so damn cool," I said. "Will it…drive?"

"Nope. I just thought you and Kaira would like somewhere to sit and relax while the rest of us get shit done." Yutika grinned at me. "*Of course*, it drives."

I would have come up with a snappy retort if my mind wasn't on overload. Instead, I went over to the sedan…equal parts awed and skeptical.

"Room 211!" Smith called out of the van's cracked window.

Kaira waved a hand to let Smith know we'd heard and then got into the passenger side of the car. I opened the driver's door. The car was already running. There was no key in the ignition, but other than that, it seemed like a normal car.

Weird.

There was even a hula girl stuck to the dash, which wiggled along with the engine's vibrations. I glanced into the rearview mirror. That's when I saw the stick figure decals on the back windshield. There were seven of them…and they bore more than a passing resemblance to each of us.

That's just showing off, I thought with an amused chuckle.

Kaira, who seemed used to this sort of thing, pulled on her seatbelt and adjusted her head rest.

"Don't get pulled over," she warned me. "I don't want to have to deal with you not having a driver's license."

I pressed on the gas, and to my surprise and relief, the car accelerated. We pulled onto Storrow Drive along with all the other cars. It was a mark of my current situation that I wasn't more thrilled by the fact that I was fully illusioned and driving a car that had just been brought into existence by a Creator. I was surrounded by more magic at this moment than some people got to experience in their entire lives. And I was with Kaira.

But then I remembered I was being framed for two murders, and I was no closer to answers than I'd been when I got arrested. And now someone else was dead.

"What a disaster," I groaned.

"This isn't your fault," Kaira said. "You're the victim here."

"Maybe if I turn myself in—"

"Then what?" she demanded. "You think the murders will stop?"

I didn't know. I just knew I had to do something—something more than chasing after the barest hope of learning something useful. I felt complicit in the murders because I was out here and free, and some madman was using me as a cover for committing all these atrocities.

"So, how do you want to do this?" Kaira asked.

I almost smiled. She knew me so well…she knew the best way to get me out of the black place my thoughts had gone was to give me a logical problem I could solve. I took the bait.

"Bobby Axelrod sounds pretty dumb for checking into a motel with his own credit card, but it also sounds like he's scared." I rubbed a hand along my stubbled jaw. "I doubt he'll just let us in to chat."

"I could call Bri to come break down the door."

"That'll just terrify him even more and we'll never get anything out of him," I said. My male pride required me to add, "Besides, I could break open the door if it came down to it."

Kaira grinned.

"I'd rather not call Michael unless we have to," Kaira said. "That way, if anyone shows up at Nancy's, he'll be there to find out what they know."

I agreed. Kaira and I would find out everything we could from Bobby Axelrod, one way or another.

"I'm thinking cop illusions would be best," I told her.

Kaira nodded. "That'll work. You want to be good cop or bad?"

That coaxed a small smile out of me. "Bad, obviously."

She grinned back. For a while, we drove in easy silence. It felt so strangely…normal.

I glanced at her, but she was staring out her window at something. Her whole body had gone rigid. That's when I saw the giant, lit billboard that had commanded her attention.

There was an image of a chubby, smiling infant. The huge text beneath the baby read, "The greatest gift to mankind. The greatest gift to your country."

I gripped the steering wheel.

The billboard was one of many efforts to get couples to start having more children. Ever since the Slaughters, the world population had been plummeting, and governments were desperate to replenish the deficit. People saw it as their national duty to choose a partner with whom they could produce viable children. It was one of the reasons why there had been an increase in violence toward homosexuals, and why couples who decided not to have children were social lepers.

Still, even that wasn't as bad as earning the brand of *baby killer* by breaking the third high law.

In any society, doing something that could kill hundreds of infants would be abhorrent. But particularly in a time when children were scarcer and more precious than ever before, even the possibility of producing a DAMND child, the infected offspring from a Natural and Magic couple, was unthinkable.

I understood people's fear and the real danger that Nat-Mag couples posed to others around them. It was why Kaira and I had been obsessive about birth control.

I had never cared much about having kids. I liked them enough, but it wasn't possible with Kaira, and I didn't want to be with anyone except her.

I believed there had been a time when Kaira wanted me enough to give up her chances of marriage and having a big family like the one she'd grown up with. But I hadn't missed the longing in her gaze whenever we had been watching TV and a happy couple with a baby was on the screen, and I'd seen the way she flipped too quickly through the wedding section of her magazines. Even if she wouldn't admit it, Kaira wanted those things. And I'd never be able to give them to her.

Now, though, she could marry a Magic and have it all.

The thought curdled in my stomach like sour milk.

Kaira stared down as her phone buzzed. I mentally shook myself, refocusing, and then looked over her shoulder as her screen filled with text. It was from a blocked number.

Kaira look down at the message, and then up at me. "It's Smith."

CHAPTER 17

Smith's text said, *Mag arrested for Alina Freeman murder definitely guilty.*

Kaira exchanged a look with me as she dialed a number.

Yutika's voice answered on the other end.

"Put Smith on," Kaira told her.

"The guy's an UnAllied," Smith said without preamble. "The dickhead was bragging about the murder. He was pissed Freeman was 'getting involved in Mag business.' Direct quote."

"Got it," Kaira said, her face twisted in disgust. "Thanks for checking on that."

"I'm texting you a picture of Bobby Axelrod so you'll know who you're looking for," Smith said. "Need anything else?"

"No, get some sleep. We'll be home in a couple of hours."

The call ended just as I pulled into the motel's parking lot. We both stared at the picture on Kaira's cell phone. It was of a slightly overweight, balding man with light blue eyes and a patchy beard.

Kaira put her phone back in her pocket. My eyes were drawn to her as her appearance started to morph. She became shorter and her skin darkened. Her beautiful features became bland and common. Her club outfit was replaced with a police uniform.

No matter how many times I saw her work, it never got old. There was something inherently beautiful in her magic that reminded me of a gifted painter or composer.

I looked down at myself and realized my appearance was altered, too. Except where Kaira looked unassuming, I was imposing. Muscles bulged from my arms, visible even through the cop uniform. I glanced in the rearview mirror and saw that I had a thick beard, which made me look the part of a cop who got answers.

"Let's do this," I said, deepening my voice and getting into character.

It wasn't hard to act the part of a guy who was pissed off and looking for answers.

We got out of the car and headed straight to Room 211. The curtains were drawn, but I could see a light on inside. I banged on the door.

"Mr. Axelrod, Boston Police," I called in an authoritative voice.

The curtain pulled back enough for me to see a more haggard, terrified version of the picture Smith had sent us.

"You're not in trouble," Kaira called. "We just want to talk to you."

"Why's there a Nat with you?" the querulous voice called from the other side of the door.

"Natural and Magic police are collaborating on this one," I said. "Open up, Mr. Axelrod."

I put my hand on my hip where my gun would be holstered if I had one. It was a threatening pose, but I wasn't feeling especially patient.

The door cracked open. I barged in before the guy changed his mind.

"You—you have no right," Axelrod stuttered.

"We have every right," I said in a bored tone. "Are you familiar with Section 228 of the Alliance's Report of Laws?"

I remembered the precise law that applied to this situation from my second-year law class, even though I was pretty sure Bobby Axelrod wouldn't have known the difference if I'd made something up.

"I—"

"It gives the police," I pointed to myself and Kaira, "the right to investigate crimes against and relating to any person within the city limits. Now, what can you tell us about Graysen Galder being framed for Penelope Heppurn's murder?"

It would have been impossible to miss the flash of recognition—and fear—that crossed Axelrod's face.

"I don't know anything about that murder," Axelrod said, his voice taking on a whiny quality.

"Bobby, please," Kaira said, her voice as soothing as mine was demanding. "It's late, and I'm sure you'd like to get some rest. Please just tell us who framed Graysen Galder and why, and we'll get out of your hair."

The man's hands were shaking. "I don't know anything about the murder."

"That's not what Nancy told us," I said.

Bobby's eyes narrowed and his shaking hands curled into fists. "What do you know about my wife? Have you arrested her? She doesn't know anything—"

I ground my teeth. This guy was all over the place. It would be a miracle if we could get him to say anything coherent.

"Start talking," I commanded.

"I can't." Bobby sunk down on one of the beds and covered his face with his hands. "I was going to come forward about everything, but they found out and threatened Nancy." His voice sunk to a whisper. "They'll kill her."

"Who will kill Nancy?" I pressed, my heart hammering.

"We can't protect your wife if we don't know who we're protecting her from," Kaira added.

"There's nothing the police can do," Axelrod snapped. "This is above your pay grade."

Kaira and I exchanged a look.

"Let's start with something simple," Kaira said. "Who do you work for, really?"

"And she's not talking about the Alliance job you quit six months ago," I added. "She's asking about the job that got you a $500,000 raise."

Axelrod's face paled further. A muscle had started to twitch below his left eye, and perspiration was gathering on his bald spot.

"I—I didn't—"

"We don't care that you have the money," I said. "We just want to know where it came from and what it has to do with Penelope Heppurn's murder."

Bobby's gaze moved between us like he was an animal caught in a trap.

"We can get Nancy into protective custody," Kaira said. "There are Mags in the department who will give her a new identity, money, and transportation to Canada. It's very safe there, and whoever is after you will never find her."

That got his attention.

"You'll do that? If I cooperate?"

"Just tell us what we need to know, and we'll make sure whatever you're involved with doesn't touch Nancy," I said.

Bobby licked his lips. I sensed the man's resolve crumbling.

"Penelope's murder," I pushed. "You knew it was going to happen beforehand. How did you know?"

"God forgive me," Axelrod whispered. "I overheard their conversation when they decided Penelope would be the first murder, and that Graysen Galder would be the one who was framed. I don't think they meant for me to hear, but the lab shares a wall with one of the conference rooms. I wasn't trying to eavesdrop. It just kind of…happened."

I clenched my fists by my sides, forcing myself not to betray any emotion.

Let the guy talk himself out, I told myself.

"They came over after the meeting, and I think they could just tell I had heard more than I was supposed to. They said that since I already knew everything, they needed my help with something else. They told me to make a potion that was basically like a strong rat poison." His Adam's apple bobbed as he swallowed. The guy was sweating so much dark patches had appeared on his shirt.

"They used my potion to kill the guy they'd hired at the same time as me. Jonas Meddlesworth." He pressed a chubby palm to his forehead. "I think they framed Graysen Galder for that murder, too."

I didn't look at Kaira, because I knew I'd see her fury if I did, and then I'd lose my own remaining shreds of self-composure.

Bobby's eyes started to water.

"I swear, I was gonna come forward and tell the cops everything. But then they threatened Nancy, and I figured the only way to keep her safe was if I disappeared, and—"

Bobby lunged for me.

I was expecting a punch to the face, but instead, he grabbed at my belt.

Not my belt, I realized as Bobby staggered back. He'd been reaching for the illusion of my gun.

"Who are you people?" he demanded.

"Call us interested parties," I deadpanned, trying not to let it show that I'd begun to panic.

"You lying bastards!"

Bobby bolted for the door. I went after him.

The struggle was brief. I was bigger, fitter, and more determined. In seconds, Bobby was back in the center of the room, looking more disheveled and dejected.

With no more point in keeping up our illusions, Kaira let them slip away. Bobby's face didn't register anything when he looked at Kaira, but as soon as he turned to me, the man's already-pale face went white as a sheet.

I folded my arms and leaned back against the wall.

"I'm sorry," Bobby whispered.

"I don't want an apology," I said. "I want answers."

Bobby shook his head.

"Enough of this," Kaira said, pulling out her cell. She tapped a few keys and then put the call on speaker.

"What's up?" Michael's deep voice asked after the second ring.

"Gray and I are at the Watertown Motel with Bobby Axelrod. He knows who set Gray up, but he isn't talking."

"I can be there in twenty. Want me to bring Bri?"

"Leave her with Nancy," Kaira said, pausing to give Bobby a meaningful look. "Just in case Bobby here needs a little extra motivation."

The call ended.

"Michael's a Level 10 Whisper," Kaira told a speechless Bobby. "Everyone talks to him. You can try to resist all you want. I think the longest it's ever taken Michael to get information out of someone was half a second." She smirked at him.

"I can't. They'll kill Nancy. You don't understand."

"Then help us understand," I ground out.

"We'll do what we can to protect you and your wife," Kaira said. "I wasn't lying about having the resources to make you both disappear. As soon as you've told us everything you know, you and Nancy will be on a plane to Canada with new files and everything you need to start a new life."

"My bosses. They'll find us. They'll—"

Bobby doubled over, clutching his stomach. He started toward the bathroom.

I followed him, unwilling to trust the guy for even a second. I'd seen enough movies to know better than to leave a key witness alone, where he might slip out of a window or climb out through an air vent or something. I doubted the guy was resourceful or skinny enough for the latter, but I wasn't taking any chances.

"I have a bad stomach," Bobby said, still holding his midsection. "Just give me a few minutes, I beg you."

I flipped on the bathroom light and looked around for any weapons or a way of sneaking out.

My search revealed only some toiletries scattered around and a tiny window that was too high and too small to be of any use for an escape. I grabbed the disposable razor on the sink—just in case the man was stupid enough to come after us with it. Convinced Axelrod wasn't going anywhere, I stepped aside. Axelrod scurried into the bathroom and shut the door. I heard the lock turn.

I paced back and forth outside the bathroom, carving a path of impatience in the stained carpet.

"He knows who's behind this," Kaira told me. "And in about ten minutes when Michael gets here, we'll know everything he knows. Just be patient."

I gave her a short nod before going back to pacing. Learning the truth behind Penelope's murder was only the first step in this nightmarish uphill battle I was fighting. The next step would be convincing this squirrely witness to go to the Alliance authorities and repeat his story. We would need evidence, enough to prove beyond a shadow of a doubt that someone else was responsible for Penelope's murder. Even then, I would still be on the hook for breaking out of prison, evading the authorities, and a half dozen other crimes. And I'd have to craft my defense without revealing who had helped me.

Even if I could prove my innocence and convince a judge to let me off with some community service, my reputation would be forever tarnished. My father's reputation was still suffering from the comparatively minor infraction of losing a Testing file. I would never get out from under the mud my name had been dragged through, even if I was somehow miraculously exonerated from the crime I'd been accused of.

Maybe Yutika could create a new identity and Kaira could illusion me to look like someone else. Although I'd need to stay within a mile of Kaira for the illusion to hold. A plastic surgeon who could permanently alter my appearance would be more practical….

An awful gurgling, choking sound came from inside the bathroom.

"Bobby?" Kaira called.

No answer.

"Axelrod." I rapped on the door. "Are you alright?"

Silence.

"Gray."

Kaira pointed at the wisps of blue smoke curling under the door.

I knocked again. When no answer came, I motioned for Kaira to get out of the way.

"Fair warning, I'm kicking in the door," I called.

For the first time in living memory, I silently thanked Coach for all the quad presses and squats he'd made me do since joining the crew team. My third kick broke the door's hinges, and the fourth sent the door slamming into the bathroom.

Blue smoke poured out of the open doorway. I saw the faint outline of Bobby Axelrod. He was lying on the floor.

CHAPTER 18

I immediately began choking on the foul-smelling smoke. It billowed out of the small bathroom, blanketing the rest of the room in a bluish fog that burned my throat and made my eyes water.

"Shit, shit, shit!" Kaira pulled the collar of her shirt over her nose and ran into the bathroom.

"Kaira," I began, but I swallowed a mouthful of smoke and was overtaken by a fit of coughing.

We had to get out of here.

Whatever we were breathing, it couldn't be good.

Axelrod was conscious…barely. His face was coated with perspiration, and his pupils were so dilated there were barely any whites left. I covered my mouth and nose with my shirt, which helped a little.

"Get out of here," I ordered Kaira, my words coming out muffled from beneath my collar.

I bent down, grabbed Axelrod underneath his armpits, and started to drag him out of the bathroom. He was awake, but limp, and his dead weight fought against me.

Once we were out of the small bathroom, Kaira grabbed his feet. Together, we half-carried, half-dragged, him to the door.

I yanked it open, gulping in the fresh night air as I pulled Axelrod outside.

"Are you okay?" I asked Kaira.

She was bent over the railing and taking great, heaving breaths of clean air.

"Fine," she managed.

I waited another few beats to make sure she was alright before I turned my attention on Axelrod.

"What did you do?" I demanded, my voice full of a desperation I didn't recognize.

"Sorry," he gasped. Bloody spittle flew out of his mouth and speckled his white, sweat-soaked shirt. "Would have killed Nancy. Had to."

This couldn't be happening. I wouldn't let it.

Fury like I'd never felt before lashed through me. "You don't get to do this. Do you hear me? I need answers! You have to—"

Axelrod was making a horrible choking noise that cut me off mid-rant. Foam, flecked with blood, spilled out of his mouth and down his chin.

That sense of helplessness I was becoming all-too familiar with gripped me in a vise. This man was dying. And if we lost him, I lost my chance of finding out the truth.

I gripped his chin in my hand, forcing his bloodshot eyes to focus on me.

"Tell me how to undo this," I commanded.

I was so goddamned sick of having no control, of being prey to the whims of others.

I yanked the man onto his side. I'd spent enough nights after parties with my crewmates to know when a person was in danger of choking on his own vomit.

It didn't help.

Come on, you bastard!

"W-won't w-work," he managed as his body began to twitch and convulse.

"Axelrod, please," I begged.

Please give me something…anything….

I heard the defeat in my own voice.

Kaira, who was kneeling on Axelrod's other side, looked at me. Her eyes were wide with fear and the same helplessness I felt.

"Please," I said again, my voice barely audible over Axelrod's choking.

"V—V—"

I couldn't tell whether he was trying to say something, or if the sound was just some effect of whatever was happening to his body.

"Vvvv—"

Axelrod's whole body jerked and then went still. The foam bubbling out of his mouth slowed to a trickle.

"No." I shook Axelrod.

"Gray—"

"No!"

I refused to look at Kaira or to hear the apology in her voice.

"What's going on out here?" a woman in a fuzzy purple bathrobe and matching slippers demanded. She was standing in the doorway of the neighboring motel room.

"Police business, ma'am," Kaira said. "We're going to need you to go back inside." Her voice was authoritative, but her hands were shaking.

Footsteps pounded the metal stairs that led up to the walkway. We couldn't stay here, and yet, I couldn't summon the strength to move.

"Kaira? Graysen?" a deep, male voice asked. "What happened?"

I knew it was Michael, but I didn't look up from the man whose body was stiffening and cooling on the cement.

"He's dead, Gray," Kaira said, tugging on my arm.

I was shaking my head. This man had all the answers. He was my salvation.

I couldn't accept that he was gone.

I forced myself to look at Axelrod's face. Blood was still leaking from his mouth, but his eyes were open and glassy. His skin was gray.

"We need to get his body back in the motel room and wipe it down," Michael said, his voice grim as he bent to pick up Axelrod's lifeless body.

"…careful," Kaira was telling Michael. "…some kind of poison."

I could barely make sense of anything that was happening around me. The man's gruesome death played in my head on repeat. It was only the thought of Kaira back in that poison-filled room that got my legs moving.

I followed them inside, where most of the smoke had dissipated. My chest felt tight as I breathed in, but it wasn't painful anymore.

"Look at this." Michael was standing just outside the bathroom.

He moved aside so Kaira and I could see in. My stomach dropped. Perched on the bathroom counter was a can of shaving cream, a bottle of cleaning fluid, and mouthwash. A foul-smelling concoction was brewing in the bathroom sink.

Axelrod was a Level 8 Alchemist. For him, turning these common products into toxic chemicals must have been child's play.

"We need to get out of here," Michael said. "Someone will have called the cops by now." He glanced at our illusions. "The real ones, I mean."

I knew he was right, but I couldn't make myself move.

"Bobby did this so he wouldn't have to tell us the truth," Kaira said in a hoarse voice as we all stared at the partly-empty bottles.

Fury, regret, hopelessness…. The emotions churned in my gut, filling my throat with bile. I wanted to punch through the wall until my fists were bloody and broken. I wanted to scream.

Except none of that would do me an ounce of good. Axelrod was dead, and with him, I'd lost my chance at answers.

"We need to get out of here," Michael said again. He was using a bath towel to wipe down all of the surfaces.

"What do we do about this body?" Kaira asked, her tone lacking its usual confidence.

I couldn't feel my legs as I went over to the phone on the side of the bed. Numbly, I picked up the receiver and dialed 9-1-1.

"9-1-1. What's your emergency?"

"There's been a suicide in the Watertown Motel," I heard myself say.

The female voice on the other line was still talking when I hung up the phone.

"Let's go."

Kaira waved a hand, and she and Michael turned into different people. I caught sight of myself in the mirror above the dresser. I wore the same face as the cop who had entered the room, except now I wore jeans and a black sweater.

A small crowd had gathered in the parking lot, where people were pointing up at Axelrod's room.

"Everything is fine," Michael said in his calming voice. "Go back to your rooms. You didn't see anything. Nothing unusual happened here tonight."

The spectators murmured in agreement. They smiled adoringly at Michael before turning and heading back to their own rooms.

We all got into the car without a word. I didn't look back as we drove out of the parking lot.

CHAPTER 19

We'd lost our only lead for the murders, and by the time we got back to the house, it was clear we weren't the only ones with bad news. Smith was monitoring three laptop screens while A.J. stared over his shoulder in open-mouthed shock.

I ducked as a stack of dirty dishes zoomed over my head and deposited themselves into the sink. A.J. waved his hands in a flourish, and the sponge and bottle of soap went to work on the dishes.

"I'm stress cleaning," A.J. announced.

A bottle of wood cleaner and a rag smacked against the wall before they started to scrub the coffee table with enough vigor to take off the varnish. Michael stepped over a broom that seemed to be doing more dancing than sweeping.

"What happened now?" Kaira asked as she, Michael, and I came into the room.

"Maybe we should tie Graysen down before we show you this," A.J. said. "I have some fuzzy handcuffs—"

"What happened?" I demanded, not in the mood.

Smith and A.J. looked at each other. Then, the blank wall filled with newspaper headlines.

UnAllied Vow to Kill One Nat a Day Until Graysen Galder is Apprehended.
Magic Community in Uproar Over Unsolved Murder of Penelope Heppurn.
Level 6 Clairvoyant Predicts first Retaliatory Nat Murder for Tomorrow, 10AM

I grasped the edge of the table to keep myself upright.

"The Mag community isn't disavowing the UnAllied's threats the way they usually would," Smith said, his face still buried in his screens. "And a record number of Mags are expected to turn out for Valencia's rally on Saturday."

I stared at the images on the wall, feeling more helpless than I ever had in my life.

Except, I wasn't helpless. There was something I could do.

I looked up, only to find the others staring at me, waiting for me to say something.

"I'm turning myself in," I said.

As soon as the words were out, I felt an enormous relief. At least I was doing something. At least I'd be able to prevent the real murderer from hiding behind me anymore. It might even save lives....

"Over my dead body." Kaira stepped in front of the door like she was going to block me from leaving.

"Our only lead is on his way to the morgue right now," I pointed out.

"So, we'll find another one. Axelrod said he had bosses. Plural. All we have to do is find one of them." She set her jaw and gave me a challenging stare as I stepped toward her.

"Kai, give me your phone." I tried to say it gently.

A single tear slid down her cheek. She pressed her back against the door, her white-knuckled grip on the door handle.

I sighed. "Kaira, get out of the way."

"No." She was furious.

A scraping sound came from somewhere behind me. I turned to see the couch sliding across the wooden floor, knocking chairs out of the way as it headed for us. Kaira stepped away from the door so the couch could take her place as a barrier between me and the exit.

"A.J., what the hell," I said tiredly. I didn't have time for this.

I bent to shove the couch aside. It didn't budge.

"A.J.," I said through gritted teeth.

"It's not happening, hun. You're not martyring yourself. Nope, nope, nope."

"It's not martyrdom, it's—"

"Do you want to do right by Penelope's family and find the real killer?" Kaira demanded.

"Of course, but—"

"And do you want your future back?"

"Yes, but—"

"These murders aren't going to stop if you turn yourself in," Kaira argued. "All you'd be doing would be getting yourself executed." She took a steadying breath. "If you care about justice for Penelope and the others, you'll stay and help us figure out who's behind the murders." She looked at me, and there was so much emotion in her eyes that the air was torn from my lungs. "I can't do this without you."

I felt the weight of those words bury into my soul, because I knew she was talking about more than just this case.

"Kai." I lowered my voice, wishing we didn't have an audience right now so I could say all the things I wanted her to hear. "You have to let me go."

Kaira shook her head, her eyes full of that stubborn determination I had always loved about her. "We're going to figure this out together, and then you can walk out that door as a free man."

"And a hero," A.J. added. "You'll probably get knighted or something."

"We're not in England, dumbass," Smith said mildly.

"So?" A.J. retorted. "That's how grateful everyone'll be. He'll be an *American* knight."

"You're wasting time," Michael told me. "Our city's under attack, and we're the only ones who know you aren't the one responsible. We need to get to work and figure out who's behind these murders."

I stood in front of the unmovable couch and stared at the set expressions of the others in the room. I knew I was defeated.

I was frustrated and angry, but I couldn't help the rush of warmth I felt toward these people. With the exception of Kaira, I barely knew any of them, and yet, they were willing to risk everything to help me. I knew they were doing it more for Kaira and the city we all loved, but it didn't matter.

A shiver went down my spine as I realized these people were probably the only ones in the country—with the exceptions of my dad and Ma—who would look at me without hatred and disgust. They were all on my side.

The layer of ice around my heart thawed. The weight of anger and injustice eased a fraction, and I felt some of my tension slide away.

With a sigh, I nodded.

Kaira gave me another furious look. "The next time you walk out that door as yourself, you'll do it as a free man going back to his life. That's the only way this works."

Kaira's phone chimed, breaking our standoff. When she answered, I could hear Yutika's frantic voice on the other end. Michael stepped forward, genuine worry on his face, as Kaira listened to the chatter on the other end of the line.

"Okay. Bri's only a few blocks away. I'll have her meet you there. We're on our way."

She hung up.

"What's wrong?" Michael demanded.

Kaira held up a finger as she dialed another number.

"Hey Kaira," Bri's voice said when the call connected.

"Bri, I need you to go to the safe house on Commonwealth. One of the Mags is having a panic attack and Yutika can't get her to calm down." Kaira pulled a sweater on over her tank top with one hand while she continued to talk into the phone. "Just keep her subdued so she doesn't hurt herself or anyone else until we get there."

"You don't want me to stay on Nancy anymore?" Bri asked.

Kaira glanced at me before turning her attention back to the phone. "Her husband's dead, so I don't think anyone will be coming after her anymore."

"Oh, right then," Bri said without missing a beat. "On my way."

"It must be the woman we picked up on Western Ave while you were at the motel," A.J. said.

I helped carry Smith's laptops and power cords as we all piled into the van.

A.J. continued, "We were on our way back to the safe house with two families—both kids who skipped their Test and had been hiding out—and we saw this lady in a hospital gown just wandering around. She was standing in the middle of traffic and was going to get killed, so we picked her up."

"And?" Michael asked, flooring the gas.

"And, the lady seemed a little unhinged. Harmless though," A.J. hurried to say as Michael gave him a death stare in the rearview mirror.

We made what should have been a ten-minute drive in five. The van lurched to a stop on the street outside an unassuming brick townhouse. Kaira illusioned us, and we made our way up the steps to the front porch. Kaira pulled out a ring of keys, unlocked the door, and ushered us inside.

"Is this place yours, too?" I asked.

"Yutika's, technically," she replied, "since she's the one who made the money we used to buy it and created the paper trail of fake documents."

I shook my head. A few days ago, I would have known exactly how I felt about all of this illegal behavior. It went against one of the founding principles of the Alliance, that Magics couldn't use their abilities to take advantage of Naturals. I believed in those principles. I believed that the Alliance was our city's—our country's—only hope of true equality between Naturals and Magics.

But that was before I'd been framed for a murder I didn't commit. That was before I'd broken out of a maximum-security prison, started a bar fight, threatened a woman with a knife, and driven a man to poison himself.

Now, I supposed, I couldn't judge any of the Six. I used to know exactly which circumstances would make me break a high law, and they all had to do with loving Kaira. Now, I had no idea how far I would go to get the answers I needed. The thought terrified me almost as much as the idea of not getting answers at all.

CHAPTER 20

An ear-splitting cry filled the house the moment the door opened. It was a keening, animal-like sound that was full of unspeakable pain. Kaira let everyone's illusions except mine fall away as we entered the large, comfortable-looking sitting room. The source of the screams was immediately apparent. A woman in a hospital gown was clawing at Bri's titanium skin as she struggled to free herself.

"I need to go!" she shrieked, kicking and writhing.

Her eyes were rolling around in her head, and I wondered if she was having some kind of psychotic break.

"Thank God!" Yutika said, jumping up at the sight of us.

"She's insane," Yutika told Michael, pointing at the woman who Bri was holding in a bear hug.

"Should I knock her out?" Bri shouted, her words barely audible over the other woman's screams.

Michael strode over, skirting around the woman's flailing limbs. He said something into her ear. She stopped screaming and fighting long enough to listen to him.

"You're safe here," Michael told the woman. "Please relax."

At the soothing command, my own tension eased. I'd been worried about something before, but now I wasn't. I watched with little interest as the woman slumped against Bri's side.

After a few more seconds had passed, my mind sharpened. I realized the spell of Michael's Whispering must have affected me. I moved to put more distance between us. I wasn't interested in anything or anyone that would dull my ability to think for myself, even if it was temporary.

"She's been drugged," Michael said.

"She probably escaped from the psych ward," Yutika said, wiping blood off the scratches on her arm.

Smith, who had set himself up with all of his laptops on the love seat, frowned at his screens. "I'm not seeing any reports of hospital or psych ward patients missing in the Boston area."

"Can you tell what kind of drug?" Kaira asked Michael.

He shook his head. "I can tell it's affecting her mental state, and that there are gaps in her conscious awareness."

"I don't mean to be callous, but if you're going to allow her to stay here, my family will need to make other arrangements."

I turned to the woman who had spoken. I hadn't even noticed when we first came into the house, but now I saw that there were what looked like two separate families, each with a high school-aged daughter, huddled on the leather couch. They were all watching the now-subdued woman with a combination of alarm and disgust.

"You're not in any danger," Kaira assured the families. "Michael is a Level 10 Whisper. If anyone can help her, it's him."

Michael was sitting on the floor next to the woman, who was half-supported by the wall at her back and Michael by her side. Her eyes had closed, but at a word from Michael, she opened them.

"What's your name?" Michael asked the woman in a soothing voice.

"Elizabeth," she replied, her voice hoarse from all the crying and screaming she'd probably been doing for the last few hours. "Elizabeth Nelson."

"What are you upset about, Elizabeth?" Michael asked.

"They took my baby, and I have to get her back."

"Where is your child now?" Michael asked in the same calming voice.

"I—I don't know," Elizabeth stammered, a hint of her crazed expression returning.

"She kept repeating that," Yutika said. "She said they took her baby and that she needed to get her back, but she couldn't remember what had happened. She keeps trying to leave and find her."

"She's only two days old. I have to get her back. She won't survive without me." Elizabeth moved to get up, but, at a word from Michael, sat back down.

"Is your baby with your husband?" Michael asked.

"I…." Elizabeth tilted her head, considering. "We're not married."

"The baby's father, then," Michael amended patiently.

Elizabeth's eyes filled with tears. "They took him, too."

"Where is he?" Michael prompted.

Tears spilled down the woman's cheeks. "They killed him."

"Who did?" Michael asked.

"I don't know," Elizabeth wailed.

Something dropped onto my head. I batted the thing out of my hair, which turned out to be a spider. Another one fell onto my arm. Yutika squealed and jumped onto the coffee table. Everyone else was wriggling and smacking their hair and clothes, like the spiders were on them, too. I looked up to see where they were all coming from.

"Holy shit."

The ceiling was covered in about a thousand spiders, ants, millipedes, and other squirming, too many-legged creatures.

"Ohmygod," Kaira said, looking more embarrassed than freaked out. She gave the families cowering on the couch an apologetic look. "This has never happened before. I swear—"

"Cockroach!" A.J. shrieked. He leaped into Bri's arms, who almost dropped him when a mouse scampered across her foot.

The mouse raced across the carpet, but it didn't disappear into some dark hole like the ones that could sometimes be seen in the BSMU study lounges. It raced right onto Elizabeth's open palm.

She cupped her hand around the creature and cuddled it to her chest.

I stared at her, uncomprehending. That was when I realized that all the insects—and two more rodents that were far too robust to be called *mice*— had congregated around Elizabeth. In a rapid turn of events, she seemed to be the only one in the room who wasn't freaking out.

"She's an Animalist," I said out loud, finally putting it together. She must not have been a very powerful one, if the only animals she could draw were the ones already living in the walls.

Just the thought had me checking my hair for more spiders.

"Elizabeth, can you ask the insects to go back where they came from?" Michael asked as he flicked a wriggling worm off his sleeve. His soothing voice was a complete contrast to the pandemonium filling the room.

Elizabeth, seeming calmer now that there were two rats perched on her knees and a ring of bugs surrounding her, nodded and gave Michael a gentle smile.

The insects departed in orderly rows, separated by species. The spiders climbed back up the silk threads hanging from the ceiling, while the others disappeared into invisible cracks in the walls and floor. Feeling vaguely nauseous, I backed all the way against the wall to avoid the dangling spiders.

"I'll uh, have exterminators here first thing in the morning," Kaira promised the scandalized Magic families. "In the meantime, would you prefer the Four Seasons or the Mandarin Oriental?"

"S-sorry," Elizabeth said. "That happens when I'm upset."

"It's alright," Michael told her.

I wasn't so sure about that. I still felt things crawling on my skin, even though all the insects were gone. From the way the others were staring at the walls and ceiling, I knew I wasn't alone.

The two families on the other side of the room were staring daggers at the Animalist.

"We need to find out what Elizabeth knows," I said to no one in particular.

And get the hell out of here.

If we didn't find out something concrete enough to give the police by tomorrow morning, a Natural was going to die because I was still on the loose.

"Maybe we were asking the wrong questions before." I glanced up at the ceiling once more and then focused on Elizabeth. "What do you remember?"

She looked to Michael, who gave her a nod.

She said, "My name is Elizabeth Anne Nelson. I was born in Waltham and moved to Boston in 2043 when I was two years old. I worked in the Alliance archives as an assistant librarian from 2061 until six months ago when my belly started to show." Her lip trembled. "And then I got fired."

"Why were you fired?" I asked with none of Michael's gentle encouragement.

Pregnant women didn't get fired for no reason. In fact, men and women who worked in the Alliance and were expecting a baby were usually given raises and promotions. Departments strove to be known as being family-friendly.

Elizabeth shook her head as tears continued to stream down her face. "I don't remember," she whispered. She swallowed. "I remember the police arresting us, and then some men in suits coming before we were taken away. They said we could either go with them willingly or be forced."

There was something about this woman's story that struck me as wrong. My lawyer sixth sense was tingling, and I had the sense that maybe this woman knew something important, after all. If only I could ask her the right questions to tease out the information I needed.

"Who were the men in the suits?" I asked. "Where did they take you?"

"They said they were—" she thought about it. "They didn't say. All they said was they were bringing us to the Lab." Her terrified look returned and she started to rock in place.

"What lab?" Kaira asked.

"I don't know!" Elizabeth wailed.

"Bobby Axelrod said something about a lab, too," I said in a low voice to Kaira while Michael calmed Elizabeth, who was near hysterics. "He and Jonas Meddlesworth were both working there. Could it be the same lab she's talking about?"

Kaira lifted a shoulder. "Maybe? But this lady doesn't look like she's involved with drugs unless she's using, but even then, they wouldn't have brought her to the lab where they make the drug...."

Maybe she had been in some kind of rehab center. That would explain the hospital gown.

High-pitched whimpering sounds were coming from Elizabeth. I felt myself cringing in anticipation of a second march of the insects.

"Michael, do something," A.J. pleaded. "My heebie jeebie quota is all used up for today."

"Here." Yutika scribbled on her sketch pad. A few seconds later, a stress ball with a smiley face plopped down onto the ground beside Elizabeth. "No more mice, okay?"

Or spiders....

Nodding, Elizabeth picked up the stress ball and squeezed it in her fist.

Thank you, A.J. mouthed to her, putting his hands together and bowing his head like he was worshipping her.

"That's interesting."

We all turned to Smith, whose gaze was flying back and forth between his open laptop screens.

"What?" Kaira asked.

"There's no record of an Elizabeth Anne Nelson anywhere. No tracker, no file, no record of her ever having worked at the Alliance."

"Maybe she forgot her own name," Yutika said. "She's obviously cracked."

"I am not!" Elizabeth snarled. "The Alchemists poison the air, and it makes us forget. And—"

"How did you escape this lab?" I interrupted what sounded like a conspiracy that belonged on one of Smith's dark web blogs.

"I found a shard of glass in my cell. I killed the man when he came in and stole his keycard." She looked at Michael, a desperate, pleading look in her eyes. "I didn't mean to kill him. I just wanted to get away."

"I know," Michael said, giving her a comforting smile. "Don't worry. You're safe now."

"I knew it," Smith gloated. "The Alliance is experimenting on Mags. Probably took her baby to—"

"Not now, Smith," Kaira warned.

"How else do you explain all of this?" Smith said, wilting a little under Kaira's gaze.

I didn't know, but I knew that there had to be a better explanation than one of Smith's conspiracy theories. I also didn't think Yutika was right, that this woman was just insane.

"Where's your boyfriend now?" I asked, still unable to shake the feeling that if I could only ask the right question, something important would be revealed.

Elizabeth's scared, confused expression softened. "Benji," she murmured, before turning her watery gaze on Michael. "They killed him."

"I know," Michael said in sympathy.

"What was Benji's last name?" I asked.

"Murell," she replied.

Smith's hands stayed folded across his chest as webpages opened themselves on his screen.

"Benjamin Murell, age twenty-five, found dead in his Boston apartment due to apparent suicide," I read off the screen.

"It wasn't suicide!" Elizabeth shouted. "They killed him!"

I waited for the skittering of tiny legs across the wood floors to go quiet before I asked, "Why would they want Benji dead?"

Elizabeth's chin wobbled as she shook her head. "We're nobodies. I'm just a Level 1 Animalist."

"And was Benji also an Animalist?" I asked, knowing I was grasping at straws.

"He was a Nat," Elizabeth said.

Every face in the room turned to her at once. Realizing her mistake, Elizabeth slapped a hand over her mouth.

"Holy guacamole," A.J. exclaimed. "You *did it* with a Nat?"

"Baby killer!" Bri shouted.

She launched to her feet. Her skin had gone full titanium, and she was starting toward Elizabeth.

"Stop it," Kaira commanded, moving to stand in front of Elizabeth, who was sobbing and quaking.

"You sick bitch," Bri gasped, titanium tears rolling down her cheeks and plunking down on the hardwood floor. She wiped a silver hand across her eyes. "Get out of my way, Kaira," she said.

Before I even thought about what I was doing, I had moved to stand beside Kaira.

"Bri, just calm down," I tried.

"My niece died because of a baby killer!"

Plink, plink, plink.

More titanium tears hit the floor and scattered.

Bri shouted, "One of your twisted freak babies was born in the same ward as my niece, and she died because of it. We never even got to bring her home. My brother and sister-in-law haven't been the same since. And it's your fault. It's your fault!"

Bri collapsed into Kaira's arms, sobbing.

Kaira hugged the other girl, murmuring soft words into her ear.

"I guess we know why the authorities were after them," Yutika said, looking at Elizabeth with disgust.

"We were in love," Elizabeth whispered.

My throat tightened. I couldn't help myself. I looked at Kaira. Her expression was guarded and she pointedly kept her gaze fixed on Bri, who still looked like she might murder Elizabeth if given half a chance.

It was a stark reminder about what it meant to break the third high law. Bri was one of the nicest, most easy-going people I'd ever met. Even when she was beating people up, she wasn't angry about it. But now….

"You had a baby together?" Kaira asked Elizabeth. Her voice wavered just a little. I doubted anyone else had noticed.

Elizabeth nodded. "I have to find her."

"My husband's a cancer survivor. His immune system is compromised!" one of the women on the other side of the room yelled. Her face was red with fury. "I don't want that DAMND baby anywhere near our family!"

My attention had been so fixated on Elizabeth, I had forgotten those other people were even here. I glanced at them now. Every one of their faces was filled with a mixture of disgust and hatred.

It was the way they'd be looking at Kaira and me if they knew.

Unbidden, the images I had seen in every health and science class since middle school crowded into my mind. Fetuses horribly deformed. Misshapen heads and fingerless hands. The graveyard in Missouri filled with tombstones. Hundreds of infant-sized caskets from a singled DAMND baby.

Kaira looked like she was having as much trouble holding herself together as I was. I had a sudden, desperate urge to wrap my arms around her. I wanted to do whatever it would take to erase that stricken look from her face. I wanted to shield her from the loathing expressions on her friends' faces.

But of course, if I so much as took her hand, the rest of the Six would be staring at us the same way they were staring at Elizabeth now…like she was filthy…a monster.

Baby killers.

I heard Kaira's shuddering breath before she said, "Yutika, work on getting Elizabeth new documents and enough money to go wherever she wants. Michael, do whatever you have to in order to convince her to forget about her child and worry about her own survival. I'll illusion her, and then we'll escort her to the airport and make sure she doesn't have any trouble getting out of the city."

"We're helping her?" Yutika squeaked in protest.

"She's a Mag in trouble," Kaira replied, her voice tight with all the emotions she was hiding.

My chest ached. I could see how much Kaira was hurting. It went against every instinct I had to let her suffer while I just stood by.

"I thought we only helped unMarked Mags," Bri added, throwing a look full of hate at Elizabeth.

"She is unMarked," Kaira said. "Otherwise Smith would have found her records."

"Are we going to start helping murderers and rapists now?" Bri asked, her voice rising.

"Would you really count her crime as equal to murder and rape?" Kaira demanded, incredulous.

"Just because her mutant child hasn't killed anyone yet, it doesn't mean that it won't," Bri shot back. She gave Elizabeth a freezing look. "Baby killer."

"This woman has lost enough," Kaira said, her tone final. "Now, get to work on her papers. Then, we're going home."

CHAPTER 21

The sun had risen by the time we'd made all the arrangements for Elizabeth and dropped her off at the airport. I was bleary-eyed with exhaustion, my joints were on fire, and I was shivering from a low-grade fever. I could tell the others were struggling, too. I'd gotten about five hours of sleep in the past three days, and I could barely see straight anymore. But the idea of sleeping, when the next murder was about to happen, was like a shot of adrenaline in my veins every time I thought about it.

I slumped onto the couch as soon as we got inside the house. The cushions dipped as the others crowded around beside me.

"We need to find out about this lab everyone seems to be involved with," I said. I was so tired my words slurred together. "Maybe if we can find the connection, we'll have something to give the police before the next murder."

"Um, it's a little late for that."

Before any of us could ask questions, headlines and images began to appear on the blank wall.

I sat up so fast my head spun.

Boston Mayor Found Brutally Slain, the top headline said. The bolded text below read, *Boston's second-term Natural mayor was found dead in his home at 7:59am. The words 'NATS GET OUT' were written in blood across his front door.*

"Oh God," Bri said.

"Shit," added Smith.

I felt my gorge rise. This was my fault. If I had turned myself in yesterday, the Mayor would still be alive.

"Do I need to block the door again?" A.J. asked Kaira, giving me a pointed stare.

I was too numb to move. I kept reading the headlines, feeling an icy stab in my heart with each one.

UnAllied Magic takes Credit for Murder. Sentenced to Death for Tuesday AM
Record Number of Magics Expected to Attend Valencia Stark's Rally on Saturday
Murder Toll: 2 Mags, 2 Nats; Convict Toll: 2 Mags, 0 Nats
Where in the World is…Graysen Galder?

"Jeez," Yutika said. "That's four murders in…."

"Four days," Michael finished.

Their words were just background noise at first; all of my attention was fixed on the headlines. Once my brain made sense of their words, I jolted to my feet. I clutched my head. I couldn't believe it had taken me this long to put the pieces together.

"Gray?" Kaira asked.

"Restrain him," A.J. called. "I'll get the handcuffs."

But I didn't go toward the door. I turned to Smith. "Pull up the Alliance's Report of Laws."

Smith's eyes moved, and the enormous PDF began to load on the blank wall.

"Go to Section 278, Article 3, 998J" I ordered.

"You're kidding, right?" Yutika asked.

"He's not," Kaira said, and I thought I heard the hint of pride in her voice.

The document scrolled across the wall until the appropriate cover page was displayed.

"Page fifteen," I said, my pulse speeding up. "Maybe sixteen."

"Well whaddya know? We got a Level 10 Brainiac on our hands." A.J. smirked. He was at the top of the stairs, a pair of pink, fuzzy handcuffs dangling from his hand.

Smith enlarged the text and started to scroll. My eyes were glued to the moving text.

"Stop," I said. "Blow up that third paragraph."

Smith extended his thumb and index finger in midair, and the text on the wall expanded.

A.J. read out loud: "The Alliance is an organization that was chosen by the people of Boston, but if at any time it no longer meets the promises of its founding principles to protect and serve both Naturals and Magics, then either group may independently choose to dissolve the organization by a two-thirds majority vote. To ensure both Natural and Magic interests are upheld, a vote for disbanding will automatically be triggered if there is an undue number of magically-motivated murders in Boston over a confined period."

The room went silent.

"Holy crap," Yutika said, effectively summing up what we were all thinking.

"It's a conspiracy," Smith said, sounding delighted. "I *told* you."

"You say everything's a conspiracy," Yutika pointed out. "You were bound to be right eventually."

"Someone's trying to take down the Alliance." I sank back down onto the couch as a wave of dizziness took hold of me.

"That's going to start a civil war," Michael said, incredulous. "Who would ever want to do that?"

For some reason, the question made me think of the last moments of Bobby Axelrod's life. As he was choking to death on his lethal concoction, he had been making a strange sound.

Vvvv.

At the time, I had thought it was just his horrible choking. But he had looked so determined, like he was trying to tell me something in the last moments of his life…something important.

Vvvv.

I buried my face in my hands while the others continued to speculate.

"Whoever it is, we need to find them before they instigate any more murders," Michael was saying. "If Graysen's right, these killings won't stop until the Alliance has been dissolved."

"How are we supposed to do that?" A.J. asked. "We still don't have the first clue about who's behind these murders."

Come on, I told myself. The answer was right there, hovering at the edge of my consciousness. I just had to reach out and grab it.

I sat up. Bobby Axelrod's last attempt at a word…that section in the Alliance's Report of Laws….

"Who has the most to gain from a civil war between Naturals and Magics?" I asked.

The others gave me a blank look.

"I'll give you a hint." I felt a grim smile pull at the corners of my mouth. "Her name begins with a 'V'."

For a few seconds, no one spoke.

A giant image popped up on the wall. We all stared at the zebra-print dress, giant leopard-print purse, wild red hair, and dark storm cloud hanging over the Alliance building.

"Valencia Stark," Kaira breathed.

CHAPTER 22

It was so obvious, I couldn't believe it hadn't occurred to me before.

Valencia Stark wanted to destroy the Alliance, which would result in the war between Naturals and Magics she'd always advocated for. It wasn't much of a leap to assume she had orchestrated a series of murders throughout the city, beginning with Penelope, to debilitate the only system that had thus far worked to bring peace between Magics and Naturals. As opposed to a few weeks ago when Valencia was the joke of the city, now, Magics were listening to her.

I clenched my fists as a burst of hatred rushed through me like wildfire. This woman was responsible for ruining my life. She was responsible for the death of four people. And she'd done it because she was trying to destroy the Alliance and replace it with her organization's agenda of intolerance and violence.

Everyone was talking at once. Cell phones, silverware, and other household items buzzed around the room as A.J. waved his hands in animation.

"What do we do now?" Bri asked. Her skin kept going from flesh to titanium and back again.

"We may be against Marking," Kaira said, "but if the Alliance falls, there will be nothing to keep Boston from slipping into the gutters."

"And when Valencia nominates herself as the new governing power of Boston, we'll be worse off than even the worst cities," I said. "She'll try to enslave Naturals."

"And Nats won't take that sitting down," A.J. added. "They'll bring in the military. Boston'll turn into another Detroit."

Michael's face paled, and I remembered Yutika telling me that Michael was from Detroit.

"So, what do we do?" Yutika asked.

"We could go to the police," Bri suggested. "Tell them what we know."

A week ago, I would have agreed with Bri. I'd believed so fully in the system that made Boston better than everywhere else in the country. Now, the memory of my arrest was too raw for me to have faith in that particular branch of law enforcement.

"Who's gonna believe us?" Smith asked.

"We don't have any proof," Kaira added.

"We can't go to the cops, I said, my mind churning. "We have to go straight to the Alliance. The BSMU's president is on the Alliance's Board of Peaceful Resolutions. If we can get him to believe us, he can tell everyone else on the board."

"Do you think he'll listen to us?" Kaira asked, her voice doubtful.

"He has to," I replied with more confidence than I felt. "It's in his job description to take any potential threat against the city's Natural and Magic populations seriously. And he's a big enough deal that everyone else on the Board will listen to him.

I had met the school's president a few times at various dinners, and I felt fairly certain that even if he felt the same way about me as the rest of the city, he'd at least listen once I told him about a threat to the Alliance. No one in the Alliance would want to risk the possibility of the organization being disbanded. He would be able to make the police arrest Valencia without hard evidence.

"Smith, can you—" I began.

"I've got his personal cell number here," Smith said with a self-important grin.

"Will he be able to trace the call?" Bri asked, biting one of her nails.

"What do you take me for?" Smith scowled at her before turning his attention to me. "You ready?"

I nodded. "Let's do this."

The Six went silent as Smith unplugged his headphones from the laptop and spun it toward me. Without touching the computer, Smith made a dial pad appear on the screen. The ring tone began. On the fourth ring, the call connected.

"Hello?"

"Dr. Pruwist, this is Graysen Galder."

Silence.

I decided not to waste time easing in.

"Sir, please don't hang up. I have reason to believe Valencia Stark has been orchestrating the city-wide murders in an attempt to enact Section 278, Article 3, 998J of the Alliance's Report of Laws for Naturals and Magics. It states that—"

"Graysen Galder," the man hissed. "Where the hell are you?"

I evaded the question. "Sir, there have been four murders in as many days, and I believe the murders will continue until the city's Magics vote to repeal the Alliance's authority. Once that happens, we'll be leaderless and without a working system of government. I believe Valencia intends to use the chaos in order to further upend peace between Magics and Naturals." And then, taking a page out of A.J.'s book of the dramatic, I said, "Valencia wants to start a war."

Out of the corner of my eye, I saw A.J. give me a thumbs-up.

Another few moments of silence passed.

"Do you have any idea what you've done?" Pruwist snarled.

The fury in his voice took me aback. "Sir?"

"You've raked the good name of this institution through the mud. The school's reputation is under fire, and it's your fault!"

I hadn't expected the school's president to be happy with me, but I had expected those feelings to take a backseat to the more pressing issue of the Alliance's destruction.

"Dr. Pruwist, the only crime I'm guilty of is evading my arrest. I have every intention of answering for that crime, but first, we need to safeguard the Alliance, and that begins with arresting Valencia Stark."

"You listen here, you pompous little shit," Pruwist said, his voice quavering with barely-contained rage. "You turn yourself in immediately. The BSMU's lawyers have prepared a statement, which you will sign, that makes it clear you acted in direct opposition to the policies and philosophy taught to students at the BSMU."

I couldn't believe it. I had just told this man about the impending deconstruction of the Alliance and the promise of more murders, and the BSMU's president was concerned about saving face?

"Haven't you been listening?" I demanded, all pretenses of politeness falling away. "The Alliance is being threatened. If any more murders take place, the whole institution could be disbanded. There will be complete chaos. No one will be able to stop Valencia and the UnAllied from taking over the city. You have to warn Director Remwald and everyone else on the Board."

"You get your ass to the police station now and sign that statement!" Pruwist bellowed.

The call ended.

I sat, stunned, wondering what the hell had just happened.

I just told the BSMU's president that the Alliance, and the entire city of Boston, was under threat. And he was worried about...optics?

No one outside of this room gave a damn about the murders. All they cared about was a neat resolution they could brag about during their press conferences.

This wasn't right. This wasn't the Alliance I knew...the one I'd built my future around. And yet, it was the only version of the Alliance I'd encountered since my arrest.

Where did that leave me? Where was I supposed to go from here?

"Should we go over his head? Get the man's boss on the phone? File a complaint?" A.J. asked.

I shook my head slowly, still overwhelmed by the spectacular failure of that conversation. "He was our best option. If he wouldn't listen, no one else will."

Saying those words out loud made something inside me break. I felt every joint in my body shriek in protest. It was all just too much. I collapsed on the floor, my body incapable of moving. The pain flooding through me made tears leak from my eyes.

"Ohmygosh what's happening?" A.J. wailed.

Somewhere through the pain, I heard Kaira's voice, clear and unpanicked. "Bri, help him onto the couch. Someone get him some ibuprofen."

The pain receded enough for me to feel ashamed.

"I'm fine," I managed through clenched teeth.

Kaira stood just within my view, not hovering, but there.

In a few more seconds, the pain passed enough for me to force myself to my feet without help, even though my entire body fought against me. I didn't want to look at any of the others and see the pity in their faces, but I also wasn't the type of person who hunched his shoulders and averted his gaze.

When I looked at Bri and Michael, who were both waiting to catch me in case I fell again, I didn't see the emotions I was expecting. There was a hardness to both of their gazes that said they had each seen their share of pain and misery, and mine was just one more tally to whatever they'd already experienced themselves. They didn't stare at the way my fingers had curled in on themselves, looking strange and unnatural, or at the way my teeth were now chattering from the fever that held me in its grip.

"I, uh, have an autoimmune disease," I said into the silent room. "It's not contagious or anything. And it isn't usually this bad."

"I'm going to make you some vegan chicken soup," A.J. announced, settling himself onto a bean bag as ingredients began to get themselves out of the fridge.

"Vegan chicken?" Yutika asked, looking skeptical. "Isn't that an oxymoron?"

"Honey girl, just you wait." A.J. gave her a sly look. "It'll cure anything you've got."

I should have felt exposed now that my secret was out. My closest friends at the BSMU hadn't known about my disease, and now a bunch of people I'd known for less than a week had seen me at my most vulnerable. Still, none of them acted weird or unnerved. I was more grateful than words could say.

"So, if no one's going to help us, then it's up to us to save our city?" Bri asked, picking up where the conversation had left off.

A bottle of ibuprofen and a glass of water flew through the air and hovered in front of me. I gave A.J. a nod of thanks before grabbing them out of the air.

"Maybe once we have hard proof, the authorities will be easier to convince," Kaira said, giving me a sympathetic glance.

"Why don't we get Michael to Whisper to Valencia, and then we record the conversation?" Yutika suggested. "If we can get a confession out of her, the police can do the rest."

"The police are probably part of this," Smith said, waving his poison detector wand over a pudding cup as he squinted suspiciously at the unbroken seal.

Yutika made a dismissive noise.

"I do like the idea of getting a confession out of her, though," Kaira said. "It'll be the fastest way to clear Graysen's name and get her arrested before she can murder anyone else."

"So, what are we waiting for?" Bri asked, her skin turning to titanium. "Let's go."

"You planning to walk to California?" Smith asked.

"Excuse me?" she turned back to look at him.

In answer, a giant image of a Delta flight boarding pass popped up on the wall. It read *Stark, Valencia* at the top, and underneath, a flight from Boston to LA was listed.

"What's she doing in LA?" Yutika asked.

"Recruiting, apparently," Smith said, displaying a news article onto the wall.

Valencia Stark's Rallying Cry for the Separation of Magics and Naturals Gaining Traction Out West, the article's title stated.

"When is she coming back?" Kaira asked.

"Her flight lands an hour before the rally on Saturday," Smith said, his eyes on his computer screen.

"Well, at least that gives us," Kaira glanced at the screen of her phone, "almost thirty hours to come up with a plan for how we're going to do this." She rubbed her eyes.

A.J. turned to Bri and frowned. "Are you crying, love bug?"

"I'm sorry." Bri sniffled. "I'm just so tired." She wiped her sleeve across her eyes.

"Alright, that's enough," Kaira said. "We all need to get some sleep before we turn into useless zombies."

"Too late," Yutika said, listing her head to the side and making a jerky, zombie-like motion as she leaned into Michael. The big guy's lip twitched like he was trying not to smile.

"We'll figure out what to do about Valencia after we've gotten some sleep," Kaira said.

I stayed motionless on the couch long after the others had gone upstairs. My mind was reeling from the revelation about Valencia and what she was planning. I was still haunted by the headlines about Boston's mayor. He was dead because I had chosen to stay hidden.

I knew Kaira was right—that the murders wouldn't stop until we'd exposed Valencia's whole sick agenda, but it didn't make me feel any better.

By the time I made it upstairs, I found Kaira already asleep on top of the covers. Her body was precariously balanced on the edge of the bed. She had one shoe on and the other off. Her shirt was half-over her head, like she'd fallen asleep while she was in the process of changing.

My heart expanded. I felt my lips curve into a smile at the sight of her, before I remembered myself and set my features.

Once upon a time, I wouldn't have hesitated to finish undressing her, tuck her under the covers, and then wrap my own body around hers. But I didn't have that right anymore. *Nor did I want it*, I reminded myself.

"Kai," I said in a low voice.

She didn't react, and I didn't have the heart to wake her.

I knelt to take off her other boot. I pulled her shirt back into place, keeping my eyes carefully averted from her chest and the bra that was peeking out. I made a valiant effort at ignoring the way her pants clung to the curves of her hips and showed off her bare stomach. I lifted her off the bed enough to free the blanket, which I pulled over her. Kaira didn't wake through any of it.

Since all I wanted to do was stand there and look at her like some kind of creepy stalker, I retreated into the bathroom and shut the door between us. I stripped off my clothes and got into the shower, using the cold water to knock some sense of reality and self-preservation back into me. I needed the distraction of the punishing cold to keep away the memories of all the times Kaira and I had used this shower together.

The 3-in-1 body wash I used—and Kaira had always teased me about—was long gone. The fifteen other bottles that I had always made fun of her for were still here. I grabbed one at random, which smelled like some kind of tropical fruit, and washed off quickly.

When I went through the bag of clothes from A.J., I was amused to find that he had been thoughtful enough to include a pair of pajamas among his other purchases. They were flannel and had what appeared to be tiny rhinoceroses all over them. But I felt more like myself—more like the person I'd been before this week—in my own clothes. So, I changed back into the shorts and T-shirt I had slept in before.

I shut off the light and climbed into bed. I stayed as far on my side as I could without falling off. I gave myself a stern, silent lecture about staying put so there wouldn't be a repeat of the last time I'd woken up with Kaira in my arms.

I had planned to stay awake for some time, wrestling with the problem of what to do about Valencia. As soon as I was surrounded by Kaira's rhythmic breathing, though, my exhaustion won out. My leaden eyes closed.

As tired as I was, I slept fitfully. My unconscious thoughts shifted from Bobby Axelrod, with the blood-tinged foam bubbling out of his mouth, to Elizabeth Nelson and her deformed, half-Natural baby.

At some point, the cold that had settled into my bones disappeared and was replaced by comforting warmth. The clean smell of jasmine made the awful images plaguing me vanish. I sunk into the blackness of deep sleep.

❋ ❋ ❋

"Um, Gray…."

I was too comfortable to move. I couldn't remember the last time I'd felt so…content. I wanted to stay just like this forever.

"Babe, wake up."

Reluctantly, I opened my eyes. My deep sense of satisfaction lifted and was replaced by horror as reality came flooding back. Kaira and I were face-to-face, and I was crushing her into me like I'd been trying to absorb her body into my own. My face was buried against her neck—I had no idea how I hadn't suffocated. Our arms and legs were all wound together so that I wasn't entirely sure which were my limbs and which were hers.

"Sorry," I muttered, inwardly cursing myself.

It took us several moments to disentangle ourselves, during which there were more awkward apologies when her hair got caught under my arm and our knees bumped as we tried to get free of each other.

"Muscle memory, I guess," I said, feeling my face burn.

"Yeah, I guess," Kaira said with a little laugh.

She looked as uncomfortable as I felt. *What the hell was wrong with me?*

Clearly, my body hadn't gotten the memo that being in love with Kaira was the worst sort of betrayal to my dad. I never should have slept in her bed in the first place. It just confused what was really a very simple matter between us. We might have a past, but we had no future together.

I resolved that I would sleep on Yutika's puke couch or wherever else I needed to from now on, so long as it wasn't within reach of *her*.

CHAPTER 23

By the time we made it downstairs, the rest of the Six were sitting around the kitchen table. They had forgone plates and were eating straight out of one of Ma's huge leftover containers. Feeling hungry for the first time in days, I grabbed a fork and joined them.

"Now that Sleeping Beauties have arrived, we better get crack-a-lacking," A.J. announced.

"Valencia," Yutika said, rubbing her hands together. "We're coming for you, bitch."

"Probably the easiest way would be to get her en route to the rally," Michael said, frowning in thought. "Yutika could make us a squad car, and we could just pull her over."

"That won't work," Smith said, his eyes on his screen and a can of grape soda in his hand. "She hired a Level 9 Energy Manipulator who she's been bringing everywhere with her."

I cursed under my breath. Energy Manipulators were the most dangerous Magics because they could absorb the ability of any other Magic and wield that power for themselves. Any Magics whose abilities had been stolen would be completely defenseless until they put enough distance between themselves and the Manipulator for the effect to wear off.

"This guy is no joke," Smith continued, his eyes darting back and forth across the screen. "He's been arrested eight times, and five of them were for suspected murders. He got off on technicalities for all of them—I think he's got some serious family money—since all the victims were Mags outside of Massachusetts."

Smith projected the man's image on the wall. The Manipulator looked like the type of person Smith had just described. He was covered in tattoos and looked like the quintessential biker with his long beard, red bandana, and leather jacket.

"Didn't anyone tell him that mohawks are so 1980s?" A.J. asked, glaring in disgust at the image.

"We can't risk getting near him," Kaira said. "If he gets a hold of any of our abilities, we're screwed."

"We'll just have to wait until the Manipulator goes home," Yutika said with a sigh.

"I don't think he does go home," Smith said. "She's paying him a thousand dollars a day, which makes me think he doesn't leave her side. He probably even sleeps on the floor of her bedroom or something."

"Where the hell is Valencia getting enough money to pay a Manipulator a thousand dollars a day?" Kaira asked, shaking her head.

It was a good question. I filed it away to consider more later.

"I guess we could get her during the rally itself," I said, hearing the doubt in my own voice. "I could distract the Manipulator while you guys get Valencia."

"Right," Yutika said. "We just show up at the rally, snatch Valencia in front of thousands of people, and then bring her somewhere long enough for Michael to Whisper to her. No sweat."

"And there are only six of us to pull this thing off," Smith grumbled.

"Not six." A.J. stood up from the couch and put a hand on his hip. "The Nat makes seven."

Everyone turned to me.

I felt a slow grin spread over my face as a beautiful smile lit Kaira's.

* * *

With twenty-four hours before the rally, no one left the living room as we scrapped together a desperate plan. A.J. zoomed in countless bowls of popcorn that he popped and drenched in vegan butter without ever leaving the comfort of his bean bag chair. There was a sizeable pyramid of Smith's empty grape soda cans growing on top of the coffee table.

At one point, Yutika fell asleep mid-drawing. Michael had to rush forward and catch her before she crashed through the soda can pyramid. The way he gently lifted her, and glared at Bri and Smith until they gave up their couch for her, left no question in my mind that feelings between the two were mutual.

An hour before we needed to leave the house, our plan was as solid as we could make it. There were too many variables and too many ways for everything to fall apart, and my nerves were like frayed threads.

Everyone else had dispersed to change into what A.J. had dubbed our "kick-ass" cop outfits. I pulled on my uniform, which Yutika had drawn in such a way that it fit me perfectly. I stared at the blank wall, which was no longer blank. Maps, schedules, and spreadsheets were projected over the white surface.

Smith had even made a flow chart, with Valencia at the top, and Penelope and the other murder victims underneath. As I studied the chart, a nagging sense ate at my mind. Something didn't add up. I just couldn't figure out what it was.

Four murders in four days. I looked at their images on the wall. Penelope Heppurn and Jonas Meddlesworth on the Magic side, and Alina Freeman and the Mayor on the Natural side. There had been some debate about whether to include Elizabeth's Nelson's boyfriend in the list of the dead, since his had been called a suicide and didn't have the same obvious magically-motivated undertones as the others.

And then there was the question of the mysterious lab where Bobby Axelrod and Jonas Meddlesworth had both worked, and where Elizabeth Nelson had been taken. I strained my mind to make a connection I was sure was there, somewhere, if only I could come at it from the right angle.

Valencia Stark's motivations were obvious. But from everything I knew about her, she didn't have the analytical mind that would be required to orchestrate the downfall of an organization as powerful as the Alliance on her own. Was it possible there was someone else pulling her strings?

We didn't have time for mistakes. If Valencia was just a distraction, and the real threat was someone more dangerous, then we might be going on a wild goose chase.

Think, Galder.

I remembered my criminal law professor, a squirrely little man who broke out in a sweat every time he talked about motives and intentionality.

"Follow the money," he'd say as he mopped his face with his jacket sleeve and paced back and forth behind the podium.

I let out a short breath.

Follow the money.

"Yutika!" I called, running for the stairs. "Smith!"

CHAPTER 24

We were all silent as our newly-formed, courtesy-of-Yutika police van inched through traffic on our way to the Alliance building. Even with our siren wailing, it was slow going. In a city that was known for horrendous traffic, today was the worst I had ever seen it.

People clogged the sidewalks and spilled out into the streets. After seeing my third "Get Graysen Galder" T-shirt, I kept my gaze firmly inside the vehicle.

Car traffic thinned once we got near the Alliance building and the blockades that lined the road. Michael, who was driving the van, rolled down his window and nodded at the cops directing pedestrians. They barely glanced at his badge and uniform before removing the barricade and letting us through.

Kaira had transformed all of our appearances so thoroughly that we'd needed to take the time to memorize each other's new faces.

Yutika had created all of our uniforms so Kaira wouldn't need to use extra energy illusioning our clothes. Yutika also drew real guns to avoid another Axelrod situation where our illusions were discovered, although we all agreed that she wouldn't draw any bullets to fill them. I'd learned that the only one of us who had ever shot a gun was Michael, and he didn't seem eager to either discuss or repeat the experience.

I adjusted my earpiece as backfeed from Smith's muttering filled my ear. I felt the way I always had before a big crew meet. My muscles were tense, and I was anxious to get to the main event and expend all of the pent-up energy inside me.

I slipped a hand into my pocket, reassuring myself that the small plastic rectangle was still there. It had taken Smith and Yutika about two minutes to design it after I'd explained what I wanted and why. I hadn't mentioned it to anyone else, since I wasn't entirely sure my desperate plan would work. But I hoped.

For the first time since my arrest, I felt like I had some measure of control.

Michael stopped the van when the crowd was too thick for us to get any closer to the Alliance steps. He cut the engine, and a deafening silence filled the car.

"Anyone have any questions?" Kaira asked.

No one did.

"Alright then." Kaira unbuckled her seatbelt. "Let's do this."

I opened the back door of the van and stepped out, adjusting my holster and bulletproof vest.

As Kaira moved past me, I put a hand on her elbow.

"Be careful," I told her.

She let her hand drop and squeezed mine for a second.

"This will all be over soon," she said quietly. A complicated smile curved her lips, and then she was gone, disappearing into the crowd before I could think of a response.

Shaking myself, I pushed through the crowd, looking for the man whose face Smith had left plastered on the wall for the past day. I tried not to look at the signs people were holding up, but they were impossible to ignore.

Nats get out was the most popular one, but there were plenty of other gems.

Mag perps apprehended, but where's Galder? another sign read.

The Alliance = Nat Governing.

Some of the signs had been magicked so they displayed footage of the murders on loop. I caught my own face on a number of them. It made me want to hunch my shoulders and duck my head, even though no one would ever recognize me with the illusion Kaira had given me.

I had never seen so many people in one place in my life. It was like how I imagined it would feel to be in Times Square on New Year's Eve.

I remembered one of Valencia's rallies I'd caught sight of on the news only a few weeks ago. There had been no more than a dozen Magics shouting and holding up signs. Now, there were thousands.

The thought of how far our city had fallen in less than a week—and how much farther it would yet fall if Valencia got her way—twisted my insides. I reminded myself she was why we were here. We were going to prove that Valencia was behind the murders. It wouldn't undo the damage that had been done to the fragile unity between Naturals and Magics, but that could be mended.

Easy peasy, as A.J. would say.

A fat, gray cloud burst into existence directly over the Alliance building. The crowd went wild.

"Welcome, newest memb-ahs of the UnAllied!" Valencia called in her classic Boston accent.

The Rain Maker would be impossible to miss, even if she wasn't standing in front of the microphone. Valencia's dress was cow-patterned today, which had A.J. babbling in my ear about the environment and bovine rights. Her signature leopard-print purse was slung over her arm as she controlled her tiny rain storm like an orchestra conductor.

I tried to tune out her bigoted speech as I scanned the crowd for the Manipulator, who should be somewhere close by.

"Down with Nats," Valencia called. "Down with the Alliance!"

The crowd cheered.

"We won't let them control us any long-ah," she continued. "I challenge each of you to come out to vote to put an end to the Alliance once and for alll!"

There was more cheering and applauding. I swallowed the bile that was rising from my stomach.

"Two-thirds vote, Mags! That's all we need to end the Alliance. That's all we need to get a real lead-ah in charge of this city. And I swear, I won't stop until Mags are the only ones left standing!"

I couldn't believe anyone could stand to listen to such filth, and yet, the crowd was eating up her every word. I could see the civilization our city had maintained for thirty years crumbling before my eyes. It took every ounce of willpower I possessed to keep from storming up those stairs and knocking Valencia unconscious just to shut her up.

Not that beating up Valencia would help my case…but damn, it would feel good.

"The vote will be held in the Mag building on Commonwealth all day Tuesday. That's in three days, people…three days until the Alliance is nothing more than a nightma-yah. I'll see you all on Tuesday!"

The crowd roared in approval, and chants of *End the Alliance* rang in my ears.

Three days. That's all we had to apprehend the real killer and pacify the angry Magics. If we failed, the Alliance would be dissolved, and we'd be thrown into civil war.

"Holy schnikey," A.J. said into my earpiece. "Three days?!"

"Let's just focus on getting Valencia," Kaira replied, her voice grim. "We'll worry about the rest later."

Valencia introduced the head of LA's UnAllied, a Level 6 Levitator. The woman hovered over the crowd as she began her speech about how the Alliance had been lying to Magics and was really just using the guise of unity to continue oppressing them.

I pressed a hand over my earpiece, trying to make out Smith's voice amid all the other sounds. He was still in the van, using a drone to keep a bird's eye view of the whole rally. There were so many people here, there was no way any of us standing in the crowd would be able to find the guy we were searching for.

"The Manipulator's standing on the bottom step of the Alliance building, on the side closer to Franklin Street," Smith said. "Wearing a Red Sox cap."

"Everyone's got a Red Sox cap," I replied, scanning the sea of people.

"Beard. Green shirt."

I pushed through a family holding signs that read *Give Galder the Chair* in glittered lettering.

I imagined the sign was figurative, since the electric chair wasn't used for executions anymore.

Smith's voice in my ear guided me as I cut through the crowd. As the only one immune to the Manipulator's magic, it would be up to me to distract the man long enough for the others to get Valencia.

My pulse jumped when I finally spotted the Manipulator.

The guy was about two feet taller and at least a hundred pounds heavier than his picture had suggested. I'd give Smith hell about it later. As I watched, a little boy tried to scoot past the man to run up the Alliance steps.

The Manipulator grabbed the back of the kid's jacket and bent until they were eye level. The man grinned, showing off the silver grills plating his teeth. The kid squealed in terror and ran back in the opposite direction.

Nice.

The Manipulator stood, cracked his knuckles, and brushed his hand against a bulge in his jacket.

"He's got a gun," Smith said.

"I see," I said, gathering myself. At least Kaira had illusioned me to look almost as big and fierce as the Manipulator himself. But the illusion wouldn't help if the other guy attacked me.

"Are you guys ready?" I asked, trying not to move my lips too much in case the Manipulator caught sight of me.

"Bri?" Kaira asked. "You ready?"

"Oh, hell yeah," she replied. "As soon as Valencia's done signing that woman's bra, I'll grab her."

I almost laughed at the disgust in Bri's voice.

"Okay, Gray. Go ahead."

I pulled the police ID off my belt and strode up to the Manipulator.

"Natural Police," I stated in a firm, cop-like voice. "Sir, I'm going to need you to come with me."

The Manipulator bared his grills, took two steps forward, and grabbed a fistful of my uniform.

"Get the fuck away from me, Nat," he snarled.

Okay, so it would seem the soft approach wasn't going to work.

I reached for my unloaded gun. At the same moment, the Manipulator pulled his gun out of his jacket and aimed it at me.

I heard Kaira scream something into my earpiece, but all of my attention was fixed on the Manipulator.

"We're surrounded by thousands of people with cell phones right now," I said, keeping my voice even. "What do you think the odds are that not a single one of them is filming this right now?"

The man's gaze shifted left and right before coming back to settle on me.

"And what do you think is going to happen to you after the video of you shooting a cop—a *Natural* cop—is pasted all over the nightly news?" I slowly lowered my gun and put it back in its holster.

"By this time tomorrow, you'll be in a holding cell awaiting execution." I smiled. "I've been told the last meal for first high law offenders is soggy green beans."

The Manipulator's hold on his gun faltered.

"Hey!"

A nearby cop—a real one—was racing toward us, his own weapon raised. The Manipulator looked at the cop, looked at me, and took off.

He blasted a path through the crowd, heedless of the people in his way.

I went after him.

"Stop," I commanded, taking the time to go around, rather than through, a family in my way.

The Manipulator looked behind him as he reached a thinner section of the crowd. He stepped off the curb and started sprinting down the street, which had been blocked off from traffic.

The Manipulator might be a powerful Magic, but his fitness wasn't anything to write home about. He certainly hadn't jogged five miles a day for the last three years like I had. As soon as I wasn't blocked in by people on every side, I closed the distance between us.

I tackled the guy from behind. The Manipulator hit the pavement face-first with me on top of him.

Not very graceful, but effective.

"Boston Natural Police," I yelled, using one hand to wrench the Manipulator's hands behind his back and the other to hold up my badge as five real cops came running down the street toward us with their weapons raised.

"Help me apprehend this asshole," I commanded the first cop to reach us, because I realized I had no idea how to actually use the handcuffs that were dangling from my belt.

"Want me to get my cah?" the cop asked in a Boston accent that was only slightly less thick than Valencia's.

"Nah, just hold him," I replied, ramping up my own Boston accent for effect. "The guy's a Mag."

"Shit, then what're we doin' with him?"

"How should I know?" I replied. "Captain told us to get him. Keep him here while I call it in."

As soon as I was sure the cop wasn't letting go of the Manipulator, I disappeared into the crowd.

"Guys?" I asked, holding my microphone up to my mouth. "Where are we at?"

"Valencia's in the cruiser. Gray, meet us on the corner of Congress and Sudbury."

I skidded to a stop and changed direction. "On my way."

CHAPTER 25

The van door opened, and I found myself squeezing onto a seat beside a shrieking Valencia Stark.

Everyone was soaked, and it took me a few confused seconds to realize that it was raining inside the van.

We had prepared for Valencia's temper tantrum, and Smith was huddled in the backseat under waterproof tarps along with all of his electronics. His voice was slightly muffled when he said, "The path ahead's clear. Gun it!"

With Michael behind the wheel, it was more of a controlled acceleration, but with the siren on our van screeching for effect, it still felt dramatic.

"I know my rights!" Valencia shouted at the top of her lungs as rain continued to soak us. "You people can't hold me. I want to talk to my lawy-ah!"

"Turn off the rain, or I'll knock you out," Bri said, scowling as she wrung out her hair.

Valencia bared her teeth, but the rain stopped falling.

It did nothing to stop the unpleasant squishing sound every time someone shifted on the seat. Valencia's tent-like dress draped over my lap, soaking me even more. The only thing that wasn't soaked was her leopard-print purse, which I realized was vinyl.

Yutika reached over and pulled a dark hood over Valencia's head so she wouldn't be able to see where we were taking her. The Rain Maker screamed and snarled, but with Bri sitting next to her, there wasn't much she could do.

After Valencia had shouted herself hoarse, the van went quiet as we drove to the warehouse on the Boston waterfront that Smith, Yutika, and

A.J. had spent several hours preparing for our purposes. As we neared the waterfront, Michael kept glancing in his rearview mirror.

"What's wrong?" Kaira demanded.

"Nothing," he muttered. "I thought we had a tail, but he just turned off."

"What'd you do with my Manipulat-ah, moth-ah fuck-ahs?" Valencia demanded, her voice slightly muffled from the hood.

"Shut up," Bri and I told her at the same time.

We got to the abandoned warehouse without incident. Michael stopped the van, and everyone except for Smith piled out.

Bri, her skin titanium once again, kept her hand locked on Valencia's wrist. Yutika punched in a code to the security system she had designed and Smith installed. The creaky old garage door slid up, and we all squished and slopped across the cement floor.

"Sit down," Bri commanded. She shoved Valencia into the chair, which was the only piece of furniture in the entire place. Valencia clutched her purse to her chest like it was a child she needed to protect.

As soon as Bri pulled off Valencia's hood, it started to rain inside the warehouse.

"Do you know how long it took me to blow out my hair this morning?" A.J. complained.

Six umbrellas zoomed in and opened themselves over each of our heads. Valencia scowled. A.J. smirked.

"There's someone coming down the road," Smith said into our earpieces.

I exchanged a look with Kaira. We weren't in an area where people just wandered around for no reason.

"I'll take care of it," Bri said. "Shut the door behind me. I'll be back in a flash."

Once she was gone, A.J. waved his fingers, and the garage door started to creak and groan as it closed.

It was cold and damp in here, more so because we were all soaked, but it was adrenaline that was giving me goosebumps now.

"Mag cops on the way," Smith said. "We've got eleven minutes before they track us down."

"Michael, you're up," Kaira said.

Michael crouched down next to Valencia. "Are you responsible for the four murders in the last week?" he asked.

I was ready for the furious expression to melt out of her gaze and for her muscles to relax, but Valencia only continued to glare at us.

The garage door, which was in the process of closing, came to a creaking stop. It hovered a few feet above the ground.

"I didn't tell you to stop," A.J. informed the door. He waved his hand. Once. Twice. The door didn't budge.

"Valencia, look at me," Michael said.

She ignored him.

"Graysen Gald-ah. You filthy Nat." Valencia spat on the ground at my feet. "I shoulda known."

I looked down at myself, only to see my illusion was gone. I looked at the others. Their illusions had disappeared, too.

Kaira met my gaze. "My illusions aren't working," she said, looking scared and confused at the same time.

The umbrellas that had been hovering over each of us dropped out of the air. I had to duck before mine hit me on the head.

I turned, and then blinked, convinced I was seeing things.

A heavy-set man who shared Valencia's wild red hair and thick-framed glasses was squirming under the door and into the warehouse. He had one arm wrapped around Bri's neck.

"He's got a knife," Bri called to the rest of us, "and my magic isn't working."

"Who are you?" A.J. demanded.

"Morons, let me introduce you to my broth-ah," Valencia said with a smirk that turned my insides. "My Level 5 *Shield* broth-ah."

Six curses filled the warehouse at once. Shields blocked any magic within a certain distance. A Level 5 was strong enough to block the power of every Magic here.

"Come near me or my sister, or pull one of your guns, and your little girl is getting her throat cut."

Shit. The Shield kept his back to the wall, so there was no chance of sneaking up on him.

Bri turned her head to look at the man out of the corner of her eye. "You're going to regret messing with me, pal."

I pulled my gun from its holster for the second time today and pointed it at Valencia's head.

"Hurt my friend, and I'll kill your sister," I told the Shield.

We all stood there, glaring at each other and too afraid to move for fear of what we'd start. My gun might be useless, but the knife the Shield was holding up to Bri's throat wasn't. We had everything to lose in this standoff.

Kaira gave me a panicked look.

What do we do?

Valencia guffawed at our obvious distress. Either she knew I wouldn't use the gun I was pointing at her, or she was too cracked to care. "My broth-ah and I just need to sit pretty until the cops show up. You're finished." She gave us the finger for added effect.

The Shield grinned, displaying crooked, yellowing teeth.

While his attention was on me and the gun in my hand, A.J. snuck around the far side of the warehouse and slipped under the garage door.

"I'll slow the cops down and give you kittens time to figure things out in here," he called once he was safely on the other side.

"Want me to go after 'im?" the Shield asked his sister.

"Psh, like you could catch him," Bri retorted. "Fat-ass."

"Stay put," Valencia barked at her brother. "Have you forgotten I'm being *threatened?*"

"I'll lower mine if you lower yours," I told the Shield.

Slowly, I dropped my arm so the gun was pointing at the floor. The Shield did the same. I let out a relieved breath.

There was the sound of a car door opening and shutting. Then, the van peeled away from the warehouse.

Valencia smirked. "Looks like you just lost your ride outta here. Too bad, so sad."

I glanced at the others in the room. I saw uncertainty and fear on their faces. They didn't have any more of an idea about what to do right now than I did. A.J. and Smith might be able to hold the cops off for a little while, but not forever. We probably had fifteen minutes, tops.

Think, I commanded myself.

We wouldn't get another opportunity to question Valencia.

As I glared at the woman who was responsible for the dead bodies piling up and my almost-execution, a desperate plan started to form in my mind.

"Yutika," I said without taking my eyes off Valencia. "Remember when I asked you to hide that sealed folder with all of the documents inside?" I didn't give her a chance to respond, since I'd never asked her any such thing. "I know we said we wouldn't show Valencia all the phone records and bank statements our Techie accessed, but I think we need them now. Can you go get them while the rest of us stay here with the Starks?"

I kept my gaze cool as my insides roiled.

Come on, Yutika, I silently begged her. *Don't let me down.*

"It's three blocks away," Yutika said in a convincing whine. "It's going to take ten minutes to get there and back."

"Then, you better hurry," I said, still staring at Valencia as I tried to hide all the thoughts and emotions I was barely containing.

"Want me to kill the bitch?" the Shield asked his sister.

"What records?" Valencia demanded, ignoring her brother. "You don't have anything on me."

"Not quite true," I said, giving Valencia a shrug and quirking my lips in a casual grin.

"Here's what we do know. You arranged the four murders as part of your grand plan to activate Section 278, Article 3, 998J and destroy the Alliance. Your plan is to build up an army of Magics who will support you becoming the new authority in this city. And then you're going to start a war between Nats and Mags."

The whole time I spoke, I watched Valencia's face. I saw no confusion or surprise, only an angry kind of acceptance.

So far, so good, I thought.

The Shield stood clutching his knife, but he didn't seem to know what we were talking about, or what he was supposed to do. I turned my attention back on Valencia.

"We also know about your boss and how he's been funding all of these murders you've arranged." My thoughts were moving about a mile ahead of the words coming out of my mouth. This would be tricky to navigate, since it was all speculation on my part. One wrong word would unravel my entire bluff.

"How did you find out about him?" Valencia asked. Her tone was hostile, but I didn't miss the fear that widened her eyes for a fraction of a moment.

"Our Techie's a Level 10," I informed her. "Did you really think we wouldn't be able to connect the dots?"

"He'll kill me if he finds out you know," Valencia whispered, digging her fingers into the plastic of her purse. "He'll think I told you."

This time, her fear wasn't a passing thing. I could almost feel it in the air surrounding her.

At that moment, Yutika squirmed under the garage door and ran into the warehouse, cradling a thick brown folder in her arms. I had to hold back from kissing her on the cheek or breaking into an A.J.-like dance.

I took the folder Yutika handed me without looking away from Valencia.

I hit the folder against my hand, letting the smacking sound speak for how many papers were inside. Then, I slowly and meticulously unsealed the envelope.

"I'm sure your employer will be more than a little pissed off when we go straight to the press with all of these phone records and money transfers." I pulled out a sheet of paper that, to Yutika's credit, really did look like a bank statement. I flashed it in front of Valencia's face. Just enough that she could see the official-ness of it, but not long enough that she could read anything written on it. "Especially when I tell the Globe that you were the one who handed over all of this evidence about your boss.

"But that's just the tip of the iceberg. Things are going to get worse for you when everyone finds out about your involvement in *the Lab*."

I held my breath.

Valencia's gasp was music to my ears.

"You know about the Lab?!"

"And what do you think your supporters are going to say when they find out about it?" I pushed.

"I don't envy the spot you'll be in when everyone finds out," Kaira said, shuddering for dramatic emphasis.

"Me neither," Bri piped up.

My smile broadened.

"Can I start stabbing people?" the Shield asked his sister.

I shrugged. "Our Techie has everything programmed to go straight to the Globe if anything happens to us. Even if you somehow manage to make it past all of us, you'll be screwed the minute the evening news breaks."

"Val, I'll gut the Nat here and now——"

"Shut up!" Valencia shrieked at her brother. To me, she asked, "Whaddya want?"

"Um kittens, we have a situation," A.J.'s voice said into our earpieces.

"We're headed back to you," Smith said. "Be ready to get in the van in exactly two minutes."

The others started to shift restlessly, but I stayed where I was.

"We want to know everything that our Techie didn't already find out," I told Valencia, tapping the folder for emphasis. "In exchange, we'll keep your name, and your connection with your boss, out of the press."

I was walking a careful line between keeping my words vague enough to avoid revealing how little I actually knew, and scaring Valencia enough that she'd give me what I needed.

She took the bait.

"I don't know his real name." Valencia's voice had gone hoarse.

"If you're going to lie to us——" Kaira warned.

"I'm not lyin'!" Valencia's lips had gone white. "All I know is that he's rich enough to fund the Lab and pay my people for the murders. We have an arrangement. He works behind the scenes, and I'm the one the public will know as the Mag war general."

Mag war general? Really?

"We already know all of that," I lied. "You'll have to tell us something we don't already have in here." I held up the folder.

"I'll tell you where the Lab is, but I don't know what goes on there. Boss never told me—"

"Address, now," Kaira ordered.

Valencia recited the address, which Kaira repeated into her microphone for Smith.

"Alright, I've got it," Smith said. "Now, get outside. A.J.'s dealing with ten cop cars, and he can't hold them much longer."

"One last question." I pinned Valencia with my stare as the others started to move toward the garage door. "The victims. How did you choose them?"

Valencia swallowed. "Bobby Axelrod and Jonas Meddlesworth needed to be silenced because they knew too much about the Lab. Axelrod was gonna whistleblow about something, and Meddlesworth was trying to extort the boss for more money." Her expression frosted over with disgust. "And the Nats were chosen because they were high profile enough to get everyone's attention."

I swallowed my fury. There would be time for that later. Right now, I needed information.

"And Penelope?" I asked through gritted teeth. "I'm pretty sure she wasn't involved with the Lab."

"That wasn't me," Valencia said, shaking her head. "I arranged the other ones, but that one was my employ-ah. He said he was going to take care of the first murder himself, personally. That's all I know."

She looked scared enough that I believed her.

The Shield yelped. He still held the knife, but he was hopping up and down on one foot. Bri stomped on his other foot before sucker-punching him in the gut. She wasn't made out of titanium, but the man still doubled over and wheezed like he couldn't take a breath. Bri smirked as she ducked under the man's flailing arms and went to join the others who were exiting the warehouse.

"Galder, *now*," Smith growled, when I didn't follow.

I slipped my hand into my pocket, closing my fist around the small rectangular object. Then, I lunged at Valencia, yelling something incoherent about my life being ruined. I collided with the Rain Maker.

"Gray!"

I looked up in time to see the Shield's knife flying through the air. It was a wild throw, and the weapon went right over my head. I continued to shout at Valencia as I let Kaira take my hand and pull me out of the warehouse. I tried to contort my features so I looked furious and desperate. Then, I slid under the garage door and sprinted to the van.

CHAPTER 26

Smith got out of the driver's seat and went back to his command module, while Yutika took his place. The rest of us piled in.

The van flew down the road. We drove for less than a minute before A.J.'s yellow jacket became visible on the road. He was facing away from us with his arms stretched up to the sky. He looked like a 3D painting of Moses parting the Red Sea…if Moses wore neon and the Red Sea was replaced by police cruisers.

Above him, ten cop cars hovered in mid-air. Their wheels spun, and they dipped and shook as the police inside shouted and banged against the doors. There were also about a thousand bullets frozen in mid-air all around A.J.

A.J., his face red and dripping with perspiration, backed toward us without lowering his arms or looking away from the cop cars.

"Michael…you…better…be…ready," A.J. said through gritted teeth.

"Ready." Michael threw open the van door and got out.

I heard the cops' screams as the cars gently lowered to the ground. There was a light patter as the bullets plunked down on the asphalt at a speed about as dangerous as hail.

"Officers, holster your weapons and listen to me." Michael didn't raise his voice, but it somehow carried.

The rest of us waited in tense silence while Michael spoke to the officers. I was afraid there were too many for Michael to control at once, but it was obvious from their silence that the Whisper had their attention.

"Police all over the city are looking for us," Smith said, pulling my attention away from Michael and the cops. "They know there's at least three Mags who were in a police van. They're everywhere."

"I have an idea." Yutika grinned as she scribbled madly on her note pad. "They won't be looking for us in this."

She tossed the finished sketch out of her window.

I watched as the black-and-white drawing hit the ground. And then the 2D vehicle lifted itself off the page and puttered a short distance away on wobbly, paper wheels. There was the sound of a tiny engine revving to life.

The 2D sketch began to expand. It looked too long to be a van, but in its miniature form, I couldn't really tell what kind of car Yutika was creating.

I heard the scraping of metal on metal as the toy-sized car began to grow. The air filled with the smell of burnt rubber and fresh paint. The paper-white vehicle became yellow as it continued to stretch up and out until a small, perfect replica of a school bus appeared before us.

Remembering what had happened last time I observed a car come to life, I backed up so I wouldn't be crushed underneath the thing when it became full size.

The bus rocked from side to side as it swelled. And then the small bus doubled…quadrupled…sextupled…in size. In less than a minute, a fully-formed school bus was parked in front of us.

The words *Boston Public Schools* appeared in black lettering on the yellow side. A small stop sign appeared beneath the driver's side window. Its red lights even flashed.

And, just like that, our new ride awaited.

"So awesome," I murmured.

"How come you never get this excited about my powers?" A.J. complained.

"Your powers are extremely cool," I assured him.

"Not as cool as mine," Yutika sing-songed.

Michael finished talking with the cops, who had all gone limp and doe-eyed. The rest of us got ourselves and all of Smith's equipment onto the school bus.

The cop cars turned around on the road and started to drive away from us. I let out the breath I'd been holding.

As Michael jogged back to the bus, he started to shrink. By the time he got to us, he was no longer the grown man he'd been. In his place was a five-year old kid with chubby cheeks and wispy blonde hair. I couldn't stop the semi-hysterical laugh that burst out of me.

When I looked around, I saw the rest of the Six were now kindergarten-aged kids, too. The one exception was Yutika, who was now a heavy-set woman with graying hair in her sixties. I looked down at myself.

I was pleasantly plump and covered with freckles. I was wearing tiny overalls and a shirt with fire trucks all over it.

Cool.

"I'm freaking adorable," I said.

Bri actually squealed in delight when she caught sight of her reflection in one of the bus's windows. "Kaira, this is the cutest illusion work I've ever seen," the little girl in a Minnie Mouse dress gushed.

"I'd call it the weirdest," Smith said from the body of a kindergarten girl.

"I've seen weirder," I said.

My thoughts immediately went back to the time when Kai and I went to the doctor's for her first birth control prescription. I had researched a Natural doctor who specialized in Magic care, so she wouldn't be able to tell I wasn't a Magic. We'd skipped school and driven out to Newton for the appointment.

We'd been delirious with laughter the whole ride to the doctor's office. Before we got out of the car, Kaira illusioned me to look just like Ma.

That had been weird.

Once we were in the exam room, I'd tried my best to imitate Ma's voice as I signed forms and exchanged pleasantries with the doctor. The results had been…disturbing.

"Jeez Louise!" A.J. screeched.

"What's wrong?" the rest of us asked at once.

"I'm *fat,*" he wailed.

"Seriously, A.J.?" Yutika demanded.

"Focus, guys. We're not out of this yet."

It was more than a little strange for a five-year-old with pigtails and Kaira's voice to be giving orders.

But she was right.

"Head back toward Commercial Street," Smith said. "I've cleared traffic, but there are more cops on the way."

"The ones I Whispered will be back," Michael warned. "They're confused, but I couldn't make them completely forget about us."

As if to emphasize his point, sirens blared from somewhere nearby.

The school bus lurched forward.

"Yutika—"

"I'm calibrating!"

The bus had reached the end of the road when the ten cop cars Michael had sent away, plus five more, came screeching around the corner. Bri pressed her five-year-old face against the glass of the window. Yutika edged the school bus onto the side of the road and slowed, but the cop cars flew right past us. No one even glanced our way.

It seemed like we all breathed at once.

Yutika kept the school bus at a normal speed as we turned onto a road with more traffic.

"Where to?" she asked, looking at us in the rearview mirror.

"The Lab," Kaira and I said together.

"We have to find out what they're doing there," I clarified. "Maybe it'll give us the proof we need to go to the authorities."

Even though we'd recorded Valencia's confession, we didn't have anything real to substantiate what she'd said. We needed concrete proof that the police wouldn't be able to explain away.

"It's only a couple of minutes from where we are now," Smith said, consulting one of his screens.

"My guess is they're making drugs to fund this so-called war," Bri said.

I nodded. It was as reasonable a theory as any.

"Nah," Smith said. "I'm guessing they're making some kind of weapon that can go up against the Nat military." He cocked his head, thinking. "Maybe they're collecting the DAMND babies to use as a biological weapon."

The thought made me sick to my stomach. I had thought the Slaughters were over and that Boston would transform the rest of the country into something better. I never dreamed that the opposite might happen—that our city would drag the rest of the country into civil war.

"We'll find out soon enough," Kaira said.

No one spoke as the school bus made the ten-minute drive to the street Valencia had given us.

"Are you sure this is right?" Yutika asked, idling the bus as we all looked out our windows.

"Yes," Smith said. His little kid frowned. "The address she gave you is halfway down the road."

The street was empty except for an abandoned parking lot and a construction site. There wasn't even a building yet, just a bunch of parked construction vehicles.

"That Rain Maker bitch lied to us," Yutika said, speaking for all of us.

I deflated. I was hoping we could solve this mystery today and turn the rest of the investigation over to the police. Now, we'd have to wait until my other plan went into effect.

How many more people would have to die in the meantime?

I'd been sure Valencia was scared enough by my threats that she'd been telling the truth, but it was obvious there was nowhere around here that could pass for a drug lab. Maybe my lawyer instincts were no good, after all.

"What do we do now?" A.J. asked.

"Let's go home." Kaira's kindergartener hung her head in defeat.

"Not to sound like a negative Nancy," A.J. said, folding his chubby arms, but that whole endeavor was a complete bust."

"Valencia basically admitted she's behind the murders and that her employer killed Penelope," Yutika said. "That should be enough for the police, right?"

"I want to wait and find out who this employer of hers is before we go to the cops," I said. "Otherwise, they might just convince themselves that Valencia was telling us what we wanted to hear because we'd threatened her."

"How are we supposed to find her employer, pray tell?" A.J. asked.

I turned around in my seat to find Smith, who was sitting in the aisle of the bus with one of his laptops balanced on the seat next to him.

Time to see if my other plan would amount to anything.

"Did it work?" I asked the Techie.

"Of course it worked," Yutika said before Smith could respond. "I'm a master Creator."

Smith nodded, a slow grin spreading across his little kid face. "Valencia's still in the warehouse."

A.J.'s pudgy little kid face squeezed into a puzzled expression. "What's that, now?"

I looked at the others. "I slipped a tracker in her purse."

For a moment, no one spoke.

"When you attacked her?" Kaira asked finally.

I nodded, feeling a grin spread over my face.

"And now that she thinks we have records of money transfers and phone calls with her mysterious boss, she's going to want to have a little meeting with him," Smith added. "All we have to do is wait to see where she goes."

"You brilliant little Nat," A.J. said in wonder as he reached over to ruffle my hair.

"I couldn't have done it without Smith and Yutika," I said.

"Handsome and humble." A.J. shook his head.

My grin widened.

"But how did you know she was answering to someone above her?" Bri asked.

"And that she was connected to the Lab that all our Magics keep mentioning?" Michael added.

I lifted a shoulder. "I didn't, exactly. I just assumed someone important was funding all of these murders, since *professional rabble rouser* isn't a career that pays in the hundreds of thousands. And I figured if Valencia was in deep enough with her employer, she'd know something about the Lab, which I'm guessing is the source of funding for this war of theirs." I took a breath. "And I assumed Valencia wouldn't want anyone knowing about the Lab."

I looked at Yutika. "Awesome job with that file, by the way."

She grinned in the rearview mirror. "I was so confused, so I just made every kind of document I could think of and shoved them in there, hoping it would be enough."

"You did great," I assured her.

"Police chatter on the radio is that they're taking Valencia downtown because of her threat about killing Nats," Smith said.

"They won't be able to charge her unless she admits she's responsible for those murders," I said.

"But at least she won't be able to come after us while she's busy with the cops," Michael pointed out.

"I'd like to see her try." Yutika pffed. "She doesn't have the resources to track us down."

"And since we're unMarked, her descriptions won't do the cops any good," Kaira added. Her gaze slid to me, and she gave me an *I told you so* look. It wasn't nearly as infuriating when it came the face of a five-year-old with pigtails.

For the first time, I didn't have a counter-argument at the ready.

"We kicked that Rain Maker's ass," Bri said, punching one tiny titanium fist into the air.

"Thanks to Gray's quick thinking," Kaira said.

This time, I was sure I didn't imagine the pride in her voice.

The full impact of what we'd accomplished in the last hour was starting to hit me. Valencia might have lied about the location of this mysterious Lab, but with the tracker, we'd be able to get all the evidence we needed. The police wouldn't be able to dispute our claims, and with any luck, Valencia would be in custody before the vote on Tuesday.

We were so close to ending all of this. I felt downright giddy.

Little kid Smith pulled out his earpiece and put on his headphones. I leaned into the aisle to see the little tracker dot blinking down the road on Smith's computer. It was headed in the direction of the Magic police station.

A slow grin spread over the Techie's face as he tapped his headphones. "The police arrested the Manipulator, too. Now they're investigating him for a dozen other crimes."

"At least we won't have to deal with him again," Kaira said with a little shudder.

"I guess there's nothing else we can do until the cops let Valencia out, huh?" Bri asked.

"There's one thing we have on the agenda for tonight." Chubby little kid A.J. tapped his patent leather shoe on the floor. "We're celebrating."

"We're celebrating getting a tracker on Valencia?" Yutika asked, raising a brow.

"Yuppers," A.J. said, "and Galder's initiation into the Six."

"Which can't be the Six anymore," Bri pointed out.

"The Nat makes Seven," Kaira said with a casual shrug, but even in a completely unfamiliar body, I saw the way her eyes smiled.

A warm feeling spread through my chest.

"We're going to need to make a few stops on the way home," A.J. announced. "I'm making burgers and my world-famous sangria tonight."

"Burgers?" Bri asked.

"Finally," Michael muttered.

"*Black bean* burgers," A.J. qualified, grinning as Michael scowled. "I guarantee after one bite you'll worship the ground I walk on. Assuming you don't already."

CHAPTER 27

Two hours, an abandoned school bus, a new van, three more illusions, and ten bags of groceries later, we were home. A.J. banished all of us upstairs to *get party ready*. My last sight of the kitchen as I headed upstairs was of the groceries zooming out of their bags and flying around the kitchen.

By the time we were all showered and changed, a huge bowl of sangria was waiting on the kitchen table. Amazing smells were coming from the stove, where various pots seemed to be cooking themselves on all burners.

Plastic solo cups filled themselves with sangria and floated through the air to each of us.

I wore a pair of dark jeans and a bright blue button-down A.J. had gotten me. I wasn't sure if it was too bold for me to pull off, but the answer to that question was cleared up the moment Kaira came down the stairs. With the way she looked at me, my gratitude to the Telekinetic knew no bounds.

Kaira was wearing a short-sleeved silver top and matching mini-skirt. It would have looked plain on anyone else, but nothing was plain on Kai. It showed off her toned legs and every fantastic curve. When she reached up to grab plates out of a cabinet, I saw the back of the shirt was crisscrossed so that whole sections of her back were bare. I took a long drink of my sangria and turned to talk to Yutika.

Music filled the house along with laughter and chatting. We stood around the kitchen counter, eating guacamole and drinking sangria, until A.J.'s self-proclaimed masterpiece was ready.

Then, we sat at the table drinking more sangria and eating what we all had to admit were the best burgers we'd ever had. When even Smith ate one—after first inspecting it with his poison scanner—A.J. fell out of his chair in a pretend-faint. He grumbled when Michael didn't catch him. Then, A.J. crowed about how he'd "turn" all of us vegan yet.

I felt more relaxed than I'd been in as long as I could remember. Even at the few BSMU crew parties I'd gone to when I wasn't holed up in my room studying, I hadn't been able to fully enjoy myself. As the team captain, and more often than not the only semi-sober one, I was the one who made sure none of my teammates got alcohol poisoning or decided to take a drunken swim in the Charles.

But I wasn't in charge of taking care of anyone tonight.

After dinner, we crowded onto the couches in the living room. We played charades before moving on to Cards Against Humanity. I didn't think I'd ever laughed so much in my entire life. I found myself sitting on the edge of one of the couches with Kaira next to me.

Our knees were touching, and neither of us moved to put more distance between us. Every time one of us leaned forward to play a card, our arms brushed. It was subtle enough that no one else in the room would notice, but even that small contact put my heart rate into cardiac arrest territory. I could tell from the color on Kaira's cheeks, and the way she reacted to the conversation around her a little too slowly, that she was as affected as I was.

The sangria hadn't been strong enough for us to feel anything more than a light buzz, which had worn off almost as fast as it came on. Still, we were all drunk off our recent victory and the promise of answers the next day. It was making Kaira and me bold in a dangerous kind of way.

I didn't care. I couldn't make myself stop.

The room erupted into shouts and raucous laughter over a particularly controversial round, but I wasn't paying attention to the game anymore. Kaira shifted slightly, bringing us close enough that our sides were touching. I moved my cards to my left hand and draped my right arm over the back of the couch. No one in the room was paying any attention to us, but even if they were, they wouldn't have been able to see when I let my hand slip down just enough for my fingertips to brush against the back of her shoulder.

Ours wasn't the only sexual tension. Michael and Yutika kept glancing at each other across the room. Their looks, unlike the way Kaira and I were touching, were anything but subtle. Bri kept fake-coughing and grinning, but they didn't even notice.

Yutika stood up mid-round of cards and announced that she was tired. She went upstairs, and ten minutes later, Michael mumbled that he was going to sleep. It would have been more convincing if his cheeks weren't bright red.

They got impossibly redder when A.J. sing-songed, "I'm not ready to be an uncle yet, so be safe."

"You did *not* just say that, Alexander James Winston the third," Bri chided, pretending to be appalled.

"You know I hate my given name." A.J. stuck his tongue out at Bri and then collapsed onto one of the bean bag chairs with a huff.

I was on the verge of losing my mind with these barely-there touches when Kaira yawned and stretched.

"I'm calling it a night," she told the room.

Bri and A.J. were having a heated argument about who the next *Magic Bachelorette* would be, and Smith was back behind his laptop screens. I didn't think any of them had even heard her.

The look Kaira gave me as she stood up would have brought me to my knees if I wasn't already sitting down.

I waited as long as I could stand before I went after her. I made it about thirty seconds.

I kept my steps casual until I made it to the stairs, which I took three at a time. She was waiting at the top. I glanced down the hall to make sure Yutika's door was closed, and then I lifted Kai into my arms.

I spun her around once, feeling her quiet laugh vibrate against my chest. And then our mouths collided.

There were three years' worth of repressed longing in our kiss. It was both everything, and at the same time, not nearly enough. I had just enough presence of mind to stifle a groan as Kai's legs hooked around my waist. I carried her down the hall without breaking our kiss.

We hadn't even gotten inside the room before we were undressing each other. I kicked the door shut behind us without taking my hands or lips from her. I turned on the old stereo to give us more privacy, since I'd never before had cause to wonder how loud we were or whether the walls were thin.

Kai finished with the buttons on my shirt and moved to my belt. I backed her farther into the room, my mouth never leaving hers.

I lifted her in my arms and carried her the rest of the way to the bed. My mind was empty of everything except for her. I covered her body with mine, using one hand to brace myself over her as the other explored curves I thought I'd never touch again. We were both gasping when I pulled back enough to look at her.

"Kaira." My voice was hoarse. "Do you want—"

"Yes," she breathed, her chest rising and falling. "Need you."

I couldn't have said it better myself. The fire between us was light years past wanting.

My hands were shaking as I slipped the shirt over her head. She was gorgeous beyond words.

"This is new," I murmured, staring appreciatively at her red lace bra.

"A girl's gotta have new lingerie. Three years is a long time."

Too long.

She moaned and arched into me as I dipped my head to kiss her through the lace.

"Damn, I've missed this," I said against her. *I've missed you.*

It was like I'd been in a coma for the last three years, and I'd just woken up. And it was Kai who had brought me back to life.

Our touches were soft, teasing. I could barely breathe as her fingers trailed down the ridges of my stomach. My heart felt like it might explode out of my chest.

It'd be worth it.

It was one of the things I had always loved about being with Kai. We both knew exactly how to touch each other, knew what the other wanted better than we knew our own desires. It had always been this way with us. The passage of time hadn't changed any of that. If anything, our connection felt somehow more powerful. There was no awkwardness or hesitation. There was only us, and the stubborn insistence of our love that refused to back down.

I love you, Kaira Hansley, I thought. They were words I couldn't say out loud, although I couldn't remember why.

I lifted her off the bed, wrapping one arm around her back to keep her steady so I could rid her of her bra.

"I love you, Gray."

I froze with my hand on the delicate clasp at her back. The fever of my lust cooled just enough for me to pull back and look at her.

My body was still desperate for her, but my brain was flashing warnings. Something was wrong about those words.

"No," I heard myself say before I even understood the horrible feeling that had flooded my system. "Don't say that to me."

And then rational thoughts and memories came crashing back in wave after wave.

"You're right. I don't know where that came from." Kaira leaned back against my arm, still breathing fast, her eyes wide with emotion. She took a shuddering breath. "I just got lost in the past for a second."

I let my arm drop, and she slid back on the bed, away from me. With the distance, my brain returned. All the hurt of what Kaira had done came back in full force. It was the mental equivalent of an ice bath.

"You never loved me," I said, my voice scratchy. "What you did—"

"I know. This was a mistake." She bit her lip. There were tears in her eyes, but she didn't let them fall. She was too stubborn for that. "Let's just forget this happened."

I pushed myself up onto my knees up so I was facing her. We were close enough to touch, but I didn't reach for her.

"My dad tried to kill himself that night."

The words slipped out before I could even process them. I'd never said them out loud—never talked about what had happened.

"Oh God," Kaira whispered. There was endless emotion in her brown eyes, but I was too overcome with my own pain to try to interpret it.

Now that I had started, I couldn't stop.

"After I left you that night, I went home and found my dad passed out on the floor with empty pill bottles and a bottle of whiskey."

Tears were sliding down Kaira's face. "Gray—"

"I thought he was dead, Kaira!" My voice broke. "His skin felt cold, and he wouldn't wake up." I squeezed my eyes shut, like it might be enough to banish the memory of that horrible night. "The EMTs told me he probably wouldn't make it. I was in the ICU with him for two days."

I opened my eyes. Kaira had a hand pressed to her mouth as tears streamed down her cheeks. I stared at a pile of clothes on the floor while I fought for control over my emotions.

"I didn't know," she whispered. "I thought—"

"What?" My voice turned harsh. "That you could walk into my dad's office wearing his face, and there wouldn't be consequences? What exactly did you think was going to happen?" It was a struggle to keep my volume below the level of the music.

"I thought he'd get demoted," she admitted, "but I didn't think he'd take it so hard. I figured he would be back in his position within the year."

"You knew my dad's job was everything to him!"

Kaira covered her face with her hands. Her slender shoulders shook.

"He still thinks he's the one who lost your file. He talks in his sleep about it, about how he was so careless and stupid. He's gotten obsessive compulsive about everything because he thinks he lost his mind that day." A harsh laugh escaped me. "And you want to know the most fucked up part? I never told him the truth, because that would have put *you* in danger."

Kaira still had her hands over her eyes, but I could read the distress in every tense muscle in her body. Still, I couldn't stop the words that kept pouring out of me.

"Do you know what kind of a son that makes me? Do you know what kind of a person? I've let my dad suffer for years because I was protecting a girl who didn't give a shit about me—"

"That's not true."

Kaira had stopped crying, but there was no fight left in her. There was an empty look to her that I had never seen before. Impossibly, it cooled my fury to the point where I could think.

And then, because I had nothing left to lose, I asked the question that had plagued me for three years.

"Why?"

"It was the only way," she whispered, her usual fire buried beneath her layers of guilt.

"Bull shit."

Kaira shook her head. Her eyes had gone impossibly wide and her face had paled.

I spoke, because it didn't seem like Kaira could, and I couldn't seem to make myself stop.

"If you had told me you wanted to destroy your file, I would have helped you do it. I would have fought you and tried to talk you out of it, but in the end, I would have helped you. Because that's what love is, Kai. It's a willingness to do anything for the other person's sake, even if it makes you less happy." I made a sound of disgust. "It isn't whatever you meant all those times you said it to me."

She had made me into a fool. I'd continued to play the fool every time I kept my mouth shut rather than telling my dad that Kaira was responsible for the lost file.

I wanted to be angry. Instead, all I felt was a bone-crushing hurt. This conversation had ripped the bandage off an old wound, and I felt like I was bleeding out.

"Oh, holy hell."

I spun around. A.J. was standing in the open doorway, his jaw hanging open.

I moved on instinct, using my body to block Kaira from view, even though I was wearing nothing except my boxers.

"Boyfriend, she's not really my type," A.J. said in a lighthearted voice, but as our gazes met, I saw pity.

Kaira scrambled off the bed, pulling the blanket around herself. "It's not what you think," she said quickly. "We were drunk, and—"

"Oh, honey." A.J. shook his head.

"It was my fault," I said, finding my voice. "I caught her by surprise."

I didn't know what the Telekinetic could read from our stricken faces, but whatever it was, it was obvious A.J. saw straight through our lies. For several, horrible seconds, we all just stared at each other.

"A.J.," Kaira said, and her voice broke.

A.J. held up a hand to silence her.

"No one knows this about me, but I actually can keep a secret." He gave us a sad little smile. "If anyone else finds out about this, it won't be because they heard it from me."

No one spoke for several long seconds.

"Oh." A.J. snapped his fingers. "The reason why I came up here in the first place."

He scowled at the stereo, and it turned itself off. The room filled with an unsettled quiet.

"Smith said the cops finally left your house and took down the wire taps," he told me. "If you want to call your dad, you can."

CHAPTER 28

After everything that had just happened with Kaira, it felt like iron claws had burrowed into my chest and were squeezing my heart into pulp.

I had never wanted to talk to my dad more than I did now. It was a little kid's thought. My dad and I had never had the kind of relationship where we confided in each other…not that I could, anyway. Still, I was homesick for my dad in a way I'd never been before.

I couldn't go home, but for the first time since my arrest, I could talk to my father.

After setting up the call on his laptop so it would be untraceable, Smith left me alone. Everyone else was already upstairs, and I was grateful for the privacy as I typed in my dad's number.

The call connected on the first ring.

"Hello?"

Even in that single word, I could hear my father's exhaustion.

"Dad, it's me," I managed, even though my throat felt like it was coated with sandpaper.

There was silence on the other end of the line for several seconds.

"Graysen, where are you?"

I shook my head. "I can't tell you that, Dad. But I'm somewhere safe, and I'm working on figuring out—"

"Graysen. You need to turn yourself in. I have a detective's card here, but you can just go on down to the station. I'll call the detective and let him know you're on your way."

The claws around my heart tightened.

"Do you think I'm guilty? Do you think I killed Penelope?"

My dad sighed. "Whether you did or didn't is irrelevant at this point."

My dad's non-answer left me struggling to catch my breath.

"How could you think I'm capable of something like that?" I asked when I finally found my voice.

"I taught you better, Graysen," my dad said, dodging my question again. "The justice system only works if we all obey the laws and authorities that keep everyone else safe."

Everyone else. Because my dad thought I was a criminal. Not a criminal, *a murderer.*

"Graysen? Did you hear me?"

"When have I ever done anything to make you think I'm capable of murder?" I asked, my voice cracking.

It had never once occurred to me that my dad would believe what people were saying about me.

"If you're innocent—"

I stopped listening after those words. The doubt…the disappointment…in my dad's voice was too much.

"So, is that a yes?" my dad asked.

"What?" I forced myself to loosen my grip on the laptop before it cracked.

"Are you going to turn yourself in? Can I call the detective and tell him you'll be down at the station in half an hour?"

"No." The word was almost inaudible. I cleared my throat. "If I turn myself in now, I'll be dead by the weekend. You know that, right?"

Silence.

"Every action has a consequence, Graysen. I taught you that. The Alliance is at a critical point right now. Let them do what they do best."

"You mean like convict an innocent?" I demanded, bitterness and disbelief sliding into place beside the hurt and betrayal.

"If you're innocent, the justice system will not fail you."

There they were again…those three words. *If you're innocent.*

"You care about the Alliance more than you care about me."

As soon as I'd spoken the words out loud, I heard the ring of truth in them. But a different, related thought stopped my words of outrage before they spilled from my lips.

Did I have any right to blame my dad for choosing something else over his son? Wasn't that exactly what I had been doing for the past three years, when I stayed silent for Kaira's sake rather than speak up for my father's?

But it wasn't just about my dad choosing the Alliance over me. My father didn't believe I was innocent.

"I'm sorry my arrest has caused you trouble," I said, falling back on the words I had meant to say before this call began.

"My son's all over the news for *murder!*"

"They're wrong about me, Dad, about everything. I've been trying to explain to you—"

"Did you kill Jonas, too? Did you think killing him for firing me all those years ago would make me feel better?"

I couldn't speak.

"If you have any respect for me as your father, you'll do the right thing," my dad said, his tone softer than it had been a moment ago.

"I'm trying to do the right thing," I said, my voice raspy.

"*Tonight*, Graysen. You'll turn yourself in tonight."

"I can't do that, Dad. I'm sorry, but I have to see this thing through. I'm close, I just need—"

"Then you're no son of mine."

"Dad," I choked.

There was a click, and the call ended.

I sat there with the computer on my lap, numb. I had no idea how much time passed. My mind was a meaningless fog.

"You okay, hun?"

I turned my head, only just now noticing A.J. was sitting on one of the bean bag chairs. I had no idea when he'd come downstairs, or how much he'd overhead.

"Kaira thought you might need some company," A.J. said, studying me, his expression full of a knowing kind of pity. "She was worried about you."

I didn't have room for any more anger or hurt. I just felt bone-weary. I wasn't sure I could speak, so I stared at the dark computer screen.

"Look, I know it's none of my business, but I just think you should know. Whatever happened between you and Kaira, she's hurting just as much as you are. Maybe even more."

"You're right," I said. "It isn't your business."

A.J. sighed and got off the bean bag. I was hoping he was taking his cue to leave, but instead, he came and sat down on the couch next to me.

"I know how people always say 'I know how you feel,' but I actually know how you feel." A.J. cocked his head to the side. "Well, at least about the part with your dad. The part with Kaira I won't pretend to understand for about five different reasons. But my mom and dad were all *We love you, A.J. We'll always support you, A.J.*"

"They accused you of murdering people, too?" I asked, my tone inflectionless.

A.J. chuckled. "No, but I honestly think my parents would have preferred that. When I was sixteen and figuring some things out, they came home early from work and saw me wearing a dress."

Cross-dressing wasn't exactly what one would call mainstream, but this was hardly the 1800s. Unless he'd been slitting small animals' throats while he was wearing a dress, I couldn't imagine why A.J.'s parents would have cared.

"And?" I asked.

"And nothing." A.J. shrugged. "My parents are one of those die-hard *our duty is to reproduce for the sake of our country* types, and I guess they realized then that I was never going to marry a woman and make lots of babies. You wouldn't believe the shit they said to me."

A.J. smiled, but I could see the pain in his eyes that hadn't faded all these years later.

"They were planning to send me to some rehab facility in Montana," he continued. "They thought intensive therapy and some *One Flew Over the Cuckoo's Nest* brain zaps would make me normal."

I didn't think I had room to cram any more hurt inside me, but I felt that grip on my heart tighten even more at the thought of what A.J. had gone through.

"I'm sorry," I said, looking at A.J. for the first time. "Your parents should have been there for you. What they did…it's…unforgivable."

A.J. lifted a shoulder. "Conventions are what give society structure and a sense of normalcy people can depend on. It's when people use those conventions as an excuse for turning off rationality and empathy that we've got problems."

"Wise words," I muttered.

"Look. What I'm trying to say is that after my parents did that to me, they stopped being my family. Family doesn't do shit like that."

I gave him a tight nod.

"It was terrifying to leave home at sixteen, but I survived, and it was the best decision I've ever made. I made it all the way from California to Boston, where I found my family…my *real* family." A.J. swept a hand around the room. "These kittens have been by my side through thick and thin, and that's what family does. And you're one of us."

My throat was too tight for me to manage a single word.

"Do you hear me, Nat?" A.J. demanded. "We're your family. And no matter what happens, we'll always have your back."

CHAPTER 29

Feminine voices filled the room as Kaira and Bri came down the stairs.

Kaira glanced at me, and her eyes filled with pain. Whether it was pain on my behalf or her own, I didn't know.

"Bri and I are going to Ma's," Kaira said. "Grandma Tashi had a visit from the dead, but she won't tell me anything over the phone because she thinks it's disrespectful." She rolled her eyes at the ceiling.

I stood up. "I'm coming."

If Grandma Tashi had anything useful to tell us, I wanted to be there to hear it.

Besides, going to Ma's would give me something to do besides sitting in front of a blank computer screen and re-living the past hour.

Kaira gave me a little shrug as she followed Bri toward the door. "Suit yourself."

I turned back to A.J. "Thank you," I said. "For everything."

A.J. nodded and gave me a little wave.

On the way to Ma's, I walked behind Bri and Kaira in silence. I tried to keep my attention on Bri's chatter so I wouldn't have to think about my dad or Kaira. The strangled hold on my heart had eased, leaving behind a dull ache that was almost worse because I didn't think it would ever go away.

Desiree and Cora met us at the door when we came into the house. They both hugged Kaira, said hello to Bri, and then looked at me. Cora gave me a shy smile. Desiree scowled and muttered something that sounded like *murderer*.

"Where's Grandma?" Kaira asked, giving the older of her two cousins a warning look.

"In the kitchen," Cora answered.

We followed the smell of onions cooking in butter, which reminded me of all the Thanksgivings I'd spent with the Hansley clan. They were happy memories. It had been before Kaira stabbed me in the back and my dad disowned me.

Ma abandoned her post at the stove to give us all warm hugs before returning to her cooking. We sat down at the table with Grandma Tashi, who was completely engrossed in the TV. It was the same looping footage I had been seeing the past several days. Reporters hounding the victims' families and speculating about where I might be hiding.

Kaira got up and switched off the TV, ignoring her grandmother's scowl.

Cora sat down at the table next to me, showing me her textbook on Alliance law. I managed a smile and thumbs-up, even though it felt like rocks had settled in my stomach. Desiree sat across from me and glared. I gave her a bright smile, which I'd learned years ago was the fastest way to annoy her.

"What are the dead saying, Grandma?" Kaira asked.

"A man by the name of Bobby Axelrod visited me."

Kaira, Bri, and I exchanged a look.

"Bobby Axelrod visited you?" I asked.

"Isn't that what I just said?" Grandma Tashi gave me a sour look.

"What did he say?" Kaira asked.

"He said," Grandma Tashi closed her eyes. "He's illusioned. It's illusioned." She opened her eyes. "He repeated those words over and over again."

"What does that mean?" Bri asked.

"I'm not an interpreter," Grandma Tashi snapped. "I'm just a Medium."

He's illusioned. It's illusioned.

Bat's chance in hell we'd ever unravel that cryptic message.

"He also said the next murder would also be an illusion."

"Um, okay," Kaira said.

I could tell Kaira wanted to say something sarcastic, but at the look her grandmother gave her, she wisely kept her mouth shut.

"Anything else?" I asked.

"Yes." Grandma Tashi turned the full weight of her glare on me. "Penelope stopped by for a visit. She was crying and begging *you* to leave her alone. Poor girl keeps re-living her murder. I don't think she'll find any peace while her killer walks the streets of our city."

That sick feeling twisted my gut again, and it had nothing to do with the way Grandma Tashi and Desiree were staring at me with accusation in their eyes. Penelope thought I was the one who had taken her life. She was scared and in some kind of dead people-limbo, and there was nothing I could do to help her.

"We've been over this, Grandma," Kaira said, her voice steel. "Gray didn't murder her."

"Did you ever even ask him if he did it?" Desiree piped up. "I mean, not that he'd tell you the truth, but I just think it's *in-sane* that you haven't asked him to his face."

"Alright, that's enough." Ma waved her wooden spoon in the air like she was brandishing a weapon. There was a furious look on her kind face. "This is backyard talk, not kitchen talk."

For a few seconds, no one moved.

"What are you waiting for?" Onions flew off the spoon. "You can continue this ugly conversation in the backyard where it belongs. Now, scat!"

Everyone, including Grandma Tashi, got up from the table and headed for the glass doors that led out into the tiny backyard.

"G-Baby, come here and give me a hand with these veggies."

I hesitated. If Grandma had anything else to say about the dead, I wanted to hear it. But I didn't dare to cross Ma when she was in a mood like this. Reluctantly, I hung back as the others filed outside.

Ma gave me a knife and about a thousand peeled carrots, gesturing for me to get to work.

I almost cut my finger off more than once because my attention kept straying to the argument that seemed to be heating up outside. Kaira was facing off against Grandma Tashi and Desiree. I couldn't hear anything, but I could tell they were shouting. Bri and Cora stood next to Kaira, looking uncomfortable.

I felt another layer of guilt add itself to the mountain I'd already accumulated.

"I'm sorry your family is fighting because of me," I told Ma.

"I've always thought of you as one of our family, G-Baby. You know that."

I nodded.

"Yours might be the name on every Mag's lips, but this simmering anger…this distrust…comes from a time long before you were even a twinkle in your parents' eyes." She stopped stirring her onions and looked out the glass windows. "Desiree's scared. And when people get scared, they have a tendency to listen to the loudest voice, even if that voice is dead wrong."

Valencia Stark.

"I'm afraid what you're seeing here is just a little slice of what's happening with Mags everywhere," Ma continued. "If these murders keep up much longer, Boston won't be any different from the rest of the country."

"I'm going to fix this," I vowed. "I just wish I wasn't the reason why Kai and Grandma Tashi are fighting."

"Kaira thinks you're worth fighting for. When it comes to the people she cares about most, she's the most loyal person in the world."

"Loyal." I heard the twinge of bitterness in my voice, and winced. "I just meant—"

Ma gave me a penetrating look and then sighed. "I know what you meant."

I stopped cutting carrots. "You do?"

A panicked look passed over Ma's face. Her gaze shifted from me to the backyard.

"Ma?" I asked, my pulse starting to race for no reason I could name.

"Nothing, G-Baby. Forget I said anything."

"What aren't you telling me?" My voice came out rougher and more demanding than I meant it to. "Please," I said more softly.

"Lord, I've held my tongue for three years. But I can't stay silent when my babies are hurting."

I didn't breathe for fear I'd somehow make Ma change her mind about whatever she was about to tell me.

"Tell me one thing first," Ma said, putting down her spoon and turning to give me her full attention. "Are you still in love with her?"

My knife clattered onto the cutting board.

Before I could form even a single word, Ma let out a heavy sigh. "That's what I thought."

"How long have you known?" I whispered.

"Since Thanksgiving, the year Kaira turned eighteen," Ma replied. "My Aunt Mimi was on the phone, and I came looking for Kaira. I saw you kissing under the crabapple tree." Her lip quirked in what might have been either amusement or disgust. "And it wasn't no chaste kiss, neither."

My face heated. I remembered that Thanksgiving, although not that specific kiss. Kai and I had just started having sex, and we couldn't keep our hands off each other.

"Kai never told me you knew," I managed.

More lies. More betrayal from someone I should have been able to trust without question.

"At the time, Kaira didn't know I knew. I figured you were just two teenagers being teenagers, and that you'd both move on soon enough. Maybe if I'd stepped in sooner, things mighta turned out different."

Sadness and regret pooled in Ma's dark eyes.

"What do you mean?" I forced out the words.

"You know I raised Kaira to make her own choices and own the consequences of those choices, just like your daddy taught you."

I nodded slowly.

"It was after Kaira's Test, before I knew she had decided to go unMarked. You had just gotten into the BSMU. She came home in the middle of the school day. With the way she was crying, I was sure there'd been a school shooting or something. She looked…broken. It ripped my heart right out."

I tried to swallow around the knot in my throat.

"She told me what she'd done to your daddy. She was crying so hard I could barely understand a word she was saying, but she said it was the only way to give you back your future."

"What?"

My knees had turned to gelatin. I could barely make sense of any of what Ma was saying.

"I think Kaira wanted to give you a life she knew you couldn't have if you kept on loving her. In her mind, doing something that would make you hate her was the only way to let you have that life."

"That makes no sense." I gripped the side of the counter until my knuckles went bloodless.

"You were made for big things, G-Baby, and once you started to climb the ranks in the Alliance like we all knew you would, you'd become a public figure. You weren't going to be able to have a big career and Kaira. Eventually, you would have had to choose. I think Kaira was trying to take the burden of that decision away from you and put it on her own shoulders."

"No," I said, because it was the only word that would come.

"A piece of her heart died after that. I don't think I've seen a real smile on my daughter's face since." Ma brushed away her own tears that had started to fall. "Of course, she had to bury all those feelings deep inside where no one but her Ma would see them." She stared out the window. "Kaira cried herself to sleep every night for months."

I was shaking my head. I remembered Kaira's dry-eyed, determined expression when she told me what she'd done. I remembered the way she let me walk out the door without a single apology or explanation. She'd just let me go.

I couldn't imagine her crying herself to sleep over me. I couldn't stand it…the thought of her, lying alone in the dark, with the same gut-wrenching pain that woke me gasping in the middle of the night. I couldn't imagine both of us, apart and defenseless against the pain of losing each other. It was enough to drive me insane.

"I ain't saying what she did was right or wrong," Ma continued. "But she did it outta love for you, G."

At that moment, the glass doors opened and the rest of the Hansley clan came back inside.

"Smith called," Bri told me. "Valencia left the police station. She's on the move."

CHAPTER 30

Bri and Kaira were talking about Valencia, but my mind was in too much of a fog for me to contribute.

When we got back to the house, it was a hive of activity. Michael and Yutika were helping Smith to pack his electronics into the van. A.J. and Bri were watching the tablet that showed Valencia's blinking tracker dot.

"Valencia stopped by her house to scurry around like a hamster in a ball, and now she's headed out to meet Big Bad Boss," A.J. said, filling us in. "At least, that's where we assume she's going. We're out of here in t-minus five seconds."

Kaira put the trays of food Ma had given us down on the counter and grabbed the van's keys from the hook by the door.

"Hold on," I said, speaking for the first time since we'd left Ma's.

When Yutika came back into the house, I said, "I need a car." It came out so gruff, I added, "Please."

"Sure," Yutika said, pulling out her sketch pad out of her back pocket.

Kaira raised an eyebrow at me.

"What kind do you want?" Yutika asked, flipping open her pad.

"Anything that drives," I said.

When Kaira headed for the van, I grabbed her elbow and pulled her away from the others. "We need to talk. Alone." It came out as a growl.

As soon as Yutika was finished with the drawing and a sleek gray sedan was idling outside, I gestured to Kaira, making it clear that was where we were headed.

"We'll follow you," I told the others, who gave me a curious look but didn't ask any questions.

Kaira didn't ask what was going on, either. Instead, she just put in her earpiece and told Smith, "Update me if there's anything we need to know."

"Valencia's on Western Ave heading toward 90," Bri said, her gaze fixed on the tablet as the others piled into the van.

I waited until Kaira illusioned me before going out the door and heading for the car.

"You're driving," I told Kaira. I didn't want to have to pay attention to anything except for her.

"Bossy," she muttered as she headed around to the driver's side.

Kaira stayed silent as I stared out the window and wrestled with everything in my head. Every so often, Smith's voice would come across our earpieces, announcing a turn Valencia had taken. When we got onto 90 heading west into the suburbs, I finally spoke.

"Turn it off," I told her, motioning to her microphone. I did the same for my own.

Kaira did as I asked, and then she glanced at me. "Are you going to tell me what's put that look on your face?"

"Ma told me."

Kaira's face paled. "What?"

In the window's reflection, I saw my illusion flicker before she got her emotions under control. Her surprise turned to anger in a heartbeat.

"She promised she'd never say anything. Why did she tell you?"

"The better question is why didn't you?"

"That would have defeated the point," Kaira snapped.

"And what was the point?" My anger rose to match hers.

"To give you what you needed."

I ground my teeth. "So, you're trying to tell me that my dad almost killing himself was what I needed?"

"I told you, I had no idea he'd do that," Kaira said. She reached up to brush her hair back, and I saw her hand was trembling. "I swear to you, if I had thought it would turn out like that, I would have found another way." She let out a shuddering breath. "I just wanted them to do a small investigation—not enough to hurt his career, just enough to make you mad enough at me to—"

"Never talk to you again?" I demanded. "I'm not some insane stalker, Kai. If you wanted to break up, you could have just told me you *wanted to break up* instead of going all psycho Illusionist in my dad's office."

"Don't you get it, Gray? I didn't want to break up with you! And if I lied to your face, you would have seen right through me." She wiped away the tears sliding down her cheeks.

"Then why lie at all? What gave you the right to make some arbitrary decision about my…our…future?"

"Remember that article the Globe published about you when we graduated high school?"

I threw up my hands. "I don't know. Vaguely?"

"Director Remwald's Successor Identified at Age 18," she said.

I nodded, remembering the bolded title of the news article. "So what? It wasn't some kind of premonition. It was a slow news week."

Kaira shook her head. "You taped it on your wall. That's when I knew. It was what you wanted. It was what you deserved, and you'd never have it if you stayed with me."

I was speechless.

"Don't you remember the fights we used to have about the Alliance?" Kaira continued. "You believe in everything they stand for, and I—"

"I believed in us," I said, my voice cracking. "This isn't about the Alliance. It's about what you did to my dad—"

"It is about the Alliance!" More silent tears tracked down Kaira's cheek. She swiped them away with a furious motion. "Stop being ignorant for two seconds and use your brain, Gray. Don't you get it? Your job was going to be to persecute people like me. Being with me was a complete contradiction to everything you believe. It would have destroyed you."

I raked a hand through my hair. "Even if it did, that was a decision for us to make together. You had no right to go do something completely insane in some misguided effort to save me."

"It was the only way," she said. "Either you would have picked me and given up on your dreams, or you would have chosen the Alliance and been destroyed with guilt for breaking my heart. Both decisions would have hurt you, and I couldn't bear it. I thought if you hated me, it would be easier for both of us."

"And was it…*easy* for you?" I bit out.

Kaira stayed silent for several seconds. Finally, she spoke.

"It feels like a thousand-pound weight on my chest every second of every day. It's even there when I sleep."

"Kai." The thought of her hurting like that, the way I'd been hurting for three years, was too much for me.

Kaira looked at me. "You know how everyone always says they want to change the world?" She laughed a little. "I knew from when we were kids that you were actually going to do it. It's one of the reasons I love you, and it was why I couldn't be the reason you left all that behind."

"It wasn't an either/or," I argued, even though all the anger had gone out of me. "I could have contributed to the Alliance and been with you."

"That's the part you never understood, Gray." She smiled without humor. "You can't accept that there's any problem out there that can't be solved with some hard work or the right approach. But this problem didn't have a solution like that. If we kept going like we were going, someone would have figured out about us. You would have either needed to go into hiding with me or face execution." She paused long enough to take a breath. "I chose this life of existing on the fringe of society, but it isn't for you. You were made to be in the thick of the Alliance. I loved you too much to take you away from all of that and just keep you for myself."

"You're wrong," I said, shaking my head.

"What would you have done when I brought unMarked refugees into our house, Gray?"

"I—" I looked at Kaira. "I don't know," I said honestly.

We didn't speak for several seconds.

"Everything's different now," I said, not knowing if it would make her feel better or worse. "I can't go back to my old life. I *am* one of your refugees now."

Kaira glanced at me, letting me see the fierce expression in her eyes.

"I promised you'd get your life back," she said. "We're going to clear your name, and then you'll have everything you lost and then some."

I thought about that. I thought about the tremendous sense of accomplishment I'd felt during my last weeks at the BSMU, and the way it felt when I got the call that I'd gotten my dream job right out of college.

And then I remembered the aching, drowning sensation that came after one of my dreams about Kaira. I thought about the part of myself that had disappeared the day I told her to get out of my life.

I had no idea what to say. I didn't know how I was supposed to feel. I was angry at her, and at myself, but I couldn't even really say why.

What she was saying changed everything…and at the same time, it changed nothing. She had done what she'd done for my sake, but she'd still ruined my dad's life in the process. I couldn't forgive that. Could I?

"What the hell am I supposed to do with this, Kaira?"

"The same thing you should have done three years ago," she replied, gripping the steering wheel and staring straight ahead. "Forget about me. Climb the ranks in the Alliance and become Director. Make the world better. Fall in love with a Nat."

"I already fell in love," I said. "I never stopped loving you."

Kaira sucked in a breath.

"Gray—"

"Are you guys seeing this?" Smith's voice came across our earpieces.

I hadn't even glanced at our surroundings. Now, I forced myself to look, mostly because I couldn't stomach the stricken, heartbroken look on Kaira's face.

We were on a quiet residential street lined with houses that were easily worth five-million or more. I saw huge brick and stone mansions with corvettes and BMWs parked in the drive. Most of the driveways were gated and had security cameras.

Kaira drew in a deep breath and switched on her mic. "Where are we?"

"Old Chestnut Hill," Smith replied. "Valencia's two houses down, and her car just disappeared."

CHAPTER 31

What do you mean, disappeared? Did Valencia find the tracker?" I asked, before remembering my mic was still turned off. I flipped the little switch and repeated my question.

"Don't think so," Smith said. "I can still sense the tracker. I think the issue is that the plot of land where Valencia's located doesn't show up on satellite imagery or seem to exist anywhere else for that matter."

"How is that possible?" I demanded.

"Must be another Techie on site," Smith replied.

"Okay, we're coming over," Kaira said.

Kaira and I didn't speak or look at each other as we got out of the car and crossed the street. When we got into the van, Bri and Smith were in the midst of a heated discussion about Smith's real name.

"Just your initials, then," Bri wheedled.

"Government spies are everywhere," was Smith's only reply.

"*Anyway*," A.J. loudly interrupted. "What's the plan?"

"Smith and I designed a teeny tiny camera," Yutika said, holding up a camera that was about the size of a button.

"It'll give us audio and visual, so we can see what's going on inside the property," Smith added. "And it'll record everything so we'll have that as evidence."

"Ooh, come to Papa." A.J. waved his hand, and the camera lifted off Yutika's palm and hovered in the air.

"Will that work if there's a Techie on the property?" Kaira asked.

If the other Techie was even close to as powerful as Smith, they would cancel out each other's abilities. It was the way it worked with Magics who had the same ability and were close in level. If that was the case with Smith and this new Techie, we'd be working blind.

"This Techie's only a Level 5 or 6," Smith said, his eyes still closed. "We're good."

The van door opened without anyone touching it, and the camera zoomed out. I lost sight of it in the sunlight.

One of Smith's laptops shifted around so the screen was facing us. I didn't know if it was Smith or A.J. controlling it, but the screen flickered, and then a dizzying blur of images came to life.

"Holy guacamole," A.J. exclaimed, his hands still moving through the air as he controlled the camera's flight. "That's the prettiest house I've ever seen."

The camera was looking down on the estate that was blocked from view of the naked eye because of all the trees. The image on the screen showed an enormous house. I counted fifteen windows, and that was just in the front.

"There!" several voices shouted at once.

The camera moved to hover in front of a window on the first floor. Valencia, easily recognizable in a hot pink dress that looked more like a tent with sleeves, was sitting at a table across from a man. Without her hair plastered down from her rain, Valencia's cherry-red mop made her look like she'd recently stuck her finger in an outlet. More importantly, it blocked our view of the man sitting across from her.

"I need to see our guy if I'm going to be able to look for matches," Smith grumbled.

"I can try opening the window a crack to get the camera inside," A.J. said. "But if the window squeaks, they'll notice."

"Do it," Kaira said.

"Here's to hoping these people believe in WD-40," A.J. muttered.

We all held our breath.

The window slid open such a small amount that the two people sitting at the table didn't even glance at it.

"Alright," A.J. murmured. "In you go."

The wobbling image on the screen sharpened. I ignored Valencia and stared at the man. Thinning white hair. Light blue eyes. Average height and weight. He looked…unnoteworthy. For some illogical reason, it pissed me off that someone so harmless-looking could be responsible for wrecking my life.

And instigating a civil war.

"Anyone recognize this man?" Kaira asked, her voice quiet.

We all shook our heads.

The image on the screen minimized, and then a database of faces popped up beside it. I watched as faces flicked across the screen too fast for me to get a good look at any of them.

"No matches in any police databases or Alliance records," Smith said.

"So, he's either a Nat without a criminal record, or he's unMarked," Yutika said.

"Can you check if he has a driver's license or passport?" I asked.

"Already did. No matches."

"We need to hear what they're saying," I said, stating the obvious.

A crackling sound filled the van.

"I can't guarantee our cops will be the only ones in the room," Valencia's voice said, as clearly as if she was in the van with us.

"Do you think the money I'm paying you was just a donation?" the man asked. "I'm paying you to make sure nothing goes wrong. I've already provided you with all of the necessary DNA evidence. There cannot be anyone else examining the body before it's cremated."

I started. I could have sworn I'd never seen this man before, but now, there seemed to be something familiar about him. I squinted at the image on Smith's laptop, but nothing about the man's appearance had changed. I was sure I'd never seen him before.

So why did I have the nagging sense that I knew him?

"But wouldn't it just be easier to do one more person like we did the oth-ahs?" Valencia asked, her voice taking on the hint of a whine. "Or you could just do another student like you did Penelope. Maybe we could even kill Graysen Gald-ah himself to get another Nat into the mix—"

Everyone in the van looked at me. I gripped the edge of my seat, grinding the fabric down into the metal frame to keep my anger in check.

"No," the man replied. "There is no other murder that will throw the city into bedlam faster. We need everyone scared and bloodthirsty enough to want a war."

I forced my fury down so I could focus on the conversation.

There was shuffling, but Valencia's body blocked our view of whatever the man passed across the table to her.

"I took the liberty of acquiring the crime photos in advance so your cops can get the body out of there faster. Remember, I want the body processed and cremated in under an hour."

We all exchanged a puzzled look. *What were they talking about?*

And what was it about this man that was seeming more and more familiar by the minute?

"Why the rush?" Valencia asked. "We have two more days until the vote."

"I'm not paying you to ask questions," the man snapped.

There it was again. Something about the authority and underlying threat in the man's expression. But no matter how hard I stared at the man's image, I didn't recognize him. And it wasn't like me to forget a face.

Valencia slid the folder the man gave her into her purse before standing up. "Well then, I guess I'll see you in two days at the vote."

"No mistakes, Valencia. All of our plans hinge on this final murder going precisely as it was meant to." The man steepled his fingers in front of him as he studied Valencia. "You will make an excellent first lieutenant for the new regime we're building. I would hate to have to replace you."

Valencia bristled, but with obvious effort, relaxed. Her high-pitched little laugh filled the van. "By this time on Tuesday, you'll be calling me Direct-ah."

"You may be the face of this organization, Valencia, but I am the neck." The man's voice dropped another octave. "You do nothing, you say nothing, unless I tell you to. Never forget that."

The angle of the camera shifted, and I caught a combination of fear and irritation flash across the Rain Maker's face.

"Get that camera out of there before he notices it," Kaira ordered.

"I'll get whatever that man just gave Valencia," Michael said, unbuckling his seatbelt.

"Forget it," Smith said. "There's at least one guard booth on the property, and I can sense cameras everywhere."

Kaira looked out the window, her attention fixated on something. When I followed the direction of her gaze, I saw she was looking at two squirrels that were chasing each other up a tree. She turned back and quirked her lip at Michael.

"How do you feel about small rodents?" she asked.

Michael's face paled.

Yutika clapped her hands in delight. "Ohmygosh, can you make him into a chipmunk?"

I blinked, and then Michael was gone. In his place was a chipmunk.

"You're *adorbs!*" Bri exclaimed.

"This is ridiculous," the chipmunk muttered in Michael's voice as it examined one of its paws.

"Wait for me," Kaira said as the chipmunk reached for the door handle. And then she turned into a chipmunk, too.

"I'm coming with you," I said, although I would much prefer to be a dog than a chipmunk. Or maybe a hawk.

"Me too," Bri said.

"Just me and Michael this time," Chipmunk Kaira told us. "I'm not as good at animal illusions, and the more I have to track, the harder they are to maintain."

"Do your earpieces and mics still work?" Smith asked, eyeing the chipmunks dubiously.

"They still work," Kaira's voice replied. One of the chipmunks put its paw to its tiny ear. "We're still the same people we were before, we're just appearing to be chipmunks to the rest of you."

"Alright, then," Smith said. "Just don't get the urge to start gnawing on any of those wires."

"That's not how illusions work, Smith," Kaira replied. "Although, I am a little a hungry. Maybe I'll just take a nibble."

Smith scowled. I tried and failed to hide my grin. Chipmunk Kaira saluted us before she and Michael jumped out of the van.

"Can we follow them with that camera?" I asked A.J. and Smith. There was no way I was letting Kaira get anywhere near the two people who were responsible for at least four murders…soon to be five…if I couldn't keep an eye on her.

In answer, A.J. waved a hand, and the tiny camera zoomed out of the van. We watched on Smith's screen as the chipmunks crossed the street.

A.J. manipulated the camera high enough that we lost sight of the chipmunks in the grass, but we had a clear view of Valencia coming down the long walkway to where her car was parked.

Valencia jerked to a stop and spun around, like someone had just touched her arm.

"Who's there?" she demanded.

"Valencia, what did that man give you?" Michael's deep voice came across our earpieces.

"Doctored crime scene photos," she answered immediately. She was still looking around for the source of the voice, but her wild expression had turned to one of peaceful contentment.

"Please put the folder on the ground in front of you," Michael said.

Valencia didn't hesitate to do as she was told. A.J. re-positioned the camera so we could see Chipmunk Michael paw at the folder's seal. Chipmunk Kaira stood behind him and looked over his shoulder as he emptied the contents. Photos spilled out onto the grass.

We all exchanged a look of horror.

The pictures showed a man, covered in blood and lying on top of a blood-stained rug. His body was mangled, but his face was untouched, so there was no mistaking the dead man in the photo.

It was Director Edwardian Remwald.

CHAPTER 32

Several things happened in quick succession.

The front door of the house opened, and the man who had been talking with Valencia stepped out onto the porch. I blinked, convinced my eyes were playing tricks on me. The man flickered, the way illusions did before they disappeared.

And then the old man was gone. In his place was a very-much alive and blood-free Director Remwald.

Someone in the van gasped. Bri shrieked, before slapping a hand over her mouth. A cold dread settled in me as I tried to make sense of what I was seeing.

Before I could try to puzzle it out, the two chipmunks on the grass turned back into Kaira and Michael. They looked at each other and then down at themselves. Kaira shook her head and said, "I can't."

Whatever had just happened to their illusions, it seemed to only be affecting Kaira's magic. Valencia was still standing motionless with that placid expression on her face.

And then I understood. Remwald was an Animate Illusionist. He had to be; it was the only explanation for why his and Kaira's illusions had faltered, while everyone else's magic remained unaffected.

"Kaira, he's an Animate Illusionist," I said into my mic.

Michael stared in surprise at Remwald, who was still watching them from the porch. As soon as Michael's attention was turned away from her, Valencia's glazed-over eyes sharpened.

"Michael," Yutika warned, holding her mic up to her lips.

But all of Michael's attention was still moving back and forth between the Director and Kaira.

Valencia reached into her purse. Moving faster than I would have thought the woman capable of, she pulled out a can and sprayed its contents into Michael's eyes.

Yutika screamed as Michael doubled over, clawing at his eyes.

Pepper spray, I thought, but it wasn't a coherent thought because all of my attention was on the five security guards racing across the lawn with guns raised.

"Kaira!" I hurled open the van door and ran.

Someone called my name, but I didn't look back. I crashed through the bushes nearest to the driveway, barely noticing as the branches tore at my clothes and skin. I stumbled out of the trees and onto the lawn. I saw Kaira rip off her sweater and press to Michael's face.

"Get down!" I yelled.

I heard the *pop pop pop* of gunfire as I ran for them. I heard Kaira's scream in my ear. I saw her fall.

"Kai!"

I threw myself onto the ground in front of her, using my own body to cover hers.

Kaira screamed again.

I hunched over her, trying to protect as much of her as I could. I flinched as the sound of bullets hitting something metallic and impenetrable came from somewhere behind us. I turned just enough to see Bri, her titanium armor in place, as she stood between us and the guards. The bullets pinged off her skin and ricocheted back at the guards, who were shouting as they tried to dodge their own bullets.

I had the vague understanding that we'd all be dead if it wasn't for Bri. Then I saw Kaira's stomach, and every other thought fled from my mind. Blood had soaked through her tank top and was covering her hands, which were pressed over a wound. A gunshot wound.

My body wanted to freeze in panic, but there was no time. I had to get her out of here.

"Come on!" Bri yelled. "I'll cover you."

I lifted Kaira in my arms and got to my feet. My chest constricted as she screamed in agony. I felt her blood soaking into my own shirt. My vision started to darken, and I had to force myself to focus.

I couldn't afford to lose my shit. Kai needed me.

Out of the corner of my eye, I saw Bri lift Michael over her shoulder. He was easily twice her size, but she held him with one arm as she used the other to gesture to me. I followed behind her, trying not to jostle Kaira when even the smallest movement was torture for her.

"Hold on, Kai," I told her as I ran.

"Come on, come on!" A.J. gestured frantically at us from the van.

I had the sense the security guards were recovering and preparing to renew their assault, but I didn't look back.

I passed Kaira to Bri before climbing in. I glanced back at the house once. The man who looked just like Director Remwald was standing on the porch, watching me. A smile full of menace crossed his face.

CHAPTER 33

"Michael," Yutika gasped from the driver's seat.

"Drive!" Five voices shouted at her.

Kaira was stretched out on the floor of the van with her head in my lap.

"Put pressure on the wound," Smith barked.

I yanked off my shirt and threw it to Bri, who was kneeling next to Kaira. When Bri started to press the shirt to her stomach, Kaira screamed.

"It's really bad," Bri said in a trembling voice.

"Find the nearest Mag hospital," I yelled at Smith, even though the Techie was sitting right behind me.

"We can't take her to a hospital," A.J. said. "We're unMarked."

"I don't give a—"

"Calm down," Yutika ordered as the van screeched around the corner. "You're making me hysterical!"

"We just need to think this through," Bri said, knocking her titanium fist against her temple.

"Mag hospital. Now!"

If Kai wasn't on my lap, I'd wrench Yutika out from behind the wheel and drive myself.

"We'll all be arrested," Michael said, his voice infuriatingly calm. "We can't take her to a hospital."

Kaira's screams had turned to moans of pain that had me on the brink of madness.

"I know a guy," Smith said before I lost my mind entirely. "He's not exactly Board certified, but he knows what he's doing."

"Then what the hell are we waiting for?" I snarled.

"He might not help. He…doesn't like people."

"I can take care of that," Michael said, rubbing at his eyes from the front.

"You sure you can Whisper when you're like this?" Yutika asked, glancing over at him as she chewed on her lip.

"Drive!" I roared.

Yutika flinched, and then she floored the gas.

The van blew through a stop sign. I tightened my arms around Kaira as a car coming in the opposite direction slammed on their brakes. There was a screech of tires and a blaring horn.

"Sorry!" Yutika cried as we raced past.

As if things couldn't get any worse, the horn was replaced by sirens and the flash of red-and-blue lights.

"Oh no, what do we do?!" Yutika asked, her face full of panic.

"Pull over," Michael commanded in a gruff voice.

He scrubbed at his eyes, which were bloodshot and still streaming tears.

A heavyset cop strolled out of the squad car, one hand resting on his weapon.

"Hands on the wheel—" he began.

"There's nothing wrong here, Officer," Michael said, leaning into the front seat and squinting at the cop as tears continued to stream down his face. "And you're going to give us a police escort so we can get to where we're going faster."

"That's right," the cop agreed, giving Michael a worshipping sort of look. "What's the address, Sir?"

Smith gave the cop an address before disappearing behind his laptop screen, muttering about the police and conspiracies.

The cop got back in his car, and Yutika floored it to keep up as the squad car blasted a path through traffic for us.

"Gray," Kaira moaned. "It hurts."

"I know, babe," I murmured, brushing her hair back from her face. "Just hold on. We're gonna get you help."

"He's like me," she said, slurring her words a little.

"Shh," I told her. "We're almost there."

"Don't let me go," she whispered, her eyes closing.

"Never," I swore, cupping her face gently with my free hand that wasn't already around her.

A.J. cleared his throat. I spared him a glance. A.J. stared meaningfully at Bri, who was giving me a strange look.

Like I cared about that right now.

"I think some music will calm us all down," A.J. announced loudly, and the radio began to play. I felt the Telekinetic's glare, but I didn't look away from Kaira. The others could have their suspicions.

"How much farther?" I growled.

"Not much," Smith replied, which had been the same answer he'd given the last three times I'd asked.

We were still going south, away from the city. And Kai was still bleeding. I had thought her screams were the worst sound I'd ever heard in my life. But she was quiet now, and that was worse.

Her caramel skin had taken on an ashy hue, and aside from an occasional shudder and incoherent words, she lay motionless in my lap.

"Just hold on," I begged her. "We're almost there."

I had nothing to do except hold her unconscious form and watch as blood continued to spread through the shirt pressed over her stomach. I didn't know much about medicine, but I knew there were vital organs in that area. Had the bullet hit one of them? How much blood could a person lose and still survive?

I kept one hand curled around her neck to feel her pulse. It was erratic, fluttering frantically one moment and then beating too slowly the next. I was losing my mind.

This was my fault. If it hadn't been for me, the Six would never have gone to that house. It was my fault that Michael got pepper sprayed…my fault that Kai was….

I couldn't even think the words.

I glanced out the window and saw that the city landscape had been replaced with long, uninterrupted swaths of forest. We passed a sign for the Blue Hills Reservation. The cop car in front of us swerved onto the shoulder. Yutika rolled down her window, and Michael leaned over her to whisper to the cop.

"Thanks," Michael told the man, who was looking at Michael's red face with a blank expression. "Go back to Boston now. Forget you ever saw us."

A puzzled look came over the cop's face. He rolled up his window and made a U-turn, going back toward the city.

"We're on the side of the road," I said, looking around.

"You think I'm going to lead the cops straight to one of the few places that's still off the grid?"

I ground my teeth, feeling murderous in a way I never had before. "Smith, I swear to God, if your paranoia keeps her like this for a second longer than she has to be—"

"Just relax," Smith snapped.

The Techie watched the squad car until it was out of sight. Then, he directed Yutika off the highway and onto a barely-paved road. I thought it would be agony for Kaira as the van dipped in and out of potholes, but she didn't react.

"Come on, Kai," I begged her. "Stay with me."

We reached an unmarked entrance that had overgrown bushes in front that scraped against the van as we bounced and jostled down the narrow driveway. It was the type of place that, if you didn't already know it was there, would be impossible to find.

I bit my cheek until I tasted blood to keep from shouting at Yutika to drive more smoothly. I knew none of what had happened was anyone's fault but my own.

I forced myself to focus on the fluttering pulse in Kaira's neck. It was weaker than it had been, but I could still feel it.

She was still with me.

The driveway led deeper into the trees until the road was no longer visible.

"You sure you aren't taking us to some axe murderer's?" Bri asked, sounding nervous as she stared out the window. Her hands and sleeves were rust-colored from Kaira's blood. Fresh blood was still leaking from the wound. My shirt was saturated with it. My stomach roiled.

There was a mansion at the end of the drive. It must have once been magnificent, but now, the dark brick of the house was barely visible through the trees and weeds that had run rampant all over the yard.

"Stop here," Smith commanded, even though we hadn't quite reached the house. "And stay in the car. I'll be right back."

"I'll come," Michael said.

"No. Just me."

"Hurry up," I commanded.

We all watched as Smith got out, walked a few yards, and then stepped over something invisible. Before he reached the house, he ducked under something else. Instead of going up to the front door, he walked around the side of the house and disappeared behind a weeping willow tree.

"How's she doing?" Michael asked, turning around to look at Kaira.

I gave him a helpless shrug.

"This is my fault," Bri said, her lower lip quivering. "If I'd just gone with you—"

"This isn't your fault," four voices said at once.

"It's mine," I said, my voice breaking.

Kaira felt so impossibly fragile in my arms. Her skin felt cool, although that might have been because of the ice filling my own veins.

I couldn't stop remembering the way I'd found my dad, curled on his side and unmoving, after he'd swallowed enough pills to kill him.

Dad was fine, I reminded myself. *Kai will be, too.*

Smith reappeared.

"All electronics need to stay in the van," he said. "Phones, mics, earpieces, and anything else you've got on you."

The others tossed their phones back into the car.

"Now, can we go in?" I ground out, far beyond the limits of my patience.

"There's a trip wire about twenty feet in front of you," Smith said calmly, like it was normal to have tripwires on one's front lawn. "Stay behind me and step where I step."

"Let me carry her," Bri told me, blowing on her fists until she turned into titanium.

I didn't want to let Kaira go for even a second, but her unconscious form was awkward to hold, and Bri could probably carry her more gently than I could. Reluctantly, I nodded.

I saw the gleam of the tripwire only after Smith squatted down and pointed it out. We stepped over it, and then under another wire closer to the house.

"Don't tell us this is your summer retreat," Yutika grumbled at Smith. She held Michael's hand, guiding him, since he could still barely keep his eyes open.

"I haven't been back here in a while," came Smith's gruff reply.

There was a narrow, overgrown path that wound around the side of the house. The front door was right in front of us, but I bit my tongue and concentrated on holding back the branches so they didn't scrape against Kaira.

When I looked up, an older man was standing in the doorway. He was watching us with eyes full of grim suspicion. Even in my distracted, panicked state, I couldn't help but notice how the man looked like an older version of Smith. He had the same too-thin frame, the same pointed chin and large, straight nose. He even had the same shoulder-length, greasy hair, except his was white instead of brown.

"Papa Smith," A.J. said in a falsely cheerful voice. "What a pleasure."

Smith grumbled something incoherent.

"If you ever mention this place to anyone, I'll have to kill you," Older Smith said, speaking for the first time.

"Maybe we should have listened to Graysen about the hospital," Bri whispered.

"At least if he tries to chain us in the basement you can break down the whole house," Yutika said in a voice loud enough for the older man to hear.

"Smith says you can all be trusted," Older Smith said. "And for your information, I don't have a basement. But if I wanted to imprison you, I could just slow your heart rates until you couldn't move."

"Why the hell are we here?" I hissed at Smith, not caring if his dad heard. I was beyond pleasantries or anything else that didn't involve fixing Kaira. "I'm not letting some quack touch her."

"Boy, I'm a Level 8 Mender," Older Smith said, standing a little straighter. He squinted at Kaira, who looked far too still in Bri's arms. "The bullet hit her liver. There's significant internal bleeding, and she's got about an hour before she's dead."

The world turned dark for an instant. Something came around my waist. Some part of me was aware that if it wasn't for A.J., I'd be on the ground right now. The other part of me was repeating the man's words in my head over and over.

"If we're done with the interview portion of today, I'd like to get to work." Older Smith made a sweeping gesture at the door.

My knees were weak as we followed Older Smith inside. A.J. kept his arm around me, supporting me even though I was far bigger.

Kaira had risked everything for me…and for what? So I could have my reputation and job back? And I'd let her. I'd let her take risk after risk for something that didn't count for jack compared to her life.

I wanted to fall to my knees and beg for her forgiveness.

I didn't have time to wonder at why the house was lit only with lanterns and candles. We followed Older Smith up dark wood stairs that creaked and groaned with age. We entered a large bedroom that looked normal, except for the fact that the only light came through the windows. There was a light switch beside the door that had been taped over.

There was a bed in the center of the room covered in a white quilt. The place looked clean enough, but there was no medical equipment or anything else that would be needed to treat a bullet wound. There was no IV pole or bags of blood cooling in a fridge. In addition to about a thousand other things, Kaira was going to need a blood transfusion.

My panic reached a fever pitch when I realized I didn't know Kaira's blood type. *Why the hell hadn't I ever asked her about it?*

"Calm down or I'm going to tell Michael to Whisper you into unconsciousness until she's fixed," A.J. muttered to me.

I hadn't moved or made a sound, but somehow, A.J. had read me right.

"This isn't your fault. Stop berating yourself," he continued.

It was my fault, but I planned to beat myself up about it later. Right now, all that mattered was fixing Kaira. I wouldn't divert any of my attention to anything else until that was done.

Releasing a shuddering breath, I gave A.J. a tight nod.

Older Smith grabbed a stack of towels, spread them over the bed, and gestured for Bri to lay Kaira down. Without taking his eyes off Kaira, Older Smith said, "Start flushing out your eyes with this." He held out a small black bottle to Michael. "That pepper spray was magically enhanced, and it'll turn you blind if you don't get it all out."

Yutika whimpered, and then she yanked Michael out of the room toward the bathroom across the hall.

Kaira's eyes fluttered open, and she gasped in pain. My heart was in my throat.

"Everyone out," Older Smith commanded.

Everyone else looked at Smith, who nodded and headed back through the door. I stayed where I was beside the bed.

Kaira moaned.

"You too," Older Smith told me.

"I won't get in your way," I said. *Unless I need to.*

"Graysen, come on," Smith said.

"I'm not leaving her." My voice came out savage and unrecognizable.

"Oh, they've got this protective brother-sister thing going on," A.J. said in a too-bright voice. "They practically grew up together."

"Gray." Kai's voice was little more than a whisper. She reached out a trembling hand for me.

"I'm right here." I knelt next to the bed so she'd be able to see me and wrapped both of my hands around hers.

Older Smith huffed in annoyance, but he waved the others out, telling them to shut the door behind them. As soon as it was just the three of us, Older Smith knelt down on the floor on the other side of the bed and started peeling my blood-soaked shirt from Kaira's stomach.

I swallowed my panic and questions about what this man was planning to do to her. It went against my every instinct, but I forced myself to stay silent.

Older Smith pulled up Kaira's shirt and stared down at the wound. I looked at the bloodied, mangled skin. Horror threatened to eat me alive.

My fault. The words circled around and around. I gripped Kaira's hands and pressed them to my lips to keep from screaming.

Older Smith sighed, rolled his shoulders, and then raised his hands so they hovered a few inches above Kaira's stomach. He closed his eyes.

I'd never had cause to learn anything about Menders, and I had no idea if this was standard practice. I hated being so ignorant…so helpless….

The temperature in the room started to rise. A gentle hum, like the buzz of a machine or a hive full of insects, filled my ears. Older Smith's breathing got louder, like he was physically exerting himself, even though he hadn't moved.

Kaira gasped and opened her eyes. "It hurts, Gray." Tears were spilling down her cheeks.

"Just a little longer." I kissed her hands. "You're doing so good."

"Quiet," Older Smith hissed.

Kaira's eyes rolled back in her head and her whole body went rigid. I bit down on my cheek. I tasted the iron tang of blood in my mouth and smelled it on the air. It was everywhere, soaking into the towels beneath Kaira and on the heap of bloody shirts on the floor.

I flinched when a small *plunk* interrupted the silence. I looked down at the floor and felt my jaw drop. Older Smith hadn't moved—hadn't touched Kai—and yet the bloodied bullet had just wriggled itself free from Kaira's stomach and fallen onto the floor. It rolled across the wood until it came to rest beside the pile of bloody clothes.

I stared at the older man. His eyes were squeezed shut, and his forehead was beaded with perspiration. I swallowed the questions that were on the tip of my tongue.

Will she be alright? What's the damage inside? What are you doing to her now?

I clenched my jaw. I didn't move, barely even breathed, for fear I'd interrupt Older Smith's concentration.

There was so much dried blood covering her stomach that it was impossible to tell what was happening, but at least the bloody patch on the towels hadn't expanded outward.

It might have just been wishful thinking, but as I watched Kaira's face, I thought I saw color come back into her cheeks. Her hands grew less icy, but I wasn't sure if that was just because I was gripping them between my own or because her blood wasn't leaking out of her anymore.

Enough time had passed that my legs were numb from kneeling in the same position. Older Smith's hands still hovered over Kaira's stomach. Aside from slight jerks of his head and his heavy breathing, he hadn't moved. The sun outside the window was setting, and still, none of us moved.

Kaira, whose breathing had been labored and too fast when we first brought her here, was now breathing like she was in a deep sleep. The pain creasing her face had disappeared. She looked peaceful and relaxed.

I pressed my lips to her hands as I willed her to be alright.

It got dark outside. There were no lights and I couldn't see Older Smith, but still, the other man stayed silent.

When Older Smith finally spoke, I started.

"She'll be more tired than usual for the next week or two while the healing finishes, but she should be ready to get back to whatever shit you're all mixed up with by the morning."

His words were gruff, but he sounded exhausted.

I was almost too scared to ask.

"Her liver?" I finally managed.

"I wouldn't suggest tequila shots," Older Smith said acidly. "But I said she'd be fine."

There was the sound of a match being lit, and then a lantern on the bedside table illuminated the room. Older Smith's face looked pale in the lantern light. When the older man got to his feet, he stumbled and had to lean against the wall for balance.

I knew I should go and help him, but I couldn't leave Kai. I was terrified that if I moved from this spot, if I looked away for even a second, I would come back to find her like she'd been before. I'd lived with enough illusion in my life to know I couldn't always trust what was before my eyes.

"Mr. Smith," I said, my voice coming out rough.

The man glanced at me.

"Thank you. I can't tell you…what this means to me." I looked at Kai, still sleeping peacefully.

The older man's eyes moved from my face to where my hands were clasped around Kaira's.

"You're a Nat."

I doubted this man was about to call the police, but I still tensed in anticipation of the disgust and horror I expected to fill his expression. I braced myself for the accusation of *baby killer*.

Older Smith made a noncommittal sound. "My magic doesn't work on Nats." He limped toward the door. "So I suggest you avoid getting yourself shot."

CHAPTER 34

Kai stirred when the door shut behind Older Smith.

"Gray?"

"I'm here, babe." I leaned over her, careful not to touch her stomach, and brushed my lips over hers.

"Mmm. I missed you calling me that." She blinked at me. "Why are you shirtless?"

I let out a choked laugh. "Kai." I bent over our clasped hands. "I'm so sorry. You have no idea—"

She reached up a hand to cup my cheek. She used her thumb to wipe away the single tear falling down my cheek.

"I'm sorry," she said.

I gave her an incredulous look. "What are you sorry for?" I traced the edges of her face with my finger, marveling at how alive she was.

"I know how awful this week has been for you, but I'm grateful for it."

"You're grateful for something that almost got you killed?" I asked, my voice breaking on that word.

I still couldn't come to grips with how close I'd come to losing her.

She nodded. "This is the first time I've felt whole in three years."

"Kai." I didn't trust myself to say more. I pressed my lips to her hand, knowing she would understand all the things I couldn't bring myself to say out loud.

She ran her fingers through my hair. "I know things will go back to the way they were as soon as we clear your name, but it was just…nice to have you back, even if it wasn't real."

"This is real," I told her, my voice sand-papery. "I never stopped loving you. Not even when I was so angry with you for what you did."

Pain flashed across her beautiful face, and I wanted nothing more than to take it away again.

I leaned down and kissed her.

The door opened, and we wrenched ourselves apart. I looked away as the rest of our friends piled into the room, staring out the window into darkness while I struggled for control over my emotions. A few seconds later, I thought I'd managed it well enough, but while Yutika and Bri hovered around Kaira, A.J. poked me in the chest. He whispered, "Unless you're ready for everyone else to know you're in love with her, wipe that expression off your face."

I gave him a puzzled look. A.J. rolled his eyes skyward. "Honestly, it is beyond me how the two of you went this long without being arrested. If you were half as obvious before as you are now…."

"I get it," I said, interrupting A.J.'s tirade. "See?" I motioned to my face. "Nothing going on here."

A.J. huffed and then sat down on the bed next to Kaira. He straightened her blankets and cooed to her like she was a little kid with the sniffles. The bed was a decent size, but I was less than thrilled about everyone crowding her after she'd just been shot. They were careful not to get near her stomach, and Kaira was smiling, so I let it be.

"Michael," Kaira said, reaching out a hand for him. He went over to the bed and stood where she could see him. At least he had the good graces not to climb on the mattress like A.J. and the girls. Michael's eyes were still a little red, but nothing like the way they'd been before.

"I'm so sorry," Kaira told him.

"Don't be," he told her, his normally stoic face twisted in regret. "It was my fault. If I'd been quicker—"

"Don't," Kaira said, shaking her head back and forth. "It was my illusion that gave us away."

I went and sat on the floor next to Smith, who was looking lost without his three computers in front of him.

"How's your dad?" I asked the Techie.

Smith gave me a sharp look. "Who said anything about him being my dad?"

"You're right," I said. "How is that man who helped Kaira? He looked pretty exhausted when he left here."

Smith huffed and stared out the dark window. After a while, he said, "Mending takes a lot out of him, especially when the wound is life-threatening."

"I don't know how it works," I said, hating my ignorance and promising myself I'd do some necessary reading after all this was over, "but if there's any way I can help…if he can take some of my energy or something—"

"Nah, he'll be fine. He just needs to sleep it off."

As if on cue, Older Smith came into the room. He was holding a tray crowded with seven bowls of ramen and a clean quilt draped over his arm. The smell of delicious broth and noodles filled the room. As if on cue, my stomach rumbled.

Older Smith set the tray down on the floor and put the quilt on the edge of Kaira's bed. He yelled at Bri, Yutika, and A.J. to *stop climbing the hell over his patient* and then left the room with a scowl.

Scrambling off the bed, Bri said to Smith, "Your dad's even scarier than you."

I thought Smith would make another comment about us assuming the older man was his father. Instead, he said, "You think I'm scary?" He sounded more than a little hopeful.

"Maybe taciturn is a better word," Yutika said with a giggle.

Smith glowered.

Kaira drank the bowl of ramen broth Older Smith had made for her, waving away all of our offers to help her. She also ate most of my noodles, since healing was apparently hungry work. I was so relieved to see her alert and acting like her normal self that it earned me another poke from A.J.

"This big brother cover story is going to get more disturbing than the truth if you keep this up," A.J. hissed at me.

I scowled.

"Oh my God," Kaira said, sitting up in bed.

I was on my feet in a second, thinking she was in pain. But all her face revealed was surprise.

She looked at me. "I almost forgot about what happened before I got shot. Director Remwald. He—I—" She waved a hand, searching for the words.

From the moment the gunshots started and Kai hit the ground, I hadn't given a single thought to it, either. Now, I remembered how the old man on the porch had transformed into the Director.

"Oh my God," I echoed her. "Remwald."

"I just figured there was some kind of funky illusion work happening," A.J. said, arching a brow. "You aren't trying to tell us that was *actually* the Alliance Director colluding with Valencia, are you?"

The moment I saw the Director standing on the stoop, I realized why I had recognized something about the old man when he was talking to Valencia. I had been trying to identify the man's face, but it was his voice I knew.

"I don't get it," Yutika said, holding up a hand. "Was one of those guards an Illusionist?"

Kai shook her head. "*Remwald* is the Illusionist. The Alliance Director is a Mag."

CHAPTER 35

So, you're telling us that Director Remwald, the most famous Nat in the world, isn't a Nat at all?" Yutika asked.

A slow, wondering grin spread across Kaira's face. "Director Remwald's an *unMarked* Mag."

"That doesn't make any sense," Bri said. "If he was a Mag, any Mag who crossed his path would have known."

"Unless he's gotten a hold of some secret Alliance compound that cloaks his magic…." Smith rubbed his hands together, thrilled by the unlikely prospect.

"Give it a rest, Smith," Michael muttered.

"How else do you explain it?" Smith challenged.

"I have no idea, but I'm sure there's a more reasonable explanation that we just haven't figured out."

"No, I'm serious," Smith persisted. "What if—"

"Remember what Bobby Axelrod told Grandma Tashi?" I interrupted before the argument got out of hand.

We could worry about that particular mystery later.

"He's illusioned. It's illusioned," Kaira repeated.

I nodded. "The *he* must have been about Remwald."

"And didn't Axelrod say the next murder would be an illusion, too?" Kaira asked.

"You think Remwald's planning to illusion himself to look dead, and then have the police whisk him away before anyone realizes he's alive?" A.J. asked, wrinkling his nose.

"More likely they're going to use another body—one that's actually dead," Smith said. "That would explain why Remwald told Valencia the body needed to be processed quickly without an autopsy."

"Do you think he's powerful enough to hold that kind of an illusion?" I asked Kaira.

She nodded. "He isn't quite as powerful as me, but he's strong enough that our illusions cancelled each other out as soon as we were standing within sight of each other."

"Are you sure that's what happened?" Michael asked.

Kaira nodded again. "It's never happened to me before, because I've always been so much stronger than any other Animate Illusionists. My illusions felt weak as soon as we stepped out of the car, but I didn't give it much thought because animal illusions are harder for me. But as soon as Remwald came out of the house, our magic crossed. That's why we both lost our illusions."

Michael pulled out three crumpled photos from his jeans pocket. They all showed the same image, just from different angles.

Director Remwald, his face on full display, was lying on a rug. I recognized the room from the numerous videos Remwald shared on social media. It was the Director's office. Remwald lay in the center of the rug embroidered with the Alliance's seal. The body was covered in blood. His entire chest cavity had been exposed, showing ribs and a pink blob that must have been his heart. Even knowing the pictures weren't real, they were difficult to look at.

"I can't believe you managed to grab those after everything that happened," Bri told Michael, sounding impressed.

"Meanwhile, if he'd gotten himself shot for the sake of a few pieces of evidence, I would have killed him again myself," Yutika grumbled.

I saw Michael slip his hand into hers and squeeze.

"Do you think these photos, along with the conversation we recorded between Remwald and Valencia, will be enough for us to go public?" Bri asked.

Everyone looked at me.

I shook my head. "There's no way for us to prove what's illusion and what's real."

I was thinking about all of the legal precedents that applied in this case, and I knew that if we presented the evidence we'd gathered to a judge, there would be about fifty ways for it to be disregarded by any half-decent lawyer.

Publicizing the pictures might interrupt Remwald's plan, at least temporarily. But with all of the evidence pointing to me as Penelope's murderer, getting people to believe anything I said would be like trying to stop a tornado with a paper fan.

Who would people believe…the Alliance Director, or an escaped convict hated by both Naturals and Magics…?

"Besides," I continued. "If we went public with these photos now, Remwald would just show his face at some public event and feign ignorance. It'd just make us look stupid."

We all stared at the photos spread out on the floor.

"And you're 100% sure the guy on the porch was *the* Director Remwald? In the flesh?" A.J. asked, grimacing at the images.

"Yes," Kaira and I said.

Kaira leaned over the side of the bed to study the images. "It's just illusion," she said, shaking her head in amazement. "I could do the same thing to myself right now."

"Please don't," I said, feeling sick at the thought.

Fake or not, I couldn't handle seeing Kai like that.

"So, that dead person could be anyone," Yutika said, her brow furrowed in thought, "and the medical examiners will never know because Valencia is going to arrange for the body to be cremated before anyone gets a good look at it?"

Kaira and I looked at each other and nodded.

"Okay, so let's just assume for a minute the two of you aren't completely off your rockers, and this is actually the Director illusioning himself so everyone will think he's dead." A.J. tapped his foot on the floor. "Why would Remwald want Boston to tear apart at the seams? What would he possibly gain by destroying the organization he's in charge of?"

"It's the right question," I agreed. "And I'm going to get the answer tomorrow."

The others looked at me.

"You mean *we're* going to get the answer tomorrow, right?" Bri planted her hands on her hips.

I shook my head, my eyes going straight to Kai.

"This is my problem, and you all have already put yourselves in too much danger with all of this."

"Bull shit," Yutika said amiably.

At the same time, Kaira said, "That's not how things work around here, Gray."

I set my features. I knew they'd try to fight me, but I wasn't giving in. Not after what had happened to Kai. "I won't let any of you get hurt…get any more hurt…for my sake."

"Why do straight guys always think everything's about them?" A.J. asked with a roll of his eyes. "Look, if it makes you feel better, tell yourself that we're *only* helping for the sake of the good citizens of Boston."

"Remwald might have made you the scapegoat for these murders," Michael said, "but if he finishes this, it'll be the whole country that suffers. We have a responsibility to do what we can to stop him."

"Besides," Yutika said, "we take care of our own. And you, Graysen Galder, are ours." She reached over and patted my leg.

"That was so beautifully poetic." A.J. pulled—of all things—a checkered handkerchief out of his pocket and dabbed his eyes.

I couldn't put into words how much their support meant to me. But I still wasn't willing to put them in danger if there was any way for me to solve this mess on my own. If I had thought more about consequences before diving headlong into something we didn't fully understand, Kai wouldn't have been shot.

"Boyfriend, have you forgotten that if we hadn't broken you out of prison, you'd be dust in the wind right now?" A.J. asked.

I hadn't forgotten.

"You don't get to tell us what to do any more than we can tell you what to do," Kaira said.

I felt my control over this conversation slipping through my fingers.

"What if something happens to one of you?" I challenged.

"We were caught unprepared today," Kaira answered. "Nothing's going to happen next time."

"At least, not to us." Bri high-fived A.J.

I knew I'd been defeated. I leaned back against the wall and sighed, deciding to wage a more private battle with Kai later when we were alone.

"You know, I used to think we were awesome when we saved unMarked Mags from arrest," Bri said. "But after we save the city and prevent a Nat-Mag war, we'll be full-on heroes."

"Psh, like we weren't already." A.J. winked at her.

"Before we all start patting each other on the back," Yutika held up a finger, "we need to figure out how we're going to stop this maniac.

Smith raised an eyebrow. "I think I might have an idea."

CHAPTER 36

An hour later, I sat in the van with Smith's laptop in front of me. We'd driven a mile down the road to make the call, since Smith's dad apparently didn't allow anything that could be used to track him on his property.

Like father like son.

"Are you sure he won't be able to figure out where we are?" I asked, my finger hovering over the mousepad.

"It's encrypted to within an inch of its life," Smith replied. "And the Techie he's got isn't half as good as me. I'm sure."

I took a deep breath, and then I started the call.

"Yes?"

"Hello, Director Remwald."

There was a pause, and then a soft chuckle. "Galder. Thank you for saving my Techie the trouble of tracking you down."

"I have something of yours," I said, tracing my finger along the edge of one of the photos. "I imagine it would be…awkward…if every news outlet in the country got a hold of these pictures. I wouldn't want you to be in the uncomfortable position of having to explain why they make you look so dead."

I could feel the pretense at humor slip away as the Director's voice hardened. "What do you want?"

"A lot of things," I replied, keeping my voice cool. "We can discuss all of them in the morning. Why don't you clear your schedule, and we'll meet at your place at nine."

"Still the big shot, even as a Nat running away from execution."

"I'm not running anywhere," I told him.

"Fine, then. Tomorrow at nine."

"If I see a single gun or any Mags that make me feel nervous, I'm turning around and going straight to the Globe," I warned.

"Understood." Remwald paused, and I tensed. "How is Kaira doing, by the way?"

I was grateful that the call was audio only so Remwald wouldn't be able to see the mixture of shock and fury I knew was flashing across my face.

Smith leaned over the computer and said, "Never better, asshole," before I could recover.

"Delighted to hear it," Remwald said. And then he ended the call.

When Smith and I got back to the house, we relayed the very short call to the others. Everyone was congratulating me, but I barely heard a word they said. A cold feeling had stolen through me. The others were busy reviewing the plan, but there was only one question that I could focus on.

How did the Alliance Director know Kaira's name?

"Alright, kittens," A.J. said, yawning and stretching. He looked at his watch. "We have exactly ten hours before this little soiree, and we're all going to need some sleep if we're going to be bright-eyed and bushy-tailed." He peered at Smith. "Is there any place for us to get some beauty rest in this haunted mansion?"

Smith nodded. "There are four bedrooms, not including my dad's and this one."

"Shotty on my own room," A.J. said, getting to his feet and trotting to the door.

"Me too," Bri announced, chasing him out. "I'll fight you for it if I have to."

"Yutika and I can share a room," Michael told Smith in a quiet voice. His face turned tomato-red. Yutika's cheeks had darkened, too, but I could tell she was happy.

"I guess that means you're with me," Smith told me.

I shook my head. "I'm going to stay here for a bit. Just in case she needs anything."

"I think we have a sleeping bag somewhere," Smith offered.

"Thanks, but I'll be fine. I don't think I'll be able to sleep until all this is over, anyway."

Smith shrugged and followed Yutika and Michael out the door, shutting it behind him.

As soon as we were alone, I told Kaira about Remwald knowing her name.

Kaira's brow furrowed, but she shrugged it off, just like I knew she would.

"Kai, you can't come with us tomorrow," I said.

She rolled her eyes. "Here we go."

"I mean it," I insisted. "I have no idea how Remwald knows who you are, but I'm not taking any more chances with you. Smith'll set you up so you can see and hear everything that's going on."

Kaira looked at me and yawned. "Are you finished?"

I felt my temper rising. How could she be so nonchalant after what had happened?

"There's no need for you to be there," I said, trying to keep my tone reasonable. "Your illusion magic doesn't work around Remwald."

She bristled. "As long as I'm there, his illusions won't work, either. He won't be able to fool you into thinking he or you all are someone else."

I opened my mouth, but she wasn't finished.

"But that's not the point, is it? The point is that Remwald tried to destroy your life, almost managed to kill me, and is trying to disassemble our whole city. Any one of those would be more than reason enough for me to be there with you."

"Kai—"

"Gray."

"You were shot," I said, more desperate than angry now.

"And now I'm better." She lifted her shirt and patted her stomach. I didn't miss her small wince.

"Please, Kai," I begged her.

She shook her head and reached her hands out to me. "I don't want to fight with you. Can you just hold me?"

"Why do you always have to be so goddamn stubborn?" I grumbled as I kicked off my shoes and climbed onto the bed.

"If memory serves, you used to think my stubbornness was sexy."

She laughed at the scowl that twisted my face.

Kaira snuggled into my chest, making it impossible for me to remember why I was mad at her. When she glanced up at me, I saw that all the humor was gone from her face.

"You know something?"

I shook my head, shivering a little when her fingers stroked my jaw.

"I thought it would be horrible if you found out the truth about why I did what I did, but now, I'm glad you know. It doesn't hurt as much anymore." She put her hand over her heart. "It'll be easier to go back to the way things were before you were arrested."

I put my hand over hers. "I don't want things to go back to the way they were." I had barely been able to walk away last time, and that was back when I thought she'd betrayed me for selfish reasons.

Kaira wound her arm around my waist. "After tomorrow, the Alliance is going to need you more than ever. And maybe, once the dust settles, we can be friends." She gave me a small smile. "You know, like those movies where the vigilante befriends the brilliant detective…in your case, lawyer…and every so often, they join forces to solve an unsolvable case."

"Friends," I repeated. The word sounded twisted and wrong. With Kai, I'd always wanted more.

After everything, though, I realized it was the best I could hope for, and more than I deserved.

Kaira had done something awful, but she'd done it with the best intentions and no knowledge of how terribly wrong it would go. And the reason she'd done it was for my sake.

She had let me walk away without argument. At the time, I had thought that made her cold and unfeeling. Now, I realized, she had done it to give me a clean break so I could go to the BSMU without any ties to her. Because that was the future I had given every indication I wanted.

Never once had it occurred to me to consider how Kaira's actions that day were completely un-Kaira-like. I had been too angry, too hurt, to ask the right questions. I had assumed the worst about her, even though she had never before given me a reason to doubt her.

For the brightest student ever to go through the BSMU, I had been unforgivably stupid.

Get the hell out of my life. I never want to see you again. The burn of acid filled my throat at the memory of the words I'd shouted at her.

And then there were the words I'd said to her the other night, when we'd both been almost-naked, and I'd told her about my dad's suicide attempt. I'd lectured her about love. *It's a willingness to do anything for the other person's sake, even if it makes you less happy*, I'd told her.

The irony of my little lecture wasn't lost on me. She had been willing to give up her happiness and accept my blame so I could have a future that would be impossible if I stayed with her.

For the first time in my life, I felt truly ashamed of myself.

"I'm such a shit," I whispered.

I tightened my arms around her. "Kai, I'm so sorry for the way I treated you. I should have known…I should have seen…that wasn't you."

The words were wholly inadequate and three years too late.

I held my breath while I waited for her to say something. When she still didn't speak, I smoothed back her hair so I could see her face. I huffed out a quiet chuckle. She was asleep.

I had never felt less deserving of the woman in my arms, but that thought only made me want to tighten my hold on her. I kissed the top of her head. The rise and fall of her chest against my own helped to calm the cyclone of thoughts swirling through my mind.

While Kaira slept, I went over our plan again and again in my head, searching for loopholes and ways it could all fall apart. Remwald needed the photos for his plan to go smoothly, and the Director was smart enough to assume I wouldn't hand over the originals until I'd gotten what I wanted. I also knew the Director wasn't just going to stand by and let Michael and I interrogate him without putting up some kind of a fight.

I considered the possibility of a Shield. If Remwald had one, Michael and the rest of our group's magic wouldn't work, but neither would

Remwald's. That would put us on an equal playing field, and Remwald wouldn't be willing to do that.

A Manipulator would be more problematic for my friends, but again, Remwald would have to know that we'd have plans in place in case he tried to screw us. Smith had copies of the photos on some kind of timer so they'd be sent to the Globe tomorrow afternoon if anything happened to us.

If something was going to go wrong, I couldn't think of what it might be.

I occupied the next several hours by going over all the questions to which we still needed answers.

Why would a powerful Magic masquerade as a Natural? *How* did he manage to fool all Magics into thinking he was a Natural?

I planned to ask the Director exactly how he had gotten away with that bit of deceit. The thought of Remwald as a Magic, and a high-level Illusionist, at that, was almost too strange to consider. But Kaira had been sure.

As I sat in bed and listened to Kaira's soft breathing, I found my thoughts continually straying to the mystery of Remwald's motives.

Regardless of how he'd come to be in charge of the Alliance, Remwald was its leader now. If the organization fell apart, the blame would at least partially fall on him. The city he was in charge of would go to hell. Why would he want that?

As the hours crept by, I still couldn't find a single weakness in our plan. And yet, I felt edgy. Remwald hadn't sounded desperate on the phone. It made me feel less certain about what we'd be walking into.

The questions of *why* and *how* continued to churn in my brain. I watched the sky out the window change from black to gray-blue, and still, I didn't have any answers.

CHAPTER 37

We all assembled in the lantern-lit kitchen at dawn. Kaira had insisted on getting out of bed and going down the stairs without help, even though she was walking in a way that told me she was still in pain. She had given me *that look* that told me any argument I might make would fall on deaf ears. So, I'd shut my mouth and clenched my fists.

By the looks of the others, no one had slept much. Older Smith stood on the edge of our group, peering at Kaira in a way that made it clear he didn't like that she was out of bed. Neither did I.

The others said their thanks to Smith's dad and headed out to the van, still discussing last-minute details of our plan. I stayed behind. Older Smith gave me a challenging glower.

"I just wanted to tell you that I'll never forget what you did for Kaira." The memory of her screams filled me with so much emotion it took me a few seconds to catch my breath. "I know it might not mean much coming from a fugitive accused of murder, but I wanted to say thank you."

I expected Older Smith to make some snide comment, but again, the man surprised me.

Older Smith looked at me in a way that made me feel like he saw straight into all the hidden parts of myself that I'd never shared with anyone except Kai. Strangely, it didn't feel as awful as it should have.

"You're welcome," Older Smith said, before walking to the door and holding it open for me. "Watch the tripwire," he warned as I headed down the steps. "And kid."

I turned back to look at him.

"Use the elliptical instead of the treadmill. Your joints will thank you for it."

* * *

In the car, Smith fitted the tiny video camera we'd used before into one of the buttonholes on my new shirt. Personally, I would have just accepted the T-shirt Older Smith offered to lend me, but A.J. had insisted on designing something dressier for my meeting with the Director. A few quick strokes from Yutika's pen had brought the striped green-and-gray button-down A.J. envisioned into reality.

Smith opened his laptop so we could all see the clear video and audio coming through the tiny camera.

"That is some damn fine work, if I do say so myself," Yutika said, squinting at the barely-visible lens tucked into my shirt. She held out her hand to Smith. After a moment's hesitation, he slapped her palm.

"The two of you really could rule the world," I told them.

Yutika grinned. Smith just grunted.

"And you're sure you'll be able to save the video and make copies while I'm still in the house?" I asked, clenching and unclenching my fists as I tried to rid myself of some of my nervous energy.

"You just do your job, and I'll do mine," Smith grumbled.

My job would be to ask all the right questions that would expose Remwald's plan. We needed evidence that would be concrete enough to be authenticated by the police. There couldn't be any question of illusion work or ambiguous admissions.

Yutika drew a second car, which popped into existence behind the van. We reviewed the plan once more, and then Kaira, Michael, and I got into the smaller car while everyone else piled into the van. No one said good-bye or good luck. The Six were treating this like another one of their jobs, and I was too nervous to say anything at all.

I drove, hoping it would give me something to focus on besides what the next few hours would bring. Kaira stretched out on the backseat and immediately fell asleep. The little walking she'd done to get downstairs and to the car had thoroughly exhausted her, and there were lines of pain creasing her forehead even in sleep. Worry and guilt over everything she was putting herself through for my sake gnawed at my insides.

It was a Saturday and there weren't many cars on the road, so my mind was free to wander to all sorts of unpleasant thoughts as we drove.

Kaira's injury and our plan somehow failing weren't the only worries occupying my mind.

If Remwald really was behind all of these murders, and his plan truly was to start a war between Nats and Mags, then what would happen when the corruption was exposed? How many other essential members of the Alliance were involved?

If my friends and I kept digging, what else would we find?

And if the Alliance wasn't made up of people who wanted true equality and unity between Nats and Mags like I'd always thought, then it meant that everything I had been working for was a lie. It would mean I gave up everything for an institution that was defunct.

The thought was too disturbing to consider for more than a passing moment. I forced my mind back to the present. I'd have answers soon enough; there was no point in worrying about what-ifs prematurely.

It was half-past eight when we reached Remwald's neighborhood.

"Are you guys in position?" Kaira asked into her mic.

"Yep," Bri replied. "If you need any backup, we'll be ready."

"Is my camera still working?" I asked.

"Yes," Smith said. "I'll start saving your recording as soon as you get out of the car."

"Alright, this is where we leave you guys," Kaira said. "We'll see you in a little while."

"Hey Graysen," A.J. said, as Kaira and Michael unhooked their mics and earpieces, and tossed them onto the backseat. "In a little while you'll be a free Nat. You better remember your lowly criminal friends when you're in your corner office in the Alliance. That's all I'm saying."

"Don't worry," I told him. "I'll still need you for fashion advice."

A.J. was still cackling as I pulled out my earpiece and threw it onto the pile with the others. Everyone in the van would be able to see and hear what was going on in the house because of my camera, but we wouldn't be able to communicate with the rest of our group. If Remwald saw the earpieces and suspected we were recording the conversation, it would defeat the purpose of this whole endeavor. Still, there was something unsettling about not having our friends' constant chatter in my ear as Remwald's gated driveway came into view.

As soon as I pulled up to the driveway, the gate slid back. The three of us were silent as we drove up the long drive. I parked right in front of the house in the turnaround, making sure the wheels were angled so we could make a quick escape if necessary.

"Ready?" I asked.

Kaira and Michael nodded, and we all got out of the car.

I only managed a single, worried look at Kaira as she walked up to the porch. Her steps were stiff and measured, like she was making a conscious effort not to double over. I could see she was breathing harder from the effort of just walking.

"Focus," she hissed at me with a scowl.

The door opened just as I raised my hand to knock. A tall, thick man who looked like a Nazi SS guard with his blonde hair and blue eyes glared at us. I wondered if he was the one who had shot Kaira. White hot fury coursed through me at the mere thought.

I felt a sharp jab in my side and glanced over at Kaira, who was giving me a furious look.

Focus, she mouthed.

"Just you three?" the man asked, and I was almost surprised that he didn't have a German accent.

"Just us," I replied, meeting the guard's challenging stare.

"If you want to come inside, I'll need to check you, first."

"Be our guest." I stepped forward.

The guard was thorough, patting down my clothes and checking my pockets. Still, he didn't notice the small camera hidden in my button. He pulled up my shirt, searching for wires. When he didn't find any, he grunted and moved on to Michael.

I felt my anger creeping up again as the guard ran his hands over Kaira. I kept my jaw tightly clenched, but when the man got near her stomach, I couldn't stop myself.

"Watch your hands," I snapped.

Kaira lifted up her shirt to show she wasn't wearing a wire. The guard glared at us for a few more seconds, and then he waved us inside the house.

Director Remwald was waiting in the foyer.

"They're clean, Sir," the guard said.

I noticed a second guard fall into step behind us.

"And what about your people?" I demanded.

"Not a single weapon, as requested," Remwald replied smoothly. "My men are Combat Mags, but they're only here to make sure I'm not harmed."

I wasn't fool enough to take the snake at his word. I inclined my head at Michael.

The Whisper stepped closer to the Director. "Are your Combat Mags planning to harm us?" he asked Remwald, holding the other man with his stare.

"Not unless you attack me," Remwald replied immediately.

Michael nodded at me. Remwald shook his head, like he was trying to shake off whatever fog Michael's influence had exerted over him.

"Fine," I said. "Should we get this conversation over with, then?"

"Follow me," Remwald replied, crossing the hallway to a room just off the foyer. It was a study with a large desk in the center of the room. Several chairs were lined up across from the desk. Gold wallpaper took up the space that wasn't covered by framed diplomas and bookshelves. The air smelled faintly of leather and old books.

The two Combat Mags followed us inside. One stood by the door while the other took up a position beside Remwald.

I would have preferred to stay standing, but I sat so Kaira would have an excuse to get off her feet.

"Where are your other friends?" Remwald asked as he settled himself in the leather seat across from us.

"Back in Boston," I lied. "Where's Valencia?"

"The same. She has another rally this afternoon."

My unease was growing by the second. Remwald wasn't demanding to see the photos. He seemed relaxed.

"Is this really him or an illusion?" I asked Kaira.

"It's him," she confirmed. "I can sense his magic, and I can't make any of my own illusions.

"I have to say, it's unsettling to be in the presence of an Illusionist as powerful as myself," Remwald told Kaira in a conspiratorial kind of way.

I gripped the sides of my chair to keep my emotions from getting the best of me.

"I can imagine how unsettling it must be for you, after all these years of parading around like a Nat," Kaira said. "Just out of curiosity, how have you managed to keep everyone from noticing you were a Mag all this time?"

Remwald smiled without humor. "My brother was a gifted Alchemist. He developed a potion to temporarily suppress magical abilities. If enough of the potion is taken, the Magic effectively becomes a Nat."

I didn't miss the look of distaste that crossed Remwald's face at the mention of Nats.

"The Alchemists on my payroll are working on a new formula that will permanently suppress magical abilities, which will be a useful weapon against any Mags who don't conform," Remwald added.

I wanted to know more about this potion, but I forced myself to stay on point. I didn't know how long we had, and I couldn't afford to waste time on questions that weren't essential.

"Do you want proof that we brought the pictures?" I asked.

Remwald lifted a shoulder. "What guarantees are you going to give me that there aren't a thousand copies on one of your Techie's computers?"

"None," I replied. "But if you do what we ask, then you have our word no one else will ever see them."

Michael pulled the pictures out from his back pocket, holding them in a way that they'd appear in the frame of my camera along with the unmurdered Remwald sitting across from us.

Remwald barely glanced at the crumpled photos as Michael slid them across the desk.

"And how much is the word of a runaway convict worth?" Remwald asked.

It took me a few seconds to rein in my temper. "I don't intend to be a convict for much longer, Remwald," I said, keeping my voice even.

"So, what do you want? A pardon?"

I shook my head. "I want you to step down as Director of the Alliance."

"Very well." Remwald's eyes twinkled in amusement.

I exchanged a quick glance with Kaira. This was entirely too simple. The prickling sense of unease was becoming a roar in the back of my mind.

"Do it," I told Michael.

Michael sat forward, leaning on the desk and holding the other man with his gaze.

"I need you to tell us the truth about all of the murders from the past week," he said.

I leaned back in my seat, making sure my camera would capture Remwald's profile.

"I illusioned myself as Graysen Galder so I could lure Penelope Heppurn to his dorm room and murder her."

I gripped the arms of my chair. Kaira made a furious sound.

"You illusioned yourself to look like me."

Remwald didn't say anything.

"Answer him," Michael commanded.

"I did," came Remwald's quick response. "And after speaking with you at the Dean's house, I knew the sound of your voice well enough to deceive Penelope."

The Director of the Alliance, the man who'd been my hero and inspiration, had killed Penelope and framed me for the crime.

"Why?" I demanded, no longer able to keep my voice dispassionate.

"Penelope was the darling of the Mag community. Her death would cause the greatest stir. It was strategic, not personal."

"Why Graysen?" Kaira asked. "You could have illusioned yourself to look like anyone."

Again, Michael had to repeat Kaira's question before Remwald replied.

"Graysen Galder was the BSMU's golden boy, and when he became the chief suspect for a magically-motivated murder, it threw the BSMU and Alliance under scrutiny. It paved the way for the other murders and resulted in more Mags joining the UnAllied."

Remwald continued, "I paid Valencia Stark from Alliance funds to carry out three other murders city-wide over the last week." His voice was inflectionless, and his gaze was a little unfocused, but his words were clear.

According to Alliance law, this recording wouldn't be admissible in court since it was a confession made under compulsion, but once this video got out, it wouldn't matter. Remwald would never be able to recover his reputation, and no judge would be able to convict me.

"What were you hoping to accomplish with these murders?" Michael asked.

"The final nail in the Alliance's coffin will come on Tuesday, right before the vote, when the Alliance Director everyone knows and loves will be brutally murdered." Remwald tapped a finger on one of the photos of his slain body. "Mags will be terrified of the repercussions from the Nat community. The vote will be unanimous, and then all the Alliance laws will become unenforceable."

"And how exactly are you going to convince the world you're dead?" I asked. "No matter how fast Valencia's dirty cops get rid of the body, someone's bound to notice it still has a pulse."

"Oh, the body will be dead. It just won't be my body." Remwald said, confirming Smith's theory. "There's another would-be whistleblower in my organization who needs to disappear."

"You mean like Jonas Meddlesworth and Bobby Axelrod?" I asked.

"Precisely," Remwald said, although the word came out in a way that made me think the Director was gritting his teeth.

"And then you'll live the rest of your life wearing that old man illusion?" I asked.

"Or any other face I choose." Remwald shrugged. "Contrary to what you may believe, I don't care about fame or notoriety. That's Valencia's domain. Even if no one knows it, I'll be the one pulling all the strings."

Remwald continued, "By the time the month is out, Boston will be worse than Detroit."

"You want Boston to become like Detroit?!" Michael demanded.

I had never seen the big guy show so much emotion. His face was twisted in rage as he jumped to his feet. He leaned over the desk and grabbed the front of Remwald's shirt. The two Combat Mags moved forward.

"Michael," Kaira said, putting a hand on his arm.

Michael took a deep, shuddering breath and sat back down. "Sorry," he muttered.

"My Techie tells me your whole family was killed in Detroit," Remwald said to Michael. "That's where my brother was killed, as well."

There was a look of pure hatred on Michael's face that I had never seen before. I felt a flood of anger on my friend's behalf, but I forced the emotions back. Now wasn't the time for righteous anger. We still needed answers.

"We need his motive," I told Michael.

"Tell us why you want Boston to become like Detroit," Michael said in a growl.

"The failure of the Alliance will lead to the outbreak of a war between Mags and Nats. With Valencia as the face of the Mag army, and with me as the brains behind the operation, the war will spread. Without the Alliance, there won't be anyone to stop Mags from wresting control from the Nats. Nats will become slaves to our will. The laws about Marking will be a thing of the past, and we can rule this city—this country—as we were meant to." Remwald let out a self-satisfied sigh. "Nats will either need to flee or submit to our rule."

"That'll never work," I told Remwald. "The US military will kill any Mag who tries to start a war."

A lazy smile crossed Remwald's face. "They'll certainly try. But I have a weapon that will outmatch the Nat Armed Forces a hundred times over."

The Director's unfocused gaze moved from Kaira to Michael. "The two of you are unMarked, which tells me you're fighting for the same cause as I am."

I saw a look of horror cross Kaira's face. "We might not agree with Marking, but we don't want a massacre."

"The war is necessary," Remwald said, folding his arms across his chest. "The old systems need to be razed to the ground. Through the chaos, our chance to take control of the Nats will emerge."

"We have what we need," I said, full of disgust.

I carefully pulled the camera out from the button of my shirt and held it up between my thumb and forefinger for Remwald to see.

"Your whole confession has already been uploaded onto three different servers and can reach every major news outlet in the country with the click of a button," I told Remwald. "Actually, our Techie probably could do it without even touching a button, but that's beside the point. The point is, either you step down as Director and disappear from the public eye— without faking your own murder—or we're going to publicize everything on this recording."

I allowed myself a moment of smugness.

Once this tape got out, Remwald, Valencia, and the rest of the UnAllied who had helped with the murders would be arrested. The vote to destroy the Alliance would never even be held. A new Director would be assigned, and this whole nightmarish week would come to an end.

I gestured at the pictures on the desk. "I don't think you'll be needing to fake your own death anymore, so I hope you didn't waste too much energy on this illusion. Your actual death will be far less dramatic."

Kaira was already heading for the door. I got up.

Remwald stayed seated. As soon as Michael stood, Remwald shook himself, and the glaze-over expression left his eyes.

"Speaking of pictures," Remwald said, "I have some that might interest you."

I turned back as Remwald pulled a stuffed manila envelope out of a drawer and overturned it on his desk. Michael's body was blocking my view of the envelope's contents, but I saw him look down at the desk. The Whisper's eyes widened, his face turned redder than it had when he told us he and Yutika would be sharing a bedroom, and then he quickly looked away.

I barely registered Michael's look of apology as he stepped away from the desk. As soon as Michael was out of the way, I had a clear view of the photos littered across the desk's glass surface. All of the air went out of my lungs.

CHAPTER 38

I had to grip the back of one of the chairs to keep myself steady.

I felt Kaira come up beside me. I heard her gasp.

I was staring down at dozens of photos of Kaira and me. They were all three or four years old, and captured us in the only place we'd ever felt safe—Kaira's Back Bay house.

I couldn't tear my eyes away from the photos. Some part of me was aware that the camera I'd put back in my buttonhole was recording all of this, and that everyone in the van could see what I was seeing. But I was too overcome with the horror of what was before me to worry about that.

None of them were explicit, per say. But given the number of pictures, I didn't doubt Remwald had some of *those* pictures, too.

Still, there was an intimacy in every one of these photos that went far beyond the physical. Every one captured our love, leaving no room for doubt about the nature of our relationship.

There was one picture of us that had been taken after one of Kaira's ballet performances. She was still in her costume with her hair in an elegant knot. I held a bunch of flowers in my hand, which I had been about to give her before she raced up the stairs to our bedroom and threw herself in my arms. The photo had captured us laughing as we kissed.

In another, I had just gotten out of the shower. I had a towel around my waist and my hair was wet. Kai's hands were on the towel, like she was about to pull it off.

There was one picture that was especially disturbing because we were asleep. We were stretched out on top of the blanket, our laptops and school books scattered around us. Kai's head was resting on my chest, and my hand was buried beneath her hair. Kai's face was turned up toward the camera, displaying a soft smile that hadn't faded in her sleep.

I was staring down at the best, most private moments in my life. And here they were, splayed out over Remwald's desk like crime scene photos.

I thought I might be sick.

I felt violated in a way I didn't know it was possible to feel. What made it worse was that Remwald had violated Kaira, too.

We had taken every precaution, been downright paranoid at times. We had gotten blackout curtains for all the windows in the house and never opened them. We made sure we never arrived at the house at the same time and didn't so much as glance at each other until we were inside with the door locked.

Even if someone had found out our secret, they wouldn't have been able to get any evidence. We were that careful.

But we hadn't anticipated a drone spying on us through the skylight of our bedroom. From the angle of the camera, and the fact that every one of these pictures showed us in the bedroom, it was obvious that's how they'd been taken.

I couldn't speak. I looked at the pictures, moments that should have belonged to Kai and me alone. It felt like the bottom had fallen out of my stomach. I could barely breathe.

"You used a drone to spy on two kids?" Kaira, who got her voice back first, demanded.

"I'm the Alliance Director," Remwald replied. "My resources are extensive."

"You sick bastard!"

Kaira crumpled a handful of the pictures in her fist and threw them at Remwald's face.

"You, Kaira Hansley, are a disgrace to all Magics," Remwald said, his voice slicing through the air like a knife.

"And you're a pedophile," she shot back.

"Hardly." Remwald's face twisted in disgust. "I gained an interest in you when I heard rumors you were the most powerful Illusionist ever recorded. I was planning to recruit you and was in the process of learning more about you before extending an offer. That's when my people discovered how you were spending your free time."

I forced my gaze away from the photos so I could meet Remwald's stare.

The Director continued, "Where others would have seen nothing but two baby killers, I saw opportunity. I knew having these pictures would serve my interests eventually."

Kaira made a choked sound. "You can't get away with spying on people in their own home. This is…it's illegal. We're under eighteen in some of those. This is child pornography. Right, Gray?"

I felt my head move back and forth, even though I couldn't form the words.

"It's perfectly legal and admissible in court," Remwald said. "Alliance law states that surveillance equipment can be used by Alliance authorities when a citizen is suspected of breaking a high law."

I felt Kaira's eyes on me. "It's true." I forced out the words.

"You think we're going to let you get away with this?" Kaira demanded.

I was grateful for her fury. At least it was more useful than my paralysis.

"You won't have much choice," Remwald replied, as steady as I was unhinged.

"Michael," Kaira said.

The Whisper, who had been standing near the door with his back to us, turned around. He gave Kaira a short nod and strode back to the desk.

"You will destroy these photos and never tell anyone about them. Do you understand?"

Director Remwald's eyes glazed over. He nodded and began to gather up the pictures.

"He probably has copies," I said, my voice coming out hoarse.

"You will destroy every copy of every one of these photos," Michael continued, annunciating every word.

"I can't," Remwald replied, his unblinking stare fixed on Michael. "I anticipated you being here. There are two more sets in sealed envelopes with people I trust. They don't know what's inside the envelopes, but if anyone tries to steal the photos or I come asking for them under duress, they'll deliver them to the Magical Law branch."

Michael gave Kaira and me a helpless look. "What do you want me to do?"

Even when I wasn't looking at the pictures, they were all I could see. I saw our carefully-laid plans crumbling to dust. I saw Kaira in a jail cell, waiting for her turn in a courtroom where lawyers would show these pictures to a roomful of people. I heard the shouts of *baby killer*, heard her guilty sentence, saw her being taken out in handcuffs….

I looked at Remwald. "What will it take to make these pictures disappear?"

"First, you will destroy all records of our conversation. Second, you will come work for me."

"Work for you…how?" I asked.

A knowing smile spread across Remwald's face. "You're someone people listen to. I want you to be the first Nat to submit to Mag authority. You can consider yourself a liaison of sorts. You'll help smooth over the transition from Nat leadership to Mag." He gave me a benevolent smile. "If you wish, you can tell yourself you'll be saving Nat lives, since anyone who doesn't submit to our rule will be killed."

"Graysen would never do that," Kaira cut in.

Remwald shrugged. "Then, I'll hand over these pictures." Remwald gave me a hard look. "You'll both be executed."

I forced myself to keep my breathing steady. I just needed to keep my panic at bay long enough to find some way out of this nightmare.

"Even if I agreed to your terms, no one would listen to me anymore," I said, grasping at straws. "You made me a fugitive, remember?"

Remwald waved a hand. "We'll blame someone else for Penelope's murder. I'll have you exonerated by the end of the week."

I exchanged a panicked look with Kaira as my mind continued to reel.

"Let me be clear," Remwald said, as though he could read my mind. "I will personally make sure Kaira doesn't illusion herself and disappear. Her trial will be fast—even faster than yours—and I'll be present so there won't be any chance of another jail break."

"You can't do this," Kaira said, pounding her fist on the desk.

"If you try to run or do anything foolish, these pictures will be all over the Internet. Anyone associated with you—your families, friends, and their families—will be implicated and arrested. You may be unMarked, Kaira Hansley, but the rest of your family is not. You can illusion them all you want, but it won't stop us from tracking them down."

"You bastard," Kaira whispered.

Remwald turned his full attention on me. "Time to choose between the two loves of your life, Galder. You can expose me and rescue your precious Alliance from the monsters who seek to destroy it, or you can save the girl you love." His mouth twisted into a knowing smile. "You have what you need to destroy me, but if you use it, we're all going down together." He leaned back against his chair and crossed his legs, looking relaxed and utterly unconcerned. "Our collective fates are in your hands, Nat."

No one spoke for several moments while the full weight of Remwald's threat came to rest on my shoulders. Either I became Remwald's slave, or Kaira died.

It was my civic responsibility to hand over the evidence we'd gathered and do what I could to save the Alliance and our city. It was what the BSMU had trained me for, and the decision I know my father would tell me to make.

And yet, in comparison with Kaira's life, none of that mattered to me. My responsibility might be to the Alliance, but my heart was all hers. I couldn't believe it had taken me this long to figure it out, but now that I knew, I didn't hesitate.

"I'll do it," I say, my voice coming out clear and strong. "Whatever you need from me, I'll do it. So long as you leave Kaira out of all of it."

"Gray, no," Kaira gasped.

Remwald just smiled, and I could tell he had known it was the choice I'd make.

Kaira pulled me into a corner of the study, even though Remwald and his Combat Mags were only a few feet away and could hear every word we spoke.

"I know you," she whispered. "You'd rather die than be Remwald's slave."

It was true, but it wasn't just my life at stake. Even if I was dead, those pictures could still be used against Kaira. And I wouldn't let that happen.

"I'm going to do whatever Remwald tells me to do," I said, feeling the bitter taste of those words in my mouth, even though I had made the only decision I could make. "And you're going to get yourself and everyone else we care about the hell out of Boston."

"I can't let you go through with this," Kaira said, frustrated tears filling her eyes.

"I'll tell you what." Remwald, still reclining in his chair and looking like he was more than enjoying the spectacle, swiveled his chair to face us. "I'll give you twenty-four hours to make a decision, since my 'death' and the vote will be happening directly after that." He smirked at me, and I saw in his eyes that he was confident my choice wouldn't change.

And he was right. I wouldn't change my mind. I clenched my hands to keep from knocking that cocky expression off Remwald's face. It was only the two Combat Mags hovering around him who were stopping me.

Remwald stood. "Twenty-four hours," he repeated. "When your decision is final, have your Techie get in touch with me." He motioned to the Combat Mags and said, "Get them off my property."

I felt an iron grip on my shoulder as I was shoved out of the study. As soon as we were outside, the guards started to laugh and congratulate each other on how Remwald had outwitted us.

"Better not wait too long to give the boss your decision, or he might throw you into MagLab with the rest of your kind of freaks," the guard behind me said.

"Shut your mouth, Barry," the Mag holding Kaira ordered.

He gave Kaira's arm a vicious tug when she didn't keep pace with him.

"Leave her alone," I snapped.

My guard pulled back his fist and hit me in the jaw with so much force I saw stars.

"Don't touch them."

I heard Michael's soft command and felt the death grip on my arm disappear, even though my vision was still hazy.

The Combat Mags stood at the edge of the lawn and blinked at us as Michael, Kaira, and I got into our car. None of us spoke as we made the ten-minute drive to the meet-up point, where the van was waiting for us. We all sat motionless for several seconds.

And then I slammed my fist into the dashboard.

"Gray, stop—"

I hit the dash again, needing the physical release so I wouldn't start clawing out my own brain.

"I'll, uh, go over there now," Michael said, his gaze fixed on the van. "Take as long as you need."

Kaira, whose hand was pressed over her mouth, nodded. I couldn't manage a single word that wasn't a curse, so I didn't say anything at all.

Michael got out of the car. As soon as we were alone, Kaira turned around in her seat to face me.

"Don't," she whispered. "I know what you're doing, and just…don't."

"What am I doing?" I asked.

"Blaming yourself. Worrying about me. I know you want to save me, but I don't want your protection. We're a team on this, Gray."

"I never wanted to put you in danger," I managed through my fury and guilt.

"And I never wanted to put you in danger. But no matter how careful we were, we both knew there was some risk of being found out." She turned away from me so I couldn't see her face. "Do you regret having been with me, given what Remwald's done?"

I let out a heavy sigh. "If I were less of a selfish bastard, I would, but I could never regret being with you."

She turned back to me, her eyes bright with emotion. "I feel the same way."

I took the hand she held out to me. We sat like that, with our fingers intertwined, as we tried to make sense of the position we'd found ourselves in.

"What do we do?" she whispered.

I shook my head. "My decision's made. I won't let anything happen to you."

With those words, simultaneous relief and dread settled on me. It was the right choice, because it was the only choice I could make. I would do anything to keep Kaira safe.

"Can we just wait a little longer?" she begged, her voice filled with a desperate kind of hope. "Just in case we can figure something else out?"

Even though I couldn't imagine anything happening in the next twenty-four hours that could make any difference, I nodded. She let out a shuddering breath as I reached up and brushed the tears from her cheeks.

"Smith, Bri, and Yutika are bound to have some questions for us," Kaira said, rubbing her eyes with the hand that wasn't laced with mine. "We owe them an explanation."

I didn't let go of Kaira's hand as we walked between the two cars. When I opened up the door, what had clearly been a heated argument abruptly cut off. Michael and A.J. gave me an apologetic look. Smith's face was hidden behind his laptop screens. Bri and Yutika both looked furious.

Bri was in her titanium form. Silver titanium tears slid down her cheeks and hit the rubber mats on the floor with soft little *plunks*. "You're baby killers," she said, her voice full of hurt and accusation. "I helped a baby killer break out of prison."

My helplessness lifted enough for me to be angry, and with no other target, I directed all of it at Bri. "That name would only apply if we'd actually had a baby, which we haven't," I snapped. "So just relax."

Kaira gave me a *don't help* look. "Bri, please," she said, her voice breaking.

Bri shook her head, titanium tears still streaming down her cheeks.

"My niece would still be alive if it wasn't for people like you." Her tears continued to fall.

I moved forward, but Kaira put a hand on my chest.

"I promise we'll never have a DAMND child," Kaira said.

I hated Bri a little for forcing Kaira to say those words. I hated how she made me feel like some kind of monster.

Bri wiped her eyes. "I won't tell anyone about you, but I can't live with someone who could someday become a baby killer...not after what my family's been through." She swallowed. "Once we get back to Boston, I'm moving out."

"I understand." Kaira looked like she was on the verge of tears herself. She took the other girl's hands in hers. "I'm sorry I didn't tell you the truth sooner. I owed you that much, and I shouldn't have accepted your help without giving you all the facts. But I won't apologize for loving Gray."

Bri jerked her chin in acknowledgment.

Kaira let go before turning her fierce gaze on Yutika. "The same applies to you. Gray and I should have told you all the truth sooner. I'm sorry for that."

Yutika looked from Kaira to me. And then, she sighed.

"I can't judge you for keeping your relationship a secret." She glanced at Michael before turning back to Kaira. "And I'm okay with you…being together. I think."

Kaira nodded.

I bit back a sarcastic response. After all, she was taking all of this better than I had a right to expect. Bri's response had been appropriate, and Yutika's more than kind…all things considered.

Kaira and I were the freaks.

"And you, Smith?" Kaira asked, pushing down one of the laptop screens so Smith's face was visible.

Smith shrugged, looking uncomfortable. "Your personal life is none of my business. Honestly, the whole baby killer thing is probably a myth the Alliance made up to hide some nefarious truth about what really happens when Mags and Nats breed."

"We're not livestock or lab rats," I felt compelled to inform the Techie.

I smacked a hand to my forehead. With everything else that had happened, I had completely forgotten about the question I'd meant to ask Smith before. The thought of lab rats brought it back to the forefront of my mind.

"Remwald's guard mentioned something about a place he called MagLab."

"Maybe it's some secret Alliance facility," Smith said, sounding more than a little thrilled by the prospect. He turned to his computer screens as he began to search.

"Nothing," Smith said after a few moments.

"What about on those dark web conspiracy blogs?" I asked.

Smith's face lit up, and then he fixed all of his attention on his screen.

"Really, Galder?" A.J. complained. "Not you, too."

Smith's eyes scanned back and forth across the screen. His eyebrows rose.

"Huh," he said finally. "There's only one post about it, but it looks legit."

"A legit conspiracy theory?" A.J. scoffed. "That's an oxymoron."

Smith ignored him. "It says there's a secret branch of the Alliance dedicated to experimenting on," he squinted at the screen, "children who are the product of Mag and Nat unions."

Kaira and I looked at each other.

"Does it say anything about where this place is?" I asked Smith, my heart thundering.

Smith shook his head. "But I can try chatting the person who posted this."

"Do it," I said. "Now."

"It's terrible etiquette to directly reach out to posters on this site," Smith grumbled.

"This is important," I told the Techie. "I need to know."

"Shouldn't we be talking about more important things, like Graysen becoming Remwald's Nat slave or him and Kaira being executed for breaking the third high law?" Yutika asked.

I couldn't explain why, but I had a sense that there was nothing more important than this. Maybe it was just my psyche's desperation for some new piece of information that would help me escape a life of servitude. All I knew was that I had to figure this out before I gave Remwald my final decision.

"Chatting right now," Smith declared, typing furiously on his keyboard.

The whole van went silent except for the tapping of Smith's fingers.

Smith frowned. "Dead end. This guy was just a janitor, and they fried his brain when he quit for family reasons. All he managed to remember was that all the employees were picked up at their homes, blindfolded, and driven to a place called MagLab."

"He's illusioned. It's illusioned," I said, repeating the words Bobby Axelrod had spoken to Grandma Tashi days ago.

The others looked at me with a puzzled expression.

"Remwald's the Illusion. What if the Lab everyone keeps talking about, this MagLab, is hidden by illusion?"

"You think Valencia was telling us the truth about the address?" Kaira asked.

"Only one way to find out," A.J. said.

"Maybe they weren't involved with drugs, like we'd thought," Kaira said, sounding excited. "We have to find it and see what Remwald's been hiding."

The more I thought about it, the more the pieces started to fit into place.

"Remember what Elizabeth Nelson told us?" I asked the others. "She'd been with a Nat, and she said she went to a lab where they took away her baby."

"She was psychotic," Yutika said, but I could hear the note of uncertainty in her voice.

"What if she was telling the truth?" I challenged. "What if the Alchemists there did something to her memory so she wouldn't be able to talk about what had really happened?"

"That would make sense why my guy doesn't remember anything," Smith said, gesturing to his computer.

"Even if all of this is true, and that's a major *if*," Yutika said, "What does it have to do with us or Remwald, or the impending war we're still trying to stop?"

"I'm not sure," I admitted.

But if this lab was half as shady as I was beginning to think, and I could find a connection between it and Remwald, I might gain some leverage to use against the Director. Finding this place was all I had left.

"Huh, that's interesting," Smith muttered. His eyes were closed and his hands hovered above his keyboard.

"What?" I demanded.

"I found something buried in the Alliance archives that mentions MagLab. The information is in the Alliance's most secure information storage system. They locked it tighter than Fort Knox, which incidentally isn't very secure. I could have gotten in as a ten-year-old. Speaking of which, we should build a bomb shelter...."

"Smith!" Six voices said at once.

Smith opened his eyes. "All I found was a two-sentence mention of MagLab and Study 249."

"Study 249?" I repeated.

"Yeah. All it says is that its findings led to the writing and ratification of the third high law."

I exchanged another look with Kaira.

"Let's just go check it out," I said to the others, "and then after, I'll make the call to Remwald."

"You want to check out a secret Alliance lab that probably doesn't exist?" Bri asked, looking skeptical.

"You don't have to come," I told her.

Bri looked at Kaira, who nodded.

"None of you have to come," Kaira said. "I have no idea what we're walking into, and it might be dangerous."

Bri hesitated. Then, she said, "I'll help you guys this last time."

"I'm with you," Yutika said.

Michael nodded.

"I'm not letting you find evidence of an Alliance conspiracy without me," Smith said.

"Danger's my middle name," A.J. said. "Let's take a field trip to MagLab."

CHAPTER 39

We drove back to the construction site we'd seen the other day. Nothing about it had changed—there was nothing to indicate the place was anything other than what it appeared.

"Let's get out and have a look around," I decided. "Park behind that construction truck so the van won't be so obvious."

Michael drove forward.

We were about a hundred feet from the truck's rear when the air around the van rippled. And then the construction site in front of us blinked out of existence. A towering, fully-formed structure appeared in its place.

Kaira swore. "If I'd thought to bring Ma here the other day, she would have sensed this illusion."

"We had no way of knowing," I told her.

And I wouldn't have wanted anyone in Kaira's family mixed up in this place.

Kaira still looked distraught, but she gave me a terse nod as we all stared at the building. It was as big as any of the office buildings in the financial district, and it had the same modern, sleek style. A row of glass doors spanned the whole width of the building. Three security guards holding machine guns paced back and forth in front of the doors.

"Reverse, reverse," Smith hissed. "Before they see us."

Michael did, and I saw the air around us ripple again as we crossed back to the other side of the illusion. We all let out a breath as the building was replaced with the construction site.

"This is so exciting," Smith said, practically bouncing in his seat. "This is my first real-life conspiracy. I told you guys, didn't I? And now we've got proof!"

Yutika rolled her eyes at the ceiling. "We're never going to hear the end of this, now."

"I wonder what other secret organizations are right under our noses," Smith said, looking around like one of them might just pop into existence.

"Can we focus on this particular non-conspiracy for the moment, please?" A.J. asked.

"I can take care of those guards," Bri said, unbuckling her seatbelt.

"Just a sec," I said. "We need to get in there without anyone seeing us."

"I can help with that." Kaira smiled.

Bri, who had been sitting across from me, disappeared.

"Where'd she go?" A.J. asked, patting the air where she'd been sitting moments before.

"Um, I'm right here. Stop touching my face." Bri's voice came from the same place she'd been before, but I couldn't see her.

"I didn't know you could make people invisible," Yutika said to Kaira.

"I can't," Kaira replied.

"Oh. I'm an ant. Eww!" Bri squealed.

I squinted down at the seat, where a black ant was sitting on its butt with its legs waving in the air.

"I really hate animal illusions," Kaira said through gritted teeth.

"Alrighty then, I'm off," the ant announced.

"Wait a minute," Michael said. "Shouldn't we make some kind of a plan before we go charging in?"

"No," I said. "Every time we make a plan, we show up, and then it all goes to hell."

And I had less than twenty-four hours before I became Remwald's slave. I didn't have time to wait.

"I agree," Kaira said. "I want to go now."

The ant made a motion that I thought might have been a thumb's up…if the ant had had thumbs. And then the van door opened, and the ant disappeared from view.

The rest of us got out of the van.

"You're coming with us?" Michael asked, looking at Smith in surprise.

"You think I'd stay in the van and miss this?" Smith replied, scowling. "Not a chance."

Bri popped back into her normal, human-sized self right in front of us. She was all glittery titanium and bouncing on the balls of her feet.

"Coast is clear," she announced.

"You're a little terrifying, you know that, right?" Yutika asked her.

"I know." Bri grinned.

Kaira let the rest of us walk ahead of her. She was trying to hide it, but I didn't miss the slight hunch in her normally-perfect ballerina posture. There was a sheen of perspiration on her face, even though it was a cool morning.

"Are you up for this?" I asked quietly enough that no one else would hear.

"I'm fine," she said in typical Kai fashion.

I didn't try to argue. I just put my arm around her waist. "Lean on me," I told her.

"I'm fine," she said again, but she let me support some of her weight.

Before we reached the doors, I saw everyone else transform into tiny ants on the ground. When I looked at myself, I realized I was one, too.

"I'm not going to be able to hold these illusions for long," Kaira said, and I could hear the strain in her voice. "Let's get inside and find someplace to hide."

One of the other ants opened one of the glass doors, and we found ourselves inside the lobby of a large building. There were high ceilings and marble floors. The place had a very sterile, office-like feel. The air even had an astringent, bleached smell.

There was an elevator bank to our left and a large security desk straight ahead. There were three chairs behind the desk, but no one was sitting in them.

I still had my arm around Kaira's waist, and I could feel her shaking from the effort of holding our illusions.

"Guys, behind the desk," I whispered.

As soon as we were out of sight of anyone coming out of the elevators, Kaira dropped our illusions.

The elevator doors dinged. I peeked out from behind the desk in time to see a man and a woman, both of whom were wearing white lab coats, exit the elevator. They walked right past the desk where we were hiding and continued down the corridor. Before they disappeared from view, I saw the man's keycard detach from his lanyard and sail back to A.J.'s hand.

Yutika flipped her pad to a new page and started to sketch like a madwoman. A few minutes later, we were all pulling on white lab coats just like the ones the man and woman had been wearing. Kaira could have illusioned our outfits, but it was obvious Yutika had noticed Kai's strain. I gave Yutika a grateful smile.

We left our hiding place and went straight for the elevators. We didn't speak until we were crowded inside and the doors had shut.

"Which floor?" Bri asked.

"Tenth floor," A.J. said. "Everything interesting is always on the top floor."

"What about the basement?" Yutika asked.

"Ooh, yeah. Creepiness points for the basement," Bri agreed.

A.J. swiped the stolen badge across the keycard pad and hit the 'B' button. A green light blinked on, and the elevator descended.

Kaira illusioned all of us so we were unrecognizable as ourselves as we descended.

The elevator dinged, and the doors opened to reveal a hive of activity. There were dozens of men and women in lab coats just like the ones we were now wearing. It looked like some kind of science lab on steroids. There were beakers filled with colorful liquids that steamed and bubbled over. There were all sorts of machines with little test tubes and petri dishes nestled inside.

Someone wearing gloves opened a vat of what I thought was probably dry ice.

"Alchemists," Kaira mouthed to me.

"I'll be right back," I whispered. I adjusted my lab coat so the camera attached to my shirt wouldn't be obstructed. Then, I walked purposefully away from the elevator bank and between a row of lab benches.

Everyone around me was too focused on their experiments to pay any attention to me. I grabbed a clipboard and pair of goggles off an empty bench and used them to look like I belonged.

I stopped behind different lab tables and pretended to make notations on my clipboard as I tried to read the small print on the computer screens over each work station.

I couldn't make sense of the formulas, since the chemical symbols on the screen weren't ones I'd learned about in my high school's AP chem class. But I did catch sight of a label on one of the beakers.

Magical reduction, 90% for 24 hours, the label read.

An identical-looking beaker beside it had a label that read *Magical reduction, 25% for 30 days*.

A hand-written note was taped to the lab table between the two beakers. On it was written, *Goal: 100% magical reduction, permanent*.

The word *permanent* was double-underlined.

Could this be the same potion Remwald had described, which took away Magics' abilities?

If such a thing were possible, it could be used to force non-compliant Magics into submission. Remwald could threaten to force them to drink the potion, and the fear of losing their magic would make them willing to do what they were told.

I remembered the look of fear on Kaira's face when she came face-to-face with Remwald at his estate and realized her illusions no longer worked. I couldn't imagine what it would do to her if the effect was permanent.

I moved on to a lab station where several of the Alchemists had gathered. I tried to be subtle as I peered around them.

All I could see was a row of petri dishes lined up on the slate counter. One of the Alchemists lifted something with a pair of tweezers. It looked like a strand of black hair. He deposited the hair into a beaker filled with a pea soup-green liquid. When the Alchemist dropped in the next ingredient, I couldn't help the shudder that went through me. It was a fingernail.

The concoction frothed and hissed. The fluid congealed, like it was putty instead of liquid. It shot straight up into the air. It reached the ceiling at least ten feet overhead, and then fell back into the beaker.

The Alchemists oohed and ahhed as they applauded the guy who had been wielding the tweezers.

"We're making history," one of the Alchemists said with a chuckle as he shook another Alchemist's hand.

"Shouldn't be much longer until we can replicate our subjects' abilities without needing any human carriers at all," the other man replied. He cleared his throat. "I'll admit I don't approve of the way we keep the mothers caged like hens."

"A necessary evil, my friend," the first replied.

I had no idea what they were talking about, but I couldn't ignore the sick feeling that was growing in the pit of my stomach. I strode back to the others, who were hovering around an empty lab table and pretending to be busy. I returned the clipboard and goggles to the bench where I'd found them.

A man carrying a tray with hundreds of petri dishes was walking by, and I paused to let him pass.

"How're the new specimens?" the other man asked without looking up from his tray.

I looked around before realizing the man couldn't be talking to anyone but me.

"Um, fine," I said.

The other man stopped in his tracks.

"You new? I haven't seen you around before."

"Yep, I just started." I studied my clipboard as my heart pounded a frantic rhythm in my chest.

I could feel the other man's scrutinizing stare even though I kept my gaze studiously fixed on my clipboard.

"Holy shit. You're not an Alchemist…you're a Nat!"

The exclamation was loud enough to attract the attention of all the surrounding Alchemists.

A desperate idea came to me before my panic got the best of me. I only hoped I was right.

"I just tested some of the magical reduction potion." I gave the man an easy grin. "Works like a charm, apparently."

The other man's pinched expression relaxed, and I knew my guess about those beakers had been right.

"Amazing," the Alchemist murmured. He picked up some kind of metal sensor from his lab table and waved it in front of me. Blinking red text appeared on the screen.

The Alchemist squinted at the text, and then his face paled.

"No, wait," I said.

It was too late.

The Alchemist lunged for his lab table and slammed his hand on a large, black button. A blaring alarm rang out as red lights all along the wall started to flash.

Other Alchemists started to race toward us. I shoved the man's tray so it went flying overhead. The Alchemists screamed and abandoned their chase as they scrambled to catch the experiments before they hit the ground.

The two Alchemists nearest to me transformed into identical replicas of Director Remwald. The men looked at each other in a desperate kind of confusion.

"Graysen, get out of there!" Kaira yelled.

As I ran toward the elevator, I realized everyone else in the room was illusioned to look like the Director, too.

I dove into the elevator with the rest of the Seven.

"It's me," I said, just in case there was any doubt, since I had no idea what I looked like right then.

"Well done, team," A.J. said, gasping for breath. "Nice and subtle."

The doors slid shut.

"You know how unsettling it is when you do that?" I asked Kaira, who spared me an exasperated look.

"We have to get out of here," Yutika said, on the verge of panic.

"No," Kaira and I said at the same time.

Pounding came from the other side of the elevator doors.

"They're going to break in!" Yutika squealed.

"I've got it locked," Smith said, his eyes closed. "They won't be able to get in."

"Tenth floor," I told A.J., who was wielding the badge.

"My heart can't take this much excitement." A.J. clutched at his chest as he swiped the stolen badge and hit the button for the tenth floor.

The light next to the sensor turned red. The elevator stayed where it was.

"Fiddlesticks," A.J. muttered.

"Try a different floor!" Bri commanded.

A.J. tried the ninth. The button turned red again.

"Hurry up!" Yutika yelled.

"Trying!" A.J. replied. "This badge doesn't get us anywhere except the basement and first floor."

"Relax," Smith said. He closed his eyes, and then the elevator started to move.

"If you could do that, then why did I bother stealing this useless thing?" A.J. demanded, tossing the badge in a dramatic arc across the elevator.

"If you'd asked, I would have told you not to bother," Smith replied without opening his eyes.

A.J. threw up his hands and huffed.

I watched the digital numbers climb until we reached the tenth floor. Bri pushed her way to the front, motioning for us to get behind her.

"Open it just a little," Bri told Smith. "I'll go check things out and come back once it's clear."

The doors opened enough for Bri to slip through. As soon as she was out, Smith closed the doors again. I listened for the sound of bullets striking her titanium skin, but it was quiet.

A few minutes later, Bri's voice came from the other side of the door. "All set, guys. Come on out."

I was the first one out of the elevator, and I tripped over something in my path. I looked down to see it was man in a guard's uniform. There were three others nearby. All of them were lying motionless. I couldn't tell if they were unconscious or dead, and I didn't much care.

"Combat Mags always think they're so tough." Bri grinned as she smoothed a crease in her dress. "But all those fancy punches don't do jack for them against someone like me."

"Remind me never to get on your bad side," A.J. told her.

"Well, stop stealing my skin products and you'll never have to find out."

"It's not my fault they make my complexion extra dewy," A.J. complained.

Before Bri could reply, the other elevator next to us dinged. Two guards burst out.

The first guard was holding the biggest knife I had ever seen. The man threw the knife, which moved through the air in a blur. It pinged off Bri's titanium skin and skittered across the floor. Bri lunged at the man. They collided. I heard the man's muffled *oof* when his fist came into contact with Bri's titanium throat. She head-butted him, and the man slumped to the floor.

The second guard took one look at his fallen partner, put his hands in the air, and backed into the elevator.

"I locked all the elevators, so no one else is getting up here until I say so," Smith said as the rest of us piled out into the hallway.

"Stay behind me," Bri ordered, her expression serious again. "There might be more of those guys already up here."

We waited behind the wall of the elevator bank while Bri went forward to clear the way.

"Oh my God."

CHAPTER 40

hat?" Kaira demanded. "Bri?"

When Bri didn't answer, we all stepped out from the safety of the wall. I braced myself for more Combat Mags or Alchemists. There were neither.

I went motionless at what I saw.

We were standing at one end of a long hallway, which was lined on either side with what looked like prison cells. Metal bars and a heavy-looking metal door enclosed each one of the cells. There must have been forty or fifty identical cells. They each contained a cot, toilet, and sink, and were eerily similar to the jail cell where I'd spent the night after I was arrested.

Dread prickled down my spine.

As I walked forward, I saw each cell contained a heavily-pregnant woman.

"What is this?" Kaira demanded. "What are they doing with all of you?"

The women sat or lay on their beds. They all wore hospital gowns just like the one Elizabeth Nelson had been wearing. Some of them watched us with little interest; the rest ignored us completely. No one answered Kaira's question.

"They're drugged," Michael said, his voice tight with anger.

He went up to one of the cells and put his hand on the bars. The woman got up from the bed and waddled over to Michael. I was concerned she might tip over. Her stomach was so round, and she moved like she was drunk.

"Careful," Michael told her, and the woman immediately righted herself.

"Their minds feel the same way Elizabeth's did, only worse," Michael told us.

I clenched my hands into fists. *What the hell were they doing to these women? And why were they doing it?*

The woman reached a hand to Michael through the bars, and he took it.

"Can you tell me what's going on here?" he asked.

The woman's words were slurred, and she struggled to keep her eyes open. "Keep us drugged until the baby's born, and then take away the baby." She patted her rounded stomach, and then her eyes closed again.

"Why? What do you they want with you and your baby?"

At Michael's question, the woman forced her eyes open.

"Baby's a Super Mag." She patted her stomach again.

"What does that mean?" Kaira asked, her voice higher than usual.

"The Alchemists were talking about carriers, too," I said, feeling a little unsteady as a terrible suspicion took root in my mind.

The woman started to cry. Michael leaned closer and murmured gentle words to her. Feeling my own tension start to melt away at the sound of Michael's voice, I shook myself and walked farther down the hall so I wasn't so close to the Whisper. That was when I noticed a manila folder tucked in a metal compartment on the wall. I grabbed it and started flipping through it.

Subject: 02144

Race: Natural

Occupation: Accountant

The next pages contained the results of an IQ test, a logic test, and a math test. From what I could tell, the woman's scores were about average.

The other pages were the results of various medical tests that seemed fairly routine. There were also ultrasound pictures of what was clearly the woman's unborn child.

There was nothing else to indicate what they would want from a pregnant accountant of average intelligence. And then, I got to the last page. There was a black-and-white image of a man, who appeared to be somewhere in his thirties. A short paragraph beneath the photo detailed that the man was a Level 1 Clairvoyant, and that he was deceased on May 15, 2070, which was a week ago.

I handed the page to Michael, feeling nauseous.

"Ask her if she knows who this man is," I told Michael.

The woman's voice was a little slurred, but her answer came immediately.

"Baby's father."

I looked at Kaira, whose eyes were wide with emotion.

I went to the next cell, falling back on logic to confirm my suspicions before I let myself react. The woman inside the cell was passed out on her cot, her protruding belly rising and falling with each breath.

Subject: 01586

Race: Magic, Level 2 Telekinetic

Occupation: High school math teacher

The following pages contained the same medical tests and ultrasound photos. The last page was of a man, also recently deceased. He was a Nat.

And that was when all doubt fled my mind. These women were here because their unborn children were the product of a half-Natural, half-Magic union.

The folder slid out of my hands, which had gone numb. I leaned against the wall before my legs gave out beneath me. I squeezed my eyes shut, desperate to erase the sudden image of Kaira's face on one of the women locked in these cells.

No, that voice shouted inside my mind. *Never.*

"Pleaseeeee!"

The terrible cry came from the next cell over, and the sound of it turned my blood to ice. Two steps brought me face-to-face with the woman in the next cell. For a moment, all I could do was stare.

She had been trying pry apart the metal bars of her cell. She'd managed to bend one of the bars slightly, but not enough for it to be useful, and that small bit of progress had cost her. Her hands were covered with blood, and many of her fingers were swollen and bent in gruesome, unnatural directions. Her face was deathly pale, but it was the expression in her eyes that stole my breath.

I'd never seen such pure suffering in all my life.

"Please," she groaned again. Her voice was scratchy, like she'd blown out her vocal cords from screaming. "Help me."

For a moment, I thought she might be in labor. But she wasn't pregnant—or at least, not obviously so. It was difficult to tell with the shapelessness of the hospital gown.

I forced my gaze away from her mangled fingers as the others hurried over.

"Get her out," Kaira said after taking one look at the woman's broken fingers.

"I don't think—" Smith began.

"Get her out. Now!"

Bri wrapped her hands around two of the bars and stretched them apart.

They metal snapped apart under the force of her grip. It took two more seconds for Bri to break enough of the bars to create a human-sized hole.

"Get the others," Kaira told Bri. To the woman, she said, "Come on. We'll help you get out of here."

The woman stayed in her cell. She even backed up a couple of steps.

"No." The woman's bloodshot eyes widened. "My newborn. They've got him downstairs. If I'm bad, they won't let me see him. Every day at six o'clock. Have to stay here and be quiet so they'll let me see him. Gotta be good. Gotta behave and drink my medicine."

Her ramblings were becoming less and less coherent.

And then, with a speed that I never would have suspected she was capable of, she reached through the hole in her cell and grabbed my shirt.

I was too surprised to react.

"Find Christopher," she begged me, her voice sounding inhuman as she forced her stretched vocal cords to the breaking point. "Get him out of here. Please."

"Your baby?" I asked, trying to get a little distance from this woman, who was seeming more insane by the minute.

"Not my baby," she said, tightening her grip on my shirt. "Christopher. Save him before they kill him."

"Who's Christopher?" I heard Michael ask the woman, although I found I couldn't tear my gaze away from her horror-stricken eyes.

"My boyfriend," she wailed. "If you don't save him, they'll kill him. Please. I can't live without him."

That's when I felt something scald my chest. I looked down and saw small flames shooting out of the woman's fingertips.

A Pyrokinetic.

I took her wrists as gently as I could and pulled them away from my shirt before she set me on fire.

"I'm so sorry," I said, because I didn't know what else to say.

My shirt was smoking, and I could still feel the searing imprints of her hands.

"We need to get out of here," Yutika's nervous voice came from somewhere behind me.

"Come on," Kaira said, her voice unsteady as she took the woman's hand. "Come with us, and we'll get your boyfriend."

Any answer the woman might have given was drowned out by the maniacal laughter of the woman in the cell across the hall. The sound of it was almost as disconcerting as the other woman's cries.

"Ha-ha-ha!" she shrieked. Giddy tears streamed down her cheeks, and her enlarged stomach shuddered with the force of her laughter. "What makes you think they'd keep your precious Nat alive?"

My gaze found Kaira's as the sick feeling inside me spread. I wanted to reach out for her, but my feet were rooted to the spot.

"Liar!" The Pyrokinetic pulled away from Kaira's grip and lunged at the other woman, who stepped back from the bars, still chuckling.

"Your child has been born. They don't need him for anything anymore," the other woman continued as she rubbed one hand over her belly. "He's probably already dead."

"Nooo!"

Bri wrapped her arms around the Pyrokinetic, who was beating at the metal bars on the other woman's cell with her fists.

"A little help, Michael," Bri said as the woman continued to flail.

Michael took one step forward. And then we were all thrown backward as a blinding flash lit up the hallway. I felt a scorching wind across my face. When I looked back at the Pyrokinetic, my stomach dropped out. I couldn't move. I could barely breathe.

She was on fire.

Her skin was luminescent, like the fire was inside her and burning its way out.

Someone let out a strangled scream.

Help her, a desperate voice in my head shouted. *Help her!*

But there was nothing to be done. She was being engulfed in flames. They were eating her alive, and if I got near her, they'd consume me, too.

There was only one thing in the world that could have ripped my attention from the horrible scene playing out before us, and that was the sight of Kaira going toward the woman.

I grabbed Kai and pulled her against me, dragging us both back until we were out of the flames' range.

"We have to do something!" Kaira struggled to free herself from my grip.

My throat felt like it was lined with jagged edges of glass. I couldn't form the words to tell her there was nothing we could do…that the woman was beyond our help. So, I wrapped my arms tighter around Kaira. Her chest heaved, and I knew she was crying.

Bri, the only one of us who could get near the flames, was trying to smother them with her titanium hands. It didn't help. A scream was lodged in my throat as I watched, helpless, as the woman's own fire consumed her.

I couldn't look away. Kaira was yelling and fighting against me.

"Christopher!" The word came out garbled and choked from the flames pouring out of the woman's throat.

And then the woman just…came apart. Bri's arms were clasped around air as the woman she'd been holding turned to small bits of flames stuttering out all over the linoleum floor.

The only remaining sounds were our ragged breathing and the mad cackling from the woman in the other cell.

I was shaking, or maybe it was Kaira shaking. We were too intertwined for me to tell the difference. I couldn't make myself let go of her, even though the danger to us had passed. I needed to say something to Kaira to make this better. But my throat wouldn't work. I felt chilled to the bone, even though the hallway had become a sauna.

The laughter abruptly cut off as a bang came from somewhere past the elevators. The pregnant women who weren't unconscious or asleep whimpered. Even the insane one who'd been laughing went to her cot as fast as her pregnant belly would allow her. She lay down and closed her eyes.

I looked up just as a door at the opposite end of the hallway burst open. Guards came pouring in.

CHAPTER 41

Go, go, go!" Bri yelled, pointing for the stairway nearest to us.

"No," Kaira gasped. "We can't leave them."

I hated to abandon them, too, but there was no time. I grabbed her hand and yanked her down the hall after the others.

Michael reached the doorway first and threw it open. I looked back and saw Bri fighting against the guards. Her tiny titanium form was a blur as she felled men twice her size with ease.

I pushed Kaira into the stairs ahead of me. Her face was drained of color, and I wasn't sure if it was because of the pain in her stomach or what we'd just seen.

"What are you guys doing?" Bri demanded as she slammed through the doorway. "Move!"

We raced down a flight of stairs to the next floor. I looked over the railing and saw more Combat Mags, these ones carrying machine guns, running up the stairs from the ground floor.

I opened the door that read *Ninth Floor* and gestured everyone inside.

As soon as the door to the stairway shut behind all of us, Bri wrenched the door handle until it snapped.

"Let's see them get in now," she said with satisfaction.

We were crowded in a small room. It felt like some sort of containment area, since the entire thing was sealed, and I noticed multiple air vents in the ceiling. There was a sliding door on one side that opened up to the elevator bank. Another sliding door led in the opposite direction, although the glass was tinted so it was impossible to see what was on the other side. There was nothing else except for two buttons next to each door. There was a red button that had "Enter" printed on it, and a green one labeled "Air."

"It feels wrong here," Yutika said.

"Too much magic," A.J. agreed.

"What do you mean, too much magic?" I asked.

"It's like the feeling when we're in a club and there are Mags everywhere," Kaira explained. "Except more powerful."

"What do you guys think?" Bri asked, her finger hovering over the red "Enter" button.

"Let's do this," I said.

The door slid open.

We found ourselves in a room that was so large I couldn't see where it ended. There were four rows of glass cubicles lined up one after another. Each cubicle had the same cot, toilet, and sink as the pregnant women's cells. Except these cubicles didn't hold women. Each one of these glass cells contained…a child.

"What the hell," Michael whispered.

The children ranged in age from about five to maybe fifteen. They all wore hospital gowns and their heads were shaved, making it difficult to tell their gender. The kids stared at us, and we stared back

"What is this?" Kaira demanded, her voice closer to hysterical than I'd ever heard it.

"You guys wait here while I make sure the place is clear," Bri said, her voice grim.

Bri made it to the second set of glass cubicles before she collapsed.

We all ran for her. I still had my arm around Kaira's waist, and I could feel her limp grow worse with every step. She sagged against me. I turned to look at her, only to see her face was covered in a sheen of sweat, and her eyes were barely open.

"Kai!"

I could see her pulse fluttering erratically.

If I hadn't been supporting her, she would have fallen. I gently lowered her to the ground and pushed up her shirt, steeling myself for the sight of her stomach covered in blood.

I found nothing except for some bruising around where the bullet had entered and left. *Was she bleeding internally?*

I put a hand to her cheek. She was burning up.

"I don't feel good," she murmured.

"Where does it hurt?" I asked her, desperate.

She didn't answer.

"Something's wrong with Kaira!" I yelled.

No one answered. I looked up, blinking through the haze of my panic. It was only then that I saw the others were also on the ground. They were all deathly still.

No, please, I thought, my mind scrambling with what to do.

I needed help. Every one of my people was passed out on the floor…possibly dying…and I had no clue what was wrong with them. I had to get them to safety—had to get them help—before I succumbed to whatever was hurting them, too.

"They're not used to the chemicals," a small voice came from my right.

I whipped around to find a little boy, maybe nine or ten years old, staring at me through the glass wall of his cell.

I didn't wait to ask questions. My breathing was growing tighter and my joints were seizing up, but I didn't know if that was from whatever had poisoned the others or the fact that panic was flooding my system.

I carried Kaira back to the little enclosed space where we'd been before. I shut the sliding door and slammed my hand down on the button labeled "Air."

There was a hissing sound, and I felt a blast of cool air coming in through the vent in the ceiling. Kaira gasped and opened her eyes.

"What happened?" she demanded, her voice a little scratchy but otherwise sounding normal.

I went weak with relief. I pressed my lips to hers once, needing the contact to reassure myself she was alright.

"Stay here," I commanded her. "Close the door as soon as I leave."

Instead of carrying them one-by-one, I grabbed Bri and Smith's hands and dragged them across the smooth, tiled floor. Kaira opened the door as soon as I was close, and I yanked their unconscious bodies inside. They both woke on a gasp, disoriented the same way Kaira had been. I didn't wait long enough to hear them speak before running back out for the others.

A.J. and Yutika were next. It took all of my strength to haul Michael's dead weight back to the little room. By the time I got Michael inside, everyone else was awake and alert.

"What the hell is going on around here?" Yutika demanded.

"There's something in the air that's poisonous," I said.

"You don't look sick," Bri pointed out.

"Maybe it only affects Mags," Kaira said.

I stared at her. I'd been so focused on getting her and our friends somewhere safe before I collapsed, too, that I hadn't given it a thought. But now that I wasn't so worried about everyone else, I realized I didn't feel even a little weak or sick. I'd never heard of a poison that hurt only Magics, but there was no other explanation that made sense.

"You all stay here," I said.

"Wait," Smith said. "Yutika, I need a tablet."

Yutika began to sketch as Smith leaned over her shoulder and made adjustments to her design. A few minutes later, a working tablet was in Smith's hands. He booted it up, and then turned it so I could see the image that flickered to life on the screen.

"It's connected to your camera now, so we'll be able to see and hear. If you run into any trouble, we'll know about it."

I nodded. "Push that 'Air' button if you start feeling sick again," I told them. "I'll be back."

CHAPTER 42

I approached the glass cubicle slowly, aware of all the kids who were staring at me with a combination of fear and curiosity.

"Can you hear me?" I asked the kid who had spoken to me before.

The little boy nodded his head.

Conscious of how I might intimidate someone so young, I sat down on the floor outside the cubicle. I tried to think about the way Michael talked to people when they were scared and channel the same kind of soothing calm.

"Thank you for helping my friends," I told the boy.

"All your friends are Mags and you're a Nat," the boy observed.

"Yes. Is that why the air doesn't make me sick?"

A nod.

I glanced up at the ceiling of the glass cubicle, looking for some kind of filtering system that would keep the cubicles free of the poisonous air. I didn't see anything of the kind.

"How come none of you are sick?" I asked.

"We are sick," the boy said. "The air makes us weak so we can't fight them."

"Who's keeping you locked in here?" It was a challenge to keep my voice even, but I didn't want to scare the kid or make him think I was angry at him.

The boy lifted a thin shoulder. "The Alliance."

I shook my head. "This can't be part of the Alliance." The Alliance was governed by laws and ethics. And this place was…barbaric.

The boy shrugged again. "We're the reason the Alliance was formed in the first place. The unity thing was just an excuse. It was really about Mags and Nats agreeing to hide people like us from the rest of the world."

I didn't know much about kids, but I could tell this child was far more intelligent and well-spoken than any normal ten-year-old of either race.

"People like you?" I asked.

The kid smirked at me, like I'd said something stupid.

"We're *Super* Mags."

The woman a floor above had said her baby was a Super Mag, too. I didn't know what that meant, but I followed the kid's gaze to the plaque on the sliding glass door. It read,

Subject: 00391

Race: Super Magic

Primary Magic: Memory Reader, Level 16

Secondary Magic: Intellect, Level 14.

I didn't understand. It was a rule of nature that every Magic only had a single ability. And the levels made no sense, besides. The most powerful Magics alive were Level 10s. Scores of 14 and 16 were…impossible.

"You've never met one of us before, have you?" the kid asked, amusement lighting his eyes.

I shook my head. "Are you all more powerful?" I glanced at the other cubicles, where the kids were still watching me.

"You mean you don't know about the third high law?" The kid's brow wrinkled. "Didn't they give you the whole intro when they brought you here?"

"What about the third high law?" I demanded, forgetting that I was trying to channel Michael.

"Babies from Mag and Nat parents are stronger."

If I hadn't been sitting down, I would have fallen.

"Those babies carry lethal bacteria," I said, forcing my throat to work even though I'd gone numb.

"That's what they want you to think. Can you imagine how crazy everything would get if lots of Super Mags were just loose on the streets?

I'm one of the weaker ones here. Subject 00451 has three different kinds of magic, all at Level 17."

I was shaking my head and couldn't stop. I must have looked like I was having a fit or something, but I couldn't make sense of what this kid was telling me.

"There have been thousands of deaths because of DAMND babies," I said, my voice sounding faraway and raspy. "There's no way all of those cases could have been falsified."

The kid actually giggled.

"I'm a Memory Reader. And I know the people in charge made up the whole DAMND thing."

"That's not possible," I persisted, because I couldn't accept that what this kid was saying might be the truth. If he was right…if there was no reason for the third high law except a fear of super-charged Magics….

The little kid seemed to be enjoying the fact that my entire world was unraveling before my eyes. "I also know that hospital staff are paid to say that some deaths are because of DAMND, when they're actually just other diseases. There is no Acriobacterial stuff. They made it up."

I dug my palms into my forehead, finding it harder to breathe by the second.

"That's the only reason for the third high law," the kid continued. "The Nats don't want Super Mags, because then they'd be at even more of a disadvantage. And the Mags in power wanted to hide anyone with mixed blood. Once they realized they could use us, they started MagLab."

My vision started to go hazy.

"Are you upset because you didn't think you could have a baby with her?"

I jerked my head up from where I'd been studying the floor tiles.

"What?"

"The pretty one in all your memories."

"You can see into my memories?" I asked, horrified at the thought.

First off, my memories were private. Second off, the ones where Kai was concerned were no place for a ten-year-old to be poking his nose.

The kid pointed a skinny finger at the plaque on his door where *Memory Reader* was typed and gave me a *duh* look.

I opened my mouth, but before I could say anything else, the sound of soft crying came from another one of the glass cages. My heart lurched into my throat at the sight of a kid, maybe half the age of the one I'd just been talking to. Her tiny palms were pressed against the glass.

"Where's my mommy?" the little girl asked me, her eyes huge and round in her too-thin face.

"I—" I looked back in the direction of my friends, but I couldn't see them through the sliding door.

"I want my mommy," the girl said, tears streaming down her cheeks.

"Okay," I told her. "Let's get you out of here, and then we'll find your mom." I glanced around at the other kids. They all had their noses pressed to the glass with forlorn gazes fixed on me. Fury at the sight of all these kids locked up like lab rats washed through me. I thought about their drugged mothers...their murdered fathers....

"Same goes for the rest of you," I told the kids. "We're getting out of here."

I got to my feet. The little girl had stopped crying and was now sucking her thumb. I gestured for her to step back from the glass door.

I grasped the door handle and yanked on it with all of my strength. It didn't budge. There was an old-fashioned lock—one that opened with a regular key, rather than a digital code that Smith might be able to hack. Cursing, I shielded my face and kicked the base of the door.

Nothing. It didn't even rattle.

The little girl began to cry again.

"It won't work," the boy from before said, his voice heavy with defeat. "It's reinforced with magic."

I grunted as I kicked at the glass again. And again.

The little girl's cry was joined by others. Some of the kids were sitting on the floor of their cells, clutching baby blankets or teddy bears as they sobbed. Others banged on the glass with their own fists. One of the older ones left a streak of blood on the glass from his frantic pounding.

Something inside me tore apart at the sound of their cries. I couldn't stand it. I thought about Kaira, stuck inside the containment room and witnessing all of this on a tablet screen. She'd be frantic by now. If I didn't get these kids out of here myself, she'd come bursting through the door, poisonous air or not.

I renewed my efforts to break through the glass, putting the strength of my entire body into each kick.

Nothing.

Abruptly, the kids stopped crying. The little girl took two wobbling steps toward her cot. She collapsed before she made it.

I heard a scream—Kai's.

"Come on!" I shouted, kicking at the glass again.

I saw the other kids had collapsed, too. I looked up and saw mist filtering in through the grates in the ceiling.

And then the door at the far end of the room burst open. People wearing HazMat suits stormed into the hallway.

I heard their muffled exclamations as they raced toward me. I turned back to the glass cubicle. I couldn't just leave these kids here, passed out and breathing poisonous air….

The sliding door where my friends were waiting opened.

"Kai, get back!" I yelled.

"Not without you." Her voice was faint, and she doubled over as she braced herself against the wall.

A shot rang out. I ducked as a bullet hit the cell next to me. The bullet bounced off the glass without making so much as a crack.

Cursing, I abandoned my fruitless attempts to break the glass.

"I'll be back," I promised the little girl—all of the kids—even though there was no one conscious to hear my promise.

"Come on!" Bri motioned me frantically.

Smith opened the elevator doors, and we raced inside. A hail of bullets struck the doors just as they slid shut.

Our harsh breathing was the only sound as the elevator descended.

We reached the lobby, and the elevator doors opened. I could see the main set of doors directly in front of us. No fewer than fifty guards holding machine guns spanned the entire width of the building, blocking our only escape route.

Every one of their weapons was pointed straight at us.

CHAPTER 43

I had never seen so many guns in my life, and every single one of them was aimed at the seven of us. It was pointless, but I still pushed Kaira behind me before raising my hands in the air. A.J., who was standing beside me, lifted his hands, too. As he did so, the guns moved. They slid out of their owners' grips and rose into the air.

Surprised and furious exclamations came from the men who were now weaponless. Some of them jumped in the air as they tried to reclaim their guns. And then, like the weapons were part of some choreographed dance, they all spun around so they were aimed at their owners. Gasps and curses came from the guards.

"Maybe I haven't made myself clear," A.J. said, his voice rising to fill the whole lobby.

He clicked his right forefinger, like he was squeezing a trigger. One of the guns fired. A row of bullets blasted into the glass wall just above the guards' heads. The men ducked and shielded their heads.

"Next ones go in your brains," A.J. called.

The guards scattered. A.J. turned the weapons in the air so that no matter where the men were, their guns were still trained on them. As soon as our path to the doors was clear, we made for the exit.

"My range is two miles," A.J. told the guards. "Keep that in mind when you consider coming after us."

As soon as we were outside, we broke into a run. We didn't stop until the air rippled, and the illusion of the construction site settled back into place. The building behind us was no longer visible. It was like it had never existed.

We needed to get out of here. And yet, as soon as we were through the illusion, we all stopped in our tracks.

"Oh my God," Bri gasped. She doubled over and threw up.

A.J. and Yutika crowded around her, patting her back and murmuring to her.

"My niece. They said a DAMND baby killed her. This whole time we thought…and now, I don't even know—" Bri retched again.

I squeezed my eyes shut, but that only made my vision of all those glass cubicles clearer in my mind. I couldn't wrap my brain around the horror of it all. Everything the boy had told me came back in a rush. And with it, the knowledge that the Alliance, which was supposed to protect and unite, had deceived us all.

Baby killers.

I had spent a lifetime learning that the crime of loving a Magic was equal in the eyes of the law to murder. Worse than murder, really, because it was the most vulnerable members of our society who were at risk.

Kaira and I had spent close to a decade sneaking around, lying to the people we cared about, and hiding what we were to each other.

I'd always known we wouldn't be able to stand up in front of our friends and family and vow to love each other forever. I'd always known we would *never* have kids.

None of that had really mattered before. It was the price for being together, and we had both been glad to pay it. But now I knew the real reason for the law. It was all about power.

A sob from somewhere nearby cut through my black thoughts. I opened my eyes, and what I saw tore through my insides in a way nothing else ever could. Kaira was on her knees, her whole body shaking with the force of her sobs.

My limbs unfroze. I crossed the space between us and sunk onto the ground in front of her. I grabbed her and crushed her to me.

I couldn't make my throat work, so instead of trying to offer comfortless words, I held her. I kissed the tears streaming down her cheeks, far beyond caring who saw.

"Our babies," Kai gasped. "Our babies would go in those glass cases."

"No." I tightened my hold on her. "Kaira, that will never happen." I pulled back and took her face in my hands, making her meet my gaze. "We're going to fix this. I swear it. We're going to fix this."

I held onto her, because if I didn't, I knew I'd go storming back inside that building without a thought of danger or consequences. My grip on Kaira was almost violent, but I could feel her nails digging into my back as she held me just as fiercely.

"They lied!" Kaira's scream was hoarse. "I want them to suffer. I want them to know what it's like to be drugged and put in cages and have the ones they love killed—"

Furious, gut-wrenching sobs wracked her body.

"I won't let those monsters lock me in a cage," she said, her voice cracking.

My mind went white with rage at the very thought.

Never! my thoughts screamed. *I'd kill every one of them and tear this whole place down with my bare hands.*

"I'd die a thousand deaths before I ever let that happen to you." Hatred and disgust burrowed deep inside me, like a thousand briars in my heart. My mind roared against the senseless horror of it all.

"You heard what that woman said about all the fathers," Kaira gasped, breathless as she fisted her hands in my shirt. "I can't survive in a world where you don't exist."

"I'm not going anywhere, and neither are you." I pressed my lips to hers, hard. "These people won't so much as lay a finger on you or the kids we end up having one day."

Kai was shaking her head back and forth.

"I could never put you or our babies in that kind of danger. We can't ever have that. We can't—"

"Listen to me," I said, my voice rough with emotion. "We're going to get the women and kids out of here and demolish this place brick by brick. Then, we're going to expose these sleazes along with Remwald and every other corrupt member of the Alliance. Okay?"

Kai nodded slowly.

I continued, "And then I'm going to marry you in front of everyone we know. And someday, we're going to have kids together. As many as you want. And they're going to grow up and go to school and play with their friends like regular fucking kids. That's a promise, Kai."

"Three," she said, wiping her eyes with her sleeve.

"What?"

"I want three kids."

I managed a choked laugh as I pressed my lips to her wet cheek. "Then we're going to need a bigger house."

CHAPTER 44

We were all numb on the ride home, going through the motions of ditching the van and trading it for two others as Kaira changed out our illusions.

I numbly accepted Bri's heartfelt apologies and listened with half an ear as the others debated what to do with this new information. I knew I'd have to deal with all of it, and soon, but for now, I couldn't think. I held Kai, needing to feel her in my arms in a way I never had before. I pressed my face into her hair, breathing in her jasmine smell that made me feel like I was home.

Once we were back in the safety of our house, we collapsed on the couches in the living room. We stared at each other in disbelief.

Kaira was the first one to speak.

"Obviously all of this…MagLab stuff…is personal for Gray and me in a way I'd never expect it to be for the rest of you. And I get that this," she gestured to the way we sat pressed against each other, "might still be repulsive to some of you. I'll understand if you don't want anything to do with this…us…anymore."

"It's not repulsive," Bri said quietly. "At least, not now that I know the third high law is BS. I mean, we've all been brainwashed." She gave us a wobbly smile. "I'm not saying I'd be cool with you guys making out in front of me yet, but just give me a little more time to get used to everything. Besides," she straightened her spine, and a fierce expression came over her face, "I'm not letting this drop until I find out what happened to my niece."

"If you think I'd sit this one out after we just learned there's a confirmed conspiracy," Smith said, "then you people don't know me at all."

Yutika let out a shaky breath. "I have a confession to make." She looked at Michael. "*We* have a confession." She covered her face with her hands, so her words were a little garbled when she said, "Michael and I have been secretly dating."

"Get outta town." A.J. clutched his chest.

"It's true," Yutika cried, having missed A.J.'s sarcasm entirely. "We didn't tell anyone because we didn't want things to get weird since we all work together."

The rest of us looked at each other. And then we started to laugh. It began as a chuckle, and then all of our emotions from the past few hours bubbled over until we were in hysterics. Tears rolled down A.J.'s cheeks as he slapped his thigh. Even Kai's devastated look softened.

"What's so funny?" Michael asked in his rumbling voice, looking a little puzzled and a lot embarrassed.

"Yeah, what's so funny?" Yutika demanded, planting her hands on her hips. "You guys didn't laugh at Kaira and Graysen."

"Come here, you silly little goose," A.J. told her, before wrapping his arms around her.

Michael made a little sound of protest when A.J. hugged him, but after a few seconds, he gave A.J.'s back a pat.

"So, what are we going to do about MagLab?" Smith asked, a slight scowl on his face. The poor guy had probably never dealt with so many emotions in his entire life.

We all sobered at that.

"We have two options," Kaira said, becoming the fierce leader of our little group once again. "We can try to figure out how to get all those women and kids out of there quietly, and then we all go into hiding." She swallowed. "Or, we can expose MagLab and all the Alliance corruption to the rest of the city and let Boston decide where we all go from here."

"I say we expose the bastards," Bri said, her skin turning to titanium.

"Agreed," Yutika said.

Michael and Smith nodded.

"Um, have you kittens forgotten Remwald's threat?" A.J. raised his eyebrows.

We all looked at him.

"The idea of exposing the Alliance is all lovely and heroic, but if we do this, Kaira and Graysen will still be on the hook for breaking a high law." His expression grew serious. "Even if people know the truth about the third high law, their prejudices won't change overnight."

I thought of those pictures splayed out across the Director's desk. The simmering rage inside me began to boil.

"We can, uh, give you a few minutes to talk by yourselves," Michael told Kaira and me. He got off the couch and gestured for the others to follow him.

As soon as we were alone, I turned to face Kai.

"A.J.'s right," she said in little more than a whisper. "Even after we tell the truth, people are still going to see us as baby killers."

I couldn't argue with that. Fear and hatred were powerful emotions, and there were plenty of both when it came to the third high law.

"Maybe we can find a way to expose Remwald and MagLab without the world finding out about us," Kai said, her eyes brightening with unshed tears. "That way, you can step into the void filled by all those corrupt leaders at the Alliance, and no one will question you."

I met her gaze. She gave me an encouraging nod, giving me permission to walk away from her again. She was giving me a way to take back the life I'd always wanted.

The life I'd *thought* I wanted.

I shook my head. "You were right." And even though the words hurt, I said, "The Alliance is flawed. It isn't what I thought it was or what I wanted it to be. Besides, I don't want the same things I used to." I ran a hand down her bare arm. "Or maybe I want what I've always wanted, but it took me this long to realize what that was."

I pulled her onto my lap, marveling at the way I wasn't afraid to hold her, even though anyone coming down the stairs could see us.

"I was so passionate about the Alliance because I wanted to make things better for Nats and Mags," I continued. "I should have known any organization that kept us apart was rotten to its core."

Her eyes searched mine.

I reached up and cupped her cheek. "I'm so sorry for the way I treated you, babe. I was angry and stupid, and I didn't bother to ask any of the right questions. I hurt you."

She put her hand over mine. "You don't need to apologize."

"I do," I insisted. "And I promise you, I'll never doubt you or be that much of an idiot again." I frowned as a new realization crept up on me. "But if I tell the truth, people will find out you're unMarked. You might not be able to hide unless you stay illusioned."

Kai combed her fingers through my hair as she met my gaze. "If we're really going to fix everything that's broken in this city, I can't do it from the sidelines anymore. I'm going to be right there by your side."

I felt warmth and pride light up my insides. I'd never been more in love with her than I was at that moment.

"We'd better tell everyone," Kai said, scooting off my lap. "We're going to need their help."

"We should call Ma first," I said. "Your family needs to know the danger they might be in once we do this."

"And your dad."

Swallowing, I nodded.

Kai pulled out her phone and called Ma. We face-timed her, and Cora and Grandma Tashi squeezed into the frame as soon as Ma picked up.

"Where's Desiree?" Kai asked.

"At Valencia's rally," Ma said, her face pinched in irritation.

"You need to get her home. Graysen and I are about to do something that could put all of you in danger…."

The call lasted more than an hour. We told the Hansley clan the gist of what we'd witnessed at MagLab and about Remwald's plans for starting a war between the two races. And Kai told Cora and Grandma Tashi about our relationship.

The Hansleys were all righteously angry at the ones who were threatening our city and supportive of our decision to expose it all. Even Grandma Tashi muttered that I was a handsome boy, which I took to mean she believed me and supported us.

"You could be in danger," I told the Hansleys.

"Don't worry about us, G-Baby," Ma said, wiping away tears. "We know how to take care of ourselves. You do what you need to do."

After that, there was a lot of grumbling and banging of pans in the kitchen while Ma muttered about them still needing dinner even if the world was coming to an end.

Shaking her head, Kai told her family she loved them and then ended the call. She handed me the phone.

I heaved a sigh, steeling myself. The last time we'd spoken, my dad had pretty much said he thought I had killed Penelope. I wasn't sure he would react any better to the news I had to share now.

"Get it over with," Kai said, lacing her fingers through mine.

Sighing again, I dialed my dad's number.

The phone rang four times before my dad picked up. I didn't turn the call to video. I didn't think I could handle seeing my dad's expression as I told him everything I had to say.

"Who is this?"

"It's me, Dad."

"Mr. Galder?" Kai reached over and took the phone from my hand. "You might not remember me, but my name is Kaira Hansley, and I lived across the street from you."

"Sure, sure," my dad said, distracted. "Ma Hansley's daughter."

Kai told him about taking out her tracker, but before she could move on to the part about stealing her file, my dad interrupted.

"So, you're fugitives together now, are you?" His voice was uncharacteristically bitter.

With Kai's hand firm and warm in mine, I told my dad everything. I started with my relationship with Kai. She interjected when I got to the part about her file. Her voice was steady, but tears tracked down her cheeks as she apologized to my dad for everything that had happened. Then, it was my turn for admissions and apologies.

I didn't apologize for protecting Kai. As guilt-ridden as I was about lying to my dad for so many years, I couldn't be sorry for the choice I had made.

Throughout our long explanation, my dad stayed silent.

We told him everything, all the way up to what we'd discovered in the last week. My dad just listened without saying a word.

"You might be in danger once everything becomes public," I finished, my voice raw from so much talking. "Go to the Hansley's. You'll all be safer together. Or, if you don't want to be with them, Kai has a safe house in Back Bay—"

"Graysen."

I had no idea it was possible for one word to hold so much disappointment. I had thought my dad was listening…that there was a chance he'd understand. But with that one word, I knew. I knew everything we'd tried to tell him had fallen on deaf ears.

"I raised you better than this," my dad said.

"Dad, please listen—"

"Don't call here again."

The line went dead.

I sat there with the phone still in my hand as an icy cold washed over me. Kai wrapped her arms around me and buried her face in my neck.

"It's my fault what's happened between you and your dad," she said, her words vibrating against my skin. "I promise, once we've taken care of the emergency with the Alliance, I'm going to help you fix things with him."

I didn't think it would be that easy, but it made everything more bearable having Kaira by my side. For the first time in a long time, I wasn't filled with doubt and a crushing sense of helplessness. I had made a choice, and I stood by it.

"You ready to do this?" Kai asked me.

I shook my head. "There's one more thing we need to work out first." I took a few moments to set aside the conversation with my dad so I could put all of my focus on Kai. "I know I don't have the right to ask after everything that's happened, but I'm going to ask anyway."

She crossed her arms and gave me a suspicious look. "If this is about me filling up our bedroom with all my clothes, then I can't help you."

I felt a small smile curve my lips, not least because she'd said *our* bedroom.

"It's not about the clothes." I took both of her hands in mine. "Kaira Hansley, will you be my girlfriend…again?"

She laughed in surprise, and then she threw her arms around my neck. "My answer to you will always be *yes*."

Those words lightened the impossibly heavy weight that had settled on my chest.

"I'm never letting you go," I warned her.

"Psh, I'd like to see you pry yourself loose from my viselike monkey grip," she replied.

"Viselike monkey grip?" I raised an eyebrow.

To demonstrate, Kai wrapped her arms and legs around me, until not even air separated us.

I held her just as tightly. When she raised her face to meet my gaze, I kissed her. It wasn't one of the soft and tender ones we'd shared the night she'd been shot. It was a heart-stopping, forget-the-world-exists kind of kiss. Everything else slipped away as we lost ourselves in each other.

"What did I say about making out?" a faraway voice complained.

We were breathless and still clinging to each other when I realized Bri was standing at the bottom of the stairs. She was scowling at us, but there was amusement rather than anger in her eyes.

The others were sitting on the stairs, and I wondered if they'd been there the whole time. I realized I didn't care, and that seemed like its own kind of magic.

"You have to admit, the Nat-Mag thing aside, they're the hottest straight couple ever made," A.J. commented.

"You mean aside from me and Michael, obviously." Yutika gave A.J. an affectionate smack on the back of the head as she skipped down the stairs.

Bri snorted. Michael blushed.

"I give it a month before your pretty faces are on the cover of Vogue," A.J. told us. "They'll do a big cover story about your love, and then all the copies will sell out, and then you'll need to hire a manager because you'll be so famous."

"Are you volunteering?" Kai asked.

"Yep. I charge twenty-five percent off the top for my invaluable advice."

"Can we be serious for a minute?" Smith broke in. "I think the best way to do this will be to hack into the National Alert system. That way, our video will reach every device country-wide."

"Remwald will have heard about what happened at MagLab by now," Kai said. "We don't have time to sit on this."

"I think he'll want to keep things quiet until the vote tomorrow," Michael said, frowning in thought. "Especially given that he knows we know the truth. He's got as much to lose as we do."

"But there's always the chance he'll send some of his Combat Mags over to disappear us," Yutika said, glancing nervously at the front door.

"I'd like to see them try." Bri cracked her knuckles.

"There's no point in waiting," I said. "I want to make sure we've made our move before he can make his."

"Well, you just factor in time to shower and change," A.J. said. "I'll lose my job as chief image consultant before I've even started if I let you hack into everyone's devices looking like *that*."

CHAPTER 45

S mith was busy piecing together the various files on his computer, while the rest of us reviewed everything Kai and I would need to say once we were on camera.

At one point, A.J. disappeared upstairs for several minutes. When came back, he announced that he'd left outfits *befitting the occasion* on Kai's bed for each of us. Then, he'd proceeded to cut my hair with a pair of scissors that wielded themselves.

"If you poke my eye out, you're fired," I informed the Telekinetic as the scissors continued their frantic work.

The scissors responded by snipping warningly in front of my face.

After, when a hand mirror zoomed in and positioned itself in front of me, I had to admit it was the best haircut I'd ever gotten.

We spent the next hour planning and strategizing before we were ready. While Smith set up the tri-pod in front of our blank wall, and Bri did jumping jacks to *work off her nerves*, Kai and I went upstairs to change.

When I saw Kai in the outfit A.J. had chosen for her, my mouth went dry. She was wearing a gray skirt that hugged her slender hips and ended just below her knees. She wore four-inch black heels with a wicked point that put her almost at eye level with me. The white blouse A.J. had picked out looked incredible against her caramel skin. The outfit was simple, professional, and made her look like the smoking hot badass she was.

"I've gotta admit, that guy knows how to pick out clothes," I said admiringly. "You're gorgeous."

"So are you," she said, checking out the tapered lines of my suit. "But don't tell A.J. His ego is bloated enough as it is."

"I *heard* that!" A.J. called from outside our room.

A few minutes later, we were all gathered in the living room. When Smith tried to tell Yutika how to work the tri-pod, she batted his hands away.

"I might not be a Techie," she grumbled, "but I can figure out how to operate a video recorder I brought into existence with my own hands, *thank you very much*."

Smith positioned himself on the couch where three laptops were set up on the coffee table in front of him. Kai and I stood in front of the blank wall and tried to breathe.

"You sure about this?" I asked. I was looking at Kai, but the question was for everyone. "We're going to start a real shit storm if we do this. Boston is going to lose the only thing that has kept it from being like every other city. The fallout is going to be…intense."

"Lucky for Boston, this city has something none of the rest of them do," Yutika said.

When we all looked at her, she said, "*Us.* Duh."

"I feel like we need some kind of high-five or chant, or maybe a logo, now that we're like an official team," Bri said.

"I'll get right on that as soon as this video is done," A.J. said.

I didn't think he was joking.

"I wonder what they'll name the movie they make about us later," Bri said, a dreamy expression coming over her face.

"Presumptuous to think we're that important," Michael grumbled.

"Please." Yutika waved a hand. "We're exposing the corruption in the most powerful organization in the country, and we're going to be the ones to help get our city through the disaster that follows. They're definitely making a movie about us."

"Ooh, I'll totally be played by Zachary Quinto's grandson." A.J. clapped his hands.

Bri scrunched up her nose. "Does he even act?"

"With a god of a grandfather like Sir Zachary, how could he not?" A.J. fanned his face.

"I'd like to have a title in mind, just so we're not caught unawares when the agents come banging down our door," Yutika said, tapping a finger against her lips in thought. "Any thoughts?"

"I know," Kai said.

We all looked at her.

She smiled at me. *"The Nat Makes Seven."*

CHAPTER 46

Everyone ready?" Smith asked.

Giving a speech in front of large crowds might be paralyzing for most people, but it energized me. I imagined every resident in the city of Boston crammed into our living room.

"Ready," I said, letting out a breath.

"Ready," Kai echoed.

When she leaned forward to straighten my tie, I stole a kiss.

"Ready." Yutika squinted through the lens of the camera. "In three, two—"

"Wait!" A.J. shrieked.

Everyone froze.

"What's wrong?" Kai demanded.

A napkin flew across the room and started to wipe my face.

"What the hell, A.J.?" I demanded, swatting at the napkin.

The napkin unfolded itself and zoomed in front of each of our faces, displaying a trace of Kai's lip gloss.

Bri snorted.

"You are unbelievable," Michael said mildly.

"I think what you mean is *thank you for saving us all incalculable regret and humiliation*," A.J. retorted. "That color is far too dark for Graysen's complexion. He's much more of a peach than a plum."

"I am neither," I assured him.

"Can we proceed, your Majesty?" Smith asked.

A.J. waved a hand. "Proceed," he said in a lofty tone.

I heard all of the phones in the room start to buzz the National Security alert as Smith hacked into every device in the country. The TV in the corner of the room, which Bri had switched on, went from the news to a blank screen.

I watched Yutika's fingers above the camera count down from three. The TV flickered, and then Kai and I appeared on the screen. I waited another second. And then I began to speak.

"Hello, America. My name is Graysen Galder. You might have seen my face on the news a time or two in the past week." I offered the camera a little smile. I felt Kai relax, and it emboldened me. "I've been accused of the magically-motivated murder of Penelope Heppurn, and I'm the chief suspect in another Magic murder. I'm taking up your time today because I have proof that Director Edwardian Remwald is responsible for the murders that took place this week. He planned and carried out the murders with the assistance of Valencia Stark."

"And I'm Kaira Hansley," Kai said, her voice clear and strong. "You haven't seen my face before because I've been unMarked since my Test, when I was Marked as a Level 10 Animate Illusionist.

"I destroyed my records and went into hiding because I believed the system of Marking hurt, rather than helped, unity between Nats and Mags. I've since learned the Alliance is being led by people who seek to perpetuate fear and distrust between our races by lying to all of us."

Kaira and I had decided not to use cue cards since we didn't want our speech to sound scripted. We'd outlined the gist of what we each intended to say, but now, hearing her speak, I knew I was looking at the future of the Alliance. I was surprised my buttons weren't literally bursting from how proud I was.

"We have more to say, but before we do, you need to know the truth about the Director of the Alliance," I said into the camera. "Edwardian Remwald is not the man he has projected himself to be, as you'll see from this recording."

I glanced up at Smith. I saw the image on the TV screen change as the Techie played the footage we'd recorded at Remwald's estate.

The video displayed Remwald, illusioned as the older man who had met with Valencia, stepping out of the house. The shot kept Remwald in focus as his illusion flickered. And then the face of the man the whole world knew as the Alliance Director was revealed.

"The Alliance Director has broken the second high law, too," Kai said. "The effect you are seeing here is two Animate Illusionists who are matched in strength cancelling out each other's Magic."

"Remwald admitted that he has been using a potion to suppress his magic, which has fooled the world into thinking he's a Nat."

There was a seamless switch as Smith started to play Remwald's confession. It was eight-and-a-half minutes of uninterrupted video. Kaira and I stayed quiet, letting Remwald's confession speak for itself.

I let silence fill the air for several seconds at the end of the video before I began to speak again.

"There's more, and it's related to a confession I want to make. I am guilty of committing a high crime, although it isn't the one I was accused of." I glanced at Kai before turning my attention back to the camera. "I'm in love with a Magic."

I felt a rush of emotion at speaking those words out loud. I'd never said them to anyone except Kai, and now, the whole country knew. I never imagined that a few simple words could infuse me with so much strength.

I could almost hear the intake of breath as every American glued to their devices watched my confession.

"Today, we learned the reason behind the third high law—that children born to Magic and Natural parents carry deadly bacteria—is a lie. We discovered a place called MagLab. It's a secret branch of the Alliance where these children are kept in isolation so they can be used in the war Remwald intends to start. The truth the Alliance doesn't want any of us to know is that children of Magic and Natural couples are more powerful. There is nothing dangerous or deadly about them. Their strength simply threatens the current balance of power, and that has scared our governing body enough to imprison and kill innocent people for the sake of keeping their secret."

I paused while Smith flashed short video clips from the footage my tiny camera had taken in MagLab.

I watched the progression on the TV screen in front of us. When the images moved on from the basement experiments to the pregnant women in the cells, I reached down and entwined my fingers with Kai's. It was an unconscious gesture, but when she squeezed my hand, it made me stand taller.

I let the pictures of the kids in those glass cages speak for themselves. After, with Smith's text noting the addresses of MagLab and Remwald's private estate scrolling across the screen, I began to speak again.

The words that came out of my mouth weren't the ones I had planned to say. In that moment, the speech I had written weeks ago, back when I was preparing to be valedictorian of the BSMU and start my new job in the Alliance, came back to mind. I was surprised to discover that much of what I'd written then still applied.

"I'm proud to be a Bostonian. But we can no longer be content with the status quo, where the corrupt rule and Magics are tracked like animals. There is a magic of new beginnings, one which we must all embrace if we want our future to be different from our past.

"The changes we need aren't going to come from the actions of a few anonymous Naturals and Magics working behind the scenes. Real change will only come when we're all ready to stand together against evil. Because our city isn't what makes us strong. It's the people who live here."

Pausing, I looked straight into the camera.

"I'm confident we're all ready to set aside old fears and prejudices in exchange for something more…something we can all truly call our own. A future that will inspire the rest of the world. A future that we'll be proud to show off to our children."

I looked at Kai, whose eyes were shining with pride in me.

For all the ways life was about to get even more complicated, I felt a tremendous sense of peace. I was surrounded by a family I'd chosen, and who had chosen me. And I had Kai. No matter what came next, I knew I wouldn't have to face it alone.

I had a desperate urge to take Kai in my arms and kiss her right then. So I did just that…because I wanted to, and because she was my goddamn girlfriend. And there in our living room, with the whole country watching, she kissed me back.

THE END

✳ ✳ ✳

Because reviews are so important for a book to be successful, please consider leaving a brief review on your favorite retailer if you enjoyed *The Nat Makes 7*. Many thanks!

* * *

Sign up for Stephanie Fazio's e-Newsletter to learn about upcoming books at:
https://StephanieFazio.com/subscribe/

Acknowledgements

The idea for this book has been kicking around in my head for a while, and I am so thrilled I finally got the chance to write it. As is the case with all of my other projects, this book wouldn't be what it is without my incredible team and all of the people who support me on a daily basis.

To Andrew Brodsky, Keith Tarrier, and Ellen Schaeffer. Thank you for being part of the team that made this book possible. I couldn't have done it without you.

To my amazing ARC team. Thank you so much for all of your support.

To Julie Gibbons and Baby Klein (who will have a real name by this book's publication!).

To my wonderful family. Thank you for all of your love and support.

To my fantastic readers, who make what I do possible.

To my wonderful husband, Andrew Brodsky, for being so much better than even the best book boyfriend.

About the Author:

Stephanie Fazio is a fantasy author. She grew up in Syracuse, New York, and prior to writing full time, she worked in the fields of journalism, secondary education, and higher education. She has an undergraduate degree in English from Colgate University and a Master's degree in Reading, Writing, and Literacy from the University of Pennsylvania. Stephanie lives in Austin with her husband and crazy rescue dog. When she isn't writing, she's getting lost in parks, hosting taco nights, or ironically and miserably losing at word games, but having fun while she does it.

Connect with Stephanie Fazio:

Visit her Website: https://www.StephanieFazio.com
Sign up for her newsletter: https://StephanieFazio.com/subscribe/

Continue the Mags & Nats series

Book 2, *Mag Subject 6*
AVAILABLE October 2020!

StephanieFazio.com

Discover other books by Stephanie Fazio

The Fount Series

The Prince's Chosen

The Forsaken's Choice

The Chosen Union

Opal Contagion Series

Opal Smoke

Opal Slayer

Opal Storm

Bisecter Series

Bisecter

Halve Human

Dusker Dark

Captain Harkibel

Mags & Nats

The Nat Makes 7

Mag Subject 6 (Oct 2020)